Praise for THAT'S NOT MY NAME

"Yvonne Navarro bestows upon us what we always most need—a novel distinguished by its generosity of feeling, sense of discovery, narrative timing and command, accuracy of phrasing, and above all its sustained power. This is an exciting, thrilling, heartfelt book."

—Peter Straub, author of *Mr. X*

"Yvonne Navarro continues to explore—and master—the realms of suspense and nightmare. Once again, she's crafted a thoroughly compelling story that doesn't let go until the last page."

—Matthew Costello, author of *Maelstrom*

"THAT'S NOT MY NAME is a truly unsettling work of fiction. The chills come not from ghosts or external threats, but from within, from the very real tricks the mind can play on itself. Do not miss this one."

—F. Paul Wilson, author of *Legacies*

"With this sly, savvy mystery, Yvonne Navarro yanks the rug of certainty from beneath the reader too many times to count, and leaves one with the ultimate nagging question: Are you positive you're who you think you are?"

—Brian Hodge, author of *Wild Horses*

ALSO BY YVONNE NAVARRO:

Final Impact

Music of the Spears

Red Shadows

YVONNE NAVARRO

THAT'S NOT MY NAME

BANTAM BOOKS

New York Toronto London

Sydney Auckland

THAT'S NOT MY NAME

A Bantam Book / June 2000

ISBN 0-553-57750-6

Published simultaneously in the United States and Canada

Bantam Books are published by Bantam Books, a division of Random House, Inc. Its trademark, consisting of the words "Bantam Books" and the portrayal of a rooster, is Registered in U.S. Patent and Trademark Office and in other countries. Marca Registrada. Bantam Books, 1540 Broadway, New York, New York 10036.

PRINTED IN THE UNITED STATES OF AMERICA

OPM 10 9 8 7 6 5 4 3 2 1

For Steven Spruill.

A gifted writer and a treasured friend
who believes in me, and without whose help
this book would be only a fraction
of what it is.

Thank you to:

Detective J. J. Bittenbinder,
formerly of the Chicago Police Department.

Don VanderSluis,
for enduring friendship and support.

My dad, Martin Cochran,
who provides that most important
thing of all,
Faith.

PRELUDE

And we forget because we must
And not because we will.

—MATTHEW ARNOLD,
"ABSENCE"

During the day, her life is filled with ups and downs and a never-ending sense of anxiety about what the next moment might bring. Mornings are sweet and bright and start with her mother's drawn but sincere smile, a soft kiss on the end of her nose, the love and laughter of the rest of her small family even though Daddy doesn't live with them anymore. As she does every weekday, Auntie K comes over in the morning and Mama goes away until a little after twelve o'clock, when she's through with the breakfast shift at the restaurant. Auntie K works afternoons in a liberry and has scattered lots and lots of books around their house—it must be millions. Auntie K is helping her learn to read and she has come to love the pretty picture books and all the wonderful words; already she knows the first five letters of the alphabet by heart.

It's when Mama comes home, Auntie K leaves, and then Daddy comes over that they all dread.

She loves Daddy, of course, and it always starts okay, with the hellos and the hugs and the kisses, a fun little present or two for them all. But her parents' conversations seem to change with the dark. As the sun drops below the tops of the neighborhood houses, their voices get louder, the tones get meaner. If movements could have sharp edges, the way her mother and father whip their hands through the air would slice each other until they bled. By the time bedtime arrives, the atmosphere is tense and cold, beyond her little girl's ability to understand, and she wonders if they did something—if they do something every night—that makes Daddy get so angry.

It is a big house and she has a room all by herself even though she would rather not be left alone. But she climbs into bed and huddles against her favorite toy, a stuffed purple elephant (it makes the adults laugh when she tries to say it: effelant*) nearly half her size. The room is dark but that's okay. The absence of light frightens her not nearly so much as the vicious words still being hurled about in the living room or the way she feels so alone when she'd rather be with the rest of her family. Because she has no choice, she can only lie there and listen, trying to draw comfort from being with her best things, her effelant, the stack of her most favorite books, her small pink slippers with the fuzzy bunny ears that wiggle over her toes when she walks. It's a good place, her room, but it isn't quite enough to chase away the sounds of the never-ending argument far down the hallway. After awhile she puts her thumb in her mouth and nurses at it, ashamed at what she knows is a babyish thing but still drawing the tiniest measure of security from the movement.*

And, as she does every night, she cries herself to sleep.

When it comes, finally, her child's slumber is surprisingly sweet and untroubled, a haven that leaves behind the shouted jealousies and battles that constantly rage between her parents. It is a cool fall night and she burrows deeper beneath the sheet and her soft pink blanket as the hours pass. Slightly past midnight, just beyond the rim of dreams, she registers a sound, something odd and out of place in what should be a silent room.

Her eyelids fly open and garbled thoughts of monsters fragment her sleepy thoughts as her body suddenly sweeps upward. The room tilts around her and she sees the ceiling, the wall, the covers on the bed. Before she can cry out a hand, familiar yet rougher than she would've ever expected, clamps over her mouth. The smell of it—Old Spice and sweat—fills her nostrils as her lips are mashed painfully against her teeth. The window, open to a damp, dark breeze, looms in front of her and her kidnapper, but as he hurries toward it his hip rams one corner of the small table her mother has painted pink to match everything else in the room. She sees the family photograph fall, along with a stack of little-girl books—Auntie K has put them everywhere—but it happens slowly, like a piece of fruit dropping into a bowl of half-chilled Jell-O. There is nothing delayed about the sound when the books and the picture hit the hardwood floor, though; the shatter of glass is immediate and shockingly loud in the darkness.

She hears her mother's cry of alarm in the other room, but the scream is cut off by the mass of the building as the girl is dragged through the open window and into the chilly outside air. There her abductor breaks into a run, turning the dull glow of the street lamps into blurred circles of light flying past overhead, like strange, moving moons. She hears the sound of his strained breathing and feels his fear in the way his fingers are too tight against her face, his large hand painful around her small rib cage. She feels herself swoop downward, as though she were on the kiddie roller coaster at the fair, then the slamming of a car door and the clamor of an overtaxed engine roar in her ears. Suddenly everything is filled with the chilly breeze from the car's fan and the sensation of speed as the rest of her family is left somewhere behind.

Man and child are swallowed up by the night.

1

Reclamation

The one person who has more illusions than the dreamer is the man of action.

—OSCAR WILDE

JANUARY 16--THURSDAY

How long have I been doing this?

Too long, Jesse Waite thought as he opened the door of the Impala. He tossed the bag of groceries—nothing more than a loaf of bread, a jar of generic peanut butter, and two packages of noodle soup—onto the backseat, then climbed inside and shut the door, shivering while he waited for the engine to warm up a little.

He knew he really ought to go on home; the gas gauge showed a half-empty tank and he needed to ration that until next Friday, needed to bring this pastime of his—following this woman around—to an end. He'd been an idiot to take off from his job, and at no time had that been more apparent than when he'd discovered that his boss had sold the failing business and folded up. Had he been gone that long? Oh, you'd better believe it. All he had to do was look at the balance in the savings account at Household Bank to get a dose of reality: It was down to almost nothing, and the checking account wasn't much better—his next grocery budget would come from hosing off an old crate of dusty bottles in the basement and returning them for the deposit. At least the car still ran, no matter how cold it was, and that was a real plus; he was going to need it.

It'd taken a bit of fancy talking on the part of his friend John about Jesse's missed work time, but he'd come through for Jesse again. Four more days and Jesse started on the night shift at MC Tooling. Taking the graveyard track would give him a two-buck-an-hour night bonus, and he'd been told they paid on Friday for work through the previous Wednesday. The rent on the townhouse was paid through January, but then he had to get things straight again, hold a job and go home once in awhile, be *Jesse* again.

But it was so *hard* to let go of what little he had—why, just a few minutes ago, he'd been in the same store with her, standing only eight feet away. It was the first time Jesse'd been so near, and it only confirmed what he suspected: It wasn't his imagination at all. This young woman could, indeed, *be* Stacey. How much of this questioning was he supposed to endure, for God's sake? He'd already gone beyond the point of pain—physical, emotional, it didn't matter what kind. Some people might have been counting the days or the weeks, maybe even the hours. Not him; Jesse just counted one thing: a lifetime. And it stretched, empty and merciless, ahead of him.

Even now—it'd been only half an hour since he watched her climb out of the Lexus and wave good-bye to the driver, that same thin guy who today was wearing a ridiculous-looking old man's cap. But it already felt like it'd been hours, days, *forever*—it was like that more and more now when he was away from her. Every time he saw this woman, she became a freeze-frame in his mind, another cherished image that he filed with the rest—the way she wore her hair, what she was wearing. Today, for instance, from just the few minutes he'd been close to her, he could close his eyes and see her outfit: a sensible brown skirt and blouse under a leather-look jacket that wasn't nearly warm enough for the temperature, a pair of tan high heels.

Jesse knew this woman, he would swear his soul on it. Everything about her was familiar and comforting, *necessary* . . . he was attuned to her every move by something inside him, a strange sort of destiny on a level so deep he couldn't even put a name to it. Like when she came out tonight . . . she'd head straight back to where she'd moved into that apartment complex down the road—with *him*—

walking by herself in the snow and the dark of early evening when he would have never left her to make the trek in these freezing temperatures; *he* would have waited and given her a ride—

It was usually his mother-in-law's words that came back to haunt him—

"What if she's not really in there?"

—to gnaw at his mind like a hyena worrying the bones of a lioness's old kill. This time, however, as the automatic exit door to the Pik-Kwik hummed open and she finally stepped outside and turned east, someone else's voice suddenly grated into Jesse's head, filled with the rasp of cigarette smoke and the nuance of what might have been, or maybe *is*—

"Hey, man, you gonna sit here and cry in your beer, or you gonna go out there and fix things up with her?"

Jesse Waite flung open the door of his car and headed toward his wife.

Okay, Nola Elidad thought. I think I remembered everything. Milk, a loaf of bread for toast in the morning, and a box of cereal. Froot Loops—she felt guilty admitting it, but she liked them. She picked her way carefully through the slush outside the entrance of Pik-Kwik, using the drier spots like little islands to head toward the shoveled sidewalk in the hope of not ruining her new tan pumps. She'd made it just to the back of the last car between her and the cleared area when a man said something from behind her.

"Stacey."

Nola stopped and looked around. It was an automatic reaction because the voice was so close and she knew the speaker was talking to her, that he expected some kind of response. "Pardon me?"

The dark-haired man a few feet away was a good deal taller than she was and handsome in a rugged, outdoorsy way. His shadow-rimmed eyes were blue like hers, but darker, and they were full of pain. "Come on, honey. Let's go home."

He reached for her hand and Nola recoiled, then

started backing away. Slush seeped into her shoes, chilling her feet instantly, but she couldn't think about that right now, or about the fact that he was between her and the relative safety of the entrance to the grocery store. Her gaze flicked around the lot, but she'd get no help there—not another soul in sight.

"Oh, no," was all she could think of to say. "You—"

"Please don't do this, Stacey," the man said. This time when he snatched at her, his movement was quicker, far too fast for her to dodge. His fingers—cold and hard even through the sleeve of her jacket—locked around her wrist and she knew she was in trouble, that this was much more than a case of mistaken identity, and that if she didn't get out of it now—

"Let me go," she managed. She pulled backward, but his hold didn't loosen. "You've got the wrong person. That's not my name." The instant the words left her mouth a sudden, sickening sense of déjà vu boiled inside her, and for a moment she couldn't function beyond this added sense of terror, a black fear so strong that Nola struggled against the urge to retch.

Then it passed and, frozen, they stared at each other. His face was a pale oval beneath the fluorescent lighting in the parking lot, the skin beneath his eyes so shadowed it might have been bruised. His mouth worked for a moment, then his expression changed and he actually looked *relieved.* "God," he croaked. "I get it now. Come on."

Before she could protest further, he was pulling her across the lot and toward a rust-beaten car idling about ten feet away. "Stop it!" Nola cried. She threw herself in the opposite direction and lost her hold on her plastic grocery bag. But she couldn't worry about that now, as she went down on the side of one leg when the man's grip tightened rather than let go. His fingers dug into her flesh through the sleeve of her coat, hard enough to bruise. "Let *go!*"

"Stacey, *please,*" the man said desperately. He dragged her back to her feet, then his arm went around her waist. Her heart was hammering so hard that she nearly couldn't breathe and a sense of weightless unreality blurred her vision as she felt her feet leave the ground—he was literally *carrying* her to his car. She tried to scream and got a mouthful of his flannel jacket as he spun her around and hugged her, closing the distance.

Nola fought then, as best she could, pitting her meager five-foot-two-inch frame against his heavier, stronger one. She tried to kick and punch and claw, even bite . . . but it was no use—he seemed impervious to her blows. No one pulled into the parking lot or came out of the store, and no one heard her choked pleas for help as he easily held her struggling body with one arm while he opened the driver's side door of the waiting car.

Then she was inside, pushed past the steering wheel like she was nothing more than laundry being stuffed into a bag. She kept going and hit the passenger door face-first, ramming her nose hard enough to bring tears to her eyes but not so hard that she forgot to fumble for the door handle and yank on it.

Nothing happened.

She slammed her hands futilely against the glass as the driver's door closed. The sound was like an explosion in her brain, but not enough to drown out her abductor's words. "Don't bother, Stacey." He sounded absurdly *tired,* as if this entire thing were a terrible ordeal for him. "The lock's been jammed for months. Fasten your seat belt."

She twisted around and stared at him, pressed herself as hard as she could against the locked passenger door. "That's not my name," she whispered. Hadn't she said that before? The edges of her vision sparkled dangerously and she was mildly surprised at the taste and feel of her own blood as it laced between her teeth—she must've bit her lip when she hit the door.

"Yes it is," he said. His voice was calm and deliberate, stubborn. The expression on his face was terrifyingly serene, as if he had nothing more to do in the world than convince her that he was right and she was wrong. "I think I know what's going on here. You've got . . . what's it called? Amnesia. You've heard of it—everybody has." The clasp on his seat belt clicked as he strapped it into place.

Nola screamed then, but the sound was cut off as his hand whipped over and covered her mouth. "Cut it *out,*" he said angrily as her lips mashed against the front of her teeth. "You're just making this harder than it has to be, and I hate having to manhandle you like this. Now would you fasten your damned seat belt?"

He released her, waiting, and disbelievingly, she shrank against the seat. How amazing, Nola thought foggily, that she could feel or notice the cold, cracked vinyl jabbing into the bare skin of her back where her sweater and jacket had climbed above the waist of her slush-stained skirt. She had lost one of her heels, and her left foot, stocking ripped and wet over scraped, bloodstained flesh, ground against an ice-splattered and dirty floor mat. In the wake of what was happening to her, she was even surprised that she could feel the pulse of pain from her split lip, but there it was.

"Damn it," her kidnapper muttered. "Boy, this is a mess if I ever saw one." He stared at her, and Nola realized that if she didn't do as he asked, he was likely to reach across her and do it himself. Was it not better to keep him at least on his own side of the car for now? Her fingers scrambled to find the buckle, but they felt thick and unwieldy, as though each digit had grown to twice its size. At last she managed to connect the two pieces, another snapping sound that seemed to be an announcement of finality. Seeing her belted securely appeased her captor and he relaxed a little, easing the white-knuckled grip he'd had on the steering wheel.

He put the car in gear and Nola had to bite her lip to stop herself from screaming again. The parking lot outside the car was still deserted beneath dark, winter-clouded skies; not a single shopper stepped from the store or climbed out of a car, yet only a moment—a lifetime—ago, when Alec had let her out of the Lexus, she could've sworn there'd been at least three people doing just that. As her abductor guided the car onto Irving Park Road and accelerated, Nola searched the street frantically for a police car, praying one would pull up next to them. She was being *kid-*

napped, for God's sake, literally taken away on a weekday afternoon! Things like this didn't happen in Roselle, and they certainly didn't happen to *her.*

Nola tried to swallow, almost choked instead. Her face still throbbed and there was a vague, high sound in her head—her racing pulse was making her ears ring. Her throat was raspy and her chest hurt from trying to breathe—maybe she'd have a heart attack and she wouldn't have to worry about what was going to happen an hour from now.

"W-what do you want?" she finally managed in a sandpaper voice. "Where are you taking me?"

He gave her a glance that was half pity, half sadness. "Home, of course. Where else?"

Home? She wouldn't have thought it possible, but the pounding of her heart increased until she could feel it in her temples, a sickly throb that was surely reminiscent of cheap liquor and worse hangovers. What would he do when he got her to his home? Rape her? Murder her? She'd loved books since she was a child and the title of one, a detective thriller, came back to her now, spearing into her thoughts and nearly cutting off her air. *Eight Million Ways to Die.* She clamped her teeth against the sob that wanted to spill from her spasming lungs.

How many ways *were* there to die?

They drove for only a few minutes, or maybe it was hours. Nola knew she should watch the road, try to follow where he was taking her and memorize the route in case she had an opportunity to escape, but reality kept intruding. What were her chances, really? She was a tiny, non-athletic woman trapped in a car with a stranger who outweighed her by probably a hundred pounds. Everything had conspired against her—her size, the high heels that had kept her from running, the empty parking lot, even the broken door lock, Was there truly a chance that she'd come out of this alive?

I'm dreaming, she thought desperately. She became more and more disoriented as images slid by the window when the car turned, then turned again, the driver guiding the vehicle in grim silence. This isn't really happening, not in my world. I'm at home and I'm sick, the flu or something, and I've got a high fever. Hallucinations, that's what these are—

"Please," she said out loud. "You got the wrong woman. Stacey isn't my name. If you let me go now, we'll just forget the whole thing. *Please.*"

"Don't worry," her kidnapper said stoically. His eyes looked straight ahead, focused on the road. "We'll work it all out. You'll see."

"There's nothing to *work* out," Nola insisted. In her mind, her voice was strong and forceful, a tone that he couldn't ignore. Her ears told her the truth—she sounded like nothing more than a mouse with its tail caught in a trap, squealing in terror as the human loomed over it with a boot heel. "I'm not who you think I am."

"Whatever you say, Stacey."

She started to protest again, then sucked in her breath when he steered the car into a parking space in front of a darkened townhouse. Wherever they were, the street lighting was minimal; when he shut off the engine, the car was sitting in a pool of silent darkness. He turned his head and looked at her.

"If you touch me, I'll scream," she whispered. She didn't know what else to say to him.

He dropped his gaze and shook his head, then reached around her and into the backseat, pulling a crumpled grocery bag up front. "I've been off work awhile so we don't have much to eat," he said. He sounded absurdly ashamed. "Some soup and peanut butter, that's about it. It'll have to do for now, but I promise it'll get better."

Then he opened the car door and got out. Cold air spilled over Nola where she cowered on the front seat, and she couldn't believe he was just standing outside expectantly, waiting for her to get out and join him.

But . . . what other choice did she have?

"Nola?"

Alec stood just inside the dark dining room of the apartment, the front door still open behind him and spilling muted light from the hallway onto the carpeting. After a long moment he remembered to flip the switch on his left, squinting at the sudden brightness when the small chandelier overhead doused the room with light.

Where was his wife? He pushed the door closed and locked it without thinking, then glanced around, first scanning the tabletop and the clutter of papers surrounding his computer, then looking toward the kitchen and the neater expanse of cleared countertops. But he didn't see a note anywhere, and that made him look automatically at his watch, although he knew already what it said—it was past eleven o'clock.

Frowning, he left his coat on and moved to the kitchen, snapped on the light and opened the refrigerator. Everything in there was the same as when they'd left that morning, and a glance at the trash bin by the wall confirmed it—the empty milk carton still rested inside, and he'd found no full one to replace it. On the counter by the toaster was the same nearly empty loaf of bread, only one slice and the heel left inside the plastic bag.

Alec stood in the kitchen for a long time, one hand gripping the handle of the still-open refrigerator door as he stared toward the living room without really seeing anything. The place had that feel to it, that certain, undeniable atmosphere of isolation that prevails in a space in which nothing has moved and no one has been home for hours. Stale, overheated air permeated every corner of the silent apartment—an easy thing when you had only three and a half rooms to start with.

What should he do? Yeah, the staff meeting had run late, but he was heading up a new committee pulled together by the school to brainstorm a special education program for the mathematics department. Those things took time, and Nola had known he wouldn't be home until past ten—she'd assured him a number of times that she didn't have a problem with the occasional overtime. These late meetings were rare, anyway—once every couple of months. This was only the second one since they'd gotten married. Beyond those two times, his week was as regular as a factory worker's . . . much like Nola's own.

He closed the refrigerator door and realized he was still holding his briefcase in his other hand. He felt like a robot as he set it on a chair, then pulled off his coat and headed for the bedroom. When he flipped on the light switch, what he found set off a small, tinny alarm inside his head. Nothing had been moved, not a single wrinkle marred the smooth, neat surface of the bed where Nola might have come home and sat on the edge to pull off her nylons. He turned and went into the bathroom but it was the same: clean, neat, the towels dry and carefully folded the way they both always left them, with no indication that she had taken an after-work shower. As an afterthought, he went back to the kitchen and peered at the front of the refrigerator door. He couldn't imagine her going back out for anything at this time of night, but if she had, maybe she'd left him a note tucked under one of the little fruit-shaped plastic magnets. Nothing.

Everything in its place, and a place for everything.

Alec couldn't get that stupid litany out of his head as he went through the apartment again, moving from room to room in time to the words running around in his thoughts. Finally they achieved a nearly singsong quality that made him stop short and massage the area of his forehead between his eyebrows. That was wrong—everything *wasn't* in its place. *Nola* wasn't in her place, and her place, her *space,* was here and waiting. Where on earth was she?

It was nearly midnight before the plainclothesman rang the doorbell. Alec, still wearing his now-rumpled suit and with his tie hanging askew, ushered the man inside, then stood lamely as the policeman glanced around and waited for him to speak. He knew he should be able to say *something*—God knew he was certainly screaming in panic inside—but he felt as if a great blanket of ice had slipped over his head and shoulders and was smothering him.

Finally, the officer pulled a notebook out of his coat

pocket and flipped it open. "Mister—I'm sorry, how do you pronounce your name?"

Alec stared at him blankly. Vaguely he thought that he should offer to shake hands, but his arms felt like dead weights hanging at his sides, far too heavy for him to lift. "What? Oh—Elidad. Like 'Ellie' and 'dad' run together."

The detective nodded. "I'm Detective Lucas Conroy. If I understand the call-in correctly, you believe something's happened to your wife?"

Alec nodded jerkily. "She . . . she hasn't come home." He couldn't stop his glance from skipping toward the front door, as though Nola would walk in at any moment. He could have stood in that same spot all night, waiting, but the detective would think he was crazy if he had to take the report while standing in the dining room the entire time. Alec waved a limp hand toward the couch in the other room. "Have a seat."

Conroy inclined his head politely and stepped into the living room, his bright gaze missing nothing as he settled on the farthest end of the couch. It dawned on Alec that except for the bedroom and bathroom, from there Conroy could see most of the apartment, take it all in and file it away in that policeman's head. A medium-built man who moved easily, the detective reminded Alec of the athletics teacher at the school; he was about the same height as Alec himself but with more muscle and thick, light brown hair going silver at the temples. His eyes, though, were different—gray and intense enough to be disturbing, cataloging everything. A good-looking guy who probably had something in his life, a wife and maybe a family. Unlike me, Alec thought with a sense of sudden, almost devastating sorrow. Because without Nola that's what I am: *nothing*. Then he realized the detective was speaking and he forced himself to push his self-pity aside long enough to listen. "I'm sorry? I—I didn't catch that."

The policeman studied him, his face expressionless. "I asked if you believe there's been foul play, Mr. Elidad. What I'm trying to establish is a reason for you to suspect something has happened to your wife"—he consulted his clipboard again—"Nola, rather than . . ." Conroy paused and Alec waited, struggling to suppress the tingling of hysteria that was snapping at the edges of his self-control. He didn't want to lose it in front of this man, didn't want *anyone*—least of all this jaded police officer—to know how much he depended on Nola's presence in his everyday life.

As the silence stretched, the detective finally set the clipboard on the cushion beside him and sat forward. "Sometimes, Mr. Elidad, a man or a woman simply decides to leave." He clasped his hands as Alec stared at him. "For reasons that are . . . not always shared with a spouse, or a boyfriend, or even a parent, a person just *goes.* Across town, or across the state line, across the country—somewhere, *any*where else. They get fed up, scared, tired, whatever, and they take off and make a new life for themselves somewhere else. What I have to ask you, bluntly, is if you think there's any chance of that having happened with your wife."

For a moment Conroy's expression changed, and Alec squeezed his eyes closed against the flash of pity he'd seen, wishing the detective had kept his careful, professional neutrality. He thought of Nola, of her quietness and her passion for privacy, of the way he'd stumbled onto her last year like a lost person in the dark discovering a light. In someone else's life, where Nola was right now might be explained in a dozen different ways; in Alec's, he could think only that the world had ended and that something terrible had happened to her. Perhaps her absence had brought an instantaneous return of his pessimistic outlook, something that Nola had changed by her simple *presence* in a life that was formerly as bland and unexciting as an unwanted library book. How would he function—how *had* he functioned—in The Time Before Nola?

Alec looked around the living room and saw the uninspired furniture, the pictures on the walls that he'd put there not because he'd liked them or cared, but only because they were something to take up space. For so long, he'd simply *been* here, existing in a day-to-day life that was as close as it came to automating human flesh, but now . . . He ran a hand over his scalp, feeling the perspiring skin between the fine hair, thinking suddenly of the fifteen years that separated him from his lovely young wife. Was that it? Had this been only a stepping-stone for her, the first taste of a life beyond that of the one she'd known as a child? Had she ultimately gotten . . . tired of him? When they'd met, Nola had told him she wanted love and security, a safe, *unchanging* place. He had offered her those things, but she was young, petite, and to his mind, very, very beautiful.

Jesus, were the things he shared with her *enough*?

Alec lifted his eyes to meet Conroy's patient gaze. "I—I don't think so," was all he could manage. "I thought she was happy. She never said otherwise."

Conroy nodded and scribbled something on his clipboard, seeming to appreciate the careful consideration Alec had given the question before answering. "Were you having a disagreement about anything? Even something small that you might otherwise think was insignificant?" Alec shook his head. "All right." Conroy made another mark on the clipboard. "And does she have relatives, a mother? Have you called her family?"

Uh-oh, Alec thought. "Well . . ."

Conroy's brow lifted. "Is there a problem?"

"Well, yes." Alec shifted uncomfortably. "I don't really know if she has any relatives," he had to admit. "She was very private about her past. It was something she didn't speak about, and she made it clear when we began dating that it would stay that way. From her attitude, I assumed her childhood was unpleasant, and that she wanted to avoid contact with her parents—and from the way she acted when she did talk about it, there was probably good reason. To be truthful, I don't even know if her parents are living."

The detective was writing rapidly now, his pen making little scratching sounds that ate at Alec's ears. "I see. And how long have you been married, Mr. Elidad?"

"Three months."

Conroy glanced quickly at him, then back to the form he was filling out. "And how long have you known your wife?"

Alec hesitated long enough for Conroy to look up again. "Just . . . a little over three months," he answered.

Now Conroy was frowning outright. "Mr. Elidad, do you know anything at *all* about her past? Where she went to school, who her friends were, her family doctor—anything?"

Reluctantly, Alec shook his head. "I—I know this looks strange, but she refused to talk about her past at all." He spread his hands helplessly. "It was just something I learned to accept about her."

Conroy sighed and closed his clipboard. "All right. I'll put out an all-points on her name within the village limits tonight, but I can't do more than that until twenty-four hours have passed unless I have a reasonable suspicion that there's been foul play. We already discussed that." Conroy waited, giving him a final chance to add something, but all Alec could do was shake his head again. The policeman got to his feet, tucked the report under one arm, and straightened his jacket. "That's about it for tonight, then. I'm sorry I can't offer you more help. If she still hasn't shown up by, let's see"—Conroy chewed his lower lip for a second while he consulted some mental clock—"nine tomorrow night, then call the station and ask for me. I'll come back out and we'll go over this again. I can't do any more until then."

Alec followed him to the door. "But you don't understand," he said desperately. "She's never late." He had to stop his hands from reaching out to clutch at the man's sleeve. "I just know something bad's happened. She has nowhere else to *go*."

Conroy stopped and regarded him solemnly. "Mr. Elidad," he said softly, "the fact is, you don't really know that." He turned and opened the door for himself. "If she's not back by nine tomorrow night," he repeated firmly as he stepped into the hallway, "call me. That's the best I can offer."

And Alec was left to stare at the cheap plastic grain of his own closed front door.

This is how, for Nola, her nightmare continued:

For some reason, shock perhaps, the world around her had shifted into high speed while she remained in slow motion. The lights going past the car, all the automobiles driven by a hundred people too single-minded about where they were going to notice the terrified face of a kidnapped woman through the window of someone else's car, the entire ride to this man's home—it all felt like it took years, *forever;* at the same time Nola was convinced that while one moment she was in her abductor's car . . .

The next she was inside his townhouse.

She had a single, painful moment of clarity about what was happening to her, and what waited ahead if she didn't do something about it. It was a turning point inside her mind, as though everything in the universe revolved around this one instant—her future, her life, the whole of whatever amount of hope she had been given that she might actually be able to survive this ordeal.

It all seemed to coalesce right after he pushed her ahead of him through the door, then casually swung the door shut with one foot. He put a hand on her arm and guided her forward a few feet before he let go again, but he wasn't being rough—more matter-of-fact, as though it were the most natural thing in the world that she should stand to one side while he walked to a closet a couple of paces away and nonchalantly shrugged off his coat.

Nola watched him do this, and everything dropped into focus.

That door behind her—the one he'd just closed without giving it a second thought—now separated her from the rest of the world and life as she had once known it. She didn't believe he'd locked it—this man seemed to expect that she would stay where she was and wait, still assumed that she was who he believed her to be rather than a total stranger he had literally stolen off the street.

In the course of one small heartbeat, Nola knew that what she did—or didn't do—right now would determine the course of the rest of her life.

Screaming inside, she scrambled for the door.

She never made it.

....

There were small things moving in the dark.

It was like being in a box or a casket—a total blackout of the senses that left her straining to hear or see or feel something other than the cold permeating her flesh. As a child, her room had been like that, completely featureless once the lights were out, leaving nothing for her to think about except the spots moving behind her own eyelids. The basement of this townhouse was the same: cold, not quite quiet, and way too dark. Only the smallest sliver of light leaked from beneath the base of the door, too far away to see except at the very top of the stairs, and too minimal for her eyes to adjust its light anywhere else.

Desperation creates its own form of bravery, and finally Nola ventured down the stairs. Each step downward felt as though she were stepping into a bottomless black pit; each time she lowered her foot she expected it to keep going and going and going, never to find the surface of the next riser. She imagined herself—with her shoes lost in the struggle that had landed her here—reaching with her freezing toes until she overbalanced and tumbled headlong into . . . absolutely nothing. She would simply fall, forever, screaming and thrashing and never feeling anything again . . .

But that had hadn't happened, of course. Instead, her courage had actually been rewarded, and her hands, outstretched for balance and sweeping the air around herself as though she were a blind person spun in the middle of an unfamiliar room, had brushed against something—a cord. A few precious seconds of fumbling and she'd found it again and pulled; it was only dim light, no more than a forty-watt bulb, that seeped through the basement, but that small bit of illumination made all the difference in the world.

It was a big enough area that the feeble light didn't reach its limits, leaving pools of darkness at the edges. Nola gritted her teeth, both as an outward sign of determination and to stop their chattering, then felt her way around a bunch of boxes stacked along the back wall. Every now and then she heard soft, scuttling noises just beyond where she stood, the movements of creatures that were living between the stacks of musty-smelling cardboard and the other odd things—tires, pipes, dirty and splintered two-by-fours—pushed against the walls. More noises made her jerk around, this time coming from the lightless area under the stairs where the furnace and water heater backed up to a frigid wall of exposed lathing and concrete blocks. She wanted to huddle next to the furnace, but it must have had a sleep timer on it; an hour or so after her kidnapper locked her down there, it cut off, then only ran for about ten out of every fifty minutes—not enough to warrant standing shoeless in the icy air along the concrete floor.

As far as Nola could tell, she was trapped. The basement had no walk-out and the one escape window she'd located was worthless, nearly blocked by a precarious stack of crumbling, unlabeled boxes. The corner that was visible was clearly nailed shut, and it looked as though dirt had filled most of the well outside the window anyway.

More noises, louder now, bolder. Were there mice down here? Or . . . rats?

Nola started to climb the stairs again but stopped halfway up. What was she going to do—beat on the door and demand to be freed? Did she really want to remind him that she was down here? Or—

The door at the top of the stairs opened without warning, flooding the narrow stairwell with sudden, shocking light. Nola shrieked in fright and scrambled back down the stairs, going for the darkest, farthest corner she could find. She could see his silhouette moving up there, backlit by the light of the house behind him, and she could hear him saying something to her but couldn't make out the words—the blood was pounding high and hard in her ears again, destroying any chance she had of comprehension. This was it, the moment of truth, and if Nola had thought the waiting was the worst, teetering on the brink of actual discovery was a thousand times more devastating. What was next? Rape, murder, torture? *What?*

Now she would find out. Now he would come down the stairs and—

The door closed again, leaving her to stand, shuddering, just beyond the edge of the pitiful pool of light thrown by the dirty overhead bulb.

It's a trick, Nola thought. He doesn't want to have to chase me down here and he thinks I'll go back up there, maybe knock on the door—then he'll open it and drag me out.

But he'd been saying something when he'd opened the door, and she'd been too terrified to hear—what had it been? She stayed where she was for a long time, determined to ignore the cold air slipping around her ankles and trying to recall his words. Calmer now, she thought she could remember a few of them, although what came back was anything but comforting—

"I have to think things out."

That had been one of the things he'd said, and hadn't he also told her that she'd be better off down here? Until when?

Until he thinks things out.

The minutes stretched, impossible to calculate in the returned darkness, but her kidnapper didn't come back. She heard footsteps across the ceiling above her, the heavy tread of a man's weight that crossed, then recrossed the room, finally fading enough to where Nola was reasonably confident that he wasn't lurking on the other side of the door up there. She climbed the stairs cautiously, thankful for the minute increase in the temperature between the floor and the upper risers. A few stairs from the top the glow from beneath the door let her see that he'd left something for her. Still afraid, half certain that the door would fly open at any second, Nola had to know what these things were. Trembling, she extended one hand, filled with the irrational fear that it was something alive, that it would leap up and—

A couple of blankets.

And what was this next to it? A bowl of some kind of noodle soup, grown cold in the time that she had hesitated downstairs. Folded next to the cheap plastic bowl was a paper napkin and a cheaper plastic spoon, soft enough to dispel any notion that she might use it for some kind of weapon.

Something else he'd said found its way back along the churning currents of her memory—

"You're probably cold. We'll talk tomorrow."

Had he really said that, or was she only imagining it?

Nola honestly couldn't say, and it didn't matter anyway. She discovered very quickly that the two thin blankets were of little use in the frigid air of the basement. She guessed the outside temperature had been only in the mid-thirties when he'd kidnapped her, and she supposed that this townhouse, being one of the cheaply built and poorly insulated developer's specials, worked both for and against her. The outside air leaked in through a thousand minuscule cracks and holes, but there was also no insulation lining the ceiling. While it was true that any heat would rise, she was fairly certain it'd be a lot colder down here if the overhead rafters had been lined with fiberglass. Ultimately, desperation overrode her terror and Nola wrapped herself in the blankets and huddled at the top of the stairs, going for every bit of the warmth of the upper floor that she could get. When he opened the door, she thought she could dodge under his arm and—

Please, she thought. Who are you kidding?

Nola shifted on the stairs and shivered, although she couldn't tell if it was from the cold or from the throbbing in her left foot. He was bigger than she—ten times stronger. Even if she could get past him, what difference would that make? There was no place to go, no way to conceal herself; by now he'd most certainly locked up all the doors and windows.

Could she fight him? Be serious. The abduction in the parking lot and her attempts to escape, the short but pitiful struggle she'd given when he'd pulled her into the house, the lunge for the door while he'd hung up his coat—not only had they all been futile, but they'd probably only angered him. Face it, Nola thought grimly, there are times in a person's life when you have to accept being outranked.

How long had it been now? Hours? For Christ's sake, she was *freezing* down here. Hypothermia, she thought dully. I'm probably going to die from exposure while *inside* a building. She was horribly thirsty, but a sip or two of the now-congealing chicken soup only made her nauseous and increased her craving for water. Worse, she had to go to the bathroom—dear God, when he finally did come for her, would she wet herself like a baby?

More time passed—minutes, an hour, who knew. She was so cold and so tired . . . even a little numb. The urge to urinate faded a bit and all she wanted was a nap, like waking in the middle of the night and being unwilling to expend the effort to get up. Even so, every sound from beyond the door, every thump and step, every creak and shift of the wood around her, made her start and lift her head.

Soon, though, Nola's exhaustion blotted out everything and, as did the stranger upstairs, she slipped into a fitful sleep cut by dark and troubled dreams.

2

Reality

The heart has eyes which the brain knows nothing of.

—CHARLES H. PERKHURST

JANUARY 17--FRIDAY

"Stacey?"

Nola jerked upright and her precarious perch on the stairs slipped; before she could lose it entirely, her abductor grabbed her shoulder and steadied her, then slipped a hand around her elbow and pulled her to a standing position. Every stiffened muscle in her body screamed in protest, both at his touch and in response to the quick, forced movement after so many hours of inactivity. Jesus, she must have been dozing—exhaustion, the cold, the fear itself all overwhelming her. How long had she slept on that small wooden stair with no sense of her tenuous balance and this madman just beyond the flimsy barrier of a cheap basement door?

"Let's go," he said, and guided her, stumbling, up the last two steps and into the house. Warm air washed over her face and her skin tingled in response; at the same time little stabs of pain shot through her fingers and toes as her circulation stepped up again.

"I have to go to the bathroom." Nola's voice was frightened and raspy. Her throat felt raw and hurt all the way around her neck when she swallowed. She almost laughed—maybe she'd caught a cold from spending the night in that basement. "Could I go to the bathroom?" she repeated.

"Of course." He pulled her along a short hallway, then stopped before a half-closed door. She flinched as his hands reached for her, but he only tugged away the heavy, sodden fabric wrapped around her shoulders. "Here, let me take those blankets. They're damp anyway." He swung the door open the rest of the way and Nola saw a small, inexpensively decorated powder room. She ducked inside and pulled the door shut, then fumbled at her skirt and the ripped remains of her nylons, nearly gasping with relief as she emptied her bladder. She had a moment of embarrassment at the knowledge that he was waiting just outside the door and could hear her using the toilet, but there was nothing she could do about it.

When she was through, Nola washed her hands and splashed water on her face, then dried off with a worn face towel hanging above the sink. Now what? She scanned the room carefully, but there was no medicine cabinet or vanity, and certainly nothing like a nail file or pair of scissors conveniently lying on the back of the commode. Nothing but the toilet itself, the sink, and the large, round mirror securely hanging on the wall above it. She could break it, but what would that accomplish? A shower of dangerous flying glass, then the man in the hallway would come barreling through the door before she could even unshield her eyes, much less choose a shard of mirror as a weapon. A stupid idea.

Her reflection looked wild, as though another woman, someone doomed and unknown, had taken over her face. Her lips and lids were swollen, the eyes themselves wide with terror and set deep within blue-black shadows. Splashing her face had only smeared grime across it, and the short brown hair framing her cheekbones was tangled and spiked with dirt and dried perspiration, her clothes undeniably filthy and reeking with the stench of fear. And she was barefoot—presumably she had left her other shoe somewhere in his townhouse, or maybe that basement. Inexplicably, that above all else made her feel vulnerable.

"Are you okay?" Beyond the pseudo-wood of the door, her kidnapper's voice was muffled, concerned. Like the face in the mirror, the trembling hand that Nola reached to grasp the doorknob seemed to belong to someone else.

Am I okay? she thought. Now . . . yes. But what about in five more minutes? Her throat constricted painfully.

Sometimes, Nola thought again, a person has to accept being outranked.

She took a deep, burning breath, then opened the door to face the man on the other side.

Jesse tried to think while Stacey was in the bathroom, but his thoughts were muddled, strained from having had only a few hours of sleep split by dreams and the disjointed thoughts and questions in his head that just wouldn't let him rest. This morning it had all come together—somewhere during the night's blackest hours, exhaustion and stress had taken over and dropped him into a deep enough slumber to clear his mind so that everything finally fell into place.

He couldn't believe he hadn't seen it before now.

He'd already been awake for an hour and a half, getting ready for a day of trying to repair the damage—to which he'd probably already added. Stacey's words came back to him again, the things that she had said in the parking lot and probably more than a few times in the ride from the Pik-Kwik back to the townhouse. She'd claimed she was someone else, although if she'd given this other identity a name, Jesse couldn't recall it. His need to bring her home had overridden everything, and then—he was ashamed to admit it, but the truth was certainly there—any chance of having a rational conversation with her had been suffocated by the anger that had risen in him when she'd resisted. What an idiot he'd been.

He should have been more understanding, should have stopped to remember that there was clearly something wrong with her. Dear God, wasn't it obvious that something had misfired inside her mind while she was hospitalized last year? All those drugs, the brain damage caused by her nearly uncontrollable fever—it must've been too much. Confused and sick, with what was left of her thoughts muddled by medication—Jesse could picture even the strong-willed

Stacey climbing out of her hospital bed and simply . . . walking away from it all, wanting nothing more than to escape all the needles and drugs and machines, all the *pain.* So she'd gone searching for the parts of her mind and life that were missing, destroyed by her sickness. And if the medical staff had been careless enough to let her slip out of there . . . of course they would arrange a massive cover-up to hide their negligence.

In retrospect, he could see the signs—the whispering among the doctors, the looks from the nurses and the staff. Or perhaps, with the power that doctors seemed to wield nowadays, the head physician had been the instigator, the one who had stepped in and mapped out the deception that would save his career when Jesse and Stacey's family would have destroyed him and that damned hospital had they known the truth. And the worst of it? All the while, his wife had been wandering somewhere, recovering from her illness but mentally unstable, without a clue about her true identity. The hospital's trump card had been knowing that Jesse would be too afraid to see Stacey's body—somewhere along the line he must have mentioned his parents' awful deaths and the shock he'd suffered as a child by having to view them in their coffins. It seemed like Stacey had been in that damned hospital forever, and Jesse had chatted with so many of the staff, he could've told anyone . . .

And now this.

Jesse had risen this morning after a final hour of restless sleep, taken a few dollars from Stacey's purse, and driven over to the convenience store a few blocks away. There he'd picked up a dozen eggs, a quart of milk, and a few other things—not much, but better than the plain toast he'd planned on having. As he drove back home, the realization of what he'd done slammed into his head with the force of a hammer. Jesus Christ—he'd been so frustrated when she'd try to run away again that he'd locked Stacey in the *basement* and left her there overnight.

What had he been thinking—why would he do something like that? Anger, perhaps. Her escape attempt had been the least of what had gotten to Jesse. It'd been seeing her with that other man, all that time of watching the two of them together, until he just . . . broke, that's all. It was easy for Jesse to see how the words of an ignorant bartender at Christmastime could come back and haunt him, could be the catalyst to make him realize it really would be possible to get her back. But Jesus—to put her in the basement . . .

She was probably freezing, hungry, and there was the ever-present and terrible danger of her getting sick again, something she did with horrid ease. What a stupid, stupid thing for him to do! In the end, nothing she had done or he had thought justified it—just look at her now: Her lips were almost blue with cold, her face was shock-white, and she could barely walk. The truth was, Stacey would *never* leave him. This whole thing wasn't even her fault. It had started with a simple strep throat that snowballed out of control. Rheumatic fever followed, then that awful miscarriage, possible brain damage—how could he have been so *stupid*? God, he ought to be shot.

She was taking an awful long time in the john. Jesse could hear the sound of water running in the sink, and he did a quick mental inventory of the bathroom—nope, nothing in there that she could hurt herself with.

"Are you okay?" he asked through the door.

No answer, but she might not have heard him over the water. Or she might just be too scared to answer—he'd let his temper get the best of him last night, but not again, not *ever*. He'd make it up to her somehow, with the first order of business being to warm her up and put a good, hot meal in her stomach to get her blood going again. After that, well, they'd have a long talk and try to work this out.

Now *that* was the scary part, the part that made Jesse pace as he tried to force all the answers into solutions that were logical, fitting with his and Stacey's lives. The first problem, obviously, was that Stacey thought she was someone else. Never mind who or why, or even what she'd been doing for the last three months; Jesse knew he had to make himself forget all that. The clearest question was what did you do for an amnesia victim?

Why, you took the person to see a doctor, of course. A psychiatrist.

Except he didn't have the money for a doctor right now, and Jesse certainly wasn't going to take her to an emergency room somewhere or, God forbid, some county-run facility. A place like either of those, and he would be expected to turn Stacey's care over to them and leave. Thanks, but he'd made that mistake three months ago, and it would damn well never happen again. His medical insurance had disappeared when his company had folded and the coverage from his new job wouldn't start for at least three months—that was the standard eligibility period in the shops around here. Yet another reason why he shouldn't have been such a fool and locked her in the basement last night. But he'd been so afraid she'd find a way to leave . . .

"Stacey?"

Still no answer, and Jesse was reaching uncertainly for the knob when it twisted and she opened the door and stepped out.

The expression of fear on her face cut Jesse all the way to the heart, and he knew it was no one's fault but his own. How much damage had he done in the so-short time that he'd had her back? More than enough, obviously—to her mind, the only thing he'd ever shown her was anger. For a second, he just stared at her, his thoughts spinning and at a loss about how to fix this. He started to open his mouth, unsure even then about what he was going to say, then it hit him.

Trista!

He would call his mother-in-law, of course, and put Stacey on the line. Surely talking to her own mother would have some effect on Stacey's memory. It was a lot to hope for, but maybe this simple thing was the key to snapping everything back. As much as he disliked Trista, she'd had her own suspicions all this time, and Jesse knew that she would be overjoyed to find out the truth about what really happened to her daughter. But what to do with Stacey in the meantime? If she went for the door again . . . well, yesterday's ordeal had done too much damage. The answer, however, was right in front of him.

"Listen, I have to do something, okay?" Stacey said nothing, her eyes watching him like a terrified doe's. He motioned back to the bathroom. "Go back in here awhile, because I don't want you down in that cold basement. I'll be right outside. Go on."

Hesitantly, she obeyed, flinching away from his touch and never taking her gaze off him as she retreated to a spot against the wall where the door wouldn't hit her on the backswing. Jesse pulled it shut, then walked the short distance to the telephone table at the juncture of where the hallway met the door to the living room, keeping an eye on the bathroom door in case Stacey decided to make another run for it. It was tearing him up to see her so frightened and he wasn't keen on having her sit in that tiny room, but he couldn't risk letting his guard down and having her try to hightail it in the middle of his conversation.

It had been a long time, so he had to look up his mother-in-law's number in the small black book in the end table drawer. He hadn't talked to Trista in months; after the hospital had lied about Stacey, Jesse had called her every now and then, even though she'd said she didn't want to talk to him. Finally he'd stopped calling as it became increasingly clear that she despised him all the more for not having allowed her to visit Stacey. And in hindsight, how stupid had that been? So much of this heartache could have been avoided. But they'd never gotten along, she'd never liked him or treated him decently, even when he and Stacey had—

"Hello? Who's this?" Trista Newman's voice was slurred with sleep, and Jesse had only a second to realize it was probably before six on a Friday morning. Damn—bad start.

"Uh, Trista, this is Jesse. I'm sorry to wake you up. I, uh, wasn't looking at the time."

Silence.

Then Trista sighed, and the sound conveyed more to Jesse than the woman could have ever said in so short a time. He could imagine her grinding her teeth, trying to be a martyr and grant him a sliver of her valuable sleep time, even though she'd never believed he was worth it. Jesse waited, willing himself not to speak; pain in his hand made him glance down and he saw that he'd wrapped the telephone cord so tightly around his palm that it was cutting off his circulation. He began to unroll it.

"It's very early, Jesse," Trista said at last. "Why are you calling?"

"Look," he said, "can we just put aside our past . . . differences, just for a minute here? I found out something important—"

"Not at this ungodly hour." The woman's voice softened for a moment. "I know you've been through a lot, and I know it's been very difficult. But it's been like that for all of us, and I can't help you anymore. The ties between us are gone and I don't *want* to, don't you understand?"

"But that's just it. What you said about Stacey was—"

"There's no point in continuing this conversation, Jesse," Trista interrupted. Had he only imagined the semi-soothing tone of her voice a moment ago? He must have, because it was certainly a world away from the hard, emotionless sounds now on the other end of the line. "This is twice I've endured this kind of loss, and I just want to *forget.* As much as I can, anyway, and you should be doing the same thing. Please—*don't* call back."

For a long, slow moment, Jesse was sure it was someone else clutching the telephone receiver and staring blankly at the layout of his living room. Was he really hearing this?

A *dial tone*?

He couldn't believe it—the old bat hadn't even given him the chance to tell her that her daughter was back after disappearing for three whole months, and the kicker was that *she* was the one who'd been right all along! Rage made him slam the receiver down so hard that a fine crack appeared along the mouthpiece, and he gripped the side of the wall and just stood there, trying to breathe past the anger and resentment that always bubbled up when he attempted to deal with his mother-in-law. *Damn*—that woman made him want to pick up the phone and just throw it! Some snide part of Trista probably saw Stacey's being gone as a good thing, freedom from a son-in-law she'd always detested because he'd taken Stacey away from her and whom she'd never believed was good enough to warrant that. For all Jesse knew, maybe she'd known Stacey was okay all this time, maybe even where she'd lived right up to the time she'd been with that guy. Some act on the telephone—she probably thought that with his blue-collar job and limited education, Stacey had found better, even if she had to "disappear" to do it. What Trista, of course, had always chosen to ignore was that Stacey had always been happy with him, had *chosen* him—

Stacey!

Jesse spun and saw that the powder room door was still closed. For a minute he'd forgotten about that, had been so caught up in the results of this horrible phone conversation he hadn't been paying attention. Now he ran a hand across his forehead and found that he was sweating despite the morning chilliness of the townhouse. How the hell was he supposed to tell Stacey that her own mother—provided she even remembered the witch—hadn't even cared to know she was back?

Maybe it wouldn't matter. In reality, Stacey hadn't gotten along with her mother any better than Jesse had—it had only been out of a strict, and as far as Jesse was concerned, undeserved sense of obligation, that his wife had contacted Trista on holidays. For now he'd keep his mouth shut about the call, and if the truth came out later, at least he could honestly say that he'd tried.

Jesse took a deep breath, then let it out slowly, determined to chase away the last of the tenseness that Trista had, as usual, managed to bring up in him. A second, long inhalation, then he stepped up to the door and pushed it carefully open. Stacey was sitting, shivering, on the closed toilet seat; she jumped when the door bumped into one of her knees and was on her feet in an instant, backing up until she was pressed against the inside wall of the tiny room. Jesse reached in and took her by the hand, wrapping her small, icy fingers in his warmer ones.

"Come on," he said as he pulled her out of the bathroom. "I'm going to make you breakfast."

A fever, Nola thought. That's it—103 degrees at least, maybe higher. How else could she explain the sense of unreality that had settled around her, that high, tinny whine in her ears that wouldn't go away? Her brain was boiling inside her skull and probably sweeping away the last of her coherence with it. She was paralyzed with fear, with indecision and confusion; beneath the table her fingers were entwined so tightly that they ached, but she was helpless to pry them apart. What was it she'd heard him saying on the other side of the bathroom door a little while ago? It had sounded like a telephone conversation—fear had already blown apart the memory in her mind, but she distinctly remembered that he'd said something like *Trista.* The name was vaguely familiar, like a puzzle piece that ought to fit somewhere in her past—the same past she'd steadfastly avoided talking to Alec about because she didn't want to admit it was full of holes in her mind, dark voids that represented chunks of time for which she couldn't, try as she might, account.

And now here she was. Her kidnapper—this madman who had ripped her from a life she'd made in which she was happy and comfortable, a life she hadn't appreciated nearly as much as she should have—moved around the small, tidy kitchen seemingly without a care in the world. He was fixing her *breakfast,* for God's sake, as though she belonged here, in a stranger's townhouse—as if they were old friends. Or . . . more.

Nola's stomach roiled and she swallowed against the sensation of nausea. The smells coming from the stove weren't helping. The hot sizzle of frying bacon and potatoes and the smell of margarine as the man broke eggs into a skillet were a constant assault on her senses, tantalizing and gut-wrenching at the same time.

"I'd forgotten about this bacon in the freezer," he said cheerfully. His big hands plucked eggs from an open carton on the counter and he broke them into a bowl, whipped them into a froth, then quickly poured the mix into a hot skillet. "It was damned near buried under the frost—I guess I'd forgotten about thawing the freezer, too. You had some money in your wallet, but I only took a couple of dollars. That's how I got the eggs and potatoes, and the margarine. Oh, and a quart of milk. But I only took what I needed, just so you know. The rest is still there." For a moment, he looked absurdly ashamed, like a little boy caught pilfering from his mother's purse. "I'll pay you back as soon as I get my first paycheck."

Nola sat numbly at the table, hands folded. She was completely, utterly baffled. This wasn't the way an abduction was supposed to work. What kind of a kidnapper *borrowed* only enough money from your wallet to buy food to fix you a hot meal? She swallowed past another sick roll of her stomach and let her gaze travel around the small room until it stopped at a pair of sliding glass doors leading to a small, shabby deck. Beyond the grimy-looking glass was a tiny yard filled with the snow-covered, withered growth of the previous season and enclosed by a dark brown fence.

Against all reason, she stared at that fence. Was it as worn as everything else around here looked, perhaps even . . . rickety? And gates—all fences had them, didn't they? The trick would be to actually get past this man and *out* the door. They were probably locked, but most patio doors had a sort of flip-up lever beneath the handle like the one on the door that led to the balcony in her and Alec's apartment. Then again, this was a ground floor; there might very well be a bar lock across the bottom, the kind that could only be opened with a key.

The man at the counter was humming cheerfully to himself, and Nola resisted the urge to clap her hands over her ears. She wondered what Alec was doing this morning—was her husband even now at the police station, filing reports and sending policemen out to search for her? The thought made Nola frown slightly. She'd never owned a camera and didn't particularly like having her picture taken. Was there even a photograph of her in the apartment? She wasn't sure.

"Here we go." Her kidnapper set a plate of food in front of her, then placed another at a spot opposite hers, effectively blocking her way to the glass patio doors. He mustn't think she was much of a threat while she was in his sight, because this time he gave her a real fork to go with her paper napkin. Milk, poured into one of those tiny glasses that had once contained a cheap shrimp cocktail, completed the meal. He took a bite of scrambled eggs, then motioned at her plate with his fork. "Go on, eat. You'll get sick if you don't."

The smell was driving Nola crazy, making her mouth water even though the condition of her stomach was questionable. She *was* hungry. In spite of the fact that she had no right to be thinking about food, that she should be thinking about *dying*, for God's sake, she was starving. Maybe, she thought dismally as she eyed the breakfast, this is my last meal. If so, she ought to make it as good as she could.

Nola picked up her fork and began to eat, and the bacon and eggs were good, and hot, and those were followed by a lightly buttered piece of toast until it all floated in the pit of her belly like a dead frog on a rotting lily pad. She kept eating anyway, afraid that stopping would anger the man who sat across from her and who concentrated on his own meal, afraid of what would happen if she said she was full, afraid of what would be said and done once the meal was over. Anxiety made her swallow too fast, and she tried to slow down; it might only stall the inevitable but every minute counted. What she intended was altogether different from reality though, and Nola's stomach would accept only a fraction of what was on the plate; ultimately she simply pushed the food around while she watched him eat everything in front of him. He ate with gusto, like a man sitting in front of his first meal after being rescued from what should have been his own execution.

"My name is Jesse," her kidnapper said unexpectedly. "Jesse Waite. I guess you don't remember me." She sat, frozen, as he pushed his chair back and stood. He picked up his cleaned plate then reached for hers and paused a second, as though he might say something about how little she'd managed to eat. Instead, he only shrugged and took it to the sink. "I'm your husband, and—"

"No," she whispered. Not loud enough, he hadn't heard—or maybe he'd chosen not to.

"—and your name is Stacey Waite," he continued stubbornly. "Your maiden name is Gardell."

"No," Nola said, a little louder this time. Her stomach roiled dangerously in response to a brief, nasty repeat of that sense of déjà vu she'd felt in the parking lot yesterday evening, a bizarre sensation of remembering the *act* of remembering—none of it made any sense. Beneath the table her hands were gripping each other, the fingernails digging brutally into her nerveless skin. "You've got the wrong woman. That's not my name." My God, Nola thought suddenly, that phrase is becoming a litany—I feel like I've said it a thousand times!

"Yes it *is*," Jesse Waite insisted. Fear razored through her, sharp enough to shorten her breath as she realized he seemed to be forcing his words through clenched teeth. Again she wondered if she was having a heart attack—she felt like God Himself was throwing little lightning bolts at her chest. At the same time, the dishes in her abductor's hands clattered against each other before he set them on the counter. "We've been married for four years. I guess I ought to know my own wife." When he lifted his head, Nola saw that his expression was almost identical to when she had first seen him in the parking lot yesterday, too filled with pain and longing, *delusion*, for him to recognize the truth. "Your name," he repeated, "is *Stacey*."

"No," she said clearly. She was terrified, yet she couldn't stop herself—she had to at least try to make him understand what he was doing here, what really *was*. "That's not true. My name is Nola, Nola Eli—"

Jesse crossed the room before Nola could finish. His

hands were on her then, the same hands that had so carefully fixed her a homemade breakfast just a quarter hour before, except that now they were gripping her by the upper arms with bruising strength.

"No it's *not.*" His voice was rising and his eyes were wild, and each time he reached the end of the sentence he emphasized it with a jerk—

"Your name is *Stacey,* Stacey Waite!"

—and a shake that sent the breakfast in her stomach rolling dangerously.

"B-b-butttt—" She gulped for air and her small hands slapped frantically at his chest, his hard stomach, anything within reach to try to break his hold. There was a sting inside her mouth as she bit her own lip, chance making her find the spot that was still tender from hitting the inside of the car door the night before.

"You stop saying that, do you understand?" Jesse Waite's voice was both loud and grim, like a roll of thunder across her eardrums. "From now on, don't even think of yourself as that person anymore—she's dead, gone for good, *forever. You are not that person!*"

The taste of blood was in Nola's mouth again, but worse than when she'd first nicked the inside of her mouth; now it was thick and heavy, stronger than it should be and sliding down her throat with sticky red tentacles—

She vomited all over both of them.

"Aw, Christ," Jesse said. "Now look what I've done." Nola retched again and he held her up when she would have sunk to the floor. Tears coursed down her face and both of them were covered in the foul-smelling bits of her barely digested breakfast. "Damn, I'm sorry, Stacey. Come on, baby, don't cry." Unbelievably, he pulled her into his arms, ignoring the mess as he held her and stroked her slick forehead, her perspiration-sodden hair. "Here." He pulled a kitchen chair away from the table and pushed her gently onto it as though she were a fragile, cracked doll that he was afraid would break. "You sit and I'll wipe up the floor. Then we'll get cleaned up."

Legs shaking, Nola huddled on the chair and held herself, trying not to shake and fighting against the urge to gag—the stench was horrible and she couldn't believe this man could stand it. But Jesse pulled off his dirtied T-shirt and used it to sop up most of the vomit around his feet, then shoved it into a plastic garbage bag. He found another rag under the sink, wet it down and damp-wiped the floor, then threw that in the bag and twisted it shut. Finally he rinsed his hands and grabbed her wrist. "I'll scrub it down later. Right now we could both use a shower, but ladies first. Come on."

Nola looked at him fearfully. Blood crusted around the inside of her lip and made her mouth throb. "A shower?" she asked in a tiny voice.

"Sure." He smiled crookedly. "You know, one of those things where the water falls on your head? We actually have one." She flinched when he wiped at the side of her mouth with his thumb; it came away smeared with red. He blinked at it for a second, then shook his head. *"Christ."*

Jesse tugged her to her feet, then supported her again when her knees threatened to buckle, half-walking, half-carrying her out of the kitchen and up a flight of stairs she hadn't noticed before at the other end of the living room. Images flew by: a small dining room with a full wall of closed drapes; a decent-sized living room that also had the drapes pulled tight over all the windows. Small things—a vase of silk flowers, a framed embroidered heart hanging on the wall, a small china knickknack—spoke of a woman's touch, although everything in the place seemed to hang under a gloomy, dusty atmosphere.

On the second floor, Jesse flicked on a light, then guided her into a windowless bathroom. "Here," he said as he pointed across the small room. "Clean towels on the rack, and there's soap and shampoo by the tub. I'll bring you some clothes." He started to step back out the door, then frowned and turned around again; Nola watched as he opened the medicine cabinet door, studied its contents for a moment, then pulled out a pair of scissors and slid them into his back pocket with a self-conscious shrug. Another few seconds and he closed the door, leaving her alone without another word.

Nola stared at the door for a long moment, then spun in a frantic circle. Nothing—it was just an ordinary bathroom like any other. How often do you find a weapon in a bathroom? He'd taken the only thing she might've used. There wasn't so much as a nail file in the cabinet, or even one of those rat-tail combs. Jesus—was this *still* happening to her?

Nola sank onto the edge of the bathtub and covered her face with her hands, sobbing silently. Did this man really expect her to willingly take off her clothes, with him in the house and able to walk in on her at any moment? Tears of frustration were still sliding down her cheeks when Jesse knocked lightly on the door, then opened it cautiously.

He watched her for a few moments but didn't say anything. After a while, he closed the toilet lid and placed a folded bundle of clothes on it. "Here," he said. "Something to change into." When she still didn't move, he knelt in front of her and forced her hands away from her face, holding them tightly when she would have leaned away from him and tilted backward into the tub. "Stacey, honey, you've got to get a grip on yourself. You're a mess—you've got puke all over you, your face is all swollen up, and you need a shower really bad. Now, you claim you don't know me, right?" He let go of one hand and hooked a finger under her chin to raise her face and force her to look at him. "Right?" Finally she nodded. "Well, then, if that's true, the last thing you want is me undressing you and washing you down in the shower."

Her mouth dropped open, but before she could find a response he stood and looked at her sternly as he let go of her other hand at last. "If you don't do it yourself, I will. Now go on."

When he left the bathroom again, Nola stood shakily and inspected the door. The lock was flimsy and would never keep him out—one more thing that was nearly useless. Still, engaging it gave her a little psychological boost that at least made her able to turn her back on the door with a false sense of security.

Steeling herself, she quickly rinsed her hands and inspected the clothes he'd left, holding them up carefully so she wouldn't smear them with any of the mess drying down the front of her now-ruined skirt and blouse. Nothing fancy—a woman's medium-weight flannel shirt with long sleeves and a faded pair of denim jeans. There was even a pair of clean white socks and a useless pair of underpants, though there was no possibility that she would wear someone else's undergarments, washed or not. The shirt was a feminine color combination for a flannel, a light lavender shot through with yellow stripes, and when she examined the neckline she found a label bearing the legend "Lovingly Handmade by Stacey."

Nola started the hot water and undressed hastily, dropping her soiled work clothes in a pile in the corner and unable to stop herself from casting quick, furtive glances over her shoulder. The man was a kidnapper and God only knew what else—she couldn't help but believe that he would bust through the door the second she was naked. In spite of the edge of panic underlying her shower, Nola found that the steaming water felt good against her skin, hot and cleansing, washing away the filth if not the fear. Warmth finally seeped through her and chased away the last of the chill from her night in the basement, and when she smelled of nothing more than soap she was reluctant to step from beneath the water. If she didn't, though, he really *would* end up coming in, so finally she dried herself and slipped into the clean clothes as quickly as she could. She frowned when they fit perfectly, with not a bulge or a baggy seam to be found.

It seemed she'd hardly finished with the last button on the shirt when Jesse knocked. "Are you decent?" he asked, his voice muffled through the door.

"Y-yes." Reluctantly she turned the lock and stepped back. Without her consciously realizing it, her fingers found each other and began twisting nervously.

The door swung in and Jesse stood waiting in the hall. His hair was damp around the edges where he'd washed his face and hands, and he'd put on a clean T-shirt and a pair of old sweatpants. He still smelled faintly of vomit and Nola couldn't help sniffing; under any other circumstances, it would have been amusing to see the flush that spread across his cheeks. "Sorry," he mumbled. "I'll take a shower in a few minutes."

He reached over and pried her hands apart, then pulled firmly on her arm until she moved into the hallway.

"Come on," Jesse Waite said. "It's time for us to talk this out."

Detective Lucas Conroy checked his watch as he pulled into the parking lot in front of the grocery store. Plenty of time—he could do his shopping and take the stuff back home, then grab a nice, hot shower before his shift. He shut off the engine and climbed out of the car, a late-model black Ford that someone in charge at the department had decided could pass as Roselle's "Joe Family Car." Right—no one with a brain would ever guess that all those antennae were for police bands, just as the silver spotlights on each side would remain a mystery to the average person.

Conroy shoved his hands in his pockets against the frosty breeze that the radio had said would grow into a full-fledged wind by late evening, winter coming back after the teasing climb of the temperatures yesterday. Some of the snow had melted to slush and with a couple more degrees, even that might have evaporated; unfortunately, the onset of dusk had made the mercury plummet again and now everything had frozen to a slick film.

Conroy glanced at a skinny kid scattering salt crystals in front of the entrance and shivering beneath a too-light jacket thrown over his Pik-Kwik apron. He'd driven over here without thinking, but the name splashed across the teenager's apron sparked a memory—this was where that teacher, Alec Elidad, had claimed he'd let his wife out to go shopping before she'd disappeared. Conroy had checked in with the desk at noon, but Elidad hadn't called yet—maybe the woman had shown up after all. Just in case, he'd double-check with the desk sergeant when he got to the station, although people with missing relatives didn't usually have the patience to wait the full twenty-four hours. He was a little surprised that he hadn't heard from the guy, but then there were a lot of things about Elidad's case, even at this early stage, that were surprising.

The inside of the building was pleasantly warm after the frigid air outside. Conroy liked this store, even though some of the prices were higher than at the Jewel in Schaumburg or at the Cub Foods up in Streamwood. They had good, regular sales, excellent meat, and a great bakery section—the Temptation Aisle, he called it—plus a small-town friendliness that more than made up for the few extra pennies he spent. At the superstores Conroy was just another face, one more check-cashing card number, move 'em in and move 'em out and who's next in line. Here they smiled and a few clerks even remembered his name.

He went up and down the aisles quickly, picking up a couple of cans of Progresso soup, some seasoned rice, and pasta and spaghetti sauce before moving to the meat section to add the requisite portion of protein to his daily diet. Not an extensive array, but then he wasn't an extensive man and his cooking needs were simple. A couple of good-looking steaks on special, a pound of hamburger. Chicken was on sale—

"Detective Conroy?"

He looked up to see one of the cashiers, a cute young woman with blue hair cut short and punky, maybe colored to match her eyes. Boy, even thirty-some-odd miles west of the city, the kids were looking stranger every day. She was standing uncertainly by his cart and glancing back toward the front of the store. "What's up?" he asked.

"Mr. Novak told me to come get you," she said. "I guess there's been an accident in the parking lot or something."

Conroy's eyebrows raised and he set the meat back in the cooler. "Is anyone hurt?

She shook her head. "I don't think so. Just a fender

bender. This one guy was backing out, and the other one didn't see, or like, couldn't stop, or something. There's an old guy out there really pitching a fit, though."

Conroy sighed and hoped that the department's purchasing agent drove one of the so-called unmarked vehicles so *he* could have his shopping—or better yet, dinner—interrupted every other day. "Okay." He gestured toward his cart. "Put the cold stuff away, would you? I'll get it after I take care of this."

Outside again, Conroy set his jaw more in annoyance than against the cold as he inspected the dentless back bumper of a BMW and listened to its owner gripe about teenagers and how they didn't look where they were going. Like Conroy, the kid stood silently, shoulders hunched and obviously wishing he were anywhere but here as he gave an occasional dismal glance at the cop and the well-dressed owner of the Beemer. Conroy let the older man, a white-haired motormouth who was obviously accustomed to bullying others, yap for awhile, then finally held up his hand for silence.

"Mr. Nieman," he said, remembering the name the man had given him the instant Conroy had stepped out of the store, "why don't we wrap this up and you can both go on your way—"

"What about the bumper of my BMW?" the man demanded. The cold had made his nose run and now Nieman squinted at Conroy and sniffed.

"What about it?" Conroy asked. "I don't see any damage, and this young man has no damage to his car, either. You—"

"He should be taught to watch where he's going!" Nieman said indignantly. "He should have stopped and waited when he saw me. I want him given a ticket and a report written up."

"Hey, wait a minute," the kid finally protested. "A ticket for what? We were hardly moving!"

"No, *you* wait!" Nieman snapped. "This is a fifty-thousand-dollar car and—"

"And *you're* the one who's going to get a ticket, unless we end this matter right here," Conroy interrupted in a hard voice.

Nieman looked shocked. "What the hell for?"

"For not yielding the right of way, to start. For not looking before you backed out of a parking spot, and for careless driving if you keep on pushing." Conroy scowled at the older man and the kid looked pleased.

"*What!*"

"*He* had the right of way, not you, Mr. Nieman. From now on, I suggest you make sure the roadway is clear *before* you back onto it. Now if you still want to file a formal report, then both of you go inside where it's warm and have your driver's licenses ready, as well as your insurance cards. You do have insurance, right?" He glanced at the teenager, who nodded. "Good. I'll fill out the report, issue your ticket, Mr. Neiman, and we'll all be on our—" He saw something out of the corner of his eye and stopped.

Nieman's mouth turned down. "Ticket? I thought you were joking!"

Conroy blinked, then shifted his attention back to the two men. "Do I look like I'm joking? This is your last chance to reconsider the wisdom of formalizing a zero-damage fender bender, so think it over carefully. If you want to go through with it, go on into the store and I'll follow you in two minutes. We'll wrap this up as quickly as possible." The man and the teenager nodded and stepped away, eyeing each other distastefully.

The detective turned and scanned the parking lot again, looking for the item that had caught his eye a moment ago. There—on the north side of the lot, crushed in the juncture where the pavement met the concrete parking hump. Glancing around, Conroy strode over and pried it free with the toe of his shoe, then squatted down to peer at it.

Flattened and smudged by dried slush, the backside almost broken in half, it was still recognizable as a woman's high-heeled shoe.

He straightened and scanned the Pik-Kwik parking lot,

looking for the remainder of a bag that had broken, an old box of clothes, something to justify the presence of this shoe in an otherwise cleared and neatly kept suburban parking area. He knew that the Kmart on Lake Street over in Addison kept a Salvation Army drop box at the far corner of its lot, and that cars were forever running over boxes and bags that people were too lazy to hoist inside the Dumpster-like contraption. But there was no drop box or garbage area here, just a trash-free expanse of cement bordered by a landscaped space of wood-enclosed gravel that held bushes and flowers in the summer.

Conroy tapped his cheekbone thoughtfully, then pulled a handkerchief from his back pocket and used it to pick up the shoe. He examined it carefully, then dropped it off in his car before heading back into the Pik-Kwik. The kid was waiting inside to tell him that Nieman had apparently decided on the wiser course of action and left. Conroy told the kid to take off and quickly finished his shopping, all the while thinking about the spattering of russet-colored stains—unmistakably blood—he'd discovered around the inside seam of the shoe.

The buzzing of the doorbell made Alec's heart leap into his throat. For a moment he was paralyzed—Nola wouldn't ring the doorbell, would she? No, she'd just let herself in, so this couldn't be her. A salesman, some kid ringing the bell just to get into the complex and cause mischief. Then again, what if Nola had lost her keys and it was her?

That thought brought all kinds of nasty possibilities and what-ifs and whys with it. Instead of pushing the buzzer, Alec ran to his apartment door and yanked it open, not registering or caring that it slammed into the metal closet doors behind it hard enough to leave a dent. He sprinted down the hall, skidded left into the front foyer and pounded down the steps to the first floor; his flash of disappointment when he saw it wasn't Nola was instantly replaced by fear as he saw Detective Conroy waiting by the doorbells. For an insane moment, Alec wanted only to turn around before the policeman saw him, run back to his safe little apartment and hide from whatever dark news the man had come to deliver. The impulse was gone instantly, and then he was at the entrance and ushering the man inside.

"Did you find her?" Alec demanded. His voice was an odd cross between a strained stage whisper and a wail. "Is she all right? Where is she?"

Detective Conroy gave him a sympathetic look, that penetrating gaze warming briefly. "No, Mr. Elidad, nothing's turned up. In fact, I came by to see if she'd returned. Since that's not the case, I think we should go upstairs so I can fill out a full report. Shall we?" He gestured at the stairs.

Alec's shoulders slumped, and he stared at the floor as he led the bigger man into the apartment building. One step at a time, he told himself as he watched his feet move. Wherever she is, he'll find her. "I stayed home from the school today," he explained. "I wanted to be here in case she called or anything. I told the administrations office to telephone me immediately if they heard from her or if something—anything at all—came up. They know what's going on."

"So you've been home all this time?"

Alec nodded. "This is the first I've even come out of the apartment. I've been afraid to be out of reach of the telephone."

When he ushered Conroy inside, he could see that the policeman noticed immediately that the place was immaculate. The scent of lemons hung on the air from furniture polish and the drapes covering the glass doors leading to the balcony were open, flooding the place with southern sunlight and showing swipes on the carpet from its recent vacuuming. Alec was suddenly embarrassed at the almost cheerful atmosphere and he felt an absurd obligation to excuse his behavior.

"We keep the drapes open in the winter to let the sun brighten the place up," he said hoarsely. He looked helpless. "Cleaning up the place . . . it gave me something to do while I . . ." He stopped as he noticed the crumpled brown bag under Conroy's arm. "What's that?"

The policeman ignored the question and moved uninvited into the living room, where he sat on the couch and pulled an ink pen from his coat pocket. "Why don't you get comfortable, Mr. Elidad. I'm going to be asking you a lot of questions, some of which you'll remember answering yesterday. I want you to answer them again, just in case you remember something now that you may not have even thought about since then. Some of them will require a little thought, but take your time—consider the answers very carefully, and let's try to get everything down at once."

"All right," Alec said. His voice was an involuntary whisper and he cleared his throat as he sank onto a chair on the other side of the small room, then bent forward until he was nearly hugging his knees. The room was warm, the afghan covering the upholstered fabric beneath his legs even warmer from the sunlight spilling on it; still, Alec wanted to pull the knitted covering around his shoulders as tightly as he could—anything to protect himself against the painful things he sensed were coming. His eyes were riveted on Conroy as the detective began asking his questions.

"What is your wife's full name, including her maiden name?"

"Nola Elidad. Her maiden name is Frayne."

Conroy began to write. "Does she have a middle name?"

"Rene," Alec answered. "But she never uses it. I don't know why. I guess she doesn't like it."

"All right. Am I correct in remembering that she's twenty-one?"

"Yes."

"Tell me again about when you last saw her. Think very carefully, and try to remember everything. Was there anything unusual going on at the time—a strange-looking car or anybody out of the ordinary in the parking lot?"

Alec swallowed and made himself pause, knowing the detective was measuring his every movement. "No, not that I recall. I last saw her yesterday, late afternoon, about . . . oh, I don't know, maybe five-thirty. That's probably about it, I guess. I picked her up from work like I always do—we only have one car—but this time I dropped her off at the Pik-Kwik so she could buy a few things. I would've gone with her but I had to go back to a staff meeting at the school. She wasn't planning on buying much, and she insisted she could walk home with the groceries." Alec's hands curled into fists on either side of his legs as he thought back on it—if only he'd known, had some kind of premonition or something. He would've never—

"So it was full dark?" Conroy asked, interrupting Alec's thoughts. "Were there any other cars in the lot? What did she say before she got out of the car?"

"To tell you the truth, I didn't even notice if there was anybody else around. I mean, I'd assume there were a few cars in the lot—the place is usually pretty busy around that time of day. As for what she said . . ." Alec frowned, trying to think around the high-level fear that had settled into his head since his wife's disappearance. "I think it was something like 'I hope your meeting goes okay. I'll see you when you get home.' "

"Okay. And she's never disappeared before or gone somewhere without telling you? Even for a few hours?"

"No. Never."

"I know she's twenty-one. Give me her date and place of birth." Conroy's pen was poised for the answer.

Alec spread his hands. "Her birthday is June eighteenth. She's always talked as though she was born in this area—DuPage County—but I can't say exactly where. I told you—she's never liked talking about her past and she always avoided answering questions about it."

The detective paused and for a moment Alec thought he might comment, but he merely kept writing. "All right. Give me a physical description, including what she was wearing yesterday. I'm going to need the most recent photograph you can come up with."

"I don't have *any* photos. We were married in a civil ceremony at the courthouse. It wasn't fancy but it meant a lot to us." He looked down at his hands, remembering how they'd talked about buying a camera at Christmas, then procrastinated. Boy, those good intentions really came back to bite you in the butt sometimes. "She has brown hair, recently cut short, and fair skin—pale, actually. Her eyes are blue with green flecks. She's small, only about five-two, and slender." For a wistful couple of seconds the room and Conroy faded out and Alec was seeing Nola in his mind, her smooth skin and small, reluctant way of smiling. He cleared his throat. "I . . . I think she's beautiful."

"What's she weigh?"

Alec looked nonplussed, then he shrugged. "I really have no idea. Maybe a hundred pounds, one-oh-five—I'm not sure."

"Do you remember what she was wearing, Mr. Elidad?"

"Sure. She had on a brown wool skirt and a white blouse, with her winter jacket, a dark brown imitation-leather thing. She has pretty conservative tastes and she didn't tend to spend a lot of money on clothes and the like."

"Was she carrying a purse? And what about a hat, gloves, shoes?"

"Her purse was almost the same as her jacket—brown, not very expensive—and her gloves are here. She forgot them yesterday morning." Alec glanced toward the front closet automatically. Wherever she was . . . were her hands cold? "Oh—shoes. Tan pumps. Since I drove her almost everywhere, she hardly ever wore boots."

"Okay." Conroy was scribbling quickly and Alec chewed on his lower lip; he didn't like the way the man had suddenly seemed to get a little tenser. Was it something he'd said? "Does she drink more than what would be considered socially acceptable? Use any narcotics? What are her hobbies?"

"No, she doesn't drink at all and I've never seen her take anything stronger than aspirin—in fact, if she has a headache, I have to coax her to do that. As far as hobbies, she hasn't shown interest in anything special other than books. She works at the Roselle Library." Despite the sun beating through the window and the baseboard heater humming behind his chair, his fingers were cold and clammy. Alec massaged them together, trying to force circulation into them. He'd hoped to introduce Nola to so many things over the coming months; for instance, she had an aptitude for the sciences that he was just discovering—as was she—and they'd been talking about getting a bird, maybe a parrot or a cockatiel, when the weather turned warm. Now . . .

Stop it, Alec told himself sharply. It isn't as though she's not coming back.

"How long has she worked there?" Detective Conroy asked.

"About three months," Alec answered, happy to turn his mind away from the darker thoughts that were trying to creep in.

"And before that?"

"I . . . don't know," he admitted. "She never said. I know she graduated from Keeneyville High. And she was talking about going back to school to get a degree in library science, but she hadn't done anything about it yet."

"Any relatives at all?"

"Like I told you yesterday, I have no idea." Alec felt a flush spread across his face. What must this policeman think of him and Nola, two people who'd gotten married but who didn't know anything about each other—while he'd been perfectly willing to talk, Nola had never asked about his history and he'd assumed that was because she was uncomfortable with her own. And now she'd disappeared.

Stop it, he told himself again. She'll be back. She *will.*

Conroy shut his eyes for a second, then placed the clipboard on the cushion next to him and gave Alec a glance that was frank enough to make him dread the detective's next words. "Mr. Elidad, do you know *anything* about your wife? You don't have any pictures, you don't know of any relatives, you don't seem to know . . . very much at all." The policeman's gaze sharpened until Alec found it nearly painful. "Can you even prove to me that you're married, Mr. Elidad? Can you show me, right now, that this woman exists?"

Something twisted inside him. "Jesus Christ, of course I can!" Alec snapped as he jerked himself out of the chair. "What do you think I am? Some kind of psychotic? You think this is a twisted game I'm playing?" He left the detective sitting where he was and strode to the bedroom, his shoes stomping against the carpet, his face a low shade of red. Prove that she existed, indeed! His hands were shaking so badly he almost couldn't grasp the knob on the bottom drawer of the chest, and when he finally caught hold of the damned thing, he pulled on it so hard the entire drawer slid free and fell to the floor.

"Shit," Alec muttered uncharacteristically. He left everything on the carpet where it had fallen, shuffling quickly through the clutter until he found their marriage certificate. As an afterthought he picked up the Banker's Life policy Nola had brought home from the library only last week, when she had reached the three-month anniversary that put the life insurance into effect. The unwanted notion surfaced that perhaps she had gone somewhere to commit suicide, but Alec pushed that thought away with more force than any of the others; only unhappy people took their own lives, and Nola was perfectly happy.

Wasn't she?

The question was a subduing one, and Alec was calmer by the time he returned to the living room. Still, when he offered the papers to Conroy his hands were shaking. "Here's our marriage certificate, and a life insurance policy Nola brought home last week."

Conroy looked interested. "She bought insurance?"

Alec sank back onto his chair and rubbed his arms. There was a chill inside him that no amount of winter sunshine or artificial heat could chase away. "No, nothing like that. It's what the library offers as a benefit, that's all."

There was a moment of silence as Conroy studied the documents, then put them on the coffee table. "I don't have much to go on, Mr. Elidad," he finally said. "It really hurts us that you can't give me a photograph. I'll put out a statewide all-points bulletin with her description, then check with the area hospitals—"

"I already did that this morning," Alec interrupted.

"And we'll check them again," Conroy said patiently, "making sure to provide a physical description to the emergency room admittance desks in case a woman comes in with no identification."

Alec swallowed, unwilling to think about the implications of his wife being brought to a hospital somewhere and labeled as "unidentified." Conroy was watching him intently, as though debating his next course of action. Then Alec saw the detective's gaze flick toward that crumpled bag that Alec had asked him about earlier. Conroy had tucked it between his leg and the arm of the couch, and a sudden, unreasonable dread filled Alec as the other man lifted it and twisted it open. Time seemed to slow to half of what was normal, as though the world had abruptly downshifted and the air around him had turned to thick, invisible gel.

"No," Alec whispered without even knowing it. "Oh, please don't."

Using only his thumb and forefinger, Conroy pulled a woman's tan pump out of the bag. "Do you recognize this, Mr. Elidad?" he asked in a low voice.

"God," Alec said miserably. His trembling hands reached for it but the detective pulled it out of his range; belatedly, Alec realized he shouldn't be touching it. As he stared, Conroy turned it over so Alec could see everything—the broken heel, the way one side was crushed nearly flat, even an ugly splatter of mud or something on the inside. Alec's blurring vision found and focused on the brand label, still readable on the inside though the shoe itself was ruined and filthy. He remembered going with his wife into the small store in Stratford Square to buy these only a couple of weeks ago, watching her try them on and thoughtfully walk around the store to make sure they were comfortable. He thought his heart was going to rip itself out of his chest when at last he raised his gaze to the detective's.

"This is Nola's."

"Okay," said the man sitting across the table. "I want you to listen to me very carefully." His voice was even and low, a world away from the person who'd seemed borderline insane in the parking lot yesterday and in the kitchen earlier today. "I already told you my name is Jesse Waite. Now I'm going to fill you in on the rest, all that stuff you can't remember. I know you probably won't be able to catch it the first time around, but that's okay. I don't expect you to. We'll work through this together, you and me." He looked at Nola as though he expected her to say something; when she didn't, he kept going, his voice as soothing as if he were talking to a cranky toddler. "My name is Jesse," he said again. "I'm twenty-seven years old, and I was born in Cook County Hospital. I'm your husband. Your name is Stacey—"

Unable to stop herself, Nola started to shake her head. Anxiety was pounding through her again, making her head hurt and her stomach twist. "No—"

Jesse stilled her movement by pressing the tip of a work-roughened finger against her lips. "Shhh. Just hear me out." She'd flinched when his hand had come near her face and had seen a brief flash of regret cross his face before he quickly lowered his hand. On the tabletop, his fingers opened and closed nervously; occasionally he reached up and rubbed at the shadows under his eyes.

"You're twenty-one and your birthday is June eighteenth," he continued after taking a deep breath. "We were married four years ago, in the chapel at St. Walter's up on Maple Street. I can show you the certificate." He blushed unexpectedly, the expression blatantly out of place given the tough man and the circumstances. "You were barely eighteen. Your mom was really pissed."

Nola did her best to keep her expression bland, but . . . dear God, how had he known her birthday? Then it clicked—her purse, of course. She didn't have a driver's license but there must have been something in there that listed it, an identification card or whatever. If only her heart would stop hammering so hard and let her *think.* There were probably any number of items in her wallet that might prove her identity to Jesse.

Or maybe, Nola thought suddenly, she should go at it from the other direction. *Jesse's* direction.

"Then t-there m-must be p-pictures," Nola made herself croak. "Of . . . us."

He looked at her in such surprise that for one sweet, short moment she thought she'd reached him. Then a *Why didn't I think of that* expression slipped across his features, followed by a tiny, one-sided smile. "Well, sure. We've got those, too." He shrugged and looked self-conscious. "I guess you don't remember that they weren't great shots. We didn't have any money for a fancy photographer, so my buddy John followed us around with his camera, but he was no great shakes at lining up the lens. But, yeah, that's a great idea—you'll need to see those. I'll dig them out of the closet later."

Nola sat across from him in silence, feeling like a marionette placed into the hands of the wrong puppeteer. If dolls had minds, she thought, this is what it would be like: plucked from one life and deposited into another—*Now you'll play house HERE!*—all at the whim of someone not necessarily in control of himself, a crazed and cruel child apt to throw down his toy and stomp on it when the doll didn't behave as desired. What if Jesse—

No, she reminded herself with a stern mental shake, don't think of him like that. He's not Jesse, or Jesse Waite, or even the man who lives here—it doesn't matter that he has a name or anything else. He's just the man who kidnapped you. He's not a person; he's a *criminal.* And don't you ever, even for the smallest of seconds, forget that.

Still . . . the kidnapper on the other side of the table reminded her of that imaginary child in some ways. He had an adult's face—handsome enough though weathered by exposure, hard work, and worry—and his strength had certainly felt like that of a grown man when he'd forced her into his car. But his eyes, the gaze that she remembered as being so hard-looking and wild when she'd first seen him in the Pik-Kwik parking lot, was now filled with something different. No matter how determined Nola was to remember that the man across the table was almost certainly insane, the light in his eyes denied that. They were wide and filled with the innocent hope of a child, clear dark blue and bright as clean ocean water. God help them both, he wasn't pretending, and he didn't—at least right now—seem mean or murderous or even particularly nuts. He just seemed . . . determined and firm in his belief that Nola was really his wife.

"Listen," Jesse finally said. "I . . . I guess I kept telling myself that you'd come around any second, that there'd be . . ." He paused and shrugged slightly. "I don't know, some kind of miracle mental flash or something. But I guess I'm going to have to accept that there isn't going to be a miracle cure. So we'll just take it one day at a time and show you all the stuff that got lost or whatever." He took a deep breath and Nola tensed, certain that he was going to reach for her hand. But he didn't, fiddling instead with the edge of the table.

"I'm sorry about locking you in the basement last night, and for shaking you this morning after breakfast. You don't remember it, but I swear I'm a reasonable man, despite how mad you've seen me get. I've never laid a hand on you before. I—I didn't even think I ever could." His gaze dropped away from hers and Nola saw his hands clench together as a flush crept across his forehead beneath the unruly crown of nearly black curls. "I just—you have to try to understand, Stacey. You've been gone for over three months, and I just about went *crazy* without you. Everyone patted me on the back and said wait it out, that time would pass and I'd be okay—hell, after a while your mom wouldn't even talk to me anymore. What kind of a way was that to be? I mean, I know she's your mother, but if I had any family left alive, I'd like to think they would've been a lot more supportive than that."

He looked over at the counter and brightened suddenly, then sprang out of his chair fast enough to make her jump and started putting together a fresh pot of coffee. He seemed to be filled with nervous energy, and Nola couldn't help thinking that the last thing he needed was caffeine. "So," he continued as he worked, "I tried to deal with it on my own and accept it, move on like they all told me I had to, but I was sinking pretty fast. And then last fall, at that carnival thing in Roselle, there you were."

Nola sat very, very still and stared at Jesse.

Last fall?

"I wasn't convinced at first," Jesse said as he ran water into the coffeepot. His voice had taken on a low, thoughtful tone, as though he was still turning over in his mind the details of what had happened. "I mean, there was a resemblance, of course, but everyone—the hospital, the doctors, even that director at Pitofsky's—told me you were dead. So I said to myself, don't be stupid, that can't be her." He shot her a quick, sad smile. "I mean, it couldn't have been, right? I knew you wouldn't have just up and left me, not after everything we'd been through. We'd never fought about anything major, and I was as crazy about you as I'd always been. You . . ." He swallowed and his voice thickened momentarily. "You seemed to, you know, still feel the same about me."

She was totally dumbstruck by the concept of this man watching her—no, *stalking* her—for months, yet beneath the rush of water Nola heard him clear his throat, as if he were on the verge of crying and didn't want her to know. And Pitofsky's—what was that?

Jesse poured the water carefully into the coffee maker, then took a filter out of a cabinet and began measuring scoops of Hill's Brothers into it. "Then yesterday," he said, "I finally got up my courage and got close enough in the store to really *see* you. And I couldn't believe it, because it really *was* you—all the stuff the doctors and the hospital and everyone else told me . . . it was all lies."

"Why?" The question burst from her lips before she knew it was going to.

Jesse frowned, but it wasn't out of bewilderment. He knew exactly what she was asking, or thought he did. "I have my theory," he said at last. "I think it has to do with medical negligence and the hospital covering it up—I don't think even your mother realizes what happened. She's far too accepting and given what happened years ago, I can't tell you how much that surprises me."

Nola started to ask what he meant, then forced herself to stop. Years ago? No—she didn't want to know. Asking about this and allowing Jesse to fill her in on all the important background information would only feed his fantasy, strengthen in his mind the foundation on which he'd built this complicated delusion. She couldn't risk putting herself in a position where she might admit to Jesse that the memory structure underneath her own life was shaky at best, had become increasingly so these last few months. If he found this out, he would use the gaps in her recollection about her family and her childhood as ammunition, and she simply couldn't bear that.

Jesse pushed the ON switch and the coffee maker gurgled to life, then he came back and sat across from her again. This time he placed his hands flat on the worn wood of the tabletop and made them relax, as if showing her that they could just *be* there, without her having to fear them. "I lost my head, is all. I never grabbed you or did anything like that before, and I never will again—I swear it. I am *not* a mean man. You know that. You have to, in your heart. Right?"

"I don't know any such thing," Nola said hoarsely. A risky statement to make, but Jesse *had* promised not to hurt her again. I'm the one who's crazy, Nola thought abruptly. I must be, to even consider accepting the vow of a madman like this.

Jesse pressed his lips together, but it was more a gesture of endurance than impatience. "I understand."

She stared at him, and he stared at her. Now what? Play along with him, of course. If she could get him to lower his guard, or to trust her, an opportunity to escape was bound to present itself. Unless he killed her first.

Don't think about that.

But . . . where was his wife? His *real* wife?

"So," Nola said carefully. Her voice was very small and he was forced to lean forward to hear it. "You said I'd been . . . sick? What was wrong with me?"

For a moment, Jesse didn't answer. "It's pretty scary," he said at last. He looked like he wanted to reach for her hands, and she quickly slipped them under the table and folded them in her lap. "But don't freak out about it too much, because as long as you don't push yourself, things'll be fine."

Nola just looked at him. "What are you talking about?"

He took a deep breath. "It's your heart," he admitted. "It's a hereditary thing, a murmur that makes your heart not as strong as it should be. This whole thing started because you came down with a cold. Such a little thing, but that's why I was so *stupid* for locking you in the basement last night. The cold . . . it escalated into a sore throat, then turned into strep." Jesse looked like he was about to cry. "You should've told me that your throat hurt that much, but I guess you were thinking about doctors' bills and useless crap like that instead of your health. I didn't even know you had it, and then it turned into rheumatic fever. I got home from work one afternoon and there you were in bed, with your temperature so high I thought you were going to go into convulsions."

Nola sat without saying a word, watching Jesse's face get whiter as he recounted the event. "I took you to the hospital, of course, and I couldn't believe you pulled through . . . but now you did. You *did*."

"But why don't I remember any of this?" Nola asked pointedly. "You're not talking about some bump on the head."

"Because of the fever." Jesse took another deep breath. "You weren't quite . . . there afterward. They said it was because the fever had been so high." He couldn't meet her eyes, as if this were the last thing in the world he wanted to tell her. "The doctors had mentioned there could be some brain damage."

"What!"

"But they said you'd probably get past it," he rushed on. "That it was only temporary."

There were a thousand questions that Nola could ask about these imaginary doctors, but she didn't dare. Everything she wanted to say to stab holes in Jesse's story felt like it would sound sarcastic and angry, but everything that came out of this man's mouth was full of pain. Maybe it was better to just let him talk it through. Her own memory gaps wouldn't matter if he eventually cornered himself with something he couldn't explain. Maybe that would be the turning point, the time when that proverbial lightbulb would go off in Jesse's head and he'd realize what a terrible mistake he'd made.

And what happened then? Was she willing to forgive and forget? You bet she was; in the crime stories on television victims were always saying that, then calling the police, but if she could get out of this townhouse with her life and limbs intact, Nola had never meant anything so much. There was no harm done here, not yet anyway, other than a scraped foot and a bitten lip. Jesse Waite certainly needed help, but she didn't believe he needed prison.

On the counter the coffee maker gave a final loud gurgle and Jesse rose and went to retrieve two mugs from the cabinet. "I was wrong to leave you alone at the hospital, I guess. But I thought you would be all right there—I mean, you were surrounded by doctors and nurses and who knows what all. I *had* to go to work because of the medical bills, the part that wasn't covered by the insurance."

She said nothing, but his voice held a plea for her understanding as he opened a jar of creamer and mixed a spoonful into each cup, then turned and placed one in front of her. Without thinking, Nola brought it to her lips and took a sip; he'd never asked her how she took her coffee, but the mix was perfect. "You could've called anyone from the hospital if you needed anything. But you didn't call, Stacey. You just . . . disappeared." Jesse's eyes misted over, as though he were about to cry. "And those bastards at the hospital, they lied and told us that you were gone. Can you imagine how anyone could be that cruel?"

In spite of all that she'd been through so far, Nola couldn't. Be that as it may, for some reason, the perfectly made mug of coffee bothered her more than anything else, and Nola set it down. She had to try again, and again, and again—as many times as it would take. "It wasn't me," she whispered. "Please—you've got the wrong woman. I—I have a life—"

"Well, of course you do," Jesse said agreeably. "If I suddenly couldn't remember who I was or where I'd come from, I'd make a new life for myself, too."

"But I have a husband!" Her voice came out loud and strident, and too late she realized the danger of throwing such a thing at him.

"Just calm down," he said quickly, but it was his own face that betrayed a gathering tension. "I . . . I guess I knew this. It's that guy I've been seeing you with all this time, right?"

Nola nodded.

"I knew this," he said again, but his expression seemed to sag. For a few moments he said nothing, then he gave a small shake of his head, as if dismissing this problem as irrelevant. His next words confirmed that. "Well, we'll just have to deal with that later," he said firmly. "It's bigamy, right? When you're married to more than one person at a time?" Nola just stared at him as he ran his hands through his hair, but he didn't seem to need an answer. "Sure, it's a problem, but we'll figure out what to do about it when we have you all straightened out again."

Nola swallowed, trying to find enough saliva to speak. "What do you mean, 'straightened out'? What are you going to do to me?" What did Jesse think it would take to convince her? Once more the question of his wife—the *real* one—sped through her mind. Where was she—had she left him, perhaps because he was having delusions or whatever? She fought the urge to give a panicked giggle. Wouldn't it be just too funny if the woman walked in the door an hour from now?

But Jesse only looked bewildered. " 'Do'? Well, nothing—all I meant was when you get your memory back." His voice trailed off for a moment, then he cleared his throat and continued. "I'd be lying if I said it didn't hurt me that you've been with someone else, but I can't blame you for something going wrong in your head, can I? I know it's not something you would have ever done otherwise." He reached across the table and gave Nola's hair a quick, wistful touch before she could pull away. "You changed your hair," he said softly. "Cut most of it off. That's too bad."

"I haven't had long hair since I was in high school," Nola said with more belligerence than she really felt. It was a lie, but he didn't know that. Did he?

Her kidnapper nodded. "Sure, Stacey. If you say so."

The fear was still there—it always had been—but the life-threatening part of it was starting to mellow into a high-level anxiety; this last amiable statement topped it with a knot of frustrated anger. Her eyes narrowed. "If my mind is so messed up," Nola suggested, "shouldn't you take me to see a doctor?"

To her surprise, he nodded. "Oh, definitely—but we can't. Not right now." She made no attempt to hide her look of disappointment, and Jesse's lips pressed together. "I'm sorry, Stacey. I can't afford something like that right now, and I won't have some hack headshrinker who can't get a job anywhere but a county facility working on my wife."

"But—"

He shook his head, stopping her words. For the first time, it really began to sink in how stubborn he could be. "When I saw you at that carnival, it was like . . ." He paused, obviously trying to find the words to make her understand. "It was like being plugged back into life," he finally explained. "But there was this whole curtain of uncertainty about it because I wasn't sure it was you. So I quit my job so I could spend all my time trying to make sure."

Nola stared at him as a chill worked its way along the back of her scalp. He'd been following her for months, he'd quit his job—Jesus, he must know everything about her and Alec. Where they both worked, what their schedules were, when they shopped—oh, definitely *that.*

"I know it was a stupid thing to do," Jesse continued in his most reasonable voice. He seemed oblivious to her expression of dismay. "But I *had* to see if it really was you, and like I said, I wasn't getting any support from anyone else, not even from your mother. Now the savings account . . . well, it's dry as dust." He look ashamed, then he brightened. "But I've got another job lined up—good timing, huh? I start the graveyard shift Monday night at a machine shop up in Bensenville. The hours are kind of a pain in the butt, but there's a night shift premium. Only problem is, there won't be insurance coverage for ninety days, so the doctor or psychiatrist visits will have to wait." He gazed at her, and his face was like a little boy's: open, honest, and begging for her approval.

"But if things aren't right with you by then, Stacey, or if you still can't remember who you are or who I am, we'll go. It's not such a long time." His eyes met hers without flinching—that stubbornness again—and Nola knew there was no way on the face of this earth that Jesse would give in.

Ninety days, she thought in mute terror.

Three months.

3

Discovery

No man is happy without a delusion of some kind. Delusions are as necessary to our happiness as realities.

—CHRISTIAN NESTELL BOVEE

JANUARY 18--SATURDAY

Never in her life would she have imagined waking up and lying on the floor, tied to someone like a dog on a leash.

Saturday morning, early, and Nola was awake, had been so for hours. To her right she could see the long side of a queen-sized bed that was nearly too big for the rather small master bedroom of this townhouse. Jesse—as much as she was determined to think of him not as a human being but as her kidnapper, her mind kept betraying her—slept soundly on the bed.

For the third or fourth time in the last half hour, Nola screwed up her courage and peered over to see if he was still asleep. Her breath caught every time she heard him shift or roll over—when he woke up, warm and rested, what then? Either he was a light sleeper or nervousness was keeping him on the edge, because every time she gave the smallest tug on the fabric belt, he made a noise in his sleep, some snuffle or groan, sometimes a string of mumbled words.

Still, it was better than being in the bed itself, where Jesse had tried to convince her to sleep last night. He'd wanted to take the floor, but Nola wouldn't—couldn't—let this happen. An abducted woman lying in her kidnapper's bed—what bigger invitation could there be to disaster? No amount of promising on his part could convince her this was a good idea, and when he'd tried to make her do it his way, Nola had backed into the corner next to the nightstand and refused to budge. When Jesse had realized that for her it was the floor or nothing, he'd hauled a huge pile of blankets out of the hallway linen closet and made her a fairly passable pallet.

The bigger fear was back inside Nola's head, the black kind that wanted to take her breath away and made her, sometimes, literally unable to hear anything around the sound of her own heartbeat. The mind was a tricky, unpredictable thing, but fantasy wasn't always fear's creator. Sometimes that was simple reality, the here and now of being dressed in an unknown woman's soft flannel nightgown in a stranger's bedroom, tethered by the belt of a bathrobe—"for her own safety"—to someone who was utterly convinced he had a husband's rights to her body. When he raped her, would he hurt her?

Another peek over the bed, but this time Nola looked longingly at the door. A fool's wish—this damned belt was tied so tightly through a small fabric loop on the gown she wore that she'd have to either tear the gown or strip—not a chance—to be free of it. The other end of it disappeared beneath the covers on the bed, and Nola had no idea where Jesse had fastened it. Even if she could pry apart the knot on her end, there was the chair under the doorknob to contend with, and Jesse had jammed it so tightly in place that the legs were sure to make enough of a racket to wake him if she moved it.

Still trapped.

No matter how much she resisted, there were so many dark possibilities to think about, with nothing else to occupy her mind. Rape was the least of it, murder . . . not even the worst. What happened when he realized that she really *wasn't* who he thought she was? How would he dispose of her body when—

Stop it!

Nola's gaze darted around the bedroom, searching for something, *anything*, to distract her. Alec—what was he doing now? Sleeping? Maybe—it couldn't be more than six in the morning. In another two hours he'd be up and making coffee in their tiny kitchen and longing, sharp and intense, suddenly filled her. On Saturdays they usually each had a cherry yogurt muffin and a blueberry donut from the Country Donuts shop on Roselle Road—Alec would stop and buy them on his way home Friday night. He'd sit by his computer at the dining room table and go through the morning paper, page by page in his methodical way; Nola would take her coffee into the living room and sit on the rocker by the sliding glass doors to the balcony, sipping and rocking as she watched the world go by on Springhill Drive. Occasionally Alec would break into her reverie and read her something he thought she would find interesting. Beyond that, neither one of them spoke much. They didn't have to, and Nola liked it just fine that way.

Propping herself on one elbow, Nola leaned over and cautiously tugged the blanket aside to once again study the belt twisting through the small loop intended for a decorative ribbon at her waist. Her fingers prodded at it, but it was useless—Jesse had pulled it so tightly she didn't think it would ever come off.

Flipping the blanket back in place, Nola sank to the floor again and squeezed her eyes shut. God, she wanted to *scream*—how was she ever going to get out of this? It wasn't even a *normal* kidnapping, if there was such a thing—instead, she had a humane abductor who cooked for her, gave her warm, clean pajamas and clothes to wear, and who had tended the scrape on her foot as though it were an agonizing wound instead of just uncomfortable. He worried repeatedly about her health and hadn't placed so much as a pinkie finger on her that might lead to rape. But he was a kidnapper nonetheless, a man who cunningly eliminated anything that might help her escape long before Nola thought of it—and wasn't it amazing how much time she'd been spending in the bathrooms while he did whatever other things needed to be done? In the time she'd been here—and God, it seemed like forever—she felt like she knew every inch of both those small rooms.

There were two more doors in here—most likely closets. She'd probably seen most of the townhouse by now, including an empty second bedroom that Jesse had locked her in while he took a shower yesterday. She hadn't been in there long, but there wasn't much to see; it had a small, curtainless sliding window on one wall that was painted shut and too high for her to get the leverage needed to pry at it. Nola could barely see over the sill, and what was out there wasn't encouraging: a second-floor view of that same meager yard, barren of color and completely isolated from any neighbors by a six-foot-high wooden fence. It didn't matter anyway, because there was nothing to stand on to hoist herself out even if she broke the glass—and then she'd have to contend with a sill full of jagged edges. The room's door had opened outward and Jesse had done something to it—another chair or something—to make sure it stayed closed.

Now, as she waited for Jesse to wake up, Nola wondered about that little room—why had it been so bare? It seemed more like it belonged to an unrented apartment than to this small and well-lived-in townhouse, as though it had been intended for something that had never come to pass. Most extra rooms attracted junk—old clothes, unpacked boxes, unfinished projects, forgotten Christmas decorations—the way a clean wall beckoned a child with dirty fingers. But not that one—

Above her, Jesse murmured something into his pillow and sighed. Nola sucked in her breath, then released it when the sound moved gently into a light snore and finally evened into a soft, barely audible drone. It should have grated on her nerves; instead, the sound gradually lulled her and the tense muscles in her shoulders eased up. After awhile, Nola cautiously drew herself into a hunched sitting position, not so that Jesse would see her if he opened his eyes, but enough so that she could gaze around the dim room.

Nothing out of the ordinary here, no flash or trash. It was clean and well cared for but worn at the edges, like the clothes Jesse had given her, the handmade shirt and faded jeans, the flowered nightgown she wore now that smelled of fresh fabric softener but had gently fraying edges along its bottom hem. Nola had expected a hodgepodge of contents, hand-me-downs or garage sale finds, but the bedroom furniture was a set of inexpensive Early American with a slightly feminine design—something a woman would have chosen and a man would have agreed to because this was where he slept and his eyes were closed most of the time anyway. The bed had a bookcase headboard and a matching nightstand, and against the wall between the two doors was a chest of drawers. Across from the foot of the bed was a full dresser supporting a mirrored hutch with four small shelves displaying a few precious trinkets. As her gaze traveled upward, Nola saw a rumpled, wallet-sized photograph tucked into one corner of the mirror.

It scared her to death, but Nola was determined to get a good look at that picture. Moving only a couple of inches at a time, she managed to get close enough to study it in the poor glow of the morning's new light, and what she saw was anything but comforting. A woman with shoulder-length dark hair, aiming a smile at the out-of-focus camera. Was she seeing what she thought, or was it just the shadowy bedroom?

No, it was impossible—a resemblance, that's all. Nola pushed the idea from her mind as she eased back and pulled the blanket up under her chin, then curled into a fetal position to build more warmth against the chill of the floor. All things considered, she felt pretty good: She was unharmed, still terrified on a primal level but oddly well-rested, almost . . . *placid.* Jesse's bedroom was comfortable and she was comfortable in it, as though it was the type of room in which she belonged, and as she waited for him to wake, Nola felt herself growing sleepy again. Finally she slipped into a half-conscious state that should have been reserved for a Saturday morning somewhere else, in an apartment she rightfully shared with another man.

It was that feeling of simple contentment, of seductive acceptance and . . . *belonging,* that was enough to horrify Nola into full wakefulness long before Jesse finally opened his eyes.

This new house, the latest in too many for her to keep track of, is dark and unwelcoming to the three-year-old who stands in the living room, shivering beneath a coat too thin for the winter weather. The memory of the girl's mother is gone, like the flame at the end of a spent matchstick; she misses . . . something, *although she's no longer sure what. A woman's face, pretty but strained, flashes in her dreams now and then, sometimes laughing, sometimes crying, but almost always ending in a scream. Because of this, she feels only pain when she thinks of her, and pushes the memories away as quickly as she can.*

Now her father, too, has vanished, another person once treasured and trusted who left her like so much trash to be swept up by someone else. She hasn't seen him in weeks, not since before when he took her to his first house, then they packed everything up and moved, then moved again. Without him, who will want her now?

But this new place, with its too-dark hallways and the smell of cigarettes, dirt, and old grease, and even the sudden disappearance of her father, doesn't terrify the child nearly as much as the woman looming over her—

"What's your name?" the woman demands.

"Ta—"

The child has never been hit before and the slap surprises her so much that she does not cry out. Instead she simply stands there, blinking and staring at the adult.

"No!" The woman's voice escalates to a shout that surrounds the girl and blots out everything else. "We've been over and over this—how many times do we have to do it again? You will not use that name in this house, young lady! Not ever again!"

She is not a willful child—quite the opposite, actually. Still, rebellion rises within her, battling with fear and a tiny growth of hatred. This is wrong and she knows it, she knows what she has been taught so far. Then again, the people who taught her that are gone, and this is her mother now, this tall, big-boned woman with the loud voice who likes to scratch and slap, and who now has no one to stop her from doing exactly that. Even so . . .

"But that's my name!" The protest is out before the child can stop it, an instinctive refusal to accept the inevitable. She is too

young to know how ineffective her objections will be, how small and powerless she is in this world filled with adults.

"Not anymore," the woman says grimly. "And your father isn't around here to spoil you, is he? Things'll be different now, missy—you can bank on that." She slides fingers tipped with talonlike nails, carefully shaped and painted, into the baby-fine brown hair on the child's head and grips it, digs in solid for the first of what will be many lessons over the coming years.

"Say the words, missy, or I swear you'll live to regret it. Say 'That's not *my name.' "*

"Alec Elidad is here to see you."

Nine o'clock on a Saturday morning—the guy wasn't wasting any time. A ridiculous thought, and Conroy chided himself for it immediately. If the positions were reversed, he'd have probably camped on the station steps all night. The desk sergeant, Drosner, had warned him that Elidad would be coming in and shoved a message from the night watch at him—Elidad had called and asked for him late last night, but Conroy had already left. Drosner had reminded Elidad that Conroy had put an APB on his missing wife and convinced him that unless he had something definite about his wife's whereabouts, there was nothing else to be gained in the middle of the night. Drosner said Elidad had reluctantly agreed to wait, but clearly not for long.

A tickle of guilt flushed through Conroy and he thought that maybe Drosner should have paged him at home. The guy's wife was gone and there might be foul play involved—Nola's blood-spotted shoe from the Pik-Kwik parking lot hinted at that—but the man was still trying to keep his head. If it was my wife, Conroy thought, I'd probably be reaming new body cavities into every cop I came in contact with. The flip side of him wondered about that, though—what would he *really* feel? Conroy wasn't married, had never even dated anyone for more than a few months at a time. Whatever attracted the ladies to his male coworkers didn't seem to extend to him, although he didn't understand why.

"I'll come out," he said into the receiver now. "Tell him

it'll be about five minutes." He hung up the phone and dug Nola Elidad's file—pitifully thin—out of the drawer. Not much inside it, and all the usual checks had come up dry. Routine computer searches had ruled out a plane, bus, or train ticket, and next up he'd check into rental cars, hotels, and the like, but he needed credit card info from the husband for a detailed run like that. This business about only knowing Nola for three months . . . why did he have this feeling that something was off-kilter about that scenario, something that went a lot deeper than boy meets girl and gets married a day later? There was no denying that *something* was missing from Alec Elidad's life—the sense of loss pervaded his spotless, somber apartment as well as everything else about him. The nagging question in the detective's head was what exactly had been lost—a wife? Or a woman who'd only pretended to be that?

Conroy sighed and went up front to get Alec Elidad.

This can't be happening, Alec Elidad thought as he saw Detective Conroy step through a door across the outer waiting room and motion to him. I'm dreaming—*hallucinating*. I'm going to wake up at any moment and find this is nothing but the worst nightmare of my life—Nola will be standing over the bed and offering me a glass of water, saying something soothing like she always does if I have a bad dream.

God . . . where *is* she?

"Mr. Elidad." Detective Conroy's voice was even and polite. "Come this way please."

Alec followed the policeman through the doorway and into a room lined with desks, not the big and noisy urban centers like the ones he saw on television programs, but small and fairly hushed, *suburban*. Everyone here kept their voices down and the few typewriters off to the side were electronic instead of the big, clacking monsters of the old days. All the desks had computer terminals on them—the difference between suburban budgets and the strapped-for-cash inner-city ones.

Detective Conroy's desk was at the far end, one of the few by a window; it was messy but not as bad as some of the others, with a sense of organization to the small piles of paper. His chair was turned toward the window and Conroy dropped onto it and spun it to face Alec in a single, smooth movement, like an oversized wolf comfortable in its lair. "Have a seat," the detective said, indicating a wooden chair at the side of the desk. Alec obeyed and found the chair, an older wooden thing styled like the teachers' chairs in school, hard and unyielding; it made him feel absurdly adolescent.

Conroy settled behind the desk and folded his hands on the blotter. "No word from your wife?"

Alec shook his head. "No, sir." He swallowed and tried to keep his voice steady. For some reason he couldn't explain, Alec had the sense that this man would never understand how utterly devastated he was about Nola's disappearance—to him it was all part of the job, just another interesting mystery to be solved. "I know you said you were going to do it, but I checked with all the hospitals around here. It gave me something to do." Alec looked at his hands for a moment. "And I went through Nola's things and her closet—nothing's missing, by the way—trying to find an address or somewhere she might have had to go to. A sickly relative I didn't know about or something." Alec shook his head. "I didn't find much."

Conroy nodded and reached to open a file drawer in his desk. He selected several forms and spread them in front of him. "All right. Then let's get a little deeper into the paperwork and that'll enable me to get a few other things started." His eyes grazed Alec. "After that we'll go over everything again to make sure we didn't miss anything. Is that all right with you?"

Alec nodded. "Of course. Anything you say."

Conroy tapped his pen against the desktop thoughtfully, then put it down and cracked his knuckles. "You said she works at the Roselle Library. Have you talked to anyone there?"

"Yes." Alec reached into the pocket of his slacks and

pulled out a folded piece of paper. "The supervising librarian, a woman by the name of Krystin Parker. I think she's Nola's boss, but she wasn't very helpful."

Conroy raised an eyebrow as he picked up his pen again and jotted down the name. "Oh? Why not?"

Alec shrugged self-consciously. "She didn't seem pleased to have to talk to me at all. I think she was afraid she was getting in the middle of some sort of domestic situation or something. She just didn't want to be involved."

"Did she say anything?"

"Not much." Alec's mouth twisted. "She did say that all personal calls to the library go through her office and Nola hadn't received any that day. But that's wrong."

Conroy raised an eyebrow. "Why is that?"

"Because I called Nola at work the day she disappeared to remind her about my staff meeting that night. I talked to her. Maybe Ms. Parker was on break or something, because someone else answered the phone and went to get Nola."

The detective sat back in his chair and chewed on the tip of his pen. "So she knew before that day that you had to go to this staff meeting?"

Alec nodded.

"And how did your wife sound when you talked to her, Mr. Elidad? Did she sound calm? Or like she was under stress?"

Alec gave it a moment before he answered, to make sure he was remembering the telephone conversation correctly and not getting it mixed up with that treasured last conversation he'd had with Nola in the car. "She sounded normal," he said finally. He folded the piece of paper he'd pulled from his pocket, then folded it again, his fingers working absently. "She didn't have a very stressful job, and she wasn't upset about me being late that night. Like I said, I knew about it ahead of time, so we hadn't made any special plans for dinner or anything." The corner of his mouth twitched. "I'm afraid we aren't a very exciting couple, Detective Conroy."

"And does that bother you, Mr. Elidad?"

Alec blinked. "I'm sorry?"

"Does that bother you?" Conroy repeated. His face was impassive. "That your wife wasn't very exciting?"

Alec flushed and glared at the man across the desk. "I didn't say I don't find my wife exciting," he snapped. "I'm quite articulate and I know how to say what I mean. And no, it doesn't bother me—it didn't bother *us*, in fact—that my wife and I didn't have a busy social life. We preferred it that way."

"No offense, Mr. Elidad," Detective Conroy said mildly. "Just covering all the bases."

Alec said nothing, afraid his voice would shake if he tried. Not find Nola exciting? If Conroy thought that, he was a fool and it only confirmed how little he knew about the Elidads and their life. Nola was *everything* to Alec, the most exhilarating thing that had ever happened to him. So what if she wasn't a Cindy Crawford beauty or an Einstein-intelligent doctoral student? They fit each other like the left and right parts of a pair of gloves.

Conroy was saying something to him again and Alec straightened. "I—I'm sorry, Detective. I didn't catch your question."

"I asked if you'd come up with anything else you thought might be helpful in trying to find her, Mr. Elidad."

"Uh—yes." Alec reached into his jacket and pulled out a small packet of papers. "It's not much, but I found the standard stuff. Her social security number on her pay stub from the library, and also a credit card statement. The credit card wasn't in the file folder with it, so it must be in her wallet. I think I already told you that she doesn't have a driver's license."

Conroy's face lifted. "But this information is a plus. We'll get that credit card number into the computer right away and see if there've been any charges on it since her disappearance."

Alec nodded and pushed the statement across the desk, watching as the detective copied down the Visa number then perused the short list of charges, all paid, on the month-old bill. There wasn't much to see: a modest amount at a local clothing store, the charge for the shoes Nola had been wearing when she disappeared, a prescription.

"This item at the Osco Pharmacy," Conroy pointed out. "Would you mind telling me what that was for?"

Alec hesitated. This was so . . . *personal.* Was it really necessary to talk about such things to this stranger? But the policeman was looking at him expectantly and it was easier to just answer. "Birth control pills," he finally said. "We'd talked about it and decided we wanted to wait a few years before having our first child. Build up some savings, get out of the apartment and into a house, that sort of thing."

"Sure." Conroy glanced at him, then back down at the Visa statement. "And did the two of you have a savings account?"

Christ, Alec thought. If the man tries to act any more casual he'll whip a baseball out of his pocket and start tossing it up and down. "Yes, we have a savings account," he said tightly. "At Harris Bank. It's got about ten thousand dollars in it, and if you check the bank records you'll see that I opened it several years ago."

"No need to get testy, Mr. Elidad."

"Testy? Is that what you'd call me?" Alec heard himself laugh and couldn't believe the bitterness in the sound. "Do you think I did something to my wife, Detective?"

Conroy put his pen on the desktop and sat back, his face unreadable. "I never said that."

"No, you didn't." Alec stared at him. "But that's the undercurrent I'm getting from you."

"I never—"

"Or maybe," Alec interrupted, "since I didn't pry into her life, you don't believe she even exists. Maybe you think I've *invented* her or something, got ahold of some . . . I don't know. Phony paperwork or something, some other woman's identity. God forbid a couple of nobodies meet and fall in love and get married right away, and God *forbid* that maybe they respect each other's privacy enough not to poke their noses into what may be a painful past!"

"Mr. Elidad—"

"Or maybe it's *me* you have a problem with." People moving around the quiet room turned to stare as Alec's voice rose, but he couldn't seem to stop it. Was it really him shouting hysterically at a detective in the Roselle Police Station? "Maybe I'm just too damned *nothing* for you to believe I could marry someone as pretty or as nice as Nola, or that she could love me? Maybe you—"

"Mr. Elidad, *sit DOWN.*"

Conroy's hands, much stronger than Alec would have expected, landed on his shoulders with startling swiftness and forced him back onto the seat of the wooden chair; he landed hard enough to feel the air *whoosh* from his lungs, and before he could draw it in to begin his tirade anew, Conroy's face, his expression surprised but not angry, was only an inch away from his.

"I think you've made your point, Mr. Elidad," Conroy said in a low voice. "I heard you quite clearly—everyone did, as a matter of fact—so if you'll get a grip on yourself, we'll continue with the questions and see if we can make some progress on finding out what happened to your wife. All right?"

Alec opened his mouth to argue, but all the fight in him was gone as quickly as it had come. In the end, all he could do was sit and nod miserably.

"Getting back to your wife's prescription," Conroy said when Alec Elidad had pulled himself under control. The outburst had caught Conroy off guard, and the memory of Elidad's words brought the detective another guilty inner flush. The man's intuition had been right: Elidad's temper tantrum had surprised him because Conroy had never thought the quiet man had it in him—

"Maybe I'm just too damned nothing *for you . . ."*

—but the fact was, Conroy realized he'd deserved the verbal slap in the face that Elidad had dealt him. He'd needed to be reminded that he was acting under the guilty-until-proven-innocent concept. There was no denying that the first suspect in a missing persons case was always the person closest to the one who'd disappeared—the spouse or significant other—but Conroy had enough experience to run this investigation without being so blatant about his thoughts.

Now Elidad blinked in confusion. "The birth control pills?"

"Who prescribed them? Was it a new doctor or someone your wife had been going to for some time?"

Elidad looked blank. "Well, I guess I don't know if it was her family physician or not. It was Nola's doctor, not mine, and she never mentioned whether she'd been seeing him for a long time or otherwise. I went into his office with her and let one of his staff draw the blood for our marriage license, but I don't recall his name offhand. I'm sure it's on the pill case in the bathroom."

Conroy nodded. "Then as soon as you get back to your apartment, you call me and give me that information, along with any telephone number on the prescription label."

Elidad suddenly looked scared. "Do you think she's sick, Detective? Maybe there was something she wasn't telling me. Her past—I guess I should have asked . . ." His voice trailed off.

Conroy put down his pen and rubbed his knuckles, resisting the urge to crack them again. Lots of people found that annoying. "I have no idea, but it can't hurt to talk to this person."

And maybe, Conroy thought as he bent to the more routine parts of the form, get the answers to a whole lot of other questions.

Dr. Crandall Yu was a pleasant man not much older than Conroy himself, and to the physician's credit he'd found time to see the detective within a couple of hours of receiving his call. His Bloomingdale practice was family-based and had a waiting room full of parents and children, lots of toys and magazines and cheerful decorations, the staff open and friendly. Unfortunately the doctor didn't know much about either Nola or Alec Elidad, and Conroy soon learned that the prescription he'd written Nola was a temporary one only; this month—January—was the last one left, and with no refills Nola would need to make an appointment with a specialist in women's health to obtain more.

"Nola Elidad wasn't a talkative woman, Detective Conroy." Dr. Yu's private office was small and unimposing, sprinkled with photographs of his wife and several small daughters. He opened an extremely thin folder on his desk and ran one finger down the papers fastened to the inside. "Ordinarily I'd say this is a matter of patient confidentiality, but there isn't much I can tell you anyway, so I suppose it doesn't matter. She seemed in fine health, had normal blood pressure, no problems or complaints. When she first came to me we ran the usual tests to start a file on a patient—"

Conroy sat forward. "When was that?"

Dr. Yu flipped a page up and scanned a blue form behind it. "A few months . . . here. The middle of October." The doctor smiled slightly. "I remember it, in fact, because it was right before she got married. We did the blood tests on both her and her husband-to-be, and that was when I gave her the short-term prescription for birth control pills. Normally I wouldn't have even done that, but the wedding was only a few days away and I couldn't get her an appointment to see a gynecologist that quickly. We set that up for the beginning of November, I gave her the three-month allotment, and I believe"—he flipped the paper forward to make sure—"that was the first and only time I saw her. I can tell you that her maiden name was Frayne. Oh—it also says her middle name is Rene."

Conroy nodded. "She made no follow-up appointment?"

"There was nothing to follow up on, Detective. The only oddity she had was a slight heart murmur, but that was nothing to worry about. Those are more common than you think. Beyond that, the blood chemistry came out normal, the urinalysis came out normal, and that was the end of it." Dr. Yu smiled. "My patients may like me, but they don't come in just to chat."

"So you don't know if she kept the appointment with the other doctor—what was his name—"

"Dr. David Ophir. And no, I don't. I can give you his number, but like me, the odds are he won't have much to tell you."

Conroy leaned forward. "Doctor, like you said, you normally wouldn't release the details of a patient's medical history. I have to tell you, though, that I'm dead-ending at every turn here. Alec Elidad's screaming because his wife is gone, but he can't give me squat about who or where she was before they met and got married—and that's the same three-month period you've got in your file here. He says Nola only worked at her job for three months, and that's next on my list. I'm not trying to violate your doctor-patient confidentiality, but if there's anything in your records that might help me find out about this woman before she came to see you, it would be a big help."

"Such as what?"

Conroy cracked his knuckles absently, then realized what he was doing and put his hands in his lap. "The names and addresses of her next of kin would be a damned good start." He looked at Dr. Yu hopefully, but the physician shook his head and closed the thin file.

"I'm afraid I can't help you there, Detective Conroy." He sounded truly apologetic but he pushed the file aside with finality. "Under the circumstances, I'd probably give you the information, but according to what Nola Elidad told us, she's an adopted child and doesn't have a clue about her real family."

Conroy felt his gut sink. "But a history of some sort, previous illnesses, the name of her adopted parents—"

"Not according to this. I checked with my staff before you got here, and Kelly—that's the receptionist—says Nola answered every question the right way. No diseases, no complaints. Alec was down as the next of kin, and everything else that had to do with family history—she just labeled 'unknown.' "

Look at her, Jesse thought. She's so pretty. God, I missed her so *much*. Aloud, he said only, "Good morning."

Stacey's head jerked toward him, and while he kept his face expressionless, he winced inside at the fear he saw there. Was it because he'd shaken her yesterday morning, or because she didn't know him? Both probably—and what had he expected? That she would get a good night's sleep in their bedroom—on the floor, no less—and wake up bright-eyed and full of the life that something in her mind had blocked out? *Hi, darling—I'm back from my three-month sojourn! Sorry I left without calling!* Right.

Now Stacey said nothing, just sat on the floor and waited with that frozen-rabbit expression. It broke his heart to see her like this, but at least she was here again, and not somewhere else with that other guy, being his wife when she should have been—always *had* been—Jesse's. For a moment a surprising sort of black rage filled him, fueled by the thought of Stacey in another man's arms, of someone else running his hands along the smooth curve of her thigh—

Jesse wasn't sure how, but he pushed the anger away—for now—and sat up against the pillows, keeping his movements slow and steady so he wouldn't frighten Stacey any more than she already was. He'd never been violent, and although he had always been a jealous man, he wasn't a fool, either. In the past, Stacey had said it made her feel loved and she'd certainly never done anything to make him not trust her. Being protective and a little possessive of the person you loved was altogether different from being mistrustful, and because Stacey had a good understanding of the difference, Jesse's jealousy had never much bothered her. The feeling Jesse was having now, this rage toward the unnamed man who had acted the part of husband to Stacey when he'd had no right, wasn't something Jesse'd thought he'd ever have to face. One way or the other, he'd have to learn to control it.

"Are you hungry?" Jesse asked as he undid the fabric belt tied around his ankle and tossed it to her. Stacey shook her head as she caught it and wound it around her waist, little spastic movements that reminded him, again, of a tiny, trapped animal. Jesus. "Well, I am." He kept his voice cheerful but not too loud; he'd never been so aware of how much of a . . . *presence* he seemed to have in the physical world before now. He pulled the quilt aside and checked surreptitiously to make sure everything that had to do with his boxers was well-covered before he stood—no sense in having her think he was a pervert or a rapist on top of everything else. The idea would have been humorous if he hadn't known that six months ago Stacey would've grabbed his boxers as he tried to climb out of bed and yanked them down to his knees, laughing the whole time.

The room was chilly and Jesse reached for a T-shirt and sweatpants, then quickly pulled them over the shorts. Stacey's heavier robe was draped over the foot of the bed and he picked it up and offered it to her. "Here," he said, "this'll keep you from getting too cold."

She took it hesitantly, her gaze never leaving his eyes, her fingers never touching his. Jesse watched her stand and quickly shrug on the robe, then close it tightly. Her hair was rumpled, her face puffy from sleep—proof that at least she'd gotten some—and he couldn't remember when he'd seen her looking so good. Sure, it had a lot to do with the fact that she'd been gone for twelve weeks, but he'd always thought his wife was the prettiest thing in town and their years of marriage hadn't changed that opinion. It shamed him to see the fear in her eyes when she looked at him.

"You feel okay?" he finally asked when she didn't say anything.

Stacey nodded reluctantly. "Y-yes."

His mouth stretched into a relieved smile. "Great." She'd always been a light sleeper, so Stacey hadn't much rumpled the pad of blankets and linens he'd fixed her to lie on. Now Jesse reached down and picked up the bottom corners of the pile. "Grab the other end," he said, "and we'll get these folded up and off the floor."

Stacey looked at him numbly for a second, then picked up her corner. They folded the linens smoothly and without speaking, always moving in the same direction without having to ask; while she didn't comment on it, Jesse wondered if she noticed this and made the connection—they'd done this same task hundreds of times in their years together. When they were finished, she waited while he set the pile of linens on the end of the dresser instead of putting them away. Face it: More than likely, Stacey would be using these again tonight. Only a dreamer would think that things between them would get fixed that quickly.

"Great," Jesse said again. He hoped his cheerfulness didn't sound too phony, but Stacey's silence was unnerving and he spoke just to hear the sound of a voice. "Let's go make some coffee." He motioned to the bedroom door and his wife moved hesitantly toward it, then paused at the dresser and peered at the Polaroid photograph tucked into the upper corner of the mirror.

"That's you," he offered, even though it was obvious. He pulled the photo free and handed it to her. "Some kid took it last summer at the Chili Fest in Hanover Park. Charged me five bucks." The boy had moved when he'd pressed the button and the shot was blurred, and Jesse still couldn't believe he'd paid that much for it. Still, the Cub Foods Store was recognizable in the background behind the food booths, and there was the smudgy image of Stacey smiling at the camera.

"It's . . . too blurred to make out," she said now. "It could be anyone."

"Well, it's not anyone," Jesse said lightly. "But you're right about it being out of focus." He tried to grin. "Kid was a con artist, though. He still got me to pay for it." Stacey didn't smile in return, just glanced again at the photo. For a second, Jesse wanted to cry, then he squashed the urge. Had he really thought this would be easy? "Anyway, I'll get down the wedding photos in a little while. We can go through them and see if that refreshes your memory."

He turned to tuck the photo back at the side of the mirror and she said something, too low for him to hear.

"What?" he asked.

"You're that sure," Stacey repeated. "That it's . . . that I'm who you think I am." She looked as if it had taken every ounce of courage she had just to speak her mind, and that *was* something completely different from the woman he'd known—Stacey Waite had never been a gal to hide her opinions.

"Absolutely," Jesse said flatly. "I think I know my own wife when I see her face-to-face." He'd said almost the same thing in the car the day before yesterday.

"Really." She stared at him and lifted her chin a little, enough to make him think that maybe the real Stacey was still in there somewhere. "If that's true, then tell me why I don't recognize my husband the same way?"

God, if only he could answer that.

That tiny, empty room again, but it gave her a chance to get a little calmer as each half hour rolled past. Nola paced its width just for something to do while she waited for her captor to perform whatever morning rituals were a part of his life. Despite the small, sliding bolt Jesse had quickly installed on the outside of the door, it was a . . . mild room, with walls painted a soft, buttery yellow and free of nail holes or the waist-high scrapes left from furniture. There was a closet that was almost too small to be useful, and in it Nola discovered a triple row of wooden rods, the spacing clearly meant for child-sized clothes. She wondered idly if the room had always been like this, or if Jesse and the missing Stacey had decorated it, perhaps hoping or planning for a baby—it seemed impossible that the room could have ever been anything but a nursery. Seeing it so empty filled her with an inexplicable sadness for Jesse and the missing woman. In some respects, Nola's mind was like that—dotted with empty spaces that she desperately wanted to fill. How terrible that for Jesse and his wife, all their hopes and dreams had disintegrated into his kidnapping a stranger from a grocery store parking lot . . . and now there was only Jesse, so utterly convinced that Nola was not Nola at all.

Nola's terror was fading bit by bit, washing away in the face of a different kind of fear. Physically, she now thought she'd probably be okay—she no longer believed that Jesse Waite would beat her, or rape her, or chop her into a hundred pieces like the tortured victims of countless killers. Her own frame of mind, however . . . that was another story. Was she strong enough to hold out against this? God help her, but so many tiny seeds of doubt had already been planted, and she had never been a strong woman. What if he actually managed to persuade her—

No! Nola pinched herself viciously on one side of her rib cage, hard enough to nearly make her cry out. I am Nola Elidad, *not* someone named Stacey. I don't know the man who's keeping me here. I *don't.*

Then why did she know how long it would be before he was finished with his morning shower?

"I'm sorry," Jesse said. Stacey must've heard him moving around outside, and she was right there when he opened the door. "Did I take too long?"

She shook her head and started to step past him, then hesitated and looked back over her shoulder and into the silent nursery. Jesse remembered a time not so long ago when they had planned how to decorate this tiny room. God, how much he had taken for granted as they'd sat on the living room floor and gone over the catalogs with glasses of decaffeinated iced tea in front of them. He'd never even thought twice about giving up real coffee and soda at the same time she had—after all, this was his baby too, and if she had to deprive herself of certain pleasures to carry it, so would he.

"Do you remember this room?" he asked her now. His voice was hushed.

Stacey gave him a quick, bewildered glance, then shook her head. For a moment she didn't say anything, but Jesse knew it was only a matter of time. His wife was a naturally curious woman—not a gossip, just someone who liked knowing the details of the world around her. It was inevitable that she'd want to know the origin of this small, yellow-walled space. "Remember what?"

Although he'd known the question was coming, Jesse found himself unable to meet her gaze. The pain was just too great, even after all these months. "It . . . was supposed to be the baby's room," he finally said in a hoarse voice. "But you lost the baby because of the fever." She frowned and he rushed on, wanting to get the worst of the news out before it simply overwhelmed him. "The doctor says you can't have any more because of your heart; it won't be able to take the strain."

"I can't have children?" she asked incredulously.

Stacey looked so stunned that he wanted to take her in his arms and hold her, but he didn't dare. She wasn't accepting of him yet, and he didn't want to start this day out badly, the way yesterday had begun. "I'm sorry," was all he could think of to say. When she looked like she was going to add something, he quickly pulled her into the hallway and shut the door. "Don't think about it right now. It's probably a lot of the reason why you'd want to forget."

"But—"

"We'll talk about it later," he said firmly. "It's—it's just as painful for me, and there's other things to deal with first. Come on." He touched her elbow and was gratified to see that this time she didn't recoil. "Let's do the easy part first. We'll get some food in our stomachs, make some coffee, and take it one step at a time."

"I can't have children?"

I'm an idiot, Nola thought angrily. How could I have asked that? Worse, how could I have even been *serious* when I did?

The makeup-free face that stared back at her from the bathroom mirror offered no answers, and Nola curled her hands into fists and wished desperately that she were the type of person who could punch the mirror, vent her frustration on something inanimate and breakable but that wouldn't fight back or end up in pain because of her temper tantrum. The pure, physical release that would come from such an act had to be immense . . . but she couldn't. Nola's mind didn't work that way: She automatically thought of flying glass and the mess that she'd have to clean up afterward, the money thrown away when Jesse had to replace the mirror. She might as well feed a twenty-dollar bill down the garbage disposal.

Nola stood for a moment and stared into the sink, feeling the pulse of blood through her temples as she tried to calm down—right now, she didn't know if she was angrier at Jesse or herself. Finally she lifted her head and pushed her face close to the mirror. "I do *not* have a bad heart," she hissed at her reflection. "Just a little heart murmur. I am *not* some woman named Stacey. My name is *Nola,* Nola Elidad, and there is absolutely no reason on the face of this earth that I can't have a child. Just like there's nothing at all wrong with my mind."

Was there?

Is this it? Jesse wondered. The moment of truth when, *finally,* his wife came back to him? Please, God, he thought, let this be the end of it, the trip wire in her mind that will fix it all. There was so *much* riding on the next few minutes, their entire future. And he wasn't a fool—he knew it could go either way. Stacey could "wake up," such as it were, or . . .

The contents of this box could send the woman he loved deeper into whatever madness had stolen her away from him to begin with.

"Okay," Jesse said. To Nola, his voice was a little too glib as she watched him pull the shoe box—more of a boot box, really—from amid a jumble of things on the bedroom closet shelf and bring it carefully down. Was he as nervous as she was? Nola could see the logo "Payless" splashed across the side, and it only strengthened her conviction: There was no way she would have stored something as important as her wedding pictures so carelessly in a box that had once held boots. An album would be more her style, something rimmed in cream-colored lace with the date embroidered across the front and their best photo embedded in the cover—

Oh bullshit, Nola thought with sudden crudeness. You'd do no such thing; for God's sake, you didn't even bother to take any photographs at all on the day you and Alec got married. If you're looking to preserve your sanity in a bad situation, don't try to do it with a lie. Self-delusion will only muck things up more.

Pulse hammering, she realized Jesse was patiently standing in front of her, expecting her to take the box from him. Beneath the fabric of her shirt, Nola felt a line of nervous perspiration suddenly trickle between her breasts despite the coolness of the room, and it was followed immediately by an unpleasant chill that swept across the back of her scalp. This man probably—*obviously*—hadn't looked at these photographs in a very long time. What would he do to her when they revealed the truth, that the woman he'd kidnapped was the wrong one? The horrifying question made her literally unable to take the box from him, and finally Jesse shrugged and motioned her to follow him.

In the living room Nola sat where he told her to, at one end of a couch covered in a print of tiny brown and white flowers. Jesse set the box on the coffee table, but he made no move to open it right away, gazing at her thoughtfully instead. If he was hoping for her to take the initiative, it was going to be a long wait: Nola had no desire to speed up what was bound to be a disastrous discovery. This was the second morning she'd been held here—what difference did a few more minutes make?

"Tell you what," Jesse said at last. "I'll go make us some hot chocolate."

Nola watched him go into the kitchen and chewed nervously on the inside of her cheek. Had he sounded as reluctant as she felt? Maybe . . . *probably*. There was no question about trying for an escape in the next few minutes—he could see everything she did because of the pass-through above the counter that separated the kitchen from the dining and living room areas. If she went for the door—dead-bolted anyway—Jesse could be out of the kitchen in a flash. He'd bring her down in three short steps, like a lion bringing down a baby antelope.

She looked around the living room, resigned to waiting for him and a cup of hot chocolate she really didn't want. This tidy townhouse . . . it was a terrifying place for her. It was filled with the same touches—tiny vases of silk flowers, crocheted pillows, blown-glass figurines—that she might have chosen had she lived in a small home such as this instead of the tiny apartment she shared with Alec. Even the clothes she wore frightened her, just because they were *there:* another clean set this morning, a different pair of jeans and a winter flannel shirt. This one was a more feminine blend of pink and yellow, and it fit her as though it'd been custom-tailored. What was the likelihood, really, of something like that happening?

High, you fool. Nola's mouth stretched into a grim line as she realized the turn her thoughts were taking yet again. He's kidnapped you because you look like his wife, she reminded herself. It stands to reason you'd be the same size—you'd better clear your head right now and start thinking about how you're going to get out of this when he realizes you're Nola Elidad, not Stacey Waite. When you won't be *good enough* anymore.

The question of what had really happened to the missing Stacey rose in her mind again and Nola mulled it over, prodding at it like a cat poking cautiously at something that might leap up and bite. She'd actually started to relax a bit around Jesse . . . but that was before these other questions had surfaced. Had Jesse killed his wife? Or was his story true and had Stacey simply walked out—perhaps driven away by some personality trait in Jesse about which Nola knew nothing? God knows, there was plenty about Jesse that Nola didn't know. Yes, he was a kidnapper, but except for when he'd grabbed her in the parking lot and shaken her up in the kitchen, he actually seemed like a nice guy. Still, in his day-to-day life, maybe those whacked-out situations weren't as infrequent as Jesse would have her believe. Maybe he lost his head a lot.

And maybe he *had* killed his wife.

Nola almost screamed when Jesse's hand cut into her vision, then she realized that all he was doing was offering her the steaming mug of chocolate. The outside of the mug was too hot to touch and he had to set it on the table before she could pick it up by the handle. He'd boiled the water and stirred in the mix, and it'd even had time for the prepackaged little marshmallows to melt—Jesus, how long had she been sitting here pondering her fate?

Jesse sat next to her without touching her, then took a deep breath. "All right," he said. "I guess we can't put this off any longer."

Nola nodded voicelessly, further unnerved by his admission that he'd been as reluctant as she. Her hands found a small pillow and she picked it up and pulled it onto her lap, plucking mindlessly at the crocheted lace along its edge. A moment later, Jesse tugged it from her hands and set it aside. "Don't do that, Stacey," he said gently. "You know the thread'll break if you keep worrying at it."

She stared at him and felt a flash of anger, nothing but childish rebellion—*I'll pick at it if I want to!*—then looked away. What was the matter with her? Kidnap victims didn't think like that. For God's sake, she should be figuring out how she was going to get out of here, fabricating some deceptively simple escape plan, not thinking about starting petty arguments.

"Okay," Jesse said, bringing her attention back to the dreaded box on the coffee table. "Let's look at our wedding pictures."

He opened the boot box and handed her the item on top. She took it automatically, then turned the small American Greetings wedding invitation over on her palm and peered at it. It was neatly filled out—*Please give us the honor of your presence on Saturday, July 27th, at St. Walter's*—and went on to list the time and details of the upcoming marriage of Stacey Loren Newman and Jesse Egan Waite.

"This isn't my handwriting," Nola said. Fear had made her voice coarse, as though she hadn't used it in a very long time, and her fingers shook a bit as she set the invitation aside.

Jesse chuckled. "Well, of course it isn't, silly. Your mom filled those out." A shadow of anger crossed his face and he looked away for a moment. "She never approved of me, not ever. Didn't make any difference to her that I would've done anything in the world for you. Even these—" He indicated the wedding invitation with a sweep of his finger. "She acted like she was doing us a big favor by writing them out." His chin lifted. "That's why we paid for everything that had to do with the wedding ourselves, so she wouldn't be able to hold it up to us later."

When Nola didn't say anything, Jesse reached into the box and pulled out the next few items, handing them to her a piece at a time: a small lace handkerchief, a short, cream-colored net veil crowned by tiny pink silk flowers and pearls, a carefully pressed white rose stored between ironed-together layers of waxed paper. She examined each curiously, then set them back on the coffee table. He paused and looked at her, his blue eyes unreadable, then lifted a five-by-eight manila envelope from the box and undid its clasp, handing it to her without pulling out the contents.

Nola swallowed and took the envelope, wondering again how Jesse was going to react when the truth of everything was revealed. The paper felt warm beneath her touch, then Nola gave herself a mental slap. It wasn't any such thing—it was her own skin temperature, rising out of anxiety . . . or perhaps the thermostat had kicked on the baseboard heater by the wall.

No more stalling.

She shoved her finger under the flap of the envelope and got a stinging paper cut on the tip of her forefinger for her trouble. Grinding her teeth against the unexpected pain, Nola kept going; she absolutely would *not* consider that stupid little wound to be an omen of things to come. Sooner or later, Jesse Waite was going to have to face the truth, and sooner or later she, Nola Elidad, was going to have to face the consequences of that truth.

When she pulled the first batch of photographs from the envelope and looked down at the one on top, Nola lost herself in a scream that seemed to go on for hours.

She was looking at herself.

....

I'll be all right, Nola thought. I can make it through this, I *can.*

Despite her determination, for a few moments more Nola could only sit and stare at the walls. Her thoughts were jumbled, but at least she was finally able to think without losing herself in the hysterics that had swept her this morning in the living room. Her eyes and face were swollen from crying and Jesse had stayed with her until a little while ago, enduring her wailing and the raging denials that had followed. Now he was doing something while he gave her a little time to herself to sort things out. Maybe he was taking a shower, running an errand, or kidnapping someone else—God only knew. And here she was again in the so-called nursery, and this time, if she wanted, Nola could browse through the photographs of "their" wedding at her leisure.

She *didn't* want to . . . but she did anyway. She *had* to.

Sitting on the chilly carpeted floor with her back against the wall, Nola reluctantly splayed the photographs on the floor in front of her crossed knees, placing them carefully next to the ones that seemed most likely to be their mates, sorting them as though she were playing a game of solitaire. The young woman in these photos wore a plain, pale pink dress, and the veil that Nola had seen earlier in the box was pinned attractively to hair that was longer than Nola's. The woman's face was obscured in a lot of the shots, either by the veil or by her hair or by just plain poor photography—it all went back to the buddy Jesse had mentioned who had tried to act as the couple's official photographer. Jesse was in most of the shots with her, wearing a dress shirt and looking happy but out of place in a dark tie and slacks—apparently he didn't own a suit coat. Most of the photos were pretty amateurish, out of focus and badly lit, but there were several pretty good ones of the two of them. One particular shot showed most of Stacey Waite's profile on the left side as she danced with her new husband.

Such a frightening resemblance.

That's all it is, Nola thought, but the voice in her head had an edge of stridency to it, the sound of someone protesting out of obstinance rather than accuracy. Was she really that certain of her own identity anymore?

This woman, Nola thought as she forced herself to study the photographs, she could be me.

The western sun slanted through the high window, brightening the color of the yellow walls until it was nearly painful against Nola's tired, swollen eyes. Now she'd been in here for . . . what? Two hours? Maybe longer, turning her back on Jesse when he'd tried to talk to her through the door, refusing to come out when he'd pleaded and ignoring the peanut butter sandwich and noodle soup he'd fixed for their lunch. Eventually she would have to leave this safe, bland little room, this little haven, and try to talk to the man who was so convinced that they belonged together that he would steal her off the street. But for now, she sat in a spot of bright sunlight and squinted at the walls.

Yellow . . . a neutral color picked for the sexlessness of an unborn child. If that child had been born, would she have remembered it?

Furious with herself all over again, Nola balled her fist and pounded on the photograph of the dancing couple that held the center place of honor in the array in front of her.

No! she thought fiercely. *No no no! I am Nola, I AM!*

But tears were coursing down her cheeks, burning a path over skin still raw from the last bout of crying.

God help her; she wasn't so sure anymore.

Jesse found enough old bottles in the basement to pay for a Sunday paper, and while he was scrounging around down there, he also found the shoe Stacey had lost in the darkness. It was tan, or at least it had been before the mud and snow from the parking lot followed by the dusty, grimy basement floor; now it was crusted with dirt and salt where it'd been soaked with slush, then scuffed along the floor mat of the car.

The sight of it, like the memory of him shaking her in the kitchen, shamed him deeply. He hadn't known it was possible to be so embarrassed, but he was. He hunted as well as he could in the poorly lit room, but he couldn't find the other shoe. This one didn't look salvageable, but it wasn't for him to make decisions about Stacey's clothes, so he put it upstairs by the back door. He'd rather throw it out and forget about her other life, but Stacey was ultimately going to have to deal with that herself—the shoes she'd been wearing were the least of the details that would have to be addressed.

He hauled the bottles upstairs in two paper bags, hesitating both times outside the door to the nursery. Jesse could hear Stacey sniffling in there, and he hoped to God she hadn't had a fit and torn up their wedding pictures—there were no copies and thinking that John would have saved the negatives was a bit like expecting the clouds to rain pigs. The scene in the living room earlier had been pretty ugly—this time it hadn't been Jesse flying off the deep end, but Stacey. She'd outright screamed when she got an eyeful of those photographs, then she'd had as close to her own temper tantrum as Jesse'd ever seen. If he hadn't grabbed her wrists, the whole box of wedding memorabilia would've gone flying across the living room.

Jesse shrugged on his jacket and hurried out to the car, juggling the bags while he fought to get the key into the iced-over lock of the trunk. He was going to have to fix that passenger door now that Stacey was back; that'd been on the "to do" list when she'd gotten sick, but when he'd spotted her in Roselle, he'd never gotten around to it. Now that there'd soon be two people riding in the car again, it was time to take care of this old problem.

With the bottles stowed in the trunk, Jesse started up the car, listening to the way the grumpy old engine turned over and thinking about the new job coming up. He had to hand it to Lou, his boss at his old job. Saying "Take all the time you need" was one thing, but Jesse had just never come back—no call, no note in the mail, nothing. Lou had called the house once or twice but Jesse hadn't had much to say to Lou's questions other than "I don't know." Finally they'd replaced him. Then, when he'd started looking for work again, Jesse found out they'd folded up. But he'd been at that job for seven years, since he was twenty and a year before he'd met Stacey, and there just wasn't anywhere else he could list on his job application. He knew the shop supervisor at the new place had talked to John, and because of whatever his friend had said, MC had offered him the job a couple of days after he'd filled out the application. He ought to call John and say thanks, but . . . again, he was too damned embarrassed about his behavior. In the space of three months, he'd turned into a real prize.

As the car warmed up, Jesse glanced around the interior and remembered the single shoe he'd found in the basement. He went over the front and back floorboards, under the front seat—everywhere, but the shoe wasn't in the car. Strange . . . the parking lot at the Pik-Kwik? If so, it was surely smashed up in the snow by now. Well, that was okay; he'd tell Stacey the truth and when he had a couple of paychecks under his belt, he'd get her some new ones if she wanted.

Although the Pik-Kwik was only five minutes away, Jesse opted for Gorski's farther west on Irving Park. He hadn't so much as thought about it at the time, but what if someone had seen him pull Stacey into the car Thursday night? It stood to reason that her husband—her *other* husband—would be looking for her, and by now he'd probably filed a whole pile of reports with the police. But he must've lucked out, because the Impala's registration was current, easily traceable to the townhouse. The first thing people went for in a bad situation on the road was a license plate number, but there'd been no cop banging on the door of his home. If the police hadn't shown up by now, there were obviously no witnesses.

No witnesses. The phrase made Jesse feel like a criminal. Was it so wrong to make your wife go home with you when that was where she belonged? This wasn't a divorce from an abusive husband or a custody fight over kids—the circumstances were different, much more complicated. Sure, he could call the police himself and tell them the whole, sordid little story—

Hi, my wife went a little out of her mind and forgot who she was. Now she's married to another man, who's probably filed a missing persons report, and we need to get this mess straightened out now that I've brought her home.

—but it was easy to see that doing so would cause the biggest heartache, short of actually thinking Stacey had been dead for three months, that Jesse had ever had. Then would come doctors, psychiatric treatment—maybe they'd put Stacey away—plus Jesse would have to deal with the other guy. Jesus. All he wanted, for now, was to get Stacey used to being home again and to work on this memory problem. Then they could take it from there.

He pulled into the parking lot in front of Gorski's Foods and got out quickly, unable to stop himself from looking around furtively as he unloaded the bottles and hauled them inside. The whole process of getting his money and heading toward the newspapers took all of three minutes but it felt like an hour; suddenly Jesse could have sworn he had a red streak across his forehead identifying him as a man who stole women off the street. It didn't help when he leaned over to pick up the first edition of the Sunday *Chicago Tribune* and a headline from the *Roselle Press* caught his eye: ROSELLE WOMAN REPORTED MISSING. There were no photographs, and Jesse was suddenly afraid that someone would notice him standing there and gawking at the article; he checked his change and saw that he had enough, so he bought both papers and hurried out of the store.

Outside he restarted the car and scanned the article, sitting and shivering as a cold that had nothing to do with the frigid temperature worked its way along his spine.

Nola Rene Elidad was reported missing by her husband Alec on Thursday night. Mr. Elidad last saw his wife in the parking lot of the Pik-Kwik grocery store on Irving Park Road, where he dropped her off to do some shopping late Thursday afternoon before going to a business meeting. He called the police that evening when he arrived home and discovered that his wife had never returned to their Springhill apartment. Nola Elidad is twenty-one years old and is described as being a petite woman with brown hair and blue eyes who weighs about one hundred pounds. Please call Detective Lucas Conroy directly at 555-2950 if you have any information as to the whereabouts of this woman.

Jesse was profoundly grateful there was no photograph—he didn't think he could stand seeing his wife's picture in the paper. On the other hand, he knew Stacey's aunt read the *Roselle Press* regularly, and it would've served Trista right to have her sister call her and tell her Stacey's picture was in the paper—especially after that farce of a telephone conversation Friday morning.

Maybe, Jesse thought, I should call again. He sat there for another moment, tapping his fingers on the steering wheel. Well, he probably would—his conscience would make him—but not for a while. As far as he was concerned, Trista didn't deserve to know the good news, not after the way she'd treated him. The article implied that there were no leads, and that, at least, made Jesse feel a little better.

He started to get out and toss the paper in the trash, but now there were too many people loading up groceries in the parking lot and at least four others coming out of the store. Jesse still felt conspicuous and paranoid—what if someone later remembered seeing him buy the paper, read the front-page article, then throw it in the store's trash bin three minutes later? Rather than chance it, he tucked the tiny local paper inside the heavier *Tribune* and headed back home. Suddenly all he could think of was Stacey, locked in that melancholy nursery with the box of photographs. What if she escaped?

Jesse hadn't been paying attention to the weather reports, and as he pulled up to the traffic light at Irving Park he saw that the earlier snow flurries had deepened into a heavier fall, enough to coat the roads and make them slick. God, everything seemed designed to make his life more difficult, right down to slowing him up as he tried to get back home. The return trip took twice as long as the old car responded to his unusually heavy acceleration by trying to skew sideways, reminding Jesse that he should've replaced the worn tires last fall. Face grim, tension singing along the muscles of his shoulders, Jesse just *knew* he was going to find the front door open when he got home, or maybe a couple of squad cars crisscrossing the walkway, armed officers ready to grab him when he got out of the Impala. If that was the way it would be, fine; what he'd done wasn't wrong and he'd stand up to anyone to defend his right to bring his wife home.

But the only thing waiting was the quiet townhouse and when he grabbed up the paper and rushed inside, he realized how unfounded his panic had been. He even spooked Stacey by clawing frantically at the nursery door, so convinced was he that she'd someone gotten the second-floor window open and crawled out that way—would she be wandering around in the snow and near-zero temperatures, dazed and cold, just asking for a return of the strep throat that had started this bout of illness?

But no, and Jesse felt like a relieved fool when he found Stacey sitting on the floor with the shoe box neatly repacked at her side while she waited for him to come home.

"So you didn't see anything out of the ordinary?"

The girl Conroy was talking to was young, no more than seventeen and probably an after-schooler. She shook her head and popped her gum. "No, but you might want to talk to Brent. He was working the registers. Maybe he seen something." She glanced around, then pointed with one multicolored fingernail. "Over there—he just came in."

The detective looked and saw a lanky young man shrug off his coat as he headed to the time clock by the cash checking counter. He gave the kid a minute or two to settle in, then went to join him. When he pulled out his badge, the boy looked surprised, but at least he didn't bolt. "What's up?"

"Are you Brent?" The teenager nodded and Conroy flipped open his notebook. "One of the girls back there says you might have seen something in the parking lot Thursday night."

Brent's expression was blank for a moment, then he frowned slightly. "Oh, I think I know what she's talking about. But I don't think it was any big thing."

"Why don't you just tell me what you saw and let me decide if it was a 'big thing.' "

The teen shrugged. "Yeah, whatever. It was just this guy and this woman, and he kind of, you know, flipped out at her in the parking lot."

"Flipped out?"

Brent shrugged again. "Well, they were, like, arguing about something, then he made her get in his car, and the next time I looked, they were gone."

Conroy scribbled in his book. "What do you mean 'made her get in his car'—did he strike her?"

"Nah, nothing like that. And I couldn't actually hear anything they said—I was busy checking people out and I only saw a little of what was going on through the window, couldn't hear anything. I only noticed it because he was, you know, waving his arms and sh—, uh, stuff." Brent glanced over his shoulder, as though suddenly remembering he was at work. "Like I said, it didn't seem like a big deal. People argue all the time, and I been told enough by my dad to keep my nose out of other people's business."

Great, Conroy thought. Another oblivious teenager. Aloud, he said, "You didn't happen to notice anything about the car, did you? Maybe even the license plate number, or part of it? The color?"

Brent shook his head. "Not a clue, man. Computers are my thing—I'm a gamer. I don't do cars."

Great, Conroy thought again. "These two people, what did they look like?"

The kid looked mildly disdainful. "I told you, I was busy checking people out. I only glanced at him, and it was dark outside. The only thing I remember was that he was waving his arms around and he looked like he was yelling at her."

Conroy started to snap at the boy, then made himself hold back. "Do you at least remember how tall he was? About?"

Another frown creased the teenager's forehead, but he looked like he was trying this time. "Well, you can't really tell through the window, but he was a lot taller than her. She didn't look like she was very big."

That was something, anyway. "Did you notice anyone else with the woman?" Conroy asked. "Before the guy she was arguing with?"

"Nah. But come to think of it, we did find a bag of groceries—some milk and bread—in the parking lot that night. It was all froze up, so we tossed it."

"Right," the detective said. He pulled a card from his wallet and offered it to the kid, who took it and peered at it curiously. "Call me right away, please, if you remember anything else?"

"So what's the deal?" the kid asked. "Like, what happened—did he kill her or something?"

So much for Dad's lessons. "A local woman is missing," Conroy said. "The last time her husband saw her was when he dropped her off in this parking lot Thursday."

"No shit." The boy looked fascinated. "What—"

"That's all we know right now," Conroy told him, stopping any more questions. "Keep my card by your register, all right?"

"Sure." Brent hunched his shoulders and shoved his hands deep into the pocket of his jeans. "Kidnapped. Wow, that sucks."

Yeah, Conroy thought as he walked away.

It sure does.

The lab results were waiting for him at the station, and Conroy discovered that his instincts had been on track: The blood splatters in the shoe were a match against the doctor's records from the test taken for the marriage license—the shoe had definitely been worn by the mysterious Nola Elidad. Now Conroy had enough evidence to support the allegation that this woman, about whom no one seemed to know anything, had been abducted against her will.

The quiet little Village of Roselle, *his* village. Yeah, it had its share of thefts and accidents and robberies, but beyond that it was a peaceful, safe place to live. Nothing more serious than the very occasional armed robbery ever took place here. In Roselle, people just didn't go around grabbing women and forcing them into their cars.

He was going to find this woman, one way or another.

JANUARY 20--MONDAY

"I need a leave of absence," Alec said hoarsely. "Until my wife is found." He had been so sure that Bill Raven, the school principal, would be understanding and sympathetic, but now all the man seemed capable of doing was fidgeting and frowning over the schedule for the upcoming semester. Jesus Christ, Alec thought, if this doesn't constitute a family emergency, what the hell does?

"That's going to be very difficult, Alec." Bill flipped a few pages ahead and his frown deepened into a scowl. "I mean, I've got two teachers out on family leave already and a third out on medical leave. The last time I checked, there were no long-term substitutes available right now—it's a bad time for everyone."

"Bad time?" Alec echoed. He choked off an unexpected string of expletives—barely—by snapping his teeth together, then got a coppery, thin wash of blood from the inside of his cheek as payment for holding his thoughts in check.

"Well, yeah." Bill sat back. "Peterlin—you remember him? The new guy who started in phys ed in September—is already out with a broken ankle. That's the medical leave I told you about. The two family leaves are pregnancies, and what with the new labor laws about that, these people can be out up to twelve weeks and we have to hold their positions for them. The budget is already stretched to its maximum for substitutes—"

"A bad time," Alec interrupted, "is having the person you're supposed to spend the rest of your life with disappear for no reason." He felt a lot more in control but while the urge to cuss the man roundly had been weeded out, the rest of what he had to say was the same. In fact, he felt an almost maniacal smile tugging at his mouth. "I don't care about the time off that other people got because they had babies, and I most certainly won't give a second thought to the school budget."

Bill looked distressed and shocked that a teacher would dare to talk to him like this, a situation Alec didn't feel a pressing need to fix. A few seconds ago he had been angry, but now Alec felt a cold, dark humor slide over him, part of that whole *I can't believe this is happening and any minute I'll wake up* undercurrent inside his head. "I know what everybody around here thinks—that we had some sort of fight and Nola walked out on me, that this is some little marital tiff that will all go away in a few days."

"Alec—"

Alec held up a hand to cut him off. "People *always* assume the worst, and you know what? *So do I.* While you're sitting there talking about the school budgets, I'm terrified that my wife is *dead,* murdered by some psycho."

"Oh, I'm certain she isn't—"

The impulse to smile was gone in an instant and Alec was on his feet without remembering leaving the chair, leaning over Bill Raven's desk with his face only a foot away from the other man's. "You're certain about *what*? That she isn't what? Then maybe you'd like to call the detective on this case and help him out. Perhaps you can even explain to him why he found one of her shoes in a grocery store parking lot. Because right now he's not too damned hopeful!"

Alec straightened and the two men stared at each other without speaking for a few moments, then the principal lowered his gaze and cleared his throat. "Take all the time you need."

"Thank you," Alec said. He'd been shouting at the end, but now his voice had leveled out and he thought he could say the rest of his parting words without screaming. "I knew you'd understand."

Two hours later Alec was already wondering if the leave of absence had been a bad idea.

At ten-thirty in the morning, the apartment was as silent and empty as a waiting tomb, and Alec realized that except for Friday, the day after Nola's disappearance, he hadn't been in the apartment alone on a weekday since he and Nola were married. The library's holidays ran with the school's—when he was home, so was she. Nola had spent slightly more time here by herself because of his staff meetings and evening programs—the occasional parents' night, various school functions in which she had little interest. In fact, it was on those nights that Alec especially looked forward to coming home, because a few hours at home by herself would invariably make Nola change something about the apartment to make it more homey. Once he found new curtains in the bedroom that matched the comforter, custom-made from matching sheets to Nola's specifications by the town's best seamstress, Helen. Another time he'd opened the front door to the smell of homemade sweet Amish corn bread, blended from some recipe Nola had run across in the newspaper. Dozens of little things that kept him looking forward to his life and his new wife and the end of an overly long day.

Alec hadn't talked to Conroy since Saturday, and now the memory of his outburst at the police station embarrassed him. He seemed to be having a lot of those lately—with Conroy, this morning with Bill Raven. It wasn't like him—there was too much stress, too many unknowns thrust into a life that had previously been quiet and content, well-planned. He should see a doctor, have his blood pressure checked; he wouldn't be surprised to find it had risen dramatically. Now he poked around the apartment, straightening this, wiping that, whatever; the place smelled heavily of furniture polish and pine cleaner and Alec was suddenly exasperated with himself. What was the purpose of scrubbing, scrubbing, scrubbing this tiny apartment—did he think Nola left him because he was too dirty? Not likely, but then . . . *where was she?*

Alec sat on the chair in the living room and stared at the double glass doors that led to the balcony, not really seeing them. Instead, his mind turned back a few months, losing the gray January skies and the frigid temperatures as he remembered the small carnival at which he'd met Nola. How ironic that it had been practically across the street from his apartment, and Alec couldn't help wonder how many other times she might have been only a block or two away from him through the years—that, he supposed, was life in the suburban equivalent of a small town.

Alec had seen them setting up the rides and gone just for something to do on a dull weekend afternoon, a diversion to get him away from math books and lesson plans. Sometimes he wished he were more physically inclined, like that coach at the school; he needed more in his life than to just knock around the apartment on the evenings and weekends when there wasn't some school function to go to . . . not that he found those all that exciting either. There actually *had* been something planned for that Saturday, but for some reason that Alec could no longer remember, the event had been postponed. That, he later decided, was the luckiest thing that had ever happened to him.

It was a great day for the carnival, with eye-watering sunlight putting a wash of warmth over a crisp and breezy sixty-degree early-autumn day, almost hot where it touched Alec's cheeks above the flannel collar of his jacket. The carnival had everything—rides and hawkers, cotton candy, jugglers, animals for the kids to pet—like a noisy, merry state fair in miniature form. Countless people, drawn by the good weather, the thrill of the rides and the smells of carnival treats, milled about the Metra parking lot off

Irving Park Road for the event, a slightly tackier version of the Taste of Roselle that the village held in the middle of summer. Alec wandered around the grounds, smiling slightly and enjoying the fun of an afternoon with something to do other than make up a math schedule or lesson plan.

The small Ferris wheel caught his attention and he got in line, waiting for his chance to see his tiny suburb from the ride's uppermost position. When his turn came, it was the same old story for someone who went to one of these things by himself, as the ride-master, a disinterested teenager with a pierced nose and an unlit cigarette shoved behind one ear, motioned him off to the side.

Two to a car, mister. Stand to the side until we find someone to pair you with.

Alec nodded and stepped back, watching the people walk past as he waited for a partner. A minute or so, sooner than expected, and . . .

There she was.

He didn't realize he'd been staring at the woman he was going to be paired with until the kid motioned at him to step up to the car.

You'll be paired with this guy.

Alec felt his cheeks redden—how rude of him—as he climbed into the small car after her, and he felt compelled to say something in the hopes that she wouldn't notice his blush. "Hi."

She glanced at him quickly, then looked away. "Hi."

A quick check of the safety straps by the ride-master and the Ferris wheel started to turn, its movements jerkier than Alec had expected. The car rocked back and forth and the young woman—she had to be at least fifteen years his junior—smiled in delight even as she held on to the side and peered at the receding ground. "They look so small already," she said distantly. "And we're not even to the top."

"They sure do," Alec agreed, but the truth was that he couldn't have said if the view from the top of the wheel was good or bad or whether the air was filled with flying purple chickens—he spent the entire time frantically rehearsing what he was going to say to the lovely young woman who sat next to him. While she watched the people far below, Alec watched her from the corner of his eye. She was small and slender, and he thought she was beautiful: Against a creamy, nearly perfect complexion, her green-blue eyes sparkled in the sunlight and red highlights glinted in her shoulder-length hair. When she smiled faintly, amused by something below that Alec didn't notice, her lightly glossed lips revealed a hint of white teeth and a promise of untapped laughter.

He managed to make a little small talk with her, not an easy thing between two shy strangers, and by the time the ride stopped—to Alec it felt like no more than fifteen seconds—he'd worked up his nerve enough to aim for the big question of the moment. Before the teenager could release the safety bar, Alec dug deeper into himself than he ever had before.

"That was fun, wasn't it?"

She started slightly, apparently surprised that he would speak to her. Then she gave another faint smile. "Yes." She hesitated, then continued. "It's . . . it's a beautiful day for the carnival."

Shyness made him want to stand there, speechless, but Alec forced himself to keep going, determined not to stutter too badly and to grab this opportunity and run with it. "I'm Alec," he made himself say. "Would you like to ride on something else? If we stay together, we won't get held out of line again."

She considered this for a moment, then to his delight and surprise, nodded her agreement. "My name is Nola," she told him. After a moment, she held out her hand.

Alec grasped it briefly then let go, afraid that even that quick touch would frighten away this small, doe-like woman. "Look over there—would you like to try that one?" She followed his pointing finger to another ride, something benign that now, months later, Alec couldn't recall. Then she shook her head, and Alec felt his stomach drop—

had she changed her mind? But no; instead, she gave him a suddenly impish grin.

"How about the roller coaster instead?"

And that had been it. They'd spent the rest of the day wandering through the carnival, with Alec basking in Nola's presence and stealing glances at her where he could, soaking in the shine of her dark hair, her smile and wide eyes. Maybe not the most romantic start to a relationship and certainly not the Tahiti of locations, but that had been the day he met his future wife. The rides had turned into a walk along the midway, and the walk into dinner on a different night. That had turned into more dinners, and eight days after meeting Nola Alec had blurted out *The Question* over veal marsala at a tiny Italian restaurant called Kathleen's on Irving Park. No rehearsing there, not even a ring, just—

Would you marry me?

—and apparently nothing much to practice for her response—

Yes.

A blood test and a week after that the deed was done; they had gone to their wedding bed in a suite at the Wyndham Hotel in Itasca new to each other, and it had been a fine and wonderful night filled with love and tenderness and the hopes of a long and wonderful future.

And now . . .

This.

Alec cried for an hour, then washed his face and headed over to see Detective Conroy.

"Your crazy man is here."

Conroy looked up when Sergeant Drosner stopped by his desk. "What?"

"You know—that Elidad guy." He mispronounced it "E-lie-dad."

Conroy was surprised at the flush of resentment that went through him, especially since it was directed not at

Elidad, but at his fellow officer. "Say, Frank," he said, careful not to change his tone. "How's Jenny doing these days?"

Drosner blinked, thrown off guard. "Fine, she's fine."

Conroy stood and fought the urge to slam his chair against the desk. He liked Drosner about as much as he liked any of the other men and women in the department, but this kind of look-down-your-nose-on-the-victim shit just burned him up sometimes. He wasn't a saint or a sap, but sometimes, like now, it made the pulse in his temple throb nastily. "That's real good, Frank." He shrugged on his sport coat and stepped around the other man, then paused and looked back over his shoulder. "Now tell me you wouldn't act just a little nuts yourself if one night you went to work and you never saw her again." He left Drosner standing there with his cheeks red, not caring whether he'd pissed him off or not.

"Mr. Elidad," Conroy said gravely when he got up to the front. "I'm glad you came. I called your apartment about ten minutes ago, but—obviously—didn't get any answer."

Elidad looked startled. "Do you have any news? Did you find her?"

Conroy shook his head, wishing he hadn't seen the look of hope that had flashed over the other man's face. "No, I'm sorry. But I did find out a few things when I talked to Dr. Yu that I think you should know. Would you come with me?"

Elidad followed Conroy back to his desk. "She's not sick, is she? She never mentioned anything was wrong."

Conroy shook his head again. "Nothing like that." He settled behind his desk and indicated the extra chair. "Have a seat." Elidad did, but he looked like a nervous bird balanced on a power line, ready to take flight at any second.

"Then . . . what?"

"According to the doctor," Conroy said as he opened his folder on the case and spread the contents—not much—out in front of him, "your wife was an adopted child. Did you know this?"

Elidad's eyebrows raised, but he didn't look all that shocked. "No, but I suppose that would explain why she was reluctant to talk about her childhood. For that matter, she very obviously never wanted to speak of her parents at all—I wonder if it was a late-life thing, and maybe the new home wasn't a happy one." He looked away for a moment. "I always figured that she would start talking about her past someday, after we were together longer."

"Well," Conroy said, "we're going to try to find out about that adoption. I've got the records and research clerk running this through the computer now. Adoption records are sometimes a little sticky to get into, but if your reason is good enough, as I believe ours is, the police department can generally do it. For all we know, the info could be readily available, and maybe Nola got a lead on her real parents and decided to go find them. In the meantime I'll be able to come up with the names of her adoptive parents and talk to them. Maybe they have some ideas—or maybe that's where she is."

Elidad smiled faintly, but the expression never reached his eyes. "A run-home-to-mama thing?"

"Maybe," Conroy said honestly. "But not for the reasons you think. Just because your wife never mentioned her adoptive parents doesn't mean that she didn't keep in touch with them. What if during her last call to them she found out that one of them was sick or something? We still don't know that she's not going to show up in a couple of days and—"

"What about the shoe?" Elidad asked quietly. "Somehow I don't think my wife has the habit of leaving one behind in the parking lot snow in January."

Conroy sighed. "There is that." He looked down and shuffled papers for a moment. "We ran it through the usual tests—"

"Tests? For what?"

"Blood, liquor, oil," Conroy said honestly. "Grease, fingerprints, semen—anything unusual. It's just a shoe, Mr. Elidad." He left out the part about the lab positively matching the blood on the shoe's seam to the marriage blood test; he'd already believed the shoe belonged to Nola Elidad and Alec, in his anguish, had missed the blood spots. Conroy saw no reason to drive a spike farther into the man.

But now Alec sat back and bitterness gave his mouth a downward twist. "I get it, Detective. Up until you talked to Dr. Yu, you weren't sure that my wife was real. Now that he's verified that much, you've transferred that opinion to the shoe, right? Maybe it isn't my wife's, maybe someone dropped it, maybe she just had the urge to throw her fucking shoes aside on a ten-degree Thursday afternoon and take off barefoot for parts unknown." He looked as disgusted as Conroy had ever seen him. "Christ, maybe I ought to just hire a private detective."

"If you think you'd get better service than what I'm offering, you're wrong," Conroy snapped. He leaned closer over the desk. "Listen, Mr. Elidad, believe it or not, I'm on your side. I'm not trying to shoot down everything you say just for the hell of it. That's part of detective work, proving that what you think might be really *is*. Anyone can walk in and say 'Here! This belonged to Nola Elidad!' and voila, maybe it's a dress covered in blood and we say 'Okay, she must be dead and now all we have to find is a body.' So maybe we stop looking as hard, because she's dead anyway . . . but guess what? She's not dead at all, she's off somewhere with an old boyfriend who beats the hell out of her, or maybe she followed a cat into an old warehouse and fell through a hole in the floor and there she is, lying down there with a couple of busted bones and hoping to God someone'll come along and help her.

"*That,* Mr. Elidad"—Conroy slapped the file shut hard enough to make Alec jump—"is why I don't intend to stop looking until we *find* your wife."

"I really can't tell you that much about her," said Krystin Parker. "She wasn't here long and she certainly didn't talk about her personal life." The librarian was tall and thin, an attractive but stiff-mannered blonde woman. She peered at Conroy over the rim of her glasses as though she'd stepped out of the pages of some 1950s book of manners. Conroy, however, wasn't convinced; there was something about the ramrod-straight back and the haughty, lifted chin that didn't quite seem natural.

"Uh-huh." Conroy made a scribble in his notebook. "And how long did she work here?"

"About . . . three months, I'd guess."

"Can you get me an exact date on that?"

Ms. Parker looked pained but went to do what he'd asked. When she came back, she held a small blue folder in her hand. "I don't normally show personnel files, but you *are* the police . . ." She hesitated a final time, God bless decorum and all that. "Besides, I checked through it first and I don't believe there's anything in here that Nola Elidad would have needed to keep private anyway. In fact, there isn't much in here at all."

"Thank you." Conroy took the folder she offered, but a quick perusal revealed little he hadn't come up with in his own searches. Damn, but this was frustrating—it was like the woman had dropped out of thin air, taken a few deep breaths, then disappeared into the same hole from which she'd come. "This employment application," he said pointedly, "is nearly blank. I don't see any previous employer or references listed."

Ms. Parker gave a fragile shrug. "There really was no need, Detective. We were looking for an entry-level library clerk, not a mathematician. Experience wasn't required. Nola was obviously an educated young woman and the position didn't involve the handling of money in any way—we were willing to take her statement that she had never worked at face value."

"I see." Conroy fingered the edge of the paper. "But weren't you at all curious about what she'd done before she applied here?"

"It's not my custom to question the personal lives of employees, Detective. She mentioned part-time college—"

"I don't see that listed here under 'Education,' " Conroy said with a raised eyebrow.

"—but I don't believe she'd done so yet," she finished with a glance that chastised him for interrupting her. She gave another birdlike shrug. "In any event, she didn't have a degree, so it wasn't pertinent. Unless she tried for a promotion at a later date, it wouldn't matter."

"I see. And high school—did you verify this?"

"It was obvious she was a high school graduate. When she listed Keeneyville High, we had no reason to question that."

Conroy frowned, picked up the small pile of paper, and tapped it against the tabletop. "You don't seem very broken up, Ms. Parker. In my experience, most employers act at least a little regretful when something happens to an employee."

For a second, the librarian looked surprised, then her expression smoothed. "I assure you, Detective Conroy, that I am as concerned as anyone else. Nola Elidad was not very sociable, but she was a polite young woman who did her job very efficiently. Beyond that, she kept to herself. Even after three months of working with her every day, none of us knew her very well."

Conroy nodded; he was beginning to think no one existed who had known Nola Elidad as more than a passing acquaintance . . . even her husband. "Thanks for your time," he said, rising and holding out the employee file.

She took the folder without offering to copy any of its meager contents, tucking it securely under one arm. "I hope I've been of some help," Ms. Parker said. A false sentiment and they both knew it.

Conroy nodded noncommittally and turned as if to go. "Oh, one other thing, Ms. Parker." She paused and looked at him expectantly, clearly surprised that their conversation wasn't over. "When Alec Elidad spoke to you on the phone, you told him that all calls to employees go through you?"

"Generally, yes."

"Generally?"

One eyebrow arched and her lips pressed together in a strangely defensive way. "The library *does* allow me a lunch hour and two breaks, Detective Conroy. While I usually stay at my desk, I do occasionally need a visit to the rest room. Now, if you'll excuse me?"

Conroy nodded without saying anything further and

watched her walk briskly away. Everything inside him was screaming that there was something wrong here, but he couldn't put his finger on what—it had to do with the job application and why on earth someone as straitlaced and politically correct as that stiff librarian would hire someone about whom she knew essentially *nothing.* At the very least, Nola Elidad's education should have been checked, because even though this was an entry-level position, it was also a county job—they had as much paperwork for this as the village did. Krystin Parker was lying . . . but about what, or why, Conroy couldn't have said.

But he damned well wasn't going to forget it.

"I have to go to work tonight."

From her place on the couch—sitting as far away from him as possible, as usual—Stacey looked up at him. For the briefest of moments there was an expression on her face that Jesse could identify all too well, and it made him cry inside to think that she would see his hours gone tonight as nothing but an opportunity to escape, or at the very least freedom from his presence.

Damn it—he was trying so hard to rebuild their lives, to bring them back to where they'd been before she'd gotten sick, before everything in their world had fallen apart without her. Maybe what he was doing wasn't the most ambitious plan for the long term, but wasn't it a good start for right now? "It's time to get some money coming in," he said. His voice was hoarse but he ignored it; it always got that way when he was feeling hurt. "There's a lot we've got to make up. We weren't in debt very far, but now we've got some bill collectors calling about leftover stuff from the hospital . . ." His voice faded. Damn, he thought again. He wasn't making this sound like a very enticing life, was he?

They'd been watching television, some inane Monday night movie that had made so little an impression on Jesse that he couldn't remember its title. Nothing about the movie had settled into his brain anyway; all he seemed able to do was sit at his end of the couch and relish the fact that his wife was sitting here too, even if she was scrunched down at the other end as though he were a snake about to strike. But he was convinced that she would outgrow that, and since he didn't have any choice, he would live with things this way for now. Who knew what she'd endured—in that other marriage, for instance—that might be a factor in her skittishness? He wondered about it, but jealousy kept him from trying to learn the down-and-dirty details.

Jesse cleared his throat and rubbed his hands, then was dismayed at how smooth they felt. Jesus, he'd been off work for so long he'd lost most of his callouses—he was probably going to tear his skin up pretty good this first week on the job. But that was okay, too. It was just another indication that things were back on track, and despite the problems still to be worked out, Jesse was so damned happy he could've wept.

"I know," he said steadily, "that it's too soon for me to be able to leave you here loose on your own. I know you still think you're someone you're not—"

"Are you going to lock me in the basement again?"

He pressed his lips together, and for a second he couldn't speak. Thanks to his idiocy, Stacey's first memory of coming back home would always be of that awful night spent in the basement. Damn. "Of course not. I'm going to put you in the nur—in the spare room, with some blankets and a pillow, something to eat." He dropped his gaze and stared at the floor, ashamed but still knowing what he had to do. "I'm going to have to lock you in, Stacey. And I'm going to shove a chair under the doorknob, just in case. I'm sorry."

God, the way she looked at him . . . if only he knew what she was thinking. On second thought, did he really need to know how much this woman, whom he had once held in his arms and loved with everything he was, now hated him?

Nola helped Jesse carry the blankets—he was so worried that she'd get cold that he brought out three of them—and a plastic pitcher of water and a paper cup. Then he added a peanut butter sandwich—another repeat of one of the items on their limited-funds menu. When Jesse pushed the door shut, Nola could see the reluctance on his face. Again that question ran through her mind: What kind of a kidnapper was he? He hadn't hurt her—she'd already discounted his panicked behavior in the beginning—raped her, beaten her, or threatened to kill her. The thought of this man writing a ransom note was ludicrous—not only would Alec not have any huge sum of money to buy her back, but money was clearly the last thing Jesse wanted.

"Jesse," she said through the door.

There was a moment of silence, as if he didn't want to admit he was standing on the other side, mentally berating himself for locking her in his dead child's room. Then he answered with a quiet "Yes?"

"There's more money in my purse, at least twenty dollars. Why don't you take it and get us some food on your way home tonight?"

He didn't answer right away. "If you're sure it's all right," he said finally. "I mean, it's your money, Stacey. I don't want you to think I'm . . . you know, stealing it or anything. I'm not like that"

"It's all right," Nola said. She felt dangerously resigned, and she hoped to God it was only a temporary thing. "If you like, you can pay me back later, when the money situation straightens itself out."

"A-all right," he said. More indecision—she could tell he wanted to be able to provide all their support. Had Stacey been a homemaker? Or had she worked and paid her portion of the household expenses? Jesse had never mentioned a job that had been abandoned by his absent wife, nor had he said anything about Stacey's coworkers calling with offers of help or comfort. Coworkers? What about friends? He hadn't mentioned anyone beyond the guy who'd taken the wedding photos, only the unseen mother-in-law who hadn't approved of their marriage. Stacey, it seemed, had been a loner.

Just like me.

Nola's head throbbed suddenly, and she frowned and massaged the bridge of her nose. Like me, she thought tiredly. But *not* me. I am who I am, just like what God said in the Bible.

"But I *will* pay you back." Jesse's voice, muffled by the cheap wooden door, startled her—she'd forgotten he was standing there, forgotten all about their conversation.

"That's fine," she said.

"Is there anything special you want?"

Nola smiled slightly, beset by a mental picture of Jesse going to the grocery store and blowing the entire twenty dollars on something ridiculously stupid—strawberry ice cream, perhaps—just because she wanted it. It probably wasn't such a far-fetched notion.

"No," she said out loud. "You choose."

"Okay," he said. "I'll, uh, see you later."

Nola didn't say good-bye; it just seemed too . . . *homey* or something—

Okay, honey, I'm off to work.

Have a good day!

Okay! You too!

—to contemplate, too rooted in a world in which she didn't belong. She looked around the small room and sighed; she was well-fed and warmly dressed, and while the prospect of sleeping on the hard floor wasn't that great, she was tired and stressed out enough to look forward to it. After all, it would be a good nine hours or more without her kidnapper in the house with her. Too bad she couldn't figure out a way—

"Stacey?"

She opened her mouth to answer, then snapped it shut. What was she thinking?

"That's not my name," she said instead. "My name is Nola."

Jesse didn't answer, and she wondered if his fists were bunched at his side in frustration. When he spoke again, however, nothing about the easy, conversational tone of his voice had changed. "I've got something here so you won't be bored." She heard the knob rattle as the chair was removed, then the small bolt was drawn back. When the door opened and Nola saw him, Jesse's face was white and pained, but he didn't look angry, just . . . hurt. He held out a battered paperback book and Nola reached for it automatically—why not? "This was, uh, one of your favorites before you got, you know, sick." He looked sheepish for bringing up the subject. "See you later," he said quickly. Then he was gone again, ready to go to the new job since early this afternoon; in less than ten seconds she heard him hurry down the stairs, then the front door opened and closed. The townhouse was, finally, utterly silent.

Nola cocked her head and listened for a few moments, then glanced at the window. Forget it—it was just as nailed shut today as it had been yesterday, and she had that same lack of desire to bleed to death in a futile attempt to haul herself over the sash and a pile of broken glass; and let's not forget this was the second floor. This was such a quiet place, considering it was part of a complex. Were these townhouses that well insulated from each other? Sure, it was close to ten-thirty at night, but she couldn't hear a sound anywhere—no televisions, crying babies, or barking dogs. She supposed it was the winter, especially harsh this year, that was making everyone hide so thoroughly.

Still, if she screamed and pounded on the walls, a neighbor or a passerby would have to hear, wouldn't they? Suddenly determined, Nola went to the wall with the window and raised her fists, then pounded on it for all she was worth—

"Help!"

And again—

"Please—somebody help me!"

She switched to reaching up and knocking frantically against the small glass panes, then went back and forth. Two minutes, three, almost five—she tried to keep it going, but her voice sounded small and insignificant, the noise on the wall and window glass pathetic and hardly worth the bruising she was giving her hands and knuckles. In the midst of another blow, Nola stopped the motion in midair. This room—how well Jesse had chosen! If she was remembering the layout of the townhouse correctly, the only outside wall in here was the one with the window. If she faced that, on her left side was the wall to the hallway, and on her right was the wall that separated this room from the bathroom. For God's sake, someone would have to be standing directly below in the backyard to hear the puny noises she'd made.

Discouraged, Nola sank to the floor and hugged herself. It was useless—she might as well be in a box in the middle of the living room. Or worse . . . what if they *had* heard her, but it hadn't mattered, hadn't prompted anyone at all to call the police? These strangely silent neighbors were the same ones who'd never noticed Jesse Waite hauling an unwilling woman into his home a few days ago. Self-imposed blindness happened all the time—what if they insisted on "minding their own business," turned their backs on the sound of her pounding because they didn't want to be involved in another couple's marriage problems?

Nola rubbed her temples and tried to think. Surely she could find a way out of this situation on her own. She might not be the strongest or most resourceful woman around, but in this case, maybe a little patience was all she needed. Perhaps she could bide her time and wait until Jesse trusted her, then slip quietly out of his life the way the true Stacey apparently had. There were issues to be resolved, not the least of which was keeping him from grabbing her all over again, but she could face that when the time came—she and Alec could move, quickly if necessary. Now somehow, it felt more important that Jesse would be crushed at losing her.

Stop it, she told herself sternly. Not only should she not be thinking that far ahead, but Jesse's reaction wasn't something she should or would have to worry about. He would deal with it because he must, and she would secretly help him by claiming that she didn't know the identity of her kidnapper or where she'd been held, would even tell them that he'd been masked the entire time so she'd never get caught in a lie about what he looked like. Given the bad memories she would associate with Roselle, she knew it wouldn't be difficult to persuade Alec to relocate—good teachers were always needed. As for herself, she was just forming her job skills and had been considering going to junior college with an eye toward a degree in library science—she'd always considered the job at the Roselle Library a temporary thing that enabled her to save money while allowing her to be around the books she'd adored since she was a child.

Yes, that was the way to do it—bide her time and wait for the right opportunity. She felt sorry for him, but she knew that if she played along, Jesse—who was so eager for Stacey to come back around—couldn't help but relax. Then she would make her move.

Her spirits lifted a bit, Nola looked down at the paperback Jesse had handed her, then her jaw dropped at the dog-eared but familiar cover: *The Flame and the Flower* by Kathleen Woodiwiss. She *knew* this old book, had in fact read it several times during her dreamy, teenaged years, a time that now felt like a century ago instead of half a decade. Nola turned it over and scanned the well-remembered text, knew that she could recite word for word the opening line. When the irony of it all sunk in a minute later, she was holding her stomach and filling the small, sad room with nearly hysterical laughter.

Jesse had given her a book about a woman held captive and then forced to marry an American ship captain in the eighteen hundreds—her kidnapper.

JANUARY 21--TUESDAY

**** WORKING. PLEASE WAIT. ****

"Outdated piece of crap," Conroy muttered.

"Come on, Lucas," a woman's voice said. "You know the system was just upgraded in September."

Conroy looked up to see Dustine Curtis, one of his coworkers, passing his desk. Normally so composed, suddenly the detective felt himself blush for no good reason. Well, there *was* a reason, but it had nothing to do with this idiotic computer. "It doesn't process fast enough," he said. Of course it did; with a Pentium upgrade, it was actually damned good equipment for a small-town police force with a hard-won budget.

"Of course it does," she said, echoing his thoughts. "Besides, you're just record hunting, not trying to animate *Toy Story*." She smiled.

"Even so," he grumbled, but he finally had to grin at the overly tolerant expression on her face. "Okay, okay. I concede."

She came around the desk and peered over his shoulder. "So what are you looking for? Still working on that missing person?"

Conroy nodded and tapped the screen. "There's not much to go on. Maiden name, social security number, but no details, very little job info. It's like this woman just appeared out of nowhere three months ago. Even her doctor doesn't know anything about her—he says she told him she was adopted." He didn't bother adding that Nola had rescheduled her appointment with Dr. Ophir, then disappeared before she could see him.

Something about the circulation system in the room changed, the heat kicking on maybe, and Conroy got a whiff of Dustine's perfume, faint and sweet. The scent made him think of Alec Elidad; did he lie awake nights and remember the scent of his wife's favorite perfume? Even sadder, Conroy could picture the quiet man standing at his dresser and opening the bottles, one by one. It wasn't such a far-fetched fantasy—Conroy himself had a sister who'd been killed in a car accident in her twenties; there was a box in his closet that he took down every now and then, and everything inside smelled like Charlie perfume. Someday the smell would fade, but then he would have the bottle itself, also in the box, to open and bring back the memory of how his sister had smelled before that awful day in a long-ago December.

"Earth to Lucas."

Conroy blinked, then foolishly blushed again. "Sorry, I was daydreaming there."

"Well," Dustine said lightly, "I hope it was a good one."

"Would you like to have dinner sometime?"

He had to hand it to her; the invitation was a fastball right out of the blue, but by God she recovered with a quick chuckle. "I guess it *was* a good one. And sure, that'd be fun."

"I'm off tomorrow," he said. Conroy hoped he didn't sound as much like an eager little boy as he thought he did.

"That'd be good," she said. "My shift ends at four." She snagged a piece of notepaper from the holder and scribbled on it. "Here's my address—you can pick me up at seven. Okay?"

"Sounds great. Anyplace special?"

"I don't know. Let's just decide then." He nodded his agreement and started to say something else, but the words were overridden by a soft trill from the beeper on her uniform belt. "Oops—work calls. I'll see you later."

Dustine hurried off and Conroy sat there, careful to keep his eyes on the computer monitor so she wouldn't turn around and catch him staring after her like an infatuated puppy. His pulse was double-timing in his throat—she wasn't the only one surprised at his invitation. Interesting the way people could do unexpected things and have no idea it was coming.

His gaze cut back to the data search field he was filling in on the computer. Speaking of unexpected things, there were folks who got married when they'd known each other only a few days.

Conroy pushed the ENTER key and watched the cursor begin flashing again, heard the hard drive thrashing as it went back and forth, sorting through the search fields he'd filled in. Finally, a good two minutes later, he got a screen of data.

NAME: NOLA RENE ELIDAD

MARITAL STATUS: MARRIED

SPOUSE: ALEC MICHAEL ELIDAD

MAIDEN NAME: NOLA RENE FRAYNE

LENGTH OF RESIDENCE AT CURRENT ADDRESS: 3 MONTHS

AGE: 21

BIRTH DATE: 6/18/78

DRIVER'S LICENSE #: NONE

It went on to list more mundane things, like the social security number Conroy already knew, home address and telephone number, where she worked. The most frustrating thing about it was that Conroy himself had keyed in most of this information. He scowled and scrolled down, then stopped when he finally found something new.

MOTHER: MARLO FRANCINE FRAYNE

FATHER: DECEASED

BIRTH CERTIFICATE RECORD NO.: ***ARCHIVED. SEE COUNTY CLERK FOR RETRIEVAL***

He stared at the screen and tugged at his collar thoughtfully. Archived? He'd never heard of such a thing—it must have something to do with the adoption, and her birth certificate wasn't something that Alec had found among her scant personal papers. And why wasn't her adoptive father's name listed? In the world of computer data, no one ever truly passed away anymore. Conroy frowned, then carefully typed in the mother's name, steeling himself for another two-minute wait. But whatever had caused the system lag with Nola's records didn't exist here, and he had the information inside of twenty seconds:

NAME: MARLO FRANCINE FRAYNE

ADDRESS: 1031 GOLDEN DRIVE, KEENEYVILLE, IL

LENGTH OF RESIDENCE AT CURRENT ADDRESS: 1 YEAR 4 MONTHS

TELEPHONE NUMBER: 630 555 9238

MARITAL STATUS: WIDOW

More info, birth date, the requisite social security and driver's license numbers, a whole list of previous addresses. Just to be thorough, he ran the license through but came up with nothing—whatever Nola's mother was or wasn't to Nola, she was still a law-abiding citizen as far as the rest of the world was concerned.

But that didn't mean Conroy couldn't pay her a visit and tell her that her daughter was missing.

If she really was.

The brooding little house that Conroy found in Keeneyville was a sad, shabby place and, flanked as it was by two well-tended residences, a scar on the face of the street and no doubt a constant annoyance to its neighbors. In summer Conroy would bet that the grass was always too long and weeds sprouted enthusiastically everywhere; now the lawn was edged with filthy snow from some long-ago shoveling, while the driveway was a map of dirty ice-rimmed holes and tire tracks . . . speaking of which, no vehicle was parked in the drive and as far as Conroy could tell there was no garage.

Nevertheless, the detective trudged along the slippery, snow-packed walkway and knocked dutifully on the door. Not a sound came from within, not even the snarling of the ill-tempered dog that the look of the place had made him expect. Unwilling to give up, Conroy worked his way around back through snow littered with trash and soggy leaves on the off chance that maybe they chopped their own wood in the backyard—a stretch, but he was already here, so why not? It was a futile effort; the back of the house was just as silent and dilapidated as the front. A routine check of the two filthy basement windows showed them locked tight and obviously not opened in years, so he went back to the car and restarted it, then sat there for about twenty minutes hoping that someone would show up. When that didn't happen either, he opted to go back to the station and call until Marlo Frayne got home—which he probably should have done to begin with.

Nola heard the key in the front door downstairs at about the same time she thought her bladder was going to explode if she had to wait any longer. She was up and standing at the nursery door when Jesse finally unlocked it, and if she hadn't been so desperate she would've laughed at the comical expression of surprise on his face when she pushed past him and beelined for the small bathroom next door. Things were bad enough and she didn't want to start peeing herself like a baby; scared or not, this man was going to get an earful when she was done.

"I almost didn't make it," she said accusingly when she came out a few minutes later. Now they were seated, again, at the breakfast table; it seemed Nola's "new" life had a very limited range, indeed.

Jesse looked absurdly ashamed, like a little boy being scolded for breaking a window with a poorly aimed baseball. "I'm sorry. They gave me all kinds of insurance forms and stuff to fill out at the end of the shift and said they had to be done right away. I would've taken care of it on my lunch break if I'd gotten them then, but the day foreman was there and he put me on a machine first thing. Said he had a rush job." He rubbed one hand across a stubbled cheek and succeeded only in making his face even dirtier—Nola hadn't known a man could be that filthy after a day at work. She couldn't help but notice that his fingers were scraped and raw beneath the grime. "You know what I think?" he asked.

"I have no idea."

"I think they were testing me out," Jesse said, ignoring the sarcastic tone of her voice. "Making sure I could do the job like I claimed *before* they wasted a whole bunch of paperwork."

Nola didn't say anything, but she supposed it made sense. She didn't know what went on in a machine shop, but she remembered the forms she'd completed for her job at the Roselle Library, all for a starting wage that was significantly less than ten dollars a hour. But the woman who'd hired her had seemed to have no doubts about her abilities, or if she had, it had made no difference; realizing what Jesse had gone through at work tonight made her wonder about that.

"Well, you can't be gone that long again without figuring out a way for me to use the bathroom," Nola said crabbily.

"Sorry," Jesse said again. He looked at his hands. "Jesus, I've got to take a shower—I don't think I could eat until I do."

Nola scowled. "You're not going to put me in the extra bedroom again, are you?"

He nodded reluctantly. "Yeah, I-I have to. But it'll be just for a few minutes—I won't take long, I promise."

"Great," she muttered.

"It's just until you know who you are, Stacey—"

"That's *not* my name!" she said hotly.

Jesse's face went as rigid as granite. "Like I just said."

Jesse felt really bad about the way he was having to treat Stacey—beyond the hours spent in the nursery while he worked, there would be more hours of inactivity for her upcoming while he slept. But what could he do? If he let her have the run of the house, she'd run all right—right out the door. And this time, because she knew he'd be looking for her, Jesse might not be able to find her. He didn't think he could bear losing his wife for a third and probably final time.

He showered and dressed inside of twenty minutes, but he could still hear Stacey pacing on the other side of the door like a caged cat. More hours of silence were coming and he couldn't say he blamed her for being downright pissed about it. If it was him, he'd probably go nuts . . . God, suddenly he wondered if he weren't unknowingly worsening her condition by imprisoning her in the very same room that had once held all their sweetest dreams.

He'd been reaching for the chair under the doorknob as that thought crossed his mind, but then Jesse turned abruptly and headed to the kitchen to retrieve the small toolbox underneath the sink. Inside he found what he wanted: the heavy household hammer and a half dozen tenpenny nails. Someday the landlord was going to raise hell about this, but Jesse'd gladly deal with that when the time came. He was taking a chance hammering this early in the morning, but better now than before his shift tonight, and it only took about four minutes to nail shut the slightly larger window in the main bedroom as tightly as the one in the nursery—both were high off the floor. Jesse remembered a couple of old two-by-fours in the basement and ran down and got them, then added those across the window from frame to frame with another handful of tenpennies. No way would she be able to pry the boards free; it didn't look like much but he could close the drapes, and with the wood between the dusty window and the inside curtains, who would notice?

Weariness and lack of sleep settled over him abruptly and Jesse ran his hands through his damp hair, letting his fingers tug the strands just enough to zing his scalp. He wasn't used to working nights—didn't particularly like it, in fact, but there was a night premium of two dollars an hour to start, and more after three months. A few days, he told himself as he went to let Stacey out, that's all—you'll be better adjusted to the hours and Stacey will start being herself again. He found himself whispering just before his fingers closed around the doorknob to the nursery.

Please, God, let it happen.

"So now I have to sit quietly for another eight hours while you sleep." Jesse raised his head and stared at her, and for a moment Nola thought she should've kept her thoughts to herself. But he only shrugged and looked away; she felt bad about giving him a hard time when he looked so obviously tired, but what about her? She hadn't asked to be thrown in this situation, hadn't asked to be his *wife*—she *wasn't*, damn it. "What am I supposed to do all that time?" she asked.

"Sleep," Jesse said shortly. "Just like me."

"Just like that—snap my fingers and voila." Nola sat very straight and looked him in the eye, determined not to reveal just how scared she was in standing up for herself. "That's what I did last night."

"I gave you a book to read."

"I fell asleep," she repeated, "because I'm not used to staying up nights—"

"Well, neither am I, okay?" he snapped. "So read your book today."

"I've already read it."

He started to retort, then his mouth closed and Nola saw an emotion flash across his face—was it hope? For a moment she didn't understand, then she knew he thought she'd already read it because she was remembering it from Stacey's point of view. "I read it when I was twelve," she said, grinding her teeth. "I don't want to read it again." She took a deep breath. "Jesse, I want to go home."

She'd never seen someone's face go white, then red, so fast. "You *are* home, Stacey." Despite his half-heartbroken, half-infuriated expression, he kept his voice low. The words, however, came out in shaking syllables.

"I'm *not* Sta—"

"I don't want to hear that!"

So much for not being shouted at; her pulse was hammering in her throat now and Nola figured she'd pushed about as far as she dared for one morning. Maybe, she thought suddenly, I just won't talk to him anymore. Let's see how he likes a few hours of silence.

"Look," Jesse said. He reached to touch her hand but she jerked away. For a moment he gazed uncomprehendingly at the place where her hand had been, then he sat back. "I didn't mean to yell at you." He didn't say anything more for a few moments, then he stood. "I'm just overtired and I've got to get some sleep. Let's go." He tried to touch her again when she rose, this time on the shoulder; when Nola recoiled, she thought she heard him give a low hiss of frustration.

But as she stepped reluctantly toward the bedroom, Nola realized that a vow of silence wasn't realistic. The hours of doing nothing over the last few days were already wearing on her psyche, and she didn't need to make it worse by cutting off the only point of communication, however unwanted, she had. "I'd like something else to read," she said.

Jesse blinked, fatigue showing in every line on his face. "Well, there's other books—"

"How about the paper?" Nola said. "At least I know I haven't read it before." They were passing the living room, and she veered slightly and plucked it off the end table where Jesse had left it. "I always read the Sunday comics." She didn't know why she'd bothered to say that; she wasn't sure she wanted him to know any personal details of her life. Then again, maybe that was *exactly* what this man needed drummed into him: that Nola Rene Elidad had indeed had such a thing as her own life, one in which Jesse Waite had never played a part.

Jesse shrugged and motioned her to go on down the hallway. "Whatever." His voice was bordering on surly, and she didn't know if it was because he was so tired or because of her intentional reference to her real life. When she stepped inside the bedroom, the same old fear welled up—was it tonight that he would force himself on her? Not likely; he looked much too beaten down by this first swing shift on his new job. But who knew what the morning would bring?

He closed the door behind them, shoved that same chair tightly under the knob, and without warning her began to undress. Nola hurriedly turned her back, suddenly very aware that she was still wearing the shirt and blue jeans he'd given her last night. "This is the last night I'm going to tie you to me," he said unexpectedly. She cast a hasty glance over her shoulder, but he was climbing out of the clean jeans he'd thrown on after his shower and wasn't looking at her. Embarrassed, Nola faced the wall again, her hand involuntarily going to the neck of the flannel shirt she wore.

"I've fixed the windows in here," he continued, "and tomorrow I'll put a lock on the outside of the door. In case you forgot, there's another bathroom over there—the door next to the closet. You can stay in here from now on and have a place to sleep and what all—I'll bring the television in and set it on the dresser. You'll be a lot more comfortable." He hesitated, then she heard the bedsprings squeak beneath his weight, followed by a rustle of the blankets. Her own pile of linens was on the floor next to the bed, still folded neatly. "There's a clean nightgown in the lower dresser drawer. I'll turn my head long enough for you to change, but let's get it over with so I can get some shut-eye."

Trembling, Nola dropped the paper next to the bed, then pulled open the drawer and yanked out the first nightgown she saw, another flannel in a faded floral print—damn, that woman had liked flannel. Lips pressed together, she looked toward the bed, but Jesse was true to his word and had his face turned in the other direction; even so, Nola had never gone through a change of clothes so fast in her life. When she was through, with her shirt and jeans clutched in one perspiring hand, she felt as though she'd run up ten flights of stairs.

"Are you decent?"

Nola tried to answer and had to clear her throat before the word would come out. "Y-yes." She finally got some air, then quickly folded the clothes into a neat pile that she left on one end of the dresser. "Yes," she repeated. She felt a little more secure, clothed at least in the dubious protection of the nightgown.

" 'kay." Jesse's voice was nearly slurred. "Same thing as last night?"

A question, and wouldn't he wake up really quickly if she said *No, it's not okay, you kidnapping bastard, and if you don't let me out of here right now, I'll start screaming.* "All right," she said instead. In less than a minute Nola was tied in the same fashion as she'd been on the previous nights; in another, Jesse was sound asleep and snoring lightly.

Jesus, would this nightmare never end?

JANUARY 22--WEDNESDAY

It took Conroy damned near all day to reach Marlo Frayne. Every time he punched her number into the telephone he thought about what he was going to say—he really *should* be telling her about her missing daughter in person, but there was still that niggling little doubt in his mind about the elusive Nola Elidad. He was probably on his twentieth attempt when the phone was finally answered on the other end.

"Yes?"

Conroy never missed a beat. "This is Detective Lucas Conroy from the Roselle Police Department. I'd like to speak with Marlo Frayne. I'm calling to—"

"What do you want?"

Conroy bit back a sharp comment—*If you'll let me talk, I'll tell you!*—and tried again. "Are you Marlo Frayne?"

"Yeah, that's me."

"I'm calling to tell you that your daughter has been reported missing by her husband. Do you have any information as to her whereabouts, or has she been in contact with you since last Thursday?"

"Why would I?" the voice on the other end demanded in a sandpaper voice. Conroy could imagine a lifetime of cigarette smoke going down the throat of the speaker, and she coughed suddenly, as though confirming his speculation; the last of his reservations about breaking the news over the telephone fled at the belligerent tone of her voice. "I haven't talked to the girl in months. She ran off and married that teacher fellow and I guess she can't be bothered with me anymore. That's what a woman gets in return for raising a child all by herself nowadays."

"Could she be with her father? I don't have his name—"

"Doesn't matter. Her father's been dead for years—dropped over right after we got married."

"And what was his name?"

"Say, how do I know you are who you say you are?" Marlo Frayne demanded suddenly. "Maybe I shouldn't be answering your questions—you could be some kind of a prevert or something."

Prevert? "I'll be glad to come back out to your place now that you're home, Ms. Frayne." Conroy put special emphasis on the word *back* so she'd know he already knew where she lived.

The line was silent for a moment, then the woman gave an irritated sigh. "Never mind. I don't suppose it makes a difference, telling you this stuff anyway. If you ask me, that man she married probably did it. That's what happens when you take up with a stranger, and him looking real clean-cut doesn't mean jack."

Conroy frowned. Jesus, he thought, don't ask. Do you really want to open up that line of questioning? "Did what?" Well, he *had* to—that was his job.

"Killed her or something," was the prompt reply. "She didn't know him from the next guy on the street, and here she is, disappeared. You said that, right?"

"Ms. Frayne, I'm going to have to come out there and talk to you in more detail about this," Conroy said firmly.

"I don't want—"

"I insist." Now it was his turn to interrupt, and there was no doubt that he meant business. "I can be there within twenty minutes."

"Shit," the woman on the phone said sullenly. "I knew I shouldn't have opened my mouth."

....

Sitting across from the woman half an hour later, Conroy thought he already understood why Nola Elidad had never talked about her parents, or at least her adopted mother. The house was as dingy and poorly kept on the inside as it was outside: walls papered in outdated patterns and carpeting gone gray with age, unwashed windows beneath equally dirty drapes and shades. And all of it covered with the yellow taint of nicotine—the small, clean apartment Nola shared with her husband at Springhill was a dream compared to this.

Marlo Frayne was a big-boned woman working her way toward heavyset, the type who layered on the makeup and hair spray and remained oblivious to the fact that it just made her look older. Still, Conroy could almost glimpse the woman she'd been twenty years earlier somewhere beneath the powder, rouge, too-bright blue eye shadow and heavy eyeliner. Overweight now, he'd bet back then she was called voluptuous and had turned more than a few heads. He wondered what color her hair had been when Nola was a child; now it was dull brown, as if it'd done nothing but soak up cigarette smoke for years until it had taken on the dirty color of used ashtrays.

"Your daughter has been missing for almost a week," he repeated now. Marlo Frayne just looked at him and waited, her pudgy face bland as she sucked on a cigarette, and Conroy had to put a mental lock on the frustration he felt. Didn't this woman even care? "I'd like to talk to you more about what you said on the phone, your speculation that her husband might have killed her."

Marlo lifted her chin slightly, and if the setting hadn't been so ludicrous, the detective would've sworn she was looking down her nose at him. "Why wouldn't he?"

"That's not the question, Ms. Frayne." He rubbed his knuckles thoughtfully and resisted the urge to crack them. "The question is actually why *would* he."

"Because he's a *stranger,* that's why." Nola's mother paused to examine her long, exquisitely manicured fingernails, then leaned forward. There was an air of familiarity about her posture and the way she cocked her head to one side as her eyes narrowed—the age-old gossip with a great and grand new rumor to spread. "Think about it—the girl was the perfect victim. She meets a man at a street fair one week and marries him the next. Where's the sense in that? Maybe he took out one of them insurance policies on her or something. She'd been going with the same boy at school for the longest time—what happened to him?"

Conroy's interest sharpened. "A boy from where—high school? What was his name?"

Marlo's hand fluttered vaguely in the air. "Yeah, it was high school. He was . . . Jimmy, Johnny—who knows? I didn't pay much attention. You know how kids are, and I never let him come over here anyway. She didn't see much of him after graduation, I made sure of that."

I'll just bet, Conroy thought. "So your daughter had a steady boyfriend but you never met him?"

Nola's mother shook her head. "No, thanks. I've got no time for stupid teenage romances and I certainly didn't want them *doing* it in my house." Her eyes were small, watery beads staring at him from across the room. "And mind you, I didn't let her go flinging around after school hours or on weekends, either. She finished high school and wanted to take classes at some college or another—waste of money, if you ask me. I wouldn't allow it. She had plenty of chores here to keep her busy."

Conroy tried to loosen the steadily tightening muscles in his jaw. No social life, practically a prisoner in this house with her adopted mother—no wonder Nola Elidad née Frayne had gotten the hell out of here. There was nothing about Marlo Frayne that seemed truly evil, just . . . *insidious,* a seedy hunger to manipulate other people. He couldn't imagine spending fifteen or twenty years in this house with this woman constantly hovering over him. "I was told by her husband that she worked," Conroy said aloud. "At the Roselle Library. They verified that she'd been there about three months. They also mentioned the college thing. Can you tell me anything more about that—if she put in an application anywhere? I'd also like to know the details about her job or jobs after high school."

"There weren't any," Marlo sneered. "I nixed that college idea when her grades weren't good enough to get her any of them grants or whatever they're called. Weren't nothing special about her, Officer, and wasn't nobody going to give her any free money—least of all me. Told her I wasn't wasting none of my savings on useless schooling for *her*." Marlo sat back huffily. "And the same went for that job business—she was going to go out and get some stupid little job that'd probably pay her minimum wage, and for what? She brought in a nice little social security check from her father every month, and all of that would've stopped." Marlo's nose lifted again in the same know-it-all expression that Conroy had seen earlier. "I told her she could keep her butt right here at home for a few years, thank you very much, and the checks from her father's social security would keep on coming until she hit twenty-one."

June 18th, Conroy thought. So Nola Frayne had given her adopted mother not quite four extra months before she'd walked out of her life forever. Good for her. He cleared his throat. "Was Nola depressed the last time you talked to her?"

Marlo gave an unpleasant snort. "I haven't talked to that girl since she got married, except for once. She'd got her an attitude when her birthday passed, like she'd become something special. Don't know why anyone would want to hire her, but she landed that job at the library, then started seeing that *man*." Marlo pronounced the word like it was something dirty. "Then she went off to work the Friday before she got hitched—left while I was sleeping. She must've had that man pick her up or took a cab or something—took all of her clothes and whatnot with her, and never came back."

Conroy kept his face impassive but he wondered about that. All of her belongings, gone in a single trip? The young woman must not have owned very much.

Marlo stubbed out her cigarette, then swung one thick arm up and let it dangle along the back of the couch, raking the material absently with those long, sharp fingernails. Conroy thought there was a hidden strength in Marlo, a hidden *meanness,* that must have been terrifying for someone as petite as Nola. "The only reason I know she got married," Marlo continued, "is that she at least had the manners to call me and tell me she wasn't coming back."

For as much misery as the girl had no doubt endured growing up, Marlo Frayne was probably lucky that's *all* Nola had done; the world was full of people who preferred more drastic ways of dealing with psychologically abusive parents. Despite his own thoughts, Conroy followed Marlo's words with notations in his book. "But she told you the man's name and what their address was."

Marlo laughed, the sound like the bark of an ill-tempered mutt. "Not quite, Detective . . . what'd you say your name was?"

"Conroy."

"Yeah, right. Anyway, no—she didn't give me her address or phone number. Never even told me her new last name, just that her husband's name was Alec."

Although he wasn't surprised, Conroy let his expression slide into a frown because he knew she would expect it. "Let me understand this, ma'am. You're telling me your daughter leaves, gets married, but doesn't tell you anything on the telephone except that she's not coming back?" Marlo just looked at him, her face carrying that same unconcerned expression. "Did you and Nola not get along?"

"I guess you could say that."

"May I ask what the problem was?"

Marlo's face hardened. "What's the difference? I don't guess I got to spread out our dirty laundry for the world."

"Of course not. But anything you say would be confidential, of course." Careful here, Conroy thought. If this woman felt he was accusing her of anything, she'd clam up so tightly a crowbar wouldn't pry her mouth open. "But it might help me get a clue to her whereabouts if I knew a little more about how she thinks—"

"No one's ever going to figure out what's in that girl's

head," Marlo said disdainfully. "You'd think she'd be grateful to me for what I done, adopting her when her father died and taking care of her all these years when she wasn't even my kid. Hardly asked for anything in return, either—just the social security check to help with the bills and her to do the housework. And look what she done."

Conroy glanced surreptitiously around the living room, but he didn't see any family pictures displayed anywhere. He decided to ask outright. "Do you have any pictures of Nola? And I'd like to see her room, if you don't mind."

"Ain't nothing to see. I cleaned it out and made it into a sewing room." Marlo looked at him resentfully, then heaved herself off the couch and went over to a battered sideboard on one wall of the dim dining room. She pulled open a drawer and rummaged through it for a moment, then drew out a creased three-by-five photo. "You want a picture, here's one," she said finally. "From her high school graduation, but it's probably the most recent. She never liked having her picture taken." She came over and handed it to Conroy, then stomped back to the couch; the detective could feel her aggravation in every vibration the old floor made under her weight.

At least the photograph she'd given him was clear, a generic yearbook picture that showed an older teenager with clear skin and blue eyes, but otherwise unremarkable features. In the picture her hair looked clean and long, hanging well past her shoulders in a typical high school style. Unlike her mother, Nola Frayne wore little makeup, and her face was honest but serious, betraying a personality far more mature than that of the usual eighteen-year-old graduate. "May I keep this?"

"Whatever."

The image in the photo didn't quite mesh with the description Alec Elidad had given him, but it only took a few seconds more for the detective to find the discrepancy. "Her hair—" Conroy started to say, but Marlo apparently knew what he was going to ask.

"She chopped it all off right after she met the guy she up

and married," Marlo cut in. "Didn't think she'd ever do such a thing. Makes you wonder, don't it," she said darkly, "what else he made her do."

"Mr. Elidad seems quite distressed over his wife's disappearance," Conroy said carefully.

"Elidad? What the hell kind of a name is that? Did she go and marry a Jew?" Disdain creased Marlo's chubby face.

Conroy blinked, caught off guard. "I didn't ask." He studied her. "You were telling me about your husband. He was—"

"Charles Frayne. He died about sixteen years ago."

Conroy frowned. "I'm not quite following the time period." He flipped a page back in his notebook and tried to find the sentence he was looking for . . . there. "You said that Nola was adopted and that her father died right afterward? Was Frayne her real name?"

"I already *told* you she wasn't my kid. She was my first husband's daughter." Marlo looked pained, as if the last thing she wanted to do was tell him these old secrets. "Charles and I adopted her."

Conroy raised an eyebrow. "What happened to her real father?"

Marlo shrugged carelessly. "He dropped dead of a heart attack not long after we was married—ticker trouble apparently runs in his family, because Nola has a heart murmur, too."

"Interesting." Conroy sat back. "So you've been twice widowed. I would've thought Nola's mother would have gotten custody of her when her father died."

Marlo gave another shrug, but this one was tense enough that Conroy could spot the lie before it came. "Stowe told me she wasn't a fit mother, that she smacked the kid around a lot, had a real bad temper. She used to lock the kid in a closet until he got home from work and he'd find all kinds of marks on her, bruises and burns and shit. I wasn't about to hand her back to that woman, and anyways, I didn't know where she was. I'd heard she was dead."

Conroy raised an eyebrow. "Who told you these things?"

"Ain't you been listening? Nola's father, of course—who else? Myself, I never met the woman, but I don't think much of someone who'd torment a baby girl like she done."

"Uh-huh." Conroy prodded absently at his lips with the tip of his pen, wondering about the child custody laws of a decade and a half ago and parental kidnapping. For someone who didn't want to give a simple last name, she sure had a lot of . . . *interesting* details to offer. "And what was her name?"

"I have no idea."

Exasperation made the policeman slap his notebook shut. "Ms. Frayne, I find it a little hard to believe you don't know the name of the birth mother of the child you say you adopted, the woman who would also—provided I've got this mess straight—be your first husband's first wife and who you're claiming abused Nola."

"I don't care what you think," Marlo Frayne said. Her voice had taken on a defensive edge. "Stowe never talked about her and I didn't care to ask."

"Stowe."

"Nola's real father."

Well, Conroy thought sourly, at least she remembered *that* much. "And his last name?"

"What difference does it make?" Marlo said. Her voice had gotten nearly belligerent. "He died when she was real young, and I spent a whole lifetime making sure Nola never knew anyone but me and Charles. She didn't even know Stowe's name. She don't know any difference and I want to keep it that way."

"She might have found out," Conroy said. His patience was really wearing thin. Could this woman find a way to be any more uncooperative? "And she may have gone—"

"I'm telling you he's dead and there ain't nowhere for her to have gone *to*," Marlo said hotly. "She doesn't know and there's no need for you to know either!" Without warning, she hauled herself to her feet. "Whyn't you just go on and leave? Let's just say I don't remember, and I got nothing more to tell you, and leave it at that."

Conroy stood just as abruptly, his shoulders vibrating with anger. In two steps he was standing in front of Marlo Frayne, nearly nose-to-nose with her, but if she expected him to raise his voice, she was way off track. Instead, he gave her a cold, cold smile.

"Oh, I think you *do* remember, Ms. Frayne. And unless you want to spend the rest of the evening down at the station with me, plus as much more time as I can stretch out of it, I think you're going to tell me what Nola's father's name was."

STOWE GARDELL

DECEASED: 3/7/82

PRE-1985 RECORDS: ***MANUAL STORAGE. SEE COUNTY CLERK FOR RETRIEVAL***

And there it ended. "Well, that's a helluva lot of help," Conroy muttered. Pre-1985 . . . yeah, just like Nola's birth certificate. So much of that stuff had been handwritten in ledger books, stacks and stacks of files, and ultimately microfiche and computer tape. Now everything was on computer hard drives, but when you started digging farther into the past, the computers didn't do any good; you were back to the good old days of footwork and it could take weeks to get a simple piece of paper. He rubbed his chin thoughtfully, then began typing again, knowing that the records were limited but hoping that the ones in the counties that made up this part of northern Illinois would be enough. He'd already done the social security number search, but there wasn't anything to see in that beyond Nola Elidad's current job.

SEARCH: NOLA GARDELL

More waiting—seemed like that's all he did in front of the computer anymore. When it finally came, the response hardly seemed worth it.

<NO MATCH>

"Shit," Conroy muttered crudely. He tried again.

SEARCH: RENE GARDELL

And again:

<NO MATCH>

"All right then, try this." He went for one of the computer commands, resigning himself to an even longer stay in front of the screen.

SEARCH: * GARDELL

The detective watched the hard drive light blink for a few moments, then gave himself a mental shake and decided to grab a cup of coffee. He doubted the computer would turn up anything he didn't already know; Nola's real father was dead and had been since she was . . . how old? Marlo hadn't said specifically, but Conroy was hard pressed to believe there was anything worth following up there—the computer search was just routine. At least now he had a picture; Conroy would run it by Alec just to be sure there was still a strong enough resemblance. If it panned out, Conroy was going to plaster this sucker up all over Roselle, and he'd plant a pile at the station houses of the surrounding burbs, too. There wouldn't be a place in the six-county quadrant this woman could hide once he got through. Wouldn't hurt to feed it to the local news stations, either.

Conroy took his time getting his java, then strolled back to his desk. He set his cup down and was surprised to find a screenful of information waiting for him.

SEARCH RESULTS: * GARDELL

STOWE GARDELL

MARLO FRANCINE GARDELL <SEE MARLO FRANCINE FRAYNE>

TRISTA GARDELL <SEE TRISTA NEWMAN>

STACEY GARDELL <SEE STACEY WAITE>

TAMMY GARDELL

Interesting. He knew about Stowe and Marlo, but who were Trista, Stacey, and Tammy? No one Marlo had mentioned, so they were probably unrelated. Had it been Stowe's wife, there would have been a maiden name displayed. But just for the fun of it, he ran the first name through the database:

SEARCH: TRISTA GARDELL

SEARCH RESULTS:

TRISTA GARDELL <SEE TRISTA NEWMAN>

All right.

SEARCH: TRISTA NEWMAN

Conroy hit ENTER, then studied the information that came up.

TRISTA NEWMAN

SPOUSE: TADD NEWMAN

<SEE ALSO KRYSTIN POWELL>

The screen went on to list Trista's address in Hanover Park and a whole host of other apparently useless information. But Krystin . . . hadn't that been the librarian's name over there at the Roselle Library? Yes, but her last name had been Parker, not Powell, so it was probably a completely different woman. Frowning, he hit the PRINT SCREEN key and waited to make sure the information was sent, then returned to the keyboard. You never knew where following a hunch could lead.

SEARCII: KRYSTIN POWELL

And the results—

KRYSTIN POWELL <SEE KRYSTIN PARKER>

—were getting screwier all the time.

Stacey was smiling at him and holding his hand as they walked back to their car at Morton Arboretum. It was the fall of the year they'd gotten married and the autumn day was beautiful, filled with the fiery colors of the dying leaves while the crisp breeze brought with it the scent of pine needles and mulch. Her fingers curled around his and every so often she gave his hand a little squeeze, just because every time she did, it made Jesse smile. Saturday afternoon and not much was wrong with the world right now, he thought as he opened the car door and got in, then reached over and opened the door for Stacey. As she started to climb inside, she paused to move the newspaper out of the way so she could sit. Then her gaze met his and Jesse saw that the look in her eyes had changed: The calm affection was inexplicably gone, replaced by mistrust and fear, and Jesus, was that hate *he saw in their blue depths—*

The newspaper!

Panic made Jesse sit straight up in bed, and for a moment he yanked wildly on the sheets that were twined around his arms and waist like sodden cotton rope. Something dragged against his foot and he made himself stop thrashing as he remembered the fabric belt tied from his ankle to the side of Stacey's nightgown; when he looked over at her, he saw she was still there, lying on her pallet of blankets with her eyes open and staring at him. While it certainly wasn't what he would have hoped for, Jesse was at least gratified to see that there was none of the animosity he'd seen in the eyes of his wife in the dream.

The newspaper.

It was lying next to Stacey on the floor, neatly folded. In

fact, it didn't even look as though she'd read it—had she? Sometime in the morning hours, while he'd slept and dreamed of a bygone life and a wife who used to be, had Stacey gone through the pages and found the tiny issue of the *Roselle Press* that he'd so foolishly shoved between its pages?

And if so, what kind of damage would it do to her mental state to see the article in the paper about "her" disappearance?

God.

Things had gone by in a double-time blur this last week, but he still remembered that Stacey had managed to create an entirely new identity for herself—new job, new husband, new *personality*. What would it do to her to see something like that article, something that she could throw up to him as written "proof" that she wasn't who he knew she was?

The shade and the drawn curtains blocked all but a sliver of the light from the small, high windows, and the lamp on the chest of drawers was off. It took several moments for his eyes to adjust to the room's dimness, and it wasn't at all comforting to realize that the whole time he'd been glaring in Stacey's direction, she'd been wide awake and looking back at him. Christ, she probably thought he was nuts, jumping up in bed like that, then gawking at her with the lights off.

He cleared the sleep from his throat. "G'morning," he rasped.

She didn't say anything, just kept looking at him and waiting, her eyes unreadable across the small space, her body in that familiar, terrified-rabbit freeze. It was horribly frustrating, because Jesse knew she was waiting for him to make a move, to grab her, hold her, or—to her mind—worse. Did she really think that's how he was?

"So," he finally managed. "Did you read the, uh, paper, or were you bored?"

For a moment Stacey didn't answer, as if she were still too busy contemplating what he was going to do. "I . . . read," she said at last. "And I did end up dozing some."

Jesse nodded. He wanted desperately to figure out if she'd seen the article, but his own thoughts weren't processing—too little sleep, too much anxiety. "Well, that's . . . that's good. Maybe you'll eventually end up on the same sleep schedule as me."

"And then what?" Stacey asked. Her voice was sharp—she'd clearly been awake for awhile. "I can just stare at the walls in the middle of the night instead of the middle of the day?"

Jesse opened his mouth to reply, but he couldn't think of anything to say. She was right, of course—it wasn't the most interesting of existences. But there was nothing he could do about it, so he couldn't offer any words of comfort. "I think I'll fix some coffee," he said instead. "Make some breakfast. You hungry?"

She only shrugged, but Jesse decided to take that as a yes. "I'm getting up." He felt ridiculous making an announcement like that, but he knew she'd want to avert her eyes. He climbed out of bed without looking at her, then flicked on the small lamp on the nightstand. Soft light filled the room and he could see, finally, the newspaper—well-thumbed—where Stacey had pushed it off to the side of her pile of blankets. Beneath his feet, the carpet felt cool, unaccountably so, but he could hear the furnace running—probably just caught the end of a neutral cycle.

He grabbed a pair of pajama bottoms to go over his boxer shorts and Stacey finally stood when he untied his end of the robe belt, moving on her own to gather up first the bedding on the floor, then the newspaper. He looked longingly at the newspaper in her hands as they made their way to the kitchen, but he was afraid to reach for it—she was *so* jumpy. No, he'd have to wait until later, when he could set aside the newspaper for recycling and not be so obvious about his curiosity.

Breakfast was strained and . . . long. Something was bothering Jesse, but Nola had no idea what it was until later, after he'd had her help him clean up the dishes from the meal she'd barely touched. Once they were finished, he'd casually—*too* casually—swept the newspaper from the table, then flipped through it before he dropped it atop the pile of old papers next to the garbage can in the kitchen. When he paused at the crisply folded *Roselle Press*—which Nola had very carefully tucked back into the *Tribune*'s financial section where she'd found it—she finally understood what had troubled him enough to keep his silence for most of the meal.

He hadn't meant for her to see that newspaper.

She almost let a triumphant smile spread across her face, then squelched it at the last instant. She needed to be in control, to know about the article and the detective's number it listed without Jesse realizing it. It was her secret, her avenue to escape, and even though she hadn't had a pencil and paper to write down the number, and despite her own doubts about her memory and the fear that she wouldn't be able to remember it, she had dealt with the situation. Like any person pushed to the limits and forced to find a way to do the impossible, she had found a way.

With an expression of relief, Nola watched Jesse turn away from the papers. She said nothing, forced her face to remain expressionless despite the grin of victory that wanted so badly to surface. She only shifted on her chair, moving her body barely enough to get away from the stinging along the outside of her left thigh—

—where she'd scratched Detective Lucas Conroy's telephone number into her skin with the chewed end of one fingernail.

Conroy had always known Dustine was attractive, the way a person knows that a coworker, someone who passes in and out of his life on an almost daily basis, dresses carefully and looks nice. But the woman who opened the door to the townhouse in East Dundee made him forget his carefully rehearsed hello speech—for a moment his mind blanked and he thought he'd gone to the wrong address.

Dustine was wearing a simple, forest green sweatshirt

over a pair of khaki slacks and low-heeled shocs—a good thing, since shc was already an inch taller than Conroy. Her makeup wasn't much different from what she wore to work: eyeliner and mascara framing deep blue eyes, a little blush, the same rich red lipstick that complimented her olive complexion and dark, curly hair. Tonight, though, something about Dustine was different—something *sparkled.* Of course, he'd never seen her outside of the station, so maybe this was how she normally was when she was away from work.

"Hi," she said. She looked over her shoulder and Conroy saw a flicker of nervousness cross her face. That puzzled him a bit—he'd never seen Dustine be anything but entirely confident—but there was no time to mull it over now. Besides, he wasn't exactly an old pro at this either. "Come on in."

Conroy smiled and stepped inside Dustine's townhouse. The foyer was large and dim, windowless except for three small vertical panes of glass on one side of the entry door. Behind Dustine, Conroy could see half-flight stairways leading both up and down. Sunlight glowed in what little he could see beyond the landings.

"May I take your coat?" she said after a moment. Her voice held another flash of that same, suppressed anxiety he'd caught earlier, and Conroy wondered if the best answer would be *No, thanks. Why don't we just go straight to the restaurant?* Maybe she would feel more comfortable—

"I'll give you a tour," she offered, taking the decision away from him.

"Okay," he said. Conroy shrugged out of the wool overcoat and handed it to her, watched as she slipped it on a hanger and put it in a closet. He followed her down the stairs into what was a family room area, then stopped, impressed at what he saw. For a lower level, the oversized room was wide open and airy, with two long, large windows. White bookcases were lined up against light-colored white walls topping an earthy Southwestern wallpaper on the bottom half and wall-to-wall cream-colored Berber carpeting. There wasn't much furniture—an overstuffed, inviting couch and two chairs matched the base color of the wallpaper and faced a big oak coffee table and a console television, while off in the corner was a small desk setup. It looked like a fabulous place to relax.

"Family room," she said simply. "I kept it light so it wouldn't end up looking like a cave down here."

"Wow," he said. "It's really nice."

"Thanks." She didn't elaborate on anything else and he followed her dutifully back up the stairs. The living area was just as bright but even more open; the great room layout combined the dining and living rooms with the kitchen off to one side and had a cathedral ceiling that soared overhead to a skylight. Kitty-corner from the large kitchen area was a fireplace, around which stretched a small sectional couch in a bright pattern of red, blue, and green—more Southwestern flavor. Another half staircase went up behind him and he glanced there curiously.

"Upstairs are two bedrooms and the master bath," Dustine told him, but made no move to show him more.

Conroy nodded and moved instead toward the dining area. "It's really beautiful, Dustine. Is it new?"

"About two years old," she began, then something moved by her feet. Conroy grinned when he saw a cat—kind of a tortoiseshell-colored thing with a face that was patterned on one side and black on the other—rub against her ankles and stare at him with light green, mistrustful eyes.

Dustine rolled her eyes, but she still smiled. "This is Pima."

Conroy dropped into a squat, but the cat wouldn't come to him. "Ah," he said. "More Southwestern stuff."

Dustine crossed her arms and for the first time since he'd arrived, Conroy saw her loosen up a little. "Actually, no. It stands for Pain in My Ass."

He laughed and stood, giving up on the idea of petting Pima as the cat hissed at him and sprang up the stairs. He looked after her, but Dustine still made no offer to show him the upper level and he didn't push it; she didn't say anything, of course, but he had the unspoken sense that she appreciated that. There was a lot more going on inside this woman than met the eye, a history that as far as Conroy knew she hadn't shared with anyone at the station. The thought of that, of unshared secrets, made him think of Nola Elidad, a mysterious woman who had appeared in Alec's life only long enough to make him fall head over heels in love with her. Now she was missing and, had it not been for the adoptive mother Conroy had found, her husband had barely been able to prove she'd ever existed in his life at all.

"Boy," Dustine said gently. "I must be absolutely mesmerizing—this is twice your mind's wandered away while we were talking."

Conroy blinked, then felt his cheeks flush in embarrassment. "I'm sorry," he said hastily. "It's work, that case—it just sort of creeps into my head at the weirdest times."

She gave him a good-natured grin. "I understand. So . . . do you want a drink, or . . ."

He shook his head. "Not unless you do. Actually, I'm kind of hungry. Why don't we just head on out?"

When he'd called earlier to get directions, Dustine had told him to pick the restaurant, a not-so-subtle way of allowing him to go as light as he wanted. He'd chosen an Italian place on Lake Street called Boccé, where he'd gone off and on through the years and where the owner, a young guy named Joey, made the best version of chicken vesuvio he'd ever tasted. Although he'd never brought a woman with him, Conroy had been in enough times that Joey recognized him now and raised an eyebrow in interest at the sight of Dustine.

Joey led them to a table by the window and as they settled themselves to look over the menu, the server brought over a complimentary carafe of Chianti; when Conroy glanced toward the entrance, Joey nodded and went back to his reservation book. After a few moments of silence, Conroy poured them each a glass of wine. "I'm sorry," he said. "I never even asked if you liked Italian food—is this place okay?"

Dustine's answering smile was reassuring. "It's fine—I love pasta." Her eyes shadowed momentarily as she glanced at the Chianti. "I don't drink much, though."

"Would you like me to get you something else?"

She shook her head. "This is okay, but you'll get most of it."

Conroy chuckled. "Not unless you want to end up driving."

"So tell me what's good," Dustine said.

"Garlic?"

She grinned. "Only if you're having some, too. I don't want to be the only person in the car on the way home who smells like an Italian kitchen."

"Agreed." Conroy glanced at the menu again, but he really knew all the best items by heart. "Chicken vesuvio, pasta with Joey's sauce, linguini with white clam sauce. If you don't like clams, try the mussels or the calamari. He makes the chicken vesuvio like no place else—big chunks of chicken in a bowl of sliced mushrooms and oversized garlic pieces over pasta. It's the best thing he has."

Dustine nodded and studied the menu for another moment, then closed it. "You know," she said. "Garlic is good for your circulation."

Conroy grinned. "I take it you're going for the chicken vesuvio?"

"You got it."

"I was hoping you'd say that. Me, too."

The food was as good as he expected it to be, the conversation excellent, Dustine's company a pleasure. The whole thing left Conroy feeling a little giddy, as though he'd drank far more than the single glass of Chianti he'd consumed over the course of the meal. Beneath that was a layer of nervousness, as though he'd lost a couple of decades and was seventeen again, sitting across from his date and fumbling for his next words, hoping to God that he wouldn't say something totally dorky. Oddly enough, Alec Elidad would float through the back of his thoughts from time to time; at first Conroy was at a loss to explain it, then he realized that it was a sort of empathy. Was this the way Alec had felt, sitting across from Nola Frayne on their first date? Conroy didn't intend to jump into anything as quickly as Alec had, but he thought he could finally at least understand the sense of loss the man now exuded, the loneliness and the desperation that were so apparent in Elidad's eyes every time Conroy saw him.

They sat companionably when they were finished, not speaking, and just watched the other people in the restaurant for awhile. Their conversation during dinner had been light and Conroy had intentionally kept it so; he wanted very much to know more about this woman, but he certainly didn't want to pry or push before she was ready. His line of work had taught him that people, even the ones who were very good at hiding, gave little signs when they were ready to open up, whether by confessing to something horrible or just bringing back a memory that would later turn out to mean nothing at all. Dustine was getting there now, leaning forward slightly, a curious light in her eyes; Conroy was gratified to see that she'd drank only about a third of her glass of wine—her interest in him came from her, not the alcohol.

"So have you always wanted to be a cop?"

It was an expected question, and one which he would eventually ask her, so Conroy wouldn't complain. For most people, the answer was long and involved, springing from some pivotal event in their lives. While he wasn't necessarily a man given to short answers, this one was surprisingly simple:

"Yes." He paused, knowing she would expect more. "Ever since I was a kid. I must've thought the uniforms were cool or something." Without thinking, he rubbed his knuckles, then cracked them. "How about you?"

If the habit annoyed Dustine, she gave no sign. She shrugged and looked at the table. "I guess it's the same with me."

"You know," he said, peering at her. "There's a hint of

something in your voice . . . I'd assumed you were from around here, but is that a southern accent I'm hearing?"

She smiled self-consciously. "Yeah, I suppose it is. I've tried valiantly to get rid of it, but sometimes it creeps back."

"So where are you from?"

"Alabama," she answered. "A little town called Harmony." She looked away and something in her eyes hardened. "Lovely place."

Conroy's eyebrows lifted. "Why don't I believe you?"

Dustine blinked, then looked embarrassed. "Sorry. I just don't have good . . . memories of it."

"Ah." Conroy sat back, watching her, then chanced another question. "Family or friends?"

His date picked at the tablecloth absently. "Both, actually. Can we . . . talk about something else? Why don't you tell me about yourself instead?"

"Sure," Conroy said agreeably. Every guy's favorite subject? Not necessarily, and he would've much rather quizzed her until he found out the details of her life—the perils of being a detective, he supposed, that relentless curiosity that often had to be curtailed. "Although there's not much interesting stuff in my past, I'm afraid. I come from a mostly Irish family. Both my parents are living and I've got three brothers and two sisters. I had another sister who was killed in a car accident about five years ago."

"Ow," Dustine said softly. "That must've been hard."

"Yeah, it was. But we're a pretty close family and that helped a lot." He hesitated, feeling awkward. "How about yours?"

She shook her head and looked away again. "It's, uh, difficult for me to get close to people."

She didn't say more and Conroy thought about this. Something to do with her memories of Harmony, no doubt. She'd talk about it when—if ever—she was ready.

"I'm sorry," Dustine said abruptly. "I don't mean to be short—"

"Don't apologize for not wanting to spill your life story to someone you barely know," Conroy told her quickly.

"That's your prerogative." Another random thought—funny how he could tell her that, after what he'd put Alec Elidad through. But that's different, he reminded himself. You can't even compare the two.

Silence then, stretching until it bordered on awkward. He opened his mouth to say something, anything, to keep the conversation going, then was relieved when the server showed up with a dessert menu. He looked at Dustine and she smiled. "How about it?" she asked. "You up for a calorie binge?"

Conroy shook his head regretfully, remembering the mini-layer of pudge around his waist that he couldn't seem to get rid of. "No way, though I'd taste whatever you have."

She studied the menu for a few moments, but ultimately shook her head. "No, I really don't think so. I just can't bring myself to be that decadent. At least on a first date."

Conroy grinned, hoping it looked natural. Did that mean what he thought it might—did she want there to be a second one? God, he thought again, I feel like a stupid twelve-year-old. Maybe getting a crush on someone really is the way to stay young.

And strangely, that thought again brought the memory of the grieving Alec Elidad—his ravaged face and hollow eyes, the thinly disguised panic in his voice during his outbreak at the station—closer to the surface of Conroy's mind. There it stayed, a nagging reminder of his own good fortune while another suffered, even as Conroy spent the rest of the evening laughing with Dustine and hoping that this date was only the start of something truly special between the two of them.

Isn't this sweet, Nola thought with ill humor. We're just like the all-American couple, sitting here and watching football.

"Is there something else you want to watch?"

She barely stopped herself from jumping, afraid that would look suspicious. He was only talking to her, for God's sake, not trying to touch her. If she kept this up, he was bound to start wondering what was the matter with her, and that would make him watch her more closely. Above all, she needed to get him to relax a little tonight, just enough for her to get to the telephone on the stand next to the powder room. She'd been studying it under the guise of watching the football game with him—she didn't know or care about the teams that were playing or know which was which—and she thought that the cord was long enough to allow her to carry the phone out of earshot and make the call she'd finally decided was necessary. She'd said that detective's number so often in her mind that it was branded there, and her fingers itched to push the buttons and hear the ring on the other end. For all her anticipation, this might be the quickest call of her life, but that was okay—she only needed to get through and say a few well-chosen words. She would count on the police to do the rest, and Jesse Waite—God help him—would just have to deal with the consequences.

But wait—Jesse had asked her a question, and she needed to answer. What was it?

"No," she said calmly. "The game is fine."

Jesse nodded and looked back at the television, then reached for the beer on the coffee table, frowning slightly when he discovered it was empty. He stood and looked at her awkwardly. "Do you, uh, want one? Or something else?"

Nola shook her head, keeping her eyes on the screen but not seeing anything. "No, thanks."

Jesse nodded. "Well, I figure it would be all right to have just one more." He looked at her. "Okay?"

Was he asking her permission? Nola blinked and finally looked at him, saw that he was standing there and waiting. Amazingly enough, that was exactly what he seemed to be doing. She opened her mouth, then shut it—she had no idea what to say, so she only shrugged. He looked disappointed, as if he'd hoped for more. A solid yes, or perhaps he would have been more pleased if she'd said *No, I don't think you should,* something to indicate she was actually interested in what he did. The truth was she really didn't think he should; he had to leave for the machine shop in about three hours and—

Where her fingers were tucked beneath her folded arms, Nola gave herself a sharp pinch.

The pain was enough to snap her back to reality. The machine shop was nothing—in a few hours Jesse Waite would be in the custody of the police and she would be on her way back to Alec. Jesse could drink all the beer he wanted.

Jesse, whose attention had been caught again by the football game, cleared his throat and ducked into the kitchen. She could hear the refrigerator door opening, the clink of bottles as he pushed stuff around and got out what he wanted. When she turned her head, she could glimpse him moving around in there through the pass-through. "Sure I can't get you anything?" he called.

"No," she said in return, a bit more sharply than she'd intended. Calm down, she reminded herself. No anxiety, no panic; just keep it slow and steady, and don't give him any reason to watch you closely or to put up his guard. "Thanks anyway," she added, making a concentrated effort to soften her tone.

He was back in what seemed like only a few seconds, settling comfortably at the other end of the couch. There was a different air about the way he sat with her tonight; he was more relaxed, on his way to integrating her—whether she wanted it or not—into his lifestyle. He was a long way from trusting her, but Nola thought there might have been enough of an improvement for her to get to that enticing telephone across the room, maybe while he was in the bathroom or something. Sooner or later that beer would have to come out of him, and she was determined that she would somehow make her call tonight—she would not spend another night locked away while he went to work like she was just a part of another day in the life of Jesse Waite.

Time dragged on and more huddles and passes flitted across the television, a series of plays and combinations for which Nola had no name. Every now and then Jesse would grin and give an emphatic "Yeah!" when one of the teams made a touchdown or a particularly good play, and Nola tried to look interested. She went to the powder room herself once, with Jesse watching her every move on the way there and back as though she were a bird that would suddenly take flight.

But her plan was working. Nola could sense it.

The first time he got up to use the bathroom, she made herself stay where she was, despite the screaming inside her head that was trying to propel her toward the telephone. To stop it, she finally bit down hard on the inside of her cheek, letting the pain and blood chase away the desire to launch herself across the room. It was too soon, it was a trap—how could it not be? And she was right, because he'd hardly closed the door behind him when he yanked it open again, looking across the room at her with a half-wild expression.

Oh no—she was too smart for that. She let her gaze linger on the television before casually turning it to him, as though his expectations were the farthest thing in the world she could, or would, meet. He tried to act as though he'd forgotten something, even came all the way back to the coffee table and shuffled around the remote and a couple of the magazines there before going back, but Nola knew better. This time he stayed inside the small bathroom for a good two or three minutes, the seconds stretching to small eternities as Nola wondered if she wasn't being a fool for not taking what seemed, in hindsight, to have been a premium opportunity.

Instead, she tucked her feet under her and waited, and her gamble that she should just stay where she was paid off. Not three seconds after she'd lifted her feet off the floor, the door to the powder room opened and Jesse stepped out. His expression was strained, as if being in that tiny room without having her in his sight for even those few minutes had been as much of an ordeal for him as not trying for the telephone had been for Nola. Relief flooded his features as soon as he saw her, and when he settled on the other end of the couch, his movements were looser and lighter, his earlier tenseness mostly disappeared. Did she have the beer to thank for that, or could she credit herself for building up his false sense of security?

Another mini-lifetime passed; why, Nola wondered with sour humor, do men always seem to have bladders the size of footballs? Then finally, *finally*, Jesse got up to use the bathroom again. She watched him from the corner of her eye as he stood and looked at her hesitantly—she purposely didn't look back—then went for the powder room and pulled the door closed behind him. The hours were passing—these damned football games dragged on forever—and pretty soon he'd probably suggest making some kind of dinner; then he'd get ready for work and Nola would face another night in the "lock-up."

Not tonight.

Nola went for the telephone.

Like countless others watching the movies churned out by Hollywood, Nola had shaken her head in disgust at the woman who stumbles and falls when she's being chased, the man who drops his keys next to the car as an attacker closes in. Her experiences with Jesse so far had been harrowing, and even terrifying, but she'd never really experienced the way fear, *true* fear born of impossible odds, could just . . . *numb* a person's senses, from her memory to her sense of hearing to the feeling in the tips of her fingers as she tried to push suddenly too-small buttons on an unfamiliar telephone.

It took a precious three seconds for her brain to kick in and give her the telephone number, the same number she'd scratched on her leg and said over and over to herself enough times so that earlier it had come to mind as easily as her social security number. She started to press the buttons but the numbers looked strange, and she stared at them stupidly for another long moment before she saw that she had the receiver upside down. At last everything started working—brain, fingers, force of will—and she jammed her fingers along the raised numbers—

Too fast!

—then had to do it over again when something went wrong and the phone blared a shrill misdial tone in her ear. Jesus—how loud was that? Could Jesse hear it? Nola almost dropped the phone back into its cradle, then decided to try again—anything was better than being locked away for another night with this crazy man, even getting *caught* was better than that. This time she made it, and the line began to ring, a dull, professional-sounding *thrum* that gave her the comforting image of a bustling police station somewhere, like a hundred she'd seen in the movies. She heard a voice on the other end as she dragged the phone cord and herself as far away from the powder room door as she could, but when she drew a ragged breath to speak, the voice kept going, the words even and calm, and so, so impersonal:

"This is Detective Lucas Conroy. I'm away from my desk at the moment, but if you'll leave me a detailed message—"

Oh, my God, Nola thought. I've got his damned *voice mail*!

His words droned pleasantly, the message lasting a hundred, no, a thousand years. She waited for the voice to stop—what else could she do?—and for some sort of beep, a signal that would indicate she could begin pleading with the machine on the other end to find someone to please please please help her out of this predicament.

Just a few seconds, maybe five, and a few tiny things clicked into her memory, slid to the forefront of her mind as the world around her blanked out and focused only on the unknown policeman's voice:

The *squeak* of the sofa springs when she'd risen.

The corresponding protest of the floorboards as she'd crossed the floor, not muffled nearly enough by the worn carpeting despite her ridiculous half-tiptoeing gait.

Nola spun and saw Jesse frozen in the bathroom doorway, his face both shocked and enraged.

Paralyzed, she clutched the telephone and saw him step toward her, then bend to pick up something on the floor. Terror made her vision wobble crazily and somewhere at the edge of her consciousness she thought the voice mail message had stopped, that she could now say something that would be profound enough to give Detective Lucas

Conroy every piece of information he would need to rush over here and save her.

"Waite," she said desperately. The sight of Jesse had stolen her air and her voice came out too low, almost inaudible. "It's—"

But the line was dead.

The end of the phone line burned in Jesse's fingers; the plastic piece that he'd reached over and unplugged felt like a tiny, razor-studded square cutting into his skin. He couldn't decide if he was more furious with Stacey for betraying him or with himself for trusting her to begin with—how stupid could he have been? Did he really think there was going to be some kind of miracle overnight cure for his wife? That because she sat and watched a football game at his side it meant the old Stacey—the one who used to fix a bowl of popcorn for them, then read a magazine while he cheered on his favorite team—was on her way back?

Fool.

"I trusted you," he said hoarsely. "I can't believe you'd let me down like this."

She said nothing, just stood there like a small, frightened animal caught in the headlights of an onrushing truck. From where he stood, Jesse could see her fingers and the way they gripped the telephone; the nails were so white from the pressure that their color nearly matched the cream-colored plastic. Her blue eyes were huge, her lips pressed together tightly enough to make Jesse think she was trying to suppress a scream.

Jesse took a deep breath, but it wasn't to calm himself or to quell the hurt or the sense of anger. Yes, he still felt that way, but more than that he suddenly just wanted to curl up and cry, to take Stacey in his arms and wail about everything they'd had and lost—their love, their marriage, their *life*. Wouldn't they ever get it back?

He cleared his throat and the sound was harsher than he intended, loud in the heavy silence. "Give me the phone, Stacey."

His wife's face twisted and finally he saw a hint of the old Stacey, the one who had stood up to him during their loudest arguments and refused to take the considerable grief he could sometimes shell out. "You want the telephone," she snapped. "Then *here*."

The only thing that kept Jesse from getting knocked in the head was that he was half-expecting her throw. He made an awkward attempt to catch the phone but failed, and the device went to the floor with a clang and a tangle of cracked plastic and cord. Jesse leaned over and picked it up, then plugged it back in. "Good throw." He held the receiver to his ear. "Now it's dead," he lied. He hung it up again and set the phone back on the table. Then he didn't know what to do—should they stand here all night, each trying to stare the other down in a weaponless match of wills?

Finally, he shook his head in disgust and went back to the couch, and after a few seconds Stacey seemed to realize that there wasn't anything for her to do but follow. The football game was still on, but Jesse no longer cared about the score or who was winning. Where a little while ago it had been a pleasant evening at home with his wife, now the time dragged; he was so wounded by what she'd done that he didn't know what to say or do. His appetite was dead but he'd have to leave for work in a couple of hours, so they both had to eat. He'd fix something in a little while, one of the same, simple meals they were stuck with until he got paid.

Maybe I ought to let her go, Jesse thought morosely. She doesn't want to be here, and that other guy can probably take better care of her. He probably makes more money than me, isn't in debt up to his eyebrows—hell, he's probably *smarter* than me.

Stacey said something to him, but his mind was so full of the thought of losing her again that it didn't register. He let it slide, not trusting himself to speak anyway. His voice might crack, and she might instinctively catch just how close he was to caving in. And he couldn't, he *mustn't*. He loved her and he needed her, and he was her husband, damn it, her *first* husband—he should have been her *only* one. And until those fools at the hospital had messed up so badly, he had been just that. Above all, he had to hold on to that knowledge, let the truth be the rope that kept him from sinking below the surface of all this misery until Stacey healed.

He had to hold on—he *had* to.

Another comment from Stacey but he missed that one, too. Something about the game? It didn't matter. Let her say whatever she wanted—she couldn't hurt him any more than she had with that attempted phone call. Who had she been trying to reach? The police, of course, but the call must not have gone through—911 used a caller identification system and Roselle was a small town. If she'd talked to someone there and they'd tracked the call, the cops would have been here by now.

But outside, the evening stayed dark and silent. Inside, Jesse was tired and emotionally drained, and he pushed himself as far away from his wife as he could, into the farthest corner of the couch. Another comment from Stacey, but this time he outright ignored it.

As much as he loved her, Jesse didn't want to talk to her for awhile.

The silence was the worst.

It reminded Nola of her mother and how when Marlo had gotten angry over something, she'd done the same thing, as Nola had gotten older. As a child Nola had endured the physical end of the spectrum and those oh-so-evil fingernails that Marlo so carefully cultivated seemed to serve no other purpose than to punish her. If they weren't digging into her scalp beneath her hair, then they were embedded in the tender skin on the underside of her upper arm. It was the perfect place for unnoticed bruises, and if Marlo thought Nola'd been particularly bad, then she'd followed her grip with a vicious twist.

When Nola had become too big to scratch or slap, Marlo

had gone for a type of cold-shoulder treatment that could extend for days on end, where she wouldn't even answer yes or no to the simplest of Nola's questions. Nola spent the time in her mother's company—at the dinner table, for instance—enduring the older woman's malevolent stares; when she finally retreated to her room, Marlo would start with the "banging," as Nola came to think of it. Everything she picked up was slammed or banged when she set it back down, and she would make her presence known to her errant daughter with her every movement—

BANG --

THUMP --

CRASH --

THUD --

—until Nola could bear it no more and would beg for forgiveness for whatever transgression she had (or hadn't) committed. Then would come the lecture, the reminders, the recriminations:

"I did everything for you after your father's death, young missy, and look how you treat me. You were nothing but an orphan, a homeless, dirty-faced little girl with no place to go and no money. I *was the one who put myself out to feed and clothe you, to see that you was raised up proper.* I *was the one who did without so you could have supplies for school and toys.* I *was the one—"*

"Jesse," Nola said. Her fingers twisted together nervously. "Please—talk to me. Say something."

"I don't have anything to say."

Well, that was something, anyway. He looked like a sullen little boy, sitting there on the couch and staring at the television not with attention, but with a focused sort of petulance, as if at any moment he might look at her and blurt "You don't like me!" like a sulking third grader.

"You must have *something* to say," Nola prompted. "If you're angry, why don't you just say so instead of bottling it all up inside?"

The look Jesse gave her was somewhere between amazement and hurt, but at least it didn't contain any of the hatred that Marlo had so expertly wielded. He opened his mouth, then closed it again, stubbornness settling over his expression a little too comfortably for Nola's liking. What was going on inside his head? It was easy to guess he was angry about the call she'd tried to make, but what would be the consequences? Was this it—the silent treatment? Or would there be more, something comparable to the physical end of what she'd grown up with from Marlo?

"I'm *sorry,* okay?"

It just came out, as it so often had with Marlo, an apology for anything and everything, take the blame for it all just to try to make it better again, get the badness *over* with and move on.

Jesse turned his face toward hers, but for a moment she thought he still wasn't going to speak. Finally his mouth worked a little. "That's all?" he asked. "That's all you have to say?"

"What do you want me to say?"

He sat forward on the couch and clasped his hands. Now he was looking at the floor rather than at her, and his next words made her stomach lurch. "I want you to promise me you won't do it again."

Now it was Nola's turn to be silent. Her first impulse was to comply—she'd been well trained by Marlo—but if she did, she was effectively cutting off what might be her only chance at escape.

Jesse glanced at her, then looked back at the floor. "I've done a lot for you, Stacey—"

I did everything for you—

"—and I'm willing to do more, I'm willing to do it *all.*"

You were nothing but an orphan—

"But you have to give something in return, too."

. . . and look how you treat me.

"I told you that if you still weren't remembering the way you should be after three months, I'd take you to see a doctor, or a psychiatrist—whatever. But you have to work with me in that three-month period, Stacey. You have to give me that. You have to *promise.*"

. . . I *was the one who put myself out* . . . I *was the one* . . .

It sounded like someone else speaking when Nola hung her head like a chastised child and, at last, said the words that Jesse wanted to hear:

"I promise."

You didn't betray Jesse, Nola thought later, much later, after he'd gone on to work and left her alone for the first time in the master bedroom. You betrayed *yourself.*

She searched the entire bedroom but found nothing she could use to pry loose the wood that Jesse had nailed across the high window, and she simply wasn't strong enough to do it bare-handed; likewise with the bedroom door—she'd watched helplessly as Jesse had installed padlock clasps on both the inside and outside. The small master bathroom had been emptied of anything useful, but at least it was there and she wasn't reduced to being able to think of nothing but her bladder for half the night. Nola never watched much television but again, at least it was *there;* when she flipped it on she found a basic cable setup that brought in a decent picture and a fairly wide variety of channels.

So here she was.

Again.

No, *still.*

" 'I promise,' " she said aloud, letting all the mockery and self-loathing she felt coalesce into that small sentence. She opened the drawer of the nightstand and stared into it without registering what she was seeing, then her eyes fed the information to her brain and she reached for the small pad of paper and the cheap ink pen. She tore off one piece and carefully put the paper back where she'd found it, then wrote Detective Conroy's telephone number on it from memory. A snide little voice inside her head said that was good, because wasn't there some doubt now about who she was? If she couldn't remember *that,* how would she remember something as basic as a telephone number?

I promise.

"Stop it," she said angrily. Her voice sounded piercing and loud in the empty room. "He *made* you do that—you're not bound to it. And you *know* who you are."

But he *hadn't* made her promise, had he? He hadn't screamed or beaten her, or threatened to throw her in the basement. She could have just as easily said nothing, given him back the same cold shoulder he'd shown her. But now . . . she'd always stuck by her word, even as a child—she'd had so many promises made and broken to her by adults that it had become unthinkable for her to *not* keep her word once she gave it.

Detective Conroy's number stared at her from the piece of notepaper.

Should she call? *Would* she?

Of course . . . provided she got the chance.

In the meantime, Nola carefully folded the paper until it was a rectangle barely an inch square and slipped it into her tennis shoe, making sure she chose her uninjured foot. Promise or not, she needed to talk to this man sooner or later; all the things that Jesse seemed to know, his behavior and her own unexpected responses—that promise, for God's sake!—were shaking her up badly. The killing blow to her self-confidence had been the wedding photographs, and she couldn't get those out of her mind. In hindsight, she called herself a fool for not simply dialing 911, but now she knew why she'd done it that way. Yes, she'd been having doubts, and she'd wanted to talk about it with someone. Who better than the detective assigned to find the missing woman who had once been her?

Nola watched television for awhile, but nothing she found could capture her attention enough to make her stop thinking about the failed telephone call, about Jesse, and most of all, about the photographs. Jesse had set the box on the dresser before he'd left, as if he'd known they would be a constant temptation, a reminder of something gone horribly wrong in her life and, possibly, in her mind. Finally Nola could stand it no longer, and she walked to the dresser and touched the box tentatively, like it was something that would burn her if she picked it up. And it would, wouldn't it? Every time she thought of its contents, her heart seemed to stutter; wouldn't going through it again burn her right down to her soul?

But she had to.

And so, long into the darkest hours of the night, Nola paged through the photos of "her" marriage.

JANUARY 23--THURSDAY

"*Wait,*" the woman's voice said on the voice mail tape. "*It's—*"

Detective Conroy cracked his knuckles thoughtfully, then rewound the tape and listened again. A wrong number? But there was something odd about the voice, a rushed tone to it that seemed out of place right before the line simply went dead—no clatter where she'd hung up. The tracing program had automatically given him the originating telephone number, and he ran it through the department's records now, then sat back and tried to digest the information the computer gave him:

JESSE AND STACEY WAITE

1152 BRYSE TRAIL

ROSELLE, ILLINOIS

Waite, Conroy thought. Where have I seen that name before? He shuffled through the stuff on his desk, feeling thankful that he was a fairly organized person. When he found the piece of paper, he held it up and studied it with a frown:

SEARCH RESULTS: * GARDELL

STOWE GARDELL

MARLO FRANCINE GARDELL <SEE MARLO FRANCINE FRAYNE>

TRISTA GARDELL <SEE TRISTA NEWMAN>

STACEY GARDELL <SEE STACEY WAITE>

Wait, Conroy thought. Or . . . *Waite*?

There'd been something going around the sitcoms awhile back, a recurring bit that he thought might have actually been turned into a game called "Six Degrees of Kevin Bacon." While the detective didn't believe it was necessarily true, in a small suburb like Roselle, where it was only during the last decade or so that the commuter trains had truly brought in new blood, it wasn't so much of a stretch to tie people together by marriage or second cousins who'd married someone else's brother.

He looked again at the paper in his hands.

STACEY GARDELL <SEE STACEY WAITE>

Perhaps it was time he paid the *Waites* a visit.

The half-full bowl of instant oatmeal slid out of his hands and the meal was ruined.

It wasn't much of a breakfast, but it was something different than eggs or the peanut butter and chicken noodle soup they'd been eating. It wasn't the waste of the food that bothered Jesse so much as the loss of the meal, which was setting up to be a good one, with his wife. She hadn't been exactly talkative since he'd gotten home this morning, but he was sure she was softening. Had that been a hint of a smile he'd seen when he was trying to decide between apple-and-cinnamon flavor or blueberry? He wasn't sure, but he ached to see one—he was used to a Stacey who laughed at every opportunity, but she hadn't smiled once since he'd found her and brought her home.

Now Stacey cried out as hot cereal poured across the thighs of her blue jeans. For a too-long moment Jesse froze, then as she started to rise from her chair he did the only thing he could think of to stop the heat of the mess on her legs—

He snatched up her glass of milk and poured it onto her lap.

It must've done the job because Stacey's yelp of pain cut off in mid-syllable and she sank bank onto her chair. Jesse stood there helplessly while she looked from him to the white and gray goo lumped onto her jeans, then back to him, as though she expected him to say something to make time turn around and reverse this idiocy.

"Well," was the only thing that would come out of his mouth.

She looked like she wanted to say something, but it never materialized.

Instead, she burst into laughter.

Jesse stayed where he was, uncertain about what to do next. Should he try to help clean her up, should he apologize, or should he laugh with her? "I'm sorry," he began. "But you were getting burned—"

"Nice pitch," Stacey gulped, then laughed again.

Jesse could hear an undertone of anxiety in the sound, but at least it was *laughter,* the first he'd heard from her in literally months. He smiled cautiously. "Looks like I hit a homer, huh?"

Stacey's laughter dwindled but a hint of a smile still whispered around her mouth. "Ugh," she said as he offered her a handful of paper towels and she swabbed at herself. "This stuff's soaked all the way through. I can't just change—I'll have to shower before you go to sleep."

"Don't you want some more oatmeal?" Jesse asked innocently. "You didn't eat."

Stacey shook her head. "Sorry, but I think I've lost my appetite for the stuff."

She rose and dropped the wadded-up towels into the bowl, and the movement was so natural that Jesse damned near watched her walk out of the kitchen on her own, almost forgot that she was virtually a prisoner and he was supposed to follow her around. The look she gave him when he did was withering, like the one a teenager would give a meddling parent; to mask his awkwardness, Jesse said, "I'll, uh, get you a set of clean towels." Stacey didn't say anything, but her expression softened a bit and she nodded as he trailed her up the stairs.

Jesse had just finished cleaning the last of the oatmeal from the floor when the doorbell rang.

His heart went into his throat and for a moment he couldn't breathe. It wasn't even nine in the morning—who could it be? The shower was already running, and he didn't think Stacey could hear the doorbell over the sound of the water—he never had—but what if her hearing was more sensitive than his? He wasn't enough of a fool not to realize that years of working in machine shops had deadened his hearing a little.

For the briefest of moments Jesse considered simply ignoring it and hoping that whoever it was would just go away, then in a sudden rush he wiped his hands on another paper towel and hurried to the door before the visitor could press the bell again. There was a peephole in the door but he didn't bother looking through it; the faster he answered, the faster the person would leave. No matter who it was, he wanted to get this over with.

The last thing Jesse expected was a police detective.

In the wake of the oatmeal disaster, he'd forgotten all about Stacey's telephone call last night, but the memory certainly came rushing back as the man on his doorstep held out a gold shield and introduced himself.

"Good morning," he said pleasantly. "Are you Jesse Waite?"

"That's me," Jesse said. He was amazed to hear that the tone of his voice matched that of the detective's: even and calm, the voice of a man on the right side of the law and without a care in the world. "What can I do for you?"

The policeman tucked his identification back into his pocket. "I'm Detective Lucas Conroy." His gaze flicked momentarily over Jesse's shoulder and into the house. "May I come in?"

"Sure." Jesse backed up a couple of steps and held open the door, no hesitation whatsoever, not a thing in the world to hide. "Would you like a cup of coffee or—"

"No, thanks." Conroy stopped just inside the door and Jesse saw the man's sharp gray eyes take in everything, a true professional. He did the same thing, trying to put himself in Conroy's eyes to see what he did: a medium-sized room decorated in a light-handed Early American, some nice touches here and there—Stacey's influence, of course. As far as Jesse could tell, there was nothing incriminating or out of the ordinary. "The reason I'm here, Mr. Waite, is that last evening there was a telephone call made from this address to my private line at the station house. There wasn't any message to speak of, but we have to investigate all calls." Detective Conroy's expression was neutral. "Can you tell me why that call was made?"

"Sure," Jesse said. "My wife did it, but it was a wrong number."

"What number was she dialing?"

"Oh, I have no idea. She's taking a shower right now, but if it's important you can hang around and ask her. But I warn you" —Jesse let a small smile turn up the corner of his mouth—*Man-to-man, you know how women are in the bathroom*—and met the policeman's eyes— "she just got in there, so it could be awhile. You might want me to pour you that cup of coffee, after all."

His heart thudded as the detective glanced around again and looked like he was considering the offer. Jesse gestured toward the kitchen, where both men could see the breakfast dishes still on the table—a couple of bowls and coffee mugs, crumpled paper towels. In the background the sound of the shower still hummed steadily through the plumbing. "I'll clean things up a bit," Jesse offered.

Detective Conroy shook his head. "No, but thanks for the offer." He reached into the breast pocket of his overcoat and pulled out a small, slightly frayed notebook, then flipped through the pages. "One more question, if you don't mind. Do you know a woman named Krystin Parker?"

Jesse blinked, caught off guard for the first time. "Sure," he said again. "She's my wife's aunt."

"Aunt?" Conroy looked as surprised as Jesse had felt.

"Her mother's sister," Jesse explained. "I really don't know her very well—Stacey and I've been married for four years, but we don't see her much. I can give you her address or phone number if you need it." He bit back the obvious question—what did Krystin have to do with anything? He'd read somewhere that the first thing cops look for in guilty people was a tendency to talk too much, to over-explain every detail.

Conroy shook his head again. "That won't be necessary, but thanks." He gave a small polite nod and turned back to the door. "Sorry if I disturbed you."

"Not at all." Jesse turned the knob and opened the door for Conroy. The policeman nodded one more time and stepped outside; Jesse resisted the urge to swing the door shut and lock it, made himself wait a few moments so he wouldn't look overanxious. In the space of that small pause—no more than three seconds—he actually thought the other man was going to change his mind and turn around. Maybe he had more questions, maybe he'd seen something inside that wasn't right and that had just now registered in his mind—the crack in the telephone on the hall table, for instance. Was it visible from the front door?

Apparently not, because the detective seemed to shrug to himself, then continued on his way. Jesse shut the front door almost gently and locked it, then leaned against the inside and took a deep breath. Sweat trickled down the inside of his T-shirt, and chilled by the outside air it felt like a frigid fingernail scratching along the center of his breastbone. He stood there for a long time, trying hard to see himself and his home through the detective's eyes. Had he seemed nervous? Or a little *too* casual? A glance around reassured him, but he still wondered about the telephone in the hallway. Had Conroy stepped inside far enough to see it . . . and perhaps notice the crack along its base from when Stacey had thrown it?

And why on earth had the man asked him about Krystin?

He hadn't spoken to her since Stacey's disappearance, just one more person who'd abandoned him when he most needed support.

He had no idea how long he stood there. He felt frozen with belated terror, suffocated by the paranoid notion that Conroy would suddenly reconsider his answers and find them wanting, turn around and start pounding on the front door, call for backup, do all those other things that the cops on television always did when in hindsight they suddenly recalled the incriminating clue. He waited and the minutes passed, and somewhere in there he realized that the sound of the shower had stopped—Stacey was finished and if Conroy came back now, there was nothing to stop the two of them from meeting.

How long had it been? More than anything Jesse wanted to push the curtain aside and look out the window, see if the detective's car was still outside, if his home was being watched. He didn't dare—it was surely the first indication of guilt when the criminal checked to see if the police were still watching him.

Damn it, Jesse thought. *I am NOT a criminal.*

Determined not to worry any more about it, he pushed away from the door and went back into the kitchen to stack the dishes in the sink.

Well, Conroy thought, there was a supreme waste of time.

He scrunched his shoulders against the January chill, still strong in the unmarked car even though he was nearly back to the station. What had he expected, anyway? People dialed wrong numbers all the time, even to police stations. In any case, had it been a true emergency, the call would have come through 911. The part that bothered him was the Krystin Parker connection, and how the woman's name kept coming up in the oddest places. It might be nothing more than what he'd first assumed—a small town and a small population, and of course lots of people had the same last name—look at the mess he'd be in had Nola Elidad's last name been Smith.

At his desk, grateful to be out of the bitter temperatures, Conroy cracked his knuckles and paged through all the computer searches he'd done over the last few days, trying to put his finger on whatever it was that was eating at him. When he set them all out on the desk and went over them, he knew it was definitely time to talk to Krystin Parker again:

STOWE GARDELL

TRISTA GARDELL <SEE TRISTA NEWMAN>

KRYSTIN PARKER <SEE KRYSTIN POWELL>

STACEY GARDELL <SEE STACEY WAITE>

TAMMY GARDELL

Was the connection between Stowe Gardell and the Waites a coincidence? His acceptance of this was only going to stretch so far, and the rope between the librarian and Nola Elidad was also getting mighty thin, indeed. He turned the names over again in his mind, then put in a few more requests, just to see what turned up:

SEARCH: TAMMY GARDELL

<NO INFORMATION>

Conroy sat back in surprise. No information—what the hell was with these Gardell names? Archived . . . yes, he could accept that even if he didn't like it, but deceased, married, *something* had to turn up on Tammy Gardell. For Christ's sake, the woman's name was right there in his papers—how could the computer say she existed on one screen, then give him nothing on the next?

"Fine," he muttered. "Try this, you bastard."

SEARCH: JESSE WAITE

A minute or two, then:

NAME: JESSE EGAN WAITE

MARITAL STATUS: MARRIED

SPOUSE: STACEY LOREN WAITE

LENGTH OF RESIDENCE AT CURRENT ADDRESS: 4 YEARS

AGE: 27

BIRTH DATE: 4/7/72

DRIVER'S LICENSE #: N155 X358 9654

MOTHER: DECEASED

FATHER: DECEASED

BIRTH CERTIFICATE RECORD NO.: WJE8472-28830071

The computer gave Jesse's address and a few other things, although there didn't seem to be anything out of the ordinary. Other than his wife, the guy seemed to have no family, nor was there anything else remarkable about him.

"Next," Conroy said absently.

SEARCH: STACEY WAITE

Then:

MARITAL STATUS: MARRIED

SPOUSE: JESSE EGAN WAITE

MAIDEN NAME: STACEY LOREN NEWMAN

LENGTH OF RESIDENCE AT CURRENT ADDRESS: 4 YEARS

AGE: 21

BIRTH DATE: 6/18/78

DRIVER'S LICENSE #: W518 8492 S47C2

MOTHER: TRISTA NEWMAN

FATHER: TADD NEWMAN

BIRTH CERTIFICATE RECORD NO.: GS/GT5984-58478278

Nothing much weird there either, except perhaps for the slash between the letters of the birth certificate. Just for giggles, Conroy smacked the birth certificate number into the computer.

<NO INFORMATION>

"Son of a bitch," he said in amazement. "Damned thing did it to me *again*!"

"My, my. Another fight with your computer?"

Dustine's amused voice came over his shoulder and despite his aggravation, Conroy grinned. "Yeah," he said. "It's become my favorite pastime." He turned and saw her smiling, felt his face go pink for absolutely no reason.

Opting for discretion, Dustine decided not to mention it. "So what's the deal?"

Conroy sighed. "It's weird. I mean, everything's supposed to be cross-linked and cross-referenced, and probably cross-glued, for God's sake. But I keep running into dead ends, information that loops around and gives me the same names or, worse, the computer tells me it has 'no information.' "

Dustine's eyebrows lifted, making her dark blue eyes reflect the glow of the overhead fluorescents. "Tell you what," she suggested. "Rather than verbally sparring with it, why don't you just put in an ALL INFORMATION request through records—let them hunt around for you and find that archived stuff."

The detective couldn't help pressing his lips together. "It's just that they take so damned *long*—"

"A couple of days at the most."

"—and if I do it myself—"

"You'll get exactly where you are now."

"I've gotten some information," he protested.

"And made progress," she added blandly.

He peered at her. "Are you laughing at me?"

"Do you see a smile?"

"I think you're laughing inside."

"You're clearly mistaken."

"Would you like to go out again?" he blurted.

"Very much," she said without missing a beat. "I'm free—"

"Tomorrow night?"

This time she did pause. It was barely noticeable, but Conroy was an old hand at reading people. "Or maybe later this week," he added hastily. "I didn't mean to be pushy."

Dustine smiled and seemed to relax a little. "Actually tomorrow would be fine, if you still want to. Same time?"

"Great."

She turned to leave, then paused and glanced back at him. "And I wasn't laughing at you."

Conroy nodded agreeably. "Of course you weren't." She walked away, and he pulled a Records Information form from the drawer and started to fill it out. He'd written in only the first two fields when he heard the unmistakable sound of her giggling as she stepped through the door into the Social Services Room. He kept doggedly writing, determined not to surrender to his own urge to laugh.

And still had to remind himself not to sit there grinning like a fool.

JANUARY 24--FRIDAY

Krystin Parker was apparently out of town for the weekend.

Conroy went by the library but the junior clerk wasn't able to offer much beyond what she'd told him over the phone—

"I'm sorry, but Mrs. Parker doesn't talk much about what she does on her own time. I only know she's gone because I overheard her talking to her husband on the telephone. I think she mentioned Wisconsin."

Wisconsin in January probably meant skiing at one of the little resorts up north, a weekend jaunt to a rented condo or townhouse with a fireplace. He might as well not bother until the work week rolled around. Conroy felt like he was a truck stuck in the mud, spinning and spinning his wheels and getting absolutely nowhere; in the meantime he felt the weight of this case hanging over him like a building thunderstorm. He hadn't been in touch with Alec Elidad because he had nothing to tell the man—no progress, no clues, *nothing*—and Conroy felt absurdly guilty about it. Each day that passed lessened the likelihood that the man's wife would be found alive—this was day nine and the God's honest truth was that he wasn't holding out much in the hope department.

If nothing else, a telephone follow-up on his records request had turned up a couple of reasons for all the weird <NO INFORMATION> responses he'd been getting. The P.D.'s Central Records Department had undergone some sort of massive software switchover and it wasn't going as well as expected. Conroy didn't understand the tech talk—the clerk complained at length about something he termed a Linux O.S. in perfect working condition until "some brain-dead moron got the idea to switch to Windows 2000." The upshot of everything was that some stuff was retrievable, other stuff wasn't; they weren't expecting to have things like birth and death records sorted out until the end of February, and Conroy's records problems might or might not be attributable to the switch—there just wasn't any way to tell.

"That's not acceptable," Conroy said flatly. He was trying to be nice but there was an icy edge to his voice that immediately halted the clerk's rant. "I have a woman missing for nine days now, and I *need* this information. Every hour that goes by is critical."

There was silence on the other end, but the answer, when it came, was the last thing Conroy expected to hear.

"There's nothing I can do," the guy on the telephone said. His voice had lost its bitter, I-hate-my-job tone and he sounded truly apologetic. "I'm sorry. The data is still there—I just can't get it off the system right now. If it's that important, the only thing I can suggest is that you call the County Clerk's Office and see if you can talk someone into going into the storage vaults and personally digging through the records. I hear that with the system down for so long, some of them are actually doing this just so they don't fall so far behind in birth certificate requests."

Conroy hung up feeling more frustrated than he had at nearly any other point in the Elidad case. "Fine," he grumbled to himself. He scanned the printouts again and his eye focused on someone else—Trista Gardell. He didn't have much info on her beyond the fact that her name kept coming up linked to the librarian's. And what about Stowe Gardell—were those two related? It seemed unlikely since the guy had died in 1982, but sometimes, if the information was old enough and there'd been no input—traffic tickets or contact with the police—a piece of information might "age itself out" of the records. This had also happened frequently in the conversion of the handwritten stuff to computer files; before microfiching documents, clerks keying in the data had unilaterally made decisions about whether or not to include information based on whether they thought it was needed or not—another reason that damned <NO INFORMATION> could be turning up. The tech that Conroy had talked to was right: The only way he was going to get the full story was to persuade someone to physically go look for it.

And in the meantime: Trista Gardell.

Conroy reentered the search and asked for the full address, then dialed the number the computer listed and waited, listening to the phone ring on the other end. Two rings, then three, four, and he felt frustration sweep him again as he heard the click of an answering machine take over. When the recorded message was through, Conroy spoke.

"This is Detective Lucas Conroy of the Roselle Police Department," he said evenly. Until he'd started to speak, he'd had no idea what he was going to say; now he decided to reveal as little as possible, only enough to get the woman to call him back. "I'm calling because I'm trying to reach Krystin Parker and I understand she's gone out of town. I need to get some more information on a young woman she hired named Nola Elidad, and I thought you might be able to help me." He gave his name again then recited his telephone number—twice—and there was nothing left to do but hang up and hope she called back.

In the meantime, Conroy got things going with one of

the records retrieval clerks. His dentist, whom he'd been seeing for decades and who never seemed to age, had once fired the just-as-timeless "You get more flies with honey than salt!" cliché at him when he'd come in cranky because of a broken filling. While he still felt his irritation had been justified, it had taken that sharp reminder from an old man to really sink it in, and Conroy had remembered the advice ever since. He was pleasant to everyone with whom he worked, whether or not he felt like it, whether or not he got two hours of sleep or ten, and even if he stepped in dog crap on the way to work. His reward was that the elderly woman in Records, Mrs. Peterson, now felt compelled to put out a little more than the ordinary effort for the nice young detective who never missed saying good morning when he walked past her each day. She had, she told him, some report deadlines to meet, but she would definitely give his request for these records, whether they were archived or needed manual retrieval, her personal attention. As she archly told him, "There is no such thing as 'no information,' Detective Conroy. That's just what these abominable computers claim."

In the meantime, though, Conroy had no choice but to wait, frustrated nearly out of his mind without the elusive histories of Stowe Gardell, Nola Gardell, Tammy Gardell, Stacey Waite, and, when he went back and tried another search, Marlo Frayne's second dead husband and Nola's stepfather, Charles Frayne. They were all secondary characters anyway, nothing more than extra cards in the hand he'd been dealt; the real prize was Nola Elidad, formerly Nola Gardell . . . who, at least on paper, almost hadn't existed before her marriage to Alec Elidad.

More banging on the computer, a growing list of names and scratch-outs and sloppy question marks. When the telephone on his desk rang, it startled Conroy enough that he dropped his pen, then had to fight to keep the telephone cord from winding around his neck when he tried to pick it up and answer the phone at the same time.

"Detective Conroy?" Mrs. Peterson's slightly high-pitched voice asked. "Is that you?"

"Yes," he assured her. "I just . . . dropped the telephone. Did you find something?"

"Not much just yet, but I did come across something I thought was unusual. I thought I would tell you about it before I continued the hunt." She sounded absolutely delighted with herself, as though someone had pinned an honorary gold badge on her.

"Great," Conroy said. "What did you discover?"

"Nothing yet on . . ." There was a pause as she apparently consulted her notes. "Nola or Tammy Gardell. But I did find a placeholder," she said smugly.

He waited, but the elderly woman didn't say anything else. "And what is that, Mrs. Peterson? What does it mean?"

"Why, it means that someone physically took those files out of the storage area," she told him. Now there was a conspiratorial tone to her voice; clearly she saw herself as his partner in the case. Conroy caught himself before he could sigh out loud. "The only thing they left was a piece of cardboard with a sign-out date on it—whoever took the files didn't bother to fill in the name section. Very sloppy." She made a tsking sound, then continued. "I can't imagine why—updating or something—but they may have very well removed the computer files as well. Perhaps that's why you can't find anything."

Conroy rubbed his eyes. "And which records did you say they took?"

"I didn't, Detective." Her voice sharpened, as though chiding him for talking down to her. "But now that you asked, they took Stacey Waite's records. There's nothing but a big old empty spot where they used to be."

Conroy frowned. "I see. Did you happen to get the date on that, what was it, placeholder?"

"Of course," Mrs. Peterson said primly. "September eleventh."

"Ah." He was silent for a moment. Finally, because he knew she was waiting, he spoke. "Great job, Mrs. Peterson. Keep up the good work."

"We're getting there."

"Definitely," he agreed. "Thank you."

He hung up and wrote the September date next to Stacey Waite's name, even though it meant nothing to him at this point. He stared at it for awhile, then shook his head at his own idiocy; he'd get nowhere by making himself nuts over it. Sometimes you had to back away from the facts and the statistics and the statements, get some air and clear your head just so something that was probably already there could find its way to the surface. That's what he needed to do—he'd been staring at this stuff for so long that his eyesight was starting to blur. Lunch, he decided, that was the answer. He'd get something to eat and try not to think about this case for an hour. Who knows what could stir up in the meantime.

Nothing stirred, but Conroy could've kicked himself when he got back and found his message indicator blinking. As luck would have it, he'd missed Trista Newman's call. Then again, listening to her voice on the machine gave him the clear impression that she probably didn't care to speak with him anyway:

"Detective Conroy, this is Trista Newman returning your call. You left a message asking about my sister Krystin and someone she hired at the library. I don't know anything about her work practices and I don't understand why you would even be asking me; therefore she's the one you need to speak with about this. Since I don't have a number where she can be disturbed this weekend, obviously you'll have to call her when she returns."

Conroy didn't miss the *clang* on the tape as the phone was slammed down, nor did he fail to note the use of the phrase "where she can be disturbed" as opposed to "where she can be reached." Cracking his knuckles absently, he sat back and listened to the message a couple of more times, but he always came away with that same impression, the one that said *Why in God's name are you bothering ME about this?* While he was still hearing alarm bells about Krystin

Parker, he'd have bet his next paycheck that Trista Newman didn't even know Nola Elidad existed.

So Trista was right: There was nothing for him to do but wait.

When Dustine opened the door, Lucas Conroy was standing there holding out a bouquet of daisies. They'd obviously come from a grocery store—he'd forgotten to take off the price sticker—and he looked nervous and completely out of place clutching at the plastic-wrapped flowers. It was endearing and funny all at the same time, and she took the flowers with a grin that widened when he stumbled over the clearly prerehearsed greeting.

"Ta-da," he said, doing his best to be gallant. "I bought—brought these for you. Well, I mean, I *bought* them, too, but . . ."

"Thank you," she said quickly, afraid his next words would be an assurance that he really had paid for them. He followed her to the kitchen and took off his coat, watching while she found a vase, then set the arrangement in the middle of the dining room table. "They're lovely," Dustine said solemnly. "Pima thanks you, too."

He blinked. "The cat?"

She nodded. "The minute we leave, she's going to eat at least two of them."

Lucas laughed, and Dustine was gratified to see him relax a bit. He looked as handsome as ever—and let's be truthful, she'd been "noticing" him awhile—but tired, as if whatever he was working on was working on him at the same time. There were shadows beneath his crystalline gray eyes that the silvery blonde of his hair only seemed to intensify, and had he lost a bit of weight? Dustine gave herself a mental smack—stop it right now, Miss Mom.

"You look really nice," he said, motioning at the burgundy patterned sweater and black slacks she wore.

"Thanks." Dustine almost laughed again—he was *so* trying to be the perfect date. "So what are we doing?" she asked. "Any ideas yet, or are we still in the winging-it stage?"

"Movie?" he suggested. He reached inside his jacket and unfolded a movie listing he'd torn from the newspaper. He spread it out on the counter and she stepped closer to him to see it, scanning the listings with him. "See anything interesting?"

"Well . . ." She hesitated.

"Come on," he prompted. "Something caught your eye—spill it."

"This one." Her finger poked at something down at the bottom.

He chuckled. "*The Matrix* at the local dollar theater?"

Dustine smiled. "I know, but it's the best thing out there. And I'll even admit that I saw it when it first came out, but I'd love to see it again. It's about a world where the people aren't really—"

"—living in the world they think they are," he finished for her.

"Oh. You've seen it, too."

He nodded, then glanced at the listings again before checking his watch. "It's a two-and-a-half-hour movie. We can just make the seven-thirty showing and have popcorn as an appetizer, then get something real to eat afterward. What do you think?"

Dustine felt like she was grinning from ear to ear. "I think it's marvelous."

They turned away from the counter at the same time and nearly bumped foreheads. She jumped a little and he reached out to steady her, and she caught herself before it happened, slammed a lid down on her reflexes before she could instinctively jerk away and, probably, offend him. For a very short moment, she thought he might try to kiss her, and she nearly panicked. I *want* him to be here, she reminded herself sharply. It's all *right—he's* all right.

"Oops," he said with a smile. "Almost knocked each other out."

She laughed lightly, but even she heard the tinge of anxiety in her voice. Her upper lip suddenly felt like she had a line of perspiration along it. "Round one?"

"Goes to you," Lucas said, and she had to give it to him for not pushing things too soon. When his hand dropped back to his side her breathing eased, and she damned herself because it was always like this when she started dating someone new—not that there had been a whole lot of "new" in her life since the brutal rape she'd endured in high school. A wonderful thing, counseling, but it hadn't been able to take her over that last hurdle, the one that would allow her to let down her guard when she found someone in whom she was truly interested; it was like scaling a damned mountain every time. The curved scar on her left breast suddenly throbbed, a short, hot jab, as if to remind her of her own dark history.

"Ready?" Lucas asked gently.

Dustine swallowed and nodded gamely, went to get her coat as he plucked his off the couch and shrugged back into it. She could see the curiosity in his eyes—reading what was in a person's head and heart was part of her job—but also the rigid self-control, a cop's determination that the job's inquisitiveness would not get the best of him and poke into where it shouldn't when he was off the time clock, a seasoned detective's inbred knowledge of when and where *not* to ask. When she came back, he helped her into her coat and hardly touched her at all, as though he knew a red flag had gone off somewhere.

The ride to the movie theater, silent except for directions, was awkward and left Dustine edgy and despondent. She liked Lucas Conroy, much more than anyone in whom she'd been interested before, yet she couldn't deny that this date seemed destined to end the same way as a dozen ones before it had—after an uncomfortable couple of hours, Lucas would say good night and, if he were the more honest type, he wouldn't bother to lie about calling her in the future. She had so wanted it to be different, but what could she do but wait it out and live with the results.

At the theater, she pulled three dollars out of her purse before Lucas could protest and handed it to the teenager inside the booth. "My treat," she said as lightly as she could. The kid didn't comment, didn't even look up as he punched a button and two tickets spun out of a slot on the counter. So much for humor.

Without warning, Lucas reached past her and knocked on the window. "Excuse me," he said loudly, then Dustine realized he had his badge out and pressed against the glass. "Are you awake in there?"

"Lucas," she said, "what are you—"

"Either I look like a cheap date or this woman just tried to bribe me, and I need a witness to decide which it is," he continued. "Tell me everything you just saw."

Dustine stared at him as the teenager's jaw dropped open in confusion. *"Lucas—"*

"C'mon, kid," he insisted, and Dustine realized that as ridiculous as he sounded, there was nothing harsh or mean in his voice. A little on the loud side to get past whatever internal monologue was going through the teenaged boy's brain, but also exaggerated enough to be unmistakably all in fun. "Cheap date or cop getting bribed. You choose."

The kid blinked and shook a not-very-clean clump of bangs off one eyebrow as an almost sly smile tugged at one corner of his face. He studied Lucas for a moment, then his gaze cut to Dustine—quick up and down—before he spoke.

"Cheap date. Sorry."

"Damn," Lucas said heartily. Dustine tried to say something but she didn't know what, and he took her by the elbow and steered her inside. "Guess that means *I* have to buy the appetizers."

Dustine finally found her voice. "Lucas, I can't believe you did that!"

"What?" he asked with the utmost innocence. "All I did was ask a question. It's what I do. I'm a detective, remember?" She let him guide her to the counter, amazed at his audacity even as he still refused to meet her eyes. When he spoke, he acted as if nothing at all had happened.

"Buttered or plain, what size, and would you like anything to drink?"

....

"I'm full of popcorn and tortilla chips," she protested. "I can't possibly eat this much food."

"Trust me," Lucas said. They were at a home-style Mexican restaurant in Roselle called La Hacienda, and the place was crowded and pleasantly noisy. "You'll eat them. You have *never* tasted tacos like this. And"—he leaned a little closer across a plastic tablecloth decorated with brightly colored tropical flowers—"you won't forget them either. In fact, when we leave your clothes will even smell a little like the kitchen."

"What!"

He laughed. "It's the price you pay for the best Mexican food anywhere."

Dustine eyed the platter before her and shook her head. Well, maybe she was still a little hungry, but three of these tacos could feed her for two meals. There was a rich, almost wine-sauce aroma coming from her shredded beef selection, and the chicken tacos Lucas had chosen, the meat obviously simmered in a different sort of sauce, smelled just as good.

"One of each," he coaxed. "Two tacos isn't a lot to ask."

"You make it sound like I'm a hospital patient who has to be persuaded to eat."

He grinned. "You're not sick, just deprived. You'll see."

"And if I *don't* think these tacos are the best I've ever tasted?"

His eyebrows shot up. "If you—why, then I'll . . ." He glanced around the restaurant. "I'll eat five whole jalapeño peppers at once."

She sat back and regarded him. "You like them, don't you? Or maybe you're just nuts."

"Yeah," he admitted. "I do like them. But not *that* much. And I don't think it's polite to ask about a man's mental condition when he's betting his taste buds on something."

Dustine snickered and started to reach for her margarita. "Oh, come on," he complained. "The suspense is killing me—my mouth has to know if these are its last moments!"

"Fine," Dustine said. She put down the drink and fiddled with her napkin, picked up her fork and tucked a bit of lettuce and rice into the first taco, then pushed some more rice around on her plate. Across from her, Lucas made a sound in his throat and she giggled, then finally relented and picked up the taco. Two bites later she had to admit that he was right—the beef was rich and heavy with flavor, melt-in-your-mouth tender. Still, she would play this out a little longer—

"Don't try it," Lucas said, amused. "It's all over your face."

Dustine laughed, a little annoyed at herself for being so obvious, but enjoying the fun. "Okay," she finally agreed. "It's true—these *are* the best tacos I've ever tasted."

"Rats, I should've made you bet something, too. I must be slipping."

"Old age," she said without looking up.

"I knew it was only a matter of time."

She glanced at him and saw him scowling comically at his tacos and she burst into laughter. He grinned then took an enormous bite, leaving her to shake her head as she watched him try to catch the food squeezing out of the other end of the soft tortilla. The stiffness and the sense of doom that she'd been feeling were gone, disintegrated by that ridiculous act back at the theater. The movie had been just as good as she remembered—actually better the second time around, when she could sit back and prepare herself for the high special effects parts, the main reason she loved science fiction movies. Maybe things would be better this time, but she wouldn't, *couldn't* let herself hope for too much.

Yet the rest of the meal went just as well, and finally they faced each other across the empty plates—God, had she really eaten all three tacos?—and ordered a second, and final, round of margaritas.

"You know," Lucas said, "I don't really know what you do, except that you don't drive a beat car."

"I work in victim counseling," she said.

"Ah." Lucas sat back. "We find the pieces and you try to put them back together."

Dustine smiled. "An interesting way of looking at it, but I suppose that fits."

"Do you like it?"

"It . . . has its rewards." He was watching her, his gray eyes intense and unreadable, their color a high contrast to the deep blue sweater he was wearing. She could imagine most women being uncomfortable under that miss-nothing gaze, but she had faced a lot worse across the desk in her office. "And its failures."

"Learning experiences," Conroy said. "Nothing is ever a failure if it makes you able to do better the next time."

"Well, you do try to tell yourself that." Maybe it was the little bit of alcohol she'd had, or simply the fact that she was so stuffed with food she just couldn't think fast enough to make up anything to get anxious over, but the silence that followed felt a little more comfortable than it had earlier in thc cvcning.

Finally, Lucas spoke, his voice punctuated by the nervous cracking of his knuckles. "Is your caseload busy right now?"

Dustine tilted her head. "It's not too bad. A couple of domestic violence cases, one rape. The truth is I end up helping a lot with the paperwork end of case processing. Why?"

"I've got this case," he told her, then smiled a little. "I'm sure that's a big surprise." She said nothing, just waited. "The one I've been digging through records on—thanks for your help on that, by the way. There's someone in Records hunting stuff down for me."

She nodded. "What else can I do?"

"The man's wife is missing," Lucas said quietly. "She's been gone for almost ten days now, and while I can't tell him this, of course, I don't believe for a minute that we're going to find her alive. It's just been too long."

"And you don't think she left on her own?"

Lucas shook his head. "No. There was a witness who saw a woman arguing with a man, then being dragged into his car."

"License plate?

Lucas pressed his lips together, "Nope. He thought

it was a family thing, an argument. It was in the Pik-Kwik parking lot and he was busy checking people out at the register."

"Self-imposed blinders," Dustine said. She was surprised at the old bitterness in her voice and lifted her drink to her lips in a vain attempt to cover it.

But Lucas missed nothing. "I bet you see that a lot."

"I've come across it before," she replied with more stiffness than she intended. She forced herself to relax, to reach for the comfort level she'd felt only a few minutes earlier. She didn't quite make it, but she was close, and that was something. "Do you want me to talk to him?"

Lucas nodded. "It would be a big help. He's rather high-strung, and I can't even imagine what he's going through. If he could talk to someone with experience, like you, it might make things easier."

"Bearable," Dustine said solemnly. "Never easy."

"Right," Lucas acknowledged. "Bearable. I'll get you his number tomorrow?" She nodded as he began gathering their coats. "Ready to head out?"

"Sure. I feel like a horse that got into the granary—faced with way too much food and I didn't have the sense to stop. I'm going to explode at any moment."

The ride back to her townhouse was quiet, but it had lost the self-consciousness of earlier. For a Friday night, the streets were nearly deserted, the cold and the dark making people prefer the warmth and comfort of their homes to entertainment. Lucas turned into her driveway, then came around and opened the door for her; the street in front of the townhouse was barely lit and his eyes, that wonderful shade of gray, picked up the glow from the occasional garage light and looked luminous and slightly scary, like a wolf's picking up the shine of the moon.

When they were at her front door, Dustine hesitated. "Would you . . . would you like to come in?" Even though she'd wanted to extend the invitation, it had taken an immense amount of effort to say the words.

Lucas searched her face. "Yes, very much. But I'm not sure I should." She blinked, trying to understand, then was caught off guard when he reached up and brushed her cheek. In the frigid winter air, his fingers were warm and dry. "There's something going on in your head that I don't know about," he continued. "I don't know what, and I don't want to push. But I'm willing to wait it out."

Dustine took a deep breath. "Come in," she said. "And I'll try to tell you about it."

"Two boys," she said. She wouldn't—*couldn't* look at him, and so she stared at her mug of herbal tea instead, tracing the pattern of the ridiculous stoneware cat face with her fingernail. "I was a senior at Harmony High and it's a small rural town, so I used to walk home. They caught me on the road just outside the town limits and dragged me into the woods. They did it because I was a girl and I wanted to be a cop, and they were two good ol' southern boys who decided it was up to them to remind me of my place in the scheme of things." Lucas didn't say anything and she risked a glance at him; across the table, his face was white and grim, his eyes even more unsettling than before. For some reason, that didn't bother her—no one with a gaze like that, full of concentrated interest, could lull a person into dropping her guard. It was almost like a brutal announcement of honesty.

"When I got home, my parents and my brother Jack didn't believe me. My mother told me to go clean myself up and she never mentioned it again, and I could tell that Jack and my dad just thought I deserved it. Once, Jack damned near said so in an argument with me." Lucas still didn't say anything, but there was no sense of his judging her. He was just letting her talk it out, tell him the parts she was ready for him to know; it was a strange thing, to reveal to a man this deepest, darkest secret of hers, this ugly hidden child that only a counselor in college had ever seen. "They tried to catch me alone again, but I got very good at staying away from them. I went on to college and took additional self-defense classes before passing the Chicago police exam and enrolling in the police academy."

"Were they ever punished?" It was the only time Lucas had spoken since she began her story, and Dustine almost didn't answer. But finally . . .

"Yes," she whispered.

"You did it," he said quietly.

She nodded and felt tears sting her eyes over the memory, old but never dulled by time, as fresh and agonizing as the deep bite wound on her breast had been the day she'd gotten it. But she would not be ashamed of what had happened, or of what she had done three years after.

"The same two, older but still stupid, and I let them think that I felt safe and didn't notice when they shadowed me the whole time, waiting for the chance to catch me alone. By then I was almost ready to graduate from the academy." She waited for him to ask what happened, but he didn't; she told him anyway. "I broke one guy's nose and cheekbone and snapped his knee, and fractured three ribs and the right wrist on the other one. Left them lying in the parking lot by the back entrance of the department store I'd stopped by, then made an anonymous call from the pay phone to the cops and reported a mugging." She looked at her hands, and still, after all these years, was vaguely surprised at the violence that had exploded from them that night. "They told the police and everyone else that they'd been attacked by out-of-towners. I . . . could have killed them, Lucas." Her voice dropped to a whisper again. "So easily."

"But you didn't," he said. "As much as you probably wanted to, you didn't." She couldn't deny the accuracy of his words as he leaned toward her. Still, he didn't touch her. "And that, Dusty, says more about you than anything else."

As serious as their conversation was, she had to smile when he said "Dusty." Only one other person in her life had ever called her that, her former college roommate and best friend, Hilary Oswin.

"And so now you're a victims' counselor yourself," Lucas said. "And I'd bet you're awfully good at it."

"I went back to school to specialize in it. I do the best I can," Dustine said. "Most times I never see the result, or whether in the long run it helps or not—the people move on with their lives, for better or worse, and leave the bad part, including me, behind."

Lucas nodded and they sat there for several minutes in companionable silence. She felt quiet and comfortable, glad that he wasn't trying to pep-talk her and drag out details that she didn't—and never would—want to reveal. The violence and humiliation she'd endured would just never be the sort of thing that would bring a man and woman closer together and, like those she'd counseled, she wanted nothing more than to relegate them to the realm of forgotten bad dreams. She wasn't sure she was ready to go beyond that either, and let's face it: There wasn't much to tell about the two failed relationships since or how most of her college classmates had assumed she was gay because her best friend was a lesbian. In some ways, she used the way people let appearances judge for them. It kept them away, especially the horny college boys, in much the same way that her two rapists had used her feminine appearance—the same old Dustine Curtis as in high school—to assume she was an easy victim for a repeat rape.

"Would you like more tea?" she asked suddenly. "I have—"

Lucas shook his head before she could finish. "Thanks anyway. I really should be going." He stood at the same time she did and took his own mug to the sink, then stepped out of the way before getting into that infamous "personal space" area. She got his coat from the front hall and he pulled it on, turned up the collar and grinned. "I think I'm going to buy a parka."

Dustine chuckled, then grew serious again. "Lucas, I'm sorry if I went too far. I . . . really didn't mean to lay so much on you tonight. I wouldn't blame you if you wanted to keep your distance, and if that's what you want, I promise that working together won't make this into a problem."

He studied her for a moment as he tucked a scarf around his neck before buttoning up. "You don't usually find something worthwhile when you take the easy way out. If it's okay with you, I think going out again is definitely worthwhile."

She hoped she didn't look silly standing there with a huge smile on her face as he gave her a brief hug, then left.

....

The story that Dustine had told him was both heartbreaking and infuriating. What the attack had done to her emotionally was incomprehensible to Conroy, even though he'd seen the results dozens of times over the course of his career. As a man who cared about her and wanted to get to know her further, as a *cop*, it made him livid to think that those two had gone free; while Dustine had been able to mete out her own form of punishment, it wasn't enough—rapists belonged in prison, not walking the streets where they might one day decide that some other woman was not quite so formidable a target.

Be that as it may, he was a decade and a thousand miles removed from what had happened to her, and while he truly wanted to fix it, he couldn't. As she had done so admirably since high school, Dustine would have to deal with it on her own. He'd gotten the sense that the rape had caused problems in her past, and now he felt honored that she had trusted him with something so personal; he also felt humbled by the unseen strength he knew must be present in that lovely woman.

Driving east on Irving Park Road, Conroy glanced at his watch—ten-thirty—tapped the steering wheel thoughtfully, then made a quick decision. Friday night but not that late, at least for a weekend; he had no particular reason to do it, but he'd go over there and see what was what. If the lights were off, he'd try another time. It would only be a short trip out of his way to stop by Jesse and Stacey Waite's townhouse, and he couldn't shake the nagging feeling that the Waite, Parker, and Frayne families were somehow connected. It might turn out to be only by marriage—a bond via the sister's-cousin's-third-husband kind of thing, but it was there somewhere; tomorrow he was determined to lay it all out and find the common thread.

Tonight, however, when he steered his Maxima to the curb, Conroy saw only a faint light burning in the Waite household, its glow visible via a row of small, horizontal windows across the top of the door. He was pulling his notebook out of the glove compartment and starting to go over what he'd scribbled in it about the Waites when out of his peripheral vision he saw the light go out. An instant later the door to the townhouse opened and Jesse Waite stepped outside, then turned and locked the door behind him. So much for advance preparation.

Conroy stepped out of his car and closed the door. Jesse Waite jumped a little at the sound, but when he saw who it was he stopped and waited for Conroy to catch up. "Evening, Mr. Waite," he said pleasantly. "I'm Detective Conroy, remember?"

"Sure," Jesse said easily. "Is there something else you needed? I don't mean to rush you, but I'm on my way to work."

Conroy nodded. "Then I won't keep you. I just had another question or two, and I wondered if I might talk to your wife—" He flipped open his notebook, as if he were looking for the name.

"Stacey," Jesse offered.

"Right."

"Well, she's already gone to bed," Jesse said doubtfully, and glanced at his watch. "If it's important, I guess you could wake her up. I have to tell you though, I can't be late for work. I just started this job Monday night."

"Ah," Conroy said. He couldn't argue with that. "I guess I'll talk to your wife some other time. Where is it you work?"

"MC Tooling in Bensenville." Jesse frowned slightly. "Detective, what's this all about? I mean, this is the second time you've stopped by—there must be some reason for it."

Conroy started to answer, then realized he couldn't—he simply didn't have a satisfactory explanation. A telephone call, Krystin Parker, Trista Newman—he knew they were linked to Nola Elidad somehow, but he couldn't quite fit it all together just yet. Rather than reply, he sidestepped. "I think I asked you about Trista Newman," he told Jesse instead. "I—"

"No," Jesse interrupted. "You asked about Krystin Parker. My wife's aunt."

The guy was sharp, Conroy thought. "Right," he said. "So you know Trista Newman, too?"

"She's my mother-in-law, Detective. Krystin Parker is my wife's aunt, and Trista is my wife's mother. Like I said, I haven't talked to her in some time." Now there was a hint of impatience in Jesse Waite's voice and Conroy saw the man's gaze flick to his watch.

"And your wife, has she talked to her mother?"

Now Jesse frowned. "I assume so. Has Trista gotten in some trouble?"

Conroy shook his head. Time to back off. "No, of course not. I was just curious." He made a show of looking at his own watch to let Jesse know that he was aware of the time. "I won't keep you, Mr. Waite. Thanks for your time."

"Sure," Jesse said. "Take it easy." He walked away and Conroy watched him stroll to an old blue Impala.

"Just one more thing, if you don't mind," Conroy called at the last instant. Jesse was climbing into the car and he stopped with the door open and looked back in Conroy's direction. Conroy stepped to where he could see Jesse Waite's features in the yellowish glow cast by one of the streetlights.

"Do you know a woman named Nola Elidad?"

"No," Jesse answered. His expression stayed the same—not so much as the twitch of an eyebrow. "Should I?"

Conroy didn't say one way or the other. "Thanks for your time," he said. Jesse nodded and closed the door; a moment later the engine of the Impala hummed to life, surprisingly quiet for such an early model. Jesse let it warm up for about thirty seconds, then pulled away; Conroy heard him coaxing the accelerator to keep it running in the ten-degree air—had Conroy not delayed him, he probably would have allowed the car to warm up a bit more.

Conroy walked back to his Maxima and sat inside for awhile, warm air blowing around him from the heater while he turned over the facts and names in his head. As much as he tried, he couldn't tie them together enough to justify waking up Stacey Waite in the middle of the night—hell, he hadn't had enough to excuse nearly making Jesse Waite late for his new job.

Still, Conroy couldn't shake the feeling that, as with Marlo Frayne, there was something dark and not quite right just below the surface of this creek, and that he was blindly stepping over it as he crossed.

JANUARY 25--SATURDAY

Had Jesse always worked nights?

She didn't think so. He didn't act as if he had; he didn't treat her as if he had. Nola had once met a woman at the library who worked the graveyard shift at the IHOP up in Hanover Park, and she'd told Nola that she slept on a sort of swing shift schedule—three or four hours when she got home in the morning, then another three or four before she went back to work. That way, she'd said, she could still have a normal life in the daytime like everyone else. Nola wished Jesse would divide his sleep like that. It would be so much easier to deal with the shorter periods of inactivity than the massive stretch of time that his working and then sleeping left her to face. Maybe it was something she could bring up. It would mean a substantial adjustment on his part, but he seemed to want to please her—

And if he did change his schedule?

Would it be any easier for her to face him—would it somehow make it *easier* for her to live with her own personal kidnapper?

She ran her fingers through her hair, then stared at her reflection in the dresser's mirror, where in one corner the fuzzy photograph still hung. Pushed off to one end of the hutch was the shoe box full of wedding photographs, and she'd gone through them every night after Jesse left for work. She *had* to look, had to hunt dutifully for that one item, that trigger, that would reveal to Jesse the truth about who she wasn't in his life.

But it was a clue she was becoming more and more convinced didn't exist.

I haven't been beaten, she thought for the hundredth time. Or raped. Or murdered.

But I haven't been found, either.

Why on earth hadn't someone noticed she was gone—hadn't *Alec* done anything more about it? She'd done her part by calling that number in the paper, and so what if she hadn't been able to leave a coherent message—they should've used caller ID to trace her location. For God's sake, Jesse had forced a woman into his house—surely someone had seen. Why hadn't anyone called the police?

The answer, whether or not she wanted to face it, might be right in front of her.

"No," Nola said out loud. *"No."*

Perhaps it was because Jesse Waite was *supposed* to have a woman—a *wife*—here.

"It's not me," Nola said grimly. Her voice had a strange echo to it in the silent bedroom, a desperate sound that didn't seem to belong to the white-faced woman in the mirror. If there was a woman in Jesse's life, a wife named Stacey as he claimed, then something had happened to her—maybe Jesse had even killed her.

Another *no,* this time unspoken. Nola just couldn't believe that—she didn't know why, but she couldn't. Despite everything he'd done, she would never be convinced that Jesse Waite was a murderer. She had seen him and she had felt his touch—both rough and gentle—and such a thing just wasn't inside his soul.

So no one questioned her presence here, but Jesse presumably hadn't done away with his spouse.

Which opened up an entirely new realm of possibility.

"No," Nola said again, and this time she could hear the faintest edge of panic in her voice, like the cry of a child too tired to dog-paddle back to the edge of the pool.

After all she had endured, after all the time that had passed and all the *nothing* that had been done to find and rescue her, Nola couldn't help but finally ask herself those crucial questions, the ones she'd danced so carefully around in her head time and time again:

What if his missing wife wasn't missing at all?

And what if Jesse Waite's wife was . . . Nola herself?

She swallowed and scrubbed at her eyes with her hands, pushing on them until they hurt and she saw gold specks spread across the darkness behind her eyelids. A useless effort, because when she opened her eyes, the dreaded box of wedding photographs was still there, like a box of undeniable evidence against her. But it wasn't just that—photographs could be doctored, and while Jesse didn't seem like a computer whiz, he could very well have friends who knew how to monkey around with image software. There was so much *more* for her brain to deal with here, so many coincidences—if this was an act, then Jesse was far, far better than anyone Nola had ever seen in the movies. He talked constantly of the things "they" had once done together, of his hopes and dreams for their future, of the plans that she had supposedly made for their lives. Except for that first terrifying twenty-four hours, everything Jesse had done had been for her benefit and comfort and safety while she "mended," and where Nola couldn't see eye to eye with him about that, she could at least see how he could *think* it was so. He'd done everything he could to make her happy short of letting her go free.

She started to reach for the box of photographs, then pulled back and sat on the edge of the bed again, staring first at it, then at the silent television screen. Each day that passed made her mind more and more like that—full of big spots as blank and gray as the screen. The more she dealt with Jesse, the more she talked to him and lived with him, the more quickly everything else—Alec!—faded.

What if Jesse was right and there really was something wrong with her, some leftover crisscross in her mental circuits courtesy of a miscarriage and an illness she couldn't remember? Except for her constant state of indecision and her low-level mistrust of Jesse, she felt fine, totally healthy, but such a thing wasn't unheard of. Because really, how much of what was going on around her and what was missing from her memory could she continue to explain away? For God's sake, wouldn't a lifetime of memories take more than just a few weeks to eliminate?

I want to go home, she thought. I want to go to Alec.

But there was something missing from her need to do so, something essential like the razored edge of urgency she'd had even as early as the night before.

Because, God forgive her, Nola couldn't remember his face.

She heard Jesse's car as he drove past the townhouse, then pulled into a parking spot. Heard was, perhaps, the wrong word; the car was quiet—she remembered that much about it—and insulated as she was by the walls of the townhouse, the idea that the engine made enough noise for Nola to make it out was ludicrous.

Nevertheless, she knew without fail exactly when he would walk in every work night. It was, she thought without a bit of humor, a lot like an animal that waits dutifully at the door for its master's return, a sort of subconscious discernment of his approach, or maybe a higher-pitched sound wave than she was even aware she could hear. Whatever it was—sound, timing, premonition—Nola was on her feet and already straining to hear the sound of Jesse's key as it turned in the lock of the front door. As he came inside she listened to the thump of his work boots and, as it had been ever since she'd been here, her stomach did a little roller-coaster drop at the thought of seeing the man who had abducted her.

Still, there was something else, something that she recognized in an offhand way as vaguely dangerous: a nebulous sense of acceptance, of *surrender*. She wanted to resist, she *did* . . . but she was so *tired* of fighting him at every turn, of struggling against the seemingly never-ending pieces of what was supposed to be her own life that he kept offering. And when he opened the door to the bedroom and Nola saw the exhaustion in his eyes, she felt no victory, just a deep, sudden sense of shame for her behavior and pity for how hard he'd worked and what he'd gotten in return for it.

"Hi," he said, in a game attempt to sound lively. "Ready for some breakfast?"

Nola started to decline, then realized that she was hungrier than she could recall being since he'd brought her here. Jesse's shoulders were slumped and his face was streaked with grime from the shop; the dirt and dust had settled into the laugh lines around his eyes to make him look older, more fragile than she knew he was. Nola felt for him, for how hard he'd tried in almost every aspect—her, his job, life in general. And what had she done to repay his efforts?

The fear was still there, yes, but now it was undercut with a shadow of doubt. As Nola stared at Jesse, she realized that Alec's face, only a few months strong in her memory to begin with, had blurred so badly that it could have easily been him with her in the blurred photo on the mirror, a faceless person, like a background extra in some badly shot black-and-white film.

And here he was, still trying so hard to be kind and understanding, *patient* with her, blinding himself to the fact that she had resisted him on every level, contradicted or disagreed with everything he'd said. It must be hard, she thought suddenly, to convince someone of something she doesn't want to believe—whether or not it's true.

"I'll fix breakfast," she said.

Jesse's eyes widened, then he must've clamped a lid on the part of himself that wanted to show surprise. His tired features smoothed over and he nodded. "Great."

She didn't really know what else to say, so she stepped past him and headed toward the kitchen. He followed without speaking, then settled onto a chair at the table and watched her move around the room. It was another no-frills breakfast, bought with the money Jesse had borrowed from her purse: a little skillet of sausages, pancakes from a mix topped by margarine and inexpensive syrup.

She'd never been good at this to begin with, and what few skills she had were rusty at best, made worse by the self-consciousness brought on by him watching her. Still, she felt unaccountably comfortable in what should have been a stranger's kitchen, moving from counter to counter, finding everything she needed in the drawers and cabinets with barely a second thought. In one way, it seemed the pancakes took forever to cook; in another, everything was ready in minutes and she was sitting across from Jesse and waiting for his reaction as he took his first bite.

"This is good," he said simply. "Thanks for fixing it."

She nodded, feeling awkward and pleased at the same time, then just picked at her own plate of food. She couldn't help noticing how tired Jesse looked; usually he showered before fixing breakfast for them both, and she was surprised to see him this way—proof of the long, hard hours he worked, ostensibly so that they could have a life together, doing it on a shift that few people wanted to deal with. He did this all while she stayed home and did basically nothing—she didn't clean or cook, or even run errands. She slept and showered, watched television, and read a lot. In short, she had contributed nothing to this household beyond the few dollars in her purse.

Did she belong here? She wasn't sure she did . . . but she was no longer sure she didn't. Yes, she'd seen Jesse fix meals in this room over a dozen times, but was that enough to make her so sure of herself when she did the same? Nola couldn't deny that she'd had a chance, just for a few moments, to snag a weapon, one of the sharp knives from the silverware drawer. Yet the thought of facing down with Jesse, of hurting him so badly, had horrified her, and she'd abandoned the impulse as soon as it had flared. He had done nothing to really hurt her, and she *had* to believe there was a better way for her to resolve this situation.

She just had to.

Jesse ate the pancakes, every bit of them, even though Stacey's cooking wasn't as good as he remembered. It was as if her time away and her memory lapse had eroded that part of her too, chipping away at her physical skills as well as her emotional instincts. He just wanted his wife back, the woman he loved and who loved him in return—he wanted her sitting next to him at the table and more, beside him in bed where he could take her in his arms.

But this was a start—how unthinkable it would have been only two or three days ago that Stacey would ever cook a meal for him again. This was a step in the right direction—a baby step, perhaps, but movement nonetheless. In many ways Stacey was now a stranger, different from before—he'd been more than a little nervous when she'd reached inside the silverware drawer. But things had turned out okay, and no matter how bone-tired he was, his heart was doing a little dance of hope.

Jesse watched her surreptitiously, thinking, as always, about how pretty she was. There was something different about her today, but he couldn't quite grasp what. Her hair was clean and brushed, she wore the familiar clothes, but . . . makeup, that was it. For the first time, Stacey had dusted a bit of color along her cheekbones and used a touch of mascara on her lashes. He felt a little stunned at this turnaround in her behavior—should he say something to call attention to it? Or should he simply accept it and act as if it was nothing new?

Which of these was the least dangerous?

It'd been almost a week since he'd thought about it, but as he ate, Jesse wondered briefly if he should try to call Stacey's mother again. Directly behind that came a hot, warning flush of anger, the memory of the woman hanging up on him before he could tell her that Stacey was back, the months of isolation when Stacey had first gone and he'd had no family of his own to whom he could turn for comfort.

Jesse took another bite of his pancakes, outwardly calm. Inside, though, he was raging. Forget it; calling Trista would be the perfect way to ruin what was so far turning out to be a pretty good day. It was undeniable that Stacey and her mother had never gotten along, and except for Easter and

Christmas Stacey had avoided contact with her. Beyond that, Stacey made a point of only calling Trista on her birthday and on Mother's Day. At first, Jesse had been uncomfortable with that, because even given the circumstances, how could you only talk to your mother three or four times a year? Then, as the years passed and he saw what happened every time the two women came together, he began to understand the damage Trista had done while Stacey was growing up.

It was tragic all the way around. His mother-in-law was a hard woman, bringing Stacey up in tough times with an alcoholic husband and another daughter who'd died as an infant from the same congenital heart problem that haunted Stacey. The death of her other daughter had, from the stories that Stacey had told him, had a profound effect on Trista. Stacey had grown up with Trista hovering over her constantly, watching her health, monitoring every move she made, demanding that she document every minute of the time she was out of the house.

For Stacey, it was a constant struggle to be free, to come out from under the oppressive weight of her mother's paranoia. She felt suffocated by the woman's fear and love, a contradictory combination that served only to drive her farther and farther away from her mother. And try as she might, Trista seemed unable to curb her tendency to monitor and control; by the time Jesse and Stacey met, the damage done to the relationship was final and irreparable. Trista had turned her anger toward Jesse, blaming him for taking her daughter away, blind to her own behavior and convinced that he was the reason Stacey wouldn't—or couldn't—spend time with her anymore. It was a never-ending argument that only worsened when Stacey became ill, culminating in a final, ugly scene at the hospital in which Trista did everything but accuse Jesse of killing her daughter.

No, Stacey wasn't ready for that yet, might not be for months. Where her daughter was involved, Trista had a way of turning on people, making the most casual, innocent conversation ripe with innuendo and anger. This morning's progress was, to Jesse's mind, not a step in the right direction, but a *leap*, and yes, his first tendency was to overreact and let an irrational feeling of hope generate a headlong rush.

Not yet. He'd wait—*they'd* wait, and see how things progressed. He wasn't about to take his wife and toss her back into the midst of hell.

JANUARY 28--TUESDAY

She'd managed, to an extent, to alter her wake/sleep routine to match Jesse's. Now Nola stayed awake nearly all night, reading, watching television, sometimes just pacing the bedroom like a caged cat. It was a force-fit to a lifestyle she'd never experienced before, but it had to be done—it was either make herself stay up, or sit and watch Jesse sleep during the day, with the lights dimmed and the television off. She had the feeling that he'd try to accommodate her if she really wanted it on, if, perhaps, she was prone to watch the soaps or the inane daytime game shows. But she wasn't, and while she'd never watched much television in the past, at least the nighttime reruns and movies on the basic cable channels could be interesting. Anything was better than picking letters for useless phrases or trying to decide which was the best of three doors to choose for someone else's prize.

The inactivity seemed to be working on Nola, placating her in a vaguely devious way that she couldn't allow herself to think about—if she did, the fear would start all over again, and the tension born of the unconscious battle of wills going on between the two of them. She was over-rested and bored despite the television choices, she'd reread *The Flame and the Flower* and anything else she could get her hands on, and there simply wasn't much else to do. She took a lot of naps, and the inactivity and lack of exercise was making her lethargic and dull, *placid.* The days with Jesse had slipped into a routine that if not altogether desired was at least steady and not unpleasant. She knew when he would come home and what to expect from him when he did, and somewhere along the line she'd lost the belief that he would ever hurt her—the man obviously worshiped her. The way he'd acted in the parking lot, then later in the kitchen . . . well, who wouldn't go a little crazy under circumstances like that? If the situation were reversed, how would *she* feel after seeing her husband get out of another woman's car after he'd been gone for three months?

Jesse came home, they ate breakfast, and then they went to sleep. There was a soothing sort of sameness about it, a comfort to the routine that Nola could count on. He locked the bedroom door, then changed while she turned her back; when he was done he slipped beneath the covers and faced the opposite wall, and this was Nola's cue to change and spread out her bedding on the floor. By the time she was ready to curl beneath her own blankets, Jesse was usually fast asleep. The last couple of days, Nola hadn't taken long to follow.

Her own shivering woke her up.

Nola pulled the blankets closer beneath her chin and tried unsuccessfully to get comfortable again—no good. The room wasn't frigid, but it was damned cold, far too chilly for the meager warmth of her blankets, especially at floor level. Was something wrong with the furnace? She sat up and looked around, as if she could tell anything from her spot on the floor of this dimly lit room. Lifting to her knees, she glanced at the clock on the nightstand—noon, they'd barely been asleep for three hours.

She peered at Jesse, but he was knocked out, completely oblivious to the temperature, and she was loath to wake him, for a number of reasons. She'd have to be blind not see how exhausted he was, and surely whatever was wrong—the furnace—could wait just a couple of more hours to be repaired. Plus, what if she woke him and he misinterpreted her actions, thought she wanted to become intimate with him? Waking him—or anyone—in the middle of what was his "night's" sleep was inviting confusion, opening an avenue for misinterpretation that she simply didn't want to chance.

But she couldn't stay here—for God's sake, she was freezing, getting chillier by the minute. Nola stood and dragged all the blankets up with her; that got her away from the worst of the cold air on the floor, but she couldn't sleep standing. There was no chair, and she certainly couldn't spread the blankets out across the top of the dresser—even if she'd been willing to try resting on the narrow piece of furniture, the mirrored hutch put an end to that notion.

She was *so* damned cold, and Jesse was such a heavy sleeper. What if . . .

No, that was insane.

But now that it was there, Nola couldn't get the thought out of her head: a soft mattress, the warmth that would build up beneath the sheets and the comforter, fed not only by her own body heat but by Jesse's.

No, she thought. I can't. I just *can't.*

It was so dark, and so quiet. She could hear his deep, even breathing. Without the background hum of the furnace, it was the only sound in the room, and everything else in the world seemed to have just turned off. Without meaning to, she reached one hand out and pushed on the bed experimentally, then pulled back and waited to see what would happen.

Nothing, of course.

Chewing her lower lip, her own breathing gone to shallow inhalations of fear, Nola sat carefully on the edge of the bed farthest away from Jesse. As insubstantial as her weight was, the mattress was old and soft enough to sink quite a bit; she squashed the urge to panic and jump up—that would only jostle the mattress and wake him for sure. Still, Jesse didn't move and his breathing didn't falter.

Nola couldn't help thinking of how warm she would be

if she just stretched out, right here at the very edge, and pulled the comforter over herself. It would only be for a few hours, and even Jesse couldn't mistake her intentions when he woke and discovered the problem with the heat.

I shouldn't be doing this, she thought, even as she carefully lifted her icy legs to the bed and slid them under the sheet. Her hands were shaking when she gently drew the comforter to her chin, but she didn't know if it was from the cold or from terror. Only a foot away, Jesse slept on, oblivious to her presence, not knowing that the woman he wanted so badly lay fearfully at his side.

And in what she would have thought was an impossibly short period of time, with her body warming and feeling inexplicably safe, Nola slipped into a deep and dreamless sleep.

Nola woke to find Jesse looking at her.

He hadn't touched her, at least as far as she could remember, and he wasn't moving; he was just lying there, facing her—she hadn't felt him roll over. He wasn't smiling; instead, there was a look of almost pathetic hopefulness on his face, an expression of need and wistfulness that was nearly heartbreaking to see.

To open her eyes and meet his, separated by mere inches, was as unnerving as it was frightening, but Jesse clearly didn't think so. He said simply, "Good morning," then rolled to the other side of the bed and climbed out, heading toward the bathroom as if having her in his bed was the most natural thing in the world. And why shouldn't he feel that way? He truly believed it was—*she* was the outsider here, the square peg that didn't seem to fit into her proper slot in this tidy little picture.

By the time he came out of the bathroom, Nola was wrapped in her robe but still sitting on the side of the bed, her knees and feet drawn up and away from the floor. The room was like a refrigerator, nearly cold enough for her to see her breath. Standing by the bathroom door, Jesse frowned and rubbed his arms as he cocked his head, listening for the nonexistent sound of the furnace running. "What the hell," he muttered. He pulled open a dresser drawer and shrugged a sweatshirt on over the T-shirt he'd slept in, then did the same thing with a pair of sweatpants. "Why don't you stay in bed until I find out what's wrong with the heat," he suggested. "No sense in you walking around and freezing, too." Nola nodded, doing her best to appear as normal as possible as her pulse beat thickly in her throat.

Without saying anything else, Jesse unlocked the bedroom door and slipped out; still amazed at her own audacity, Nola barely registered the sound. No, she couldn't stay in this bed—that was unthinkable. Despite the cold air in the room, she rose and dressed, rushing into a pair of jeans and a sweater in case Jesse finished and returned sooner than expected. Then she sat there, waiting and thinking and trying to remember if Jesse had touched her at any time while she had been in his bed. Did she recall him throwing an arm across her shoulders? She thought so, but wouldn't she have woken immediately? Maybe not; this single episode of sleeping on the bed had made her realize how uncomfortable she'd been during those days of sleeping on the floor.

There was a clank from the furnace, then the reassuring sound of it humming to life again. Nola waited, and a minute or so later Jesse opened the bedroom door and came in; he looked relieved and vaguely happy, a walking indication that, at least for today, he felt things were going okay in his world. "Found it," he told her. "Belt slipped off the fan motor and the safety switch made the burners shut down. I got it back on and tightened everything up—it ought to be okay now." His voice turned serious. "Sorry you got cold. You could've woken me up, you know."

Nola opened her mouth to reply but couldn't think of any way to explain why she hadn't; instead, she just shrugged and looked at her hands while he stepped to the other side of the bed and changed his clothes. "It ought to be warm in here in no time," Jesse said cheerfully. "At least by the time we figure out what to make for supper. Any ideas?"

Again, Nola could think of nothing. "N-no," she managed. "I don't really care."

"Well, we'll figure it out. You want to brush your teeth?" When she nodded, Jesse did something she never would've expected. While she stared, he stepped to the door and unlocked it, then paused. "I'll be in the kitchen," he said simply.

And he walked out and left her alone in the unlocked bedroom.

Jesse tried very hard not to make a big deal about it.

Still, for hours, parts of that Tuesday afternoon when he'd woken and found Stacey lying next to him in the bed were dreamlike, like something happening below the surface of an anesthesia haze—the laughing gas he'd once gotten during a visit to the dentist's office. Everything had a sort of tingling, slightly buzzing *edge* to it, yet it had nothing to do with anticipation. It was simply a live-for-the-moment kind of feeling, enjoy what happened while the feeling lasted, all the while knowing that at any moment the sensation could end and might not be repeated.

When he'd first realized she was in bed with him, he'd wanted to shout with joy and take her in his arms. A short-lived impulse though, and it had died only a few moments later at the fearful look on her face when she'd opened her eyes and caught him staring at her; instead he'd simply said good morning and gotten up. But this was making progress, all right—surely to God it'd only be a little while before he and Stacey could have their normal life back again and she'd forget all this nonsense about being that other woman.

But what were they going to do about her being married to someone else? Was that real? As much as he hated to acknowledge it, he was going to have to—she still thought her name was Nola Elidad, and while she didn't have a driver's license, there was a Visa card, a library card, and a few other miscellaneous things. Jesse felt a twinge of guilt when he thought about that Detective Conroy and how he'd asked about the Nola Elidad personality. But Jesse hadn't lied to him, not really—

"Do you know a woman named Nola Elidad?"

"No. Should I?"

He *didn't* know a woman named Nola Elidad; he knew a woman, his wife, named Stacey Newman Waite. Knew her inside out, what was in her head and her heart right down to her dreams for the future and the way she sighed when they made love. Nola Elidad was a stranger, someone else's wife, and also someone who didn't really exist—no, he didn't know her at all. Stacey was the woman who had married another man, who had lost her memory and tried, admirably, to rebuild a life out of nothing. And those were the same memories he was convinced were best left to wither and die as he carefully steered her back on the road to her true identity.

"I was thinking I'd go to the grocery store today," Jesse said. "I like to shop when it's not crowded, but I won't be gone long, maybe an hour." He sounded lighthearted, as though he didn't have a care in the world. "Is there something special you want?"

"I thought we didn't have any money," Nola said. The words came out automatically, before she had time to sort them out. *We?* No, not *we.* Well, maybe temporarily. She would only be here for a little while longer; she might as well learn to live with it and make the best of the situation. If she went along with Jesse instead of fighting him at every turn, wouldn't it just make things easier on both of them until she could get back home?

"We don't have a lot of cash," he admitted, his tone taking a more serious note. "But I've gotten paid and we're not starving. By the way, I put your money back in your purse."

"I . . . wasn't worried about it."

They stood there awkwardly for a second or two, then Jesse cleared his throat. "You want anything from the store?" he repeated. "Some special kind of soup, or lunch meat or something?"

Nola thought for a second before shaking her head, then she couldn't resist a tiny smile. "Anything but noodle soup and peanut butter." It bothered her a little that she couldn't think of a single thing she preferred over anything else—surely she'd had favorite foods, hadn't she?—but in the scheme of things, that really was a minor problem.

"Fast food?" he suggested. "I could stop on the way back—"

"Seems kind of silly to do that when you're coming from the grocery store," Nola said. "I've never been much on that greasy food, anyway."

Jesse nodded. "I know. I just thought you were tired of eating the same stuff."

She shrugged. "Whatever you want to get will be fine."

Jesse hesitated, then finally shrugged. "Okay. Where do you, uh, want to . . . ?"

His voice trailed away and Nola realized that he intended to lock her up again. She felt a flash of anger at him, but it was gone immediately. Of course he would do that. The things that had happened overnight—her sleeping in his bed, him leaving her in the unlocked bedroom while he went to the kitchen—these were all baby steps between the two of them, the start of . . .

What?

"The nursery," she said out loud. She hadn't even known she was going to say that. "But I want to get the wedding pictures out of the bedroom first."

Jesse looked puzzled, but he didn't question her. "Sure. Whatever you want." He waited while she got the shoe box containing the pictures, then stood at the nursery door indecisively as she settled Indian fashion on the floor with the box in front of her. They stared at each other for a moment, then he cleared his throat. "Before I go, can I get you some water, or tea—"

"I'm fine, Jesse. Go on to the store."

"Right," he said, and when he closed and locked the door he had an almost comically guilty expression on his face.

Nola listened to the sounds of him leaving, then sat motionless as the silence of the empty townhouse rushed in to fill the space he'd left behind. Creaks and snaps, the constant warming and cooling of the heated wood and metal pitched against the frigid outside temperatures; it was probably impossible, but she imagined she could even hear the hum of the refrigerator from the downstairs kitchen, and over that came the heavier, welcome thrum of the furnace kicking on. It was like being in a sort of self-sufficient universe, isolated but provided for, lonely but not really alone.

And the key to all of it, to freedom, could very well be in the box in front of her.

Nola slid the box closer, centering it in front of her feet. She knew what was in here, so there was no reason to hesitate or be afraid. Now it was a matter of satisfying, once more, her curiosity, of examining again in her mind all those unspoken observations that had been piling up since Jesse had brought her here and she'd calmed enough to return to clear thinking.

Everything was still in there, the same as it had been the last time she'd looked. Again, no surprises.

The invitation.

The handkerchief and veil.

The carefully dried rose.

And, of course, the wedding pictures.

She peered at each one closely, more carefully than she ever had, looking for . . . something, *any*thing, that would tell her the identity of the woman in almost all of them. *Was* it her? Or was it someone else? She'd heard the claim that everyone had a double somewhere, but she couldn't believe that. Even if it were true, it was unlikely a person would ever meet up with his or her twin—the odds were just too astronomical.

But then who was the woman in the pictures?

Nola spread them out, then sorted them. The first stack—by far the largest—contained couple shots, "her" and Jesse in all of the usual wedding poses. The second pile was smaller but still plentiful—shots of her alone or with one or two other people, including a couple of older women whom she, of course, couldn't place. Jesse had told her that one of these women, although she couldn't remember which, was her mother; the other was her mother's sister and thus her aunt. The disturbing thing was that while she wouldn't admit it to Jesse, they *did* look vaguely familiar, especially the taller of the two. Admitting this, even to herself in this solitary room, was a tremendous thing, akin, perhaps, to the child removing his finger from the hole in the dam.

Did she know these two women? If so, she *wanted* to remember them, needed desperately to do so, but as hard as she tried—even to the point of closing her eyes and clenching her fists—all she got for her trouble was a delicate bead of sweat across her upper lip, an odd thing in the cool air wafting along the nursery's floor. The pictures were so . . . *there,* so undeniable; it didn't matter that some of them were too dark or a little out of focus—there were plenty that were shot dead-on, full-face poses that left no room for argument. If only she'd had a beauty mark or a mole or something, *anything,* to which she could have pointed. But there was nothing; only a complexion that had been clear of teenage acne since her sophomore year in high school. She felt as if there were something perpetually just out of her reach, but instead of that "something" being a useless piece of trivia, it was the most important thing in her life.

Nola went through the photos again. Whatever she was hoping to find, however, remained hauntingly out of reach, no matter how many times she stared at the images, at the faces—including her own—that gave evidence to a marriage she couldn't remember. Yet there it was, there it *always* was, every time she tried to deny it.

Enough—for God's sake, how many times could she go through this stuff before she had to accept, as much as she didn't want to, that something wasn't right here? Even if she couldn't bring herself to completely believe Jesse, there was no denying a hundred little things that made her wonder if he wasn't telling the truth, if the problem wasn't, indeed, her? Her face, her memory—even the clothes he had for her fit perfectly. She gathered the pictures and the other pieces of memorabilia and arranged them all back in the shoe box, tucking everything in place and making sure nothing got smashed.

This little room, she thought as she stood with the box in her hands and looked around at the empty nursery, was full of old and unforgotten ghosts. She didn't know where Jesse had stored the box of wedding photographs before he'd brought her here, but this was where she wanted this box of lost memories to stay from now on.

They put the groceries away together, like any man and wife would do. In a way it was almost an adventure for Nola, but in another it seemed like the most natural routine in the world—unpacking the plastic bags and seeing what her "husband" had bought, opening the cabinets and putting things away, all interspersed with a little bit of chitchat, so mundane that later she wouldn't be able to recall what they'd talked about. Either she'd been watching Jesse more closely than she'd realized or he stored things in the most logical places, because she had no problem figuring out where the items should go. Still, he'd bought a lot of things she never would have thought of—she'd never been the most inspired of cooks. Tortillas and turkey sausage on sale and packages of spicy beans and rice, ground beef, spaghetti, and mushroom-flavored sauce, wheat biscuits and a jar of peach butter instead of jelly—everything here was new, and the truth was, she was looking forward to trying it. Things hadn't been that bad so far, and if it meant surviving and finding herself, surely she could play house with Jesse Waite for a few more weeks. If this—

Suddenly Jesse's hands were on her shoulders.

Nola froze and opened her mouth to scream. His mouth covered hers, his tongue barely slipping across the inside of her upper lip. She felt him touch her hair lightly, then he let her go.

She couldn't speak but her face must have said a lot; Jesse's expression went from happy to dismayed in an instant and he backstepped, quickly putting distance between the two of them as he shoved his hands in his pockets. "I—I'm sorry," he said hastily. "I shouldn't have done that. Guess I got carried away—I would never make you do anything if you didn't want to. Just forget it happened, okay?"

She nodded shakily and turned back to the counter, now acutely aware of his presence in the small kitchen in a way that she hadn't been moments before. Play house? How stupid—she couldn't believe she'd even had that child's phrase in her mind. Adults didn't "play house" like kids and she'd do well to remember that, even as she tried to put Jesse's loss of control out of her head. After all, Jesse Waite wasn't a *real* kidnapper, was he? Someone like that would have done what he wanted to a long time ago, and be damned to her protests; she'd have been raped and God knows what else by now. But Jesse wasn't like that—he'd accepted her unwillingness and moved on. "Just forget it," he'd said, and Nola believed his promise that it wouldn't happen again.

But she couldn't forget it, not then, and not later, after he'd left for work and she sat unseeingly in front of the television and felt again in her mind the warmth and taste of his lips against hers.

"We don't have anything yet, Mr. Elidad," Detective Conroy told him. "But that doesn't mean we've given up."

Alec looked at the policeman and said nothing. He felt

nearly paralyzed, as if someone had injected his entire body with a dose of novocaine that just wouldn't wear off. Perhaps it was better this way—God help him when it all sank home. A movement from the edge of his peripheral vision made him turn his head, and he felt absurdly proud of himself for registering the arrival of a female police officer. "I'd like you to talk with Officer Curtis," Conroy continued. "She works a lot with family counseling and social services."

Alec nodded, then realized the woman was holding out her hand. He shook it and felt the warmth of her skin against his, and it made him want his wife all over again.

"Hello, Mr. Elidad," Officer Curtis said. "It's nice to meet you, although I'm sorry it couldn't be under better circumstances."

Alec nodded again. Neutral ground so far; he still felt safely ensconced in his little web of numbness, protected against further pain. If Nola were dead, he reasoned, Conroy would have pulled him into a private office and told him the news as soon as he'd arrived. The detective was a straightforward kind of guy.

Officer Curtis snagged a chair from another desk and pulled it closer to the two of them, then sat and faced Alec. In her hands was a piece of paper and she held it out to him; when Alec took it, he found himself staring at his wife's face . . . but not. He frowned and held the paper closer, trying to figure out what wasn't quite right about the image.

"It's an age-progression image," Conroy explained. "The original photograph came from your wife's adopted mother, and it was taken in high school. From what you told us, now she has shorter hair, but beyond that we're going on computerization. We—"

"The hair isn't right." Alec's voice sounded like he was trying to talk around a cheese grater. He cleared his throat and tried again. "It's still too long and she doesn't wear it like this. She pulls it back from her forehead."

Officer Curtis nodded. "Excellent. I knew that if we

worked with you, we could update the image, give it more accuracy." She handed him a black marker. "If you would, try and sketch in the way Nola wears her hair now. Is there anything else?"

Alec took the marker and made a few none-too-straight lines, wondering if his poor drawing skills were going to be of any help. When he was finished, he stared at the paper image for a few more moments, then shook his head. "Not really. She looks older now, but I suppose it's the hairstyle that's doing it. Her face hasn't really changed."

Conroy took the paper from him and studied it, then gave it to Officer Curtis. "We're going to have this photograph made into a poster that will be circulated in Roselle and the surrounding suburbs and, unless you have some objection, released to the media."

Conroy's look was questioning, but Alec had no reason to object. "Fine," he said.

"There are a couple of community groups who will help tack it around the area," Officer Curtis said. "On telephone poles, grocery store bulletin boards, places like that. Anyplace we can get your wife's picture has the potential to turn up someone who's seen her."

"Fine," Alec said again.

Officer Curtis leaned forward on her chair. "Mr. Elidad, I'd like you to talk with some people in a support group. I think they would be able to help you through this, connect you to people with whom you could share your feelings and who've also gone through the same type of situation."

Alec frowned. "A psychiatrist?"

She shook her head. "Not at all. There's generally a counselor at the meetings, but he or she just leads the discussion and steps in only if it's necessary—for instance, if someone's having a particularly difficult or emotional time."

Alec looked at his hands and said nothing. He could barely talk about what he was going through with Detective Conroy. How could he open himself to utter strangers?

"It's something to think about," Officer Curtis said and

offered him a business card, as if she'd known what was running through his mind. "You can call the number on the card anytime and leave a message, and the counselor leading the discussion at the time you call will get back to you."

He looked at the card without really seeing what was on it, then shoved it in his pocket. "It's not you?" he asked. "You're not involved in this?"

"No," she answered. "I'm one of the department's counselors, but not in this field."

"Mr. Elidad," Conroy interjected. "I really recommend that you take Officer Curtis's suggestion. Tough situations like the one you're faced with are so much easier to get through when you have the support of people who've been through the same thing. It helps to talk about how you're feeling, how you're going to deal—" Conroy stumbled a little on his words then, and Alec looked up from the card in time to see the policewoman give her coworker a sharp glance.

"Wait a minute," Alec said before Conroy could continue. He sat up very, very straight. "How I'm going to *deal*? With what? What's that supposed to mean?"

He couldn't miss the look the two police officers exchanged. "Mr. Elidad," Conroy said reluctantly, "I have to tell you that statistically this situation isn't very favorable. While we definitely believe Nola was taken against her will, it's unlikely that your wife was kidnapped for monetary gain because we haven't received a ransom note."

Alec sat, frozen, and for a long time he wasn't able to make his vocal cords work. "Statistically?" he managed at last. "This *situation*? How much colder or more distanced can you make yourself?" His mouth twisted. "Oh, I'm sorry—I forgot. You don't think my wife is still alive, and this is just a job to you." He wrenched his gaze away from Conroy and concentrated instead on his hands, willing them to unclench. If they didn't relax, he was afraid he'd start pounding on the desktop. He felt enraged at their surrender, and Officer Curtis's next words only made it worse.

"That's why it's really important for you to become involved in a support group, Mr. Elidad." She pushed something forward on the desk and Alec found himself looking at another business card, a duplicate of the previous one. "These people are experts at helping families—men just like yourself as well as women and children—through the loss of a spouse or a loved one. They understand how difficult it is and the importance of being in a group environment—"

"And you?" Alec interrupted. He couldn't keep the bitterness out of his voice. "Is this something you're into, too?"

Office Curtis shook her head. "No, sir. My area is violent crimes support. I counsel the surviving victims."

"Great," Alec said. He stood abruptly, leaving the business card where it was. "But you know what? I don't *need* counseling from this group, or from you, or from anyone. My wife isn't dead, she's *alive.* You people may have given up on this, but I haven't." Conroy and Officer Curtis looked at him, but said nothing. Even more furious, Alec gestured angrily at the age-progression image of Nola lying in front of Conroy. "I know what this is—just some little sideline to placate the significant other, part of the same old routine that will keep me quiet while time passes and I lose hope and stop coming around."

The detective sat forward, cutting off whatever else Alec had been about to say. "That's not the case at all, Mr. Elidad. I admit that we are no longer convinced that there will be a positive outcome to this sit—ah, to finding your wife," he amended. If nothing else, Alec felt a bit gratified that the man had heard his shot about being distant. "But we don't waste our time on stalling. We're having the posters made and distributed because no matter what happens, we would like to find your wife for you."

Officer Curtis pointed at the business card. "The support group," she said again, "can help—"

"Absolutely not," Alec said coldly. "I don't belong in it. My wife isn't dead, so I have no reason to talk to them." He turned on his heel, hoping he looked a lot sharper than he felt, and walked out of the building.

FEBRUARY 1--SATURDAY

Jesse saw the poster early Saturday morning on his way home from work.

Until then he'd been pretty jazzed about everything: another paycheck, the upcoming weekend with Stacey, all the progress they'd made that week. Yeah, maybe they weren't exactly living as man and wife—yet—but they were getting there. She was no longer acting like a terrified deer around him, afraid of his every move. She'd even decided on her own to continue sleeping in the bed, and in return, Jesse felt like he could be himself more and more, tell a few jokes, gently crack away at the exterior shell of the stranger who had taken over his wife in his efforts to find the real woman inside.

But now there it was.

His wife's face, in a slightly off-kilter black-and-white photograph, stared back at him from the wall by the lottery machine in the convenience store where he'd stopped to pick up a Saturday newspaper.

Everything he'd counted on shook and fell in that single moment, especially the crazy idea that maybe they could actually go *out* this weekend, take in a movie or something. There was a little dollar theater up in Hanover Park called The Tradewinds that showed second-run flicks and had pretty decent popcorn; for a small place, they usually had at least two, sometimes three movies showing simultaneously—good variety for cheap. It was seldom crowded and Jesse thought it was a great place to take Stacey for her first jaunt outside since her return.

But now, *this* . . .

Jesus, what a setback. How long would he have to keep Stacey hidden in the townhouse now? He'd never counted on seeing her picture in the local stores beneath the glaring caption *"Missing/Abducted"* in big, bold letters. And while he didn't get close enough to read it because he was afraid someone would notice him, Jesse knew there were more details on the poster and a number to call—perhaps the same one that had been in the newspaper. Slightly more than two weeks, and now he felt like someone had stepped in and stolen all that improvement away.

Still stunned, Jesse hung around the magazine rack for a few minutes, casting furtive glances at the wall bearing Stacey's likeness. Maybe no one else would notice, but to him it was obvious that they'd come up with a picture of her from high school and fiddled with it to make her look older. It didn't work; even from here, Jesse could pick out the parts that had been painted, or airbrushed, or whatever they called it. He thought the effect was gruesome, a parody that ruined everything about her.

Damn, Jesse thought as he flipped through the magazine selection without seeing anything. Stacey was still *so* sick—all she'd needed was a little more time to get past the amnesia and remember herself, who she *really* was. For her to be out of the townhouse now and start talking to people or, God forbid, see one of these posters, would be disastrous; it would only be a way for other people to reinforce her notion that she was someone she wasn't. He swallowed and wandered away from the magazine rack, barely remembered to buy his paper before going back to the car. He hated treating Stacey like this, keeping her locked up and isolated like a prisoner, but he had no other choice. She would never heal unless she had a solid, uninterrupted dose of the way they'd functioned as a family on which to build her memories. For her own good, especially now, Jesse would have to make sure she was kept isolated, including from the newscasts if possible. There hadn't been much on them about her—maybe they were just too close to the problems of Chicago to be interesting—but he wasn't taking any chances with this new development.

Disappointed all the way to his core, Jesse Waite headed back home to what was left of his small life.

....

He was twelve years old when everything that made up his world was destroyed by a drunken woman one Friday night. The Big Event—he would capitalize it just that way for the rest of his life—happened while he was safe at home with a baby-sitter, a generously built seventeen-year-old named Susie who sat on the phone with her boyfriend all evening while he watched reruns of old sitcoms like My Favorite Martian *and* M*A*S*H *on Channel 9 (and her—oh boy, did he keep an eye on her).*

He wasn't a firsthand witness to The Big Event, but he heard about it afterward and imagined that it went something like this:

Even on a Friday, Garvey and Rebecca Waite were not late-nighters, so it wasn't too far after eleven when they left P.J.'s Pizza on Irving Park Road. They were both full and a little sleepy, and Dad had drunk more than a few too many beers; Mom was driving, not because Dad thought it was a good idea but because an Itasca judge had told him they'd yank his license if the cops caught him DUI again. Garvey was the kind of guy who hated the whole idea of having to depend on his wife, or for that matter, any woman to cover his tracks, but the idea of losing his driver's license generated just enough fear to ease him beyond his obstinacy. Mom took it all in stride and silence, as she had every Friday night for most of her marriage; she still thought the two times that Garvey had raised his hand to her were a secret, but her son wasn't stupid and he'd heard the sound on both occasions—flesh hitting flesh—through the flimsy wall of his bedroom and had known it instantly for what it was. But he also knew his place in his dad's world and he wisely said nothing; part of him, however, hated the old man just a bit because of it.

Still, it didn't look to be a bad ride home. Garvey Waite was pretty drunk but he wasn't feeling particularly mean on this fine, late-summer night. They were driving an old Cadillac, one of those wonderful big boats from the seventies; all the windows were down to get the breeze and the radio was probably playing. Mom might have been singing along with a tune from the oldies station they both liked so much, her voice low and sweet, right in key with the music. Maybe Dad said something to her—"Hey, you know that boy is gettin' real good at football," was always Jesse's favorite fabrication—and she turned her head toward him and maybe she smiled a little. At least Jesse liked to think so.

Because he hoped to God neither one of them saw the Buick Centurion that hit them head-on.

Another old beater rumbling down the road like a tank, this one driven by a woman too liquored up to walk, much less drive or, God forbid, understand what that broken yellow line in the middle of the road really meant. The hell of it was that she—and the two toddler-aged kids in the backseat—came out of it with only a few bruises and messed-up hair, while Jesse's mom and dad were catapulted through the windshield like a couple of fastballs hit dead-on by a hotshot batter. Seat belts just weren't the rage that they are today and Garvey and Rebecca Waite ended up in front of their car, their bodies tucked amid the shattered glass in the crevice of twisted metal created by the two vehicles. What was left of them looked a lot like butchered beef and wasn't fit for a twelve-year-old boy to see.

Susie was still on the telephone—complaining about how the Waites were two hours late—when the police knocked on the front door. Finding out about The Big Event was enough to get her to finally hang up, but there was no compassion in her for Jesse; she was a teenager and he was only the regular Friday night job she'd just lost. She went home and the two cops stayed until someone from the Glen Ellyn field office of the Department of Child and Family Services arrived at four a.m. and picked him up.

Three days later his temporary custodian took him to his parents' funeral. Their caskets, inexpensive, cloth-covered pine, were end to end in the dimly lit viewing room and all his dad's drinking buddies from the construction site were there with their wives. They put their heavy hands on his shoulders and made a lot of promises they never kept, all the while looking at the wall, the ceiling, the floor, the chairs—anywhere but at Jesse or at the pathetic corpses that used to be his mom and dad.

Amazingly, both caskets were open. The room's low light and the heavy makeup slathered over his parents' skin wasn't enough to hide the lines of stitching and the dark bruising beneath it; what wasn't clear on the surface was filled in quite nicely by Jesse's imagination. Jesse touched his mom's hand and was amazed at how cold and stiff she was. He stared first at her, then at his father, unwilling to believe this had happened, unable to pull his gaze away from the fake, peachy tint brushed over their dead, expressionless faces, the dry, ridiculous color painted on their lips.

This image would blot out every other memory of his parents for the rest of his life.

4

Denial

If you have to keep reminding yourself of a thing, perhaps it isn't so.

—CHRISTOPHER MORLEY

FEBRUARY 4--TUESDAY

While Jesse was at work, Nola went through everything in the bedroom.

Drawers, closet, shelves, bathroom cabinets. She even got down on her hands and knees and peered under the bed, found herself looking at dust bunnies and one lost, lonely sock. She didn't know what she was looking for—a weapon, perhaps? Something to even the odds between her tiny frame and Jesse's burlier one . . . not that she'd ever use it, anyway. She didn't find that, but she found plenty of other stuff.

She'd felt not like a burglar but a voyeur of the worst kind, a pervert searching for the most intimate of secrets. She found everything from plain underwear to a pale aqua nightgown trimmed with lace and carefully wrapped in a plastic bag, obviously the outfit Stacey Waite had worn on her wedding night. Nola unwrapped it with a kind of reverence and held it up to herself in front of the mirror, and found no comfort in the realization that it was exactly what she might have chosen—the color was perfect for her skin, the length and style were alluring but not lewd, the fabric invited touch.

She rewrapped it and tried not to think about the memory it brought up in her, the unrelated one where Jesse had kissed her in the kitchen last week. Instead she went on with her search, discovering trinkets she couldn't recall and more clothes that looked familiar but might have been so only because they looked like a hundred thousand others in by-mail catalogs. She found nail clippers and old coins, inexpensive costume jewelry and one or two pair of real gold earrings, and . . .

Jesse's wedding ring.

With a start, Nola twisted the plain wedding band on her own finger and saw that it matched the one in the drawer. Why wasn't he wearing it? Work, of course—she didn't know much about what he did, but catching it on one of the machines he ran was an invitation to losing his finger. That he hadn't made her take hers off was odd; he had to know that it bound her to Alec, not him. Apparently he'd chosen to ignore that, to pretend it was a symbol of that which it was not.

Or was it?

Nola pulled off her ring and placed it on the dresser next to Jesse's, then stared hard at the pair. They were just inexpensive wedding rings; of course they would seem to match—they and countless others in the world. What she was looking at here wasn't strange coincidence or destiny, it was just unavoidable. As she put Jesse's ring away, what troubled her more was not that they matched, but that the face of the man who had placed hers on her finger was, now, nebulous in her memory.

And it didn't help to find the photo albums on the closet shelf.

At first she hadn't noticed them because of the way the door opened into the closet. A pretty good-sized walk-in, the closet was stuffed with a combination of men's and women's clothes—clearly Stacey and Jesse Waite didn't believe in throwing anything away. The shelves were neatly stacked with boxes, linens stored in zippered plastic bags and other odds and ends, and the photo albums were in the right back corner, the one blocked when the door was open. Nola didn't find them until she turned on the inside light, then pushed the door closed to get a look at a dress hanging on the rod. The instant she saw the albums, the dress—and everything else in the closet—was forgotten.

There were only two books, older, and they weren't thick, so it didn't take long to page through them. Some of the photos inside were of herself as a child—no matter how she wanted to fight it, there was no mistaking that. The other people she didn't know, yet now she had a nagging sense that she'd seen both the two women—younger versions of the ones from the wedding photos whom Jesse had identified as her mother and her aunt—before. From the dress and hairstyles of the adults, she was probably looking at fifteen years ago or longer. The places in the photos weren't familiar—various living rooms and holidays, a park, someone's backyard—but they weren't important. What mattered was that as hard as Nola wanted to believe otherwise, there was simply no way that Jesse Waite could have had pictures like these if she hadn't been in his life before last month.

But why couldn't she remember it?

She tried—God, how she tried. Sitting on the closet floor with the naked lightbulb burning above her like some kind of spotlight in a police interrogation room, Nola scrunched her eyes shut and concentrated on pushing her mind back, searching for memories she *knew* had to be there somewhere. She didn't need Alec, not right now—she needed *pre*-Alec, something, *anything* from the time before they'd met. When Jesse had brought her here, she'd spent so much time concentrating on how to best act in order to stay alive day to day, how not to anger him, that it had never occurred to her that she might lose herself along the way.

Her mother.

The most logical person on whom to focus, but Nola's mental search brought no warmth or love, no vision of being held or taught or loved like the child in the photo album obviously was. Pre-Alec memory did not seem to exist—before her increasingly ambiguous recollection of him was nothing but a huge black hole that was filled with soul-wrenching pain and terror. When she pushed at it anyway, tried to force herself beyond the edge of that abyss, Nola fancied she could hear a voice shrieking in her head—it might or might not have been her own—and feel someone's fingernails scraping along the surface of her skin, especially her scalp. The sensation made her so nauseated that she nearly vomited on the closet floor.

Shaking, Nola put the albums away, then rolled into a ball on top of the bedspread. She had books to read, but no television—Jesse'd thought he was being surreptitious but she'd seen him twist off the end of a wire to the cable connection in the bedroom the other day. She didn't know why he'd do such a thing, but guessed it was something on television from which he wanted to shield her—he was so very protective. Now the TV worked only on the connection in the living room and he was stalling on getting the bedroom cable connection "fixed," so Nola was left with way too much time to think. Yet she dared not contemplate the things she most wanted to think about.

If she couldn't think about her mother, then she'd think about Alec.

He was tall, with brown hair and eyes, and—

Nola frowned.

Was he tall? As tall as Jesse?

She tried to picture herself standing next to him, reached for the feeling of having his arm around her or holding his hand, but nothing happened. At five-foot-two, almost everyone was taller than she was, but she no longer knew how *much* taller Alec had been. Had he been affectionate? Had they *ever* held hands? Damn it, she couldn't remember that either. Suddenly Jesse's claims didn't seem so outrageous, because if she had truly lived a life with Alec, it must have been short indeed to fade so quickly.

No matter how she tried, Nola couldn't honestly recall his face.

She sat straight up on the bed, suddenly angrier at her circumstances than she'd been in weeks. It was Jesse doing that to her, with his constant, unspoken adoration, it was this townhouse, with all its comfortable nooks and crannies and the same decorating that she could've easily done herself, and it was the everyday we're-all-just-fine routine into which she'd so blandly slipped. Her memories of her life before this place were wearing away, like rock eroding under the constant flow of a gentle but never-ending wind.

Could she really just sit back and let that happen?

"Jesse, we need to . . . talk." It took everything she had to get those words out, and the look on his face—something between hope and terror—nearly made Nola change her mind.

"All right," Jesse said. His voice was even, but she knew it was an effort for him to keep it that way. They were in the kitchen and he pulled out the chair she usually sat on. Nola lowered herself to it, thinking that even the fact that she *had* a usual chair in Jesse's house was why she had to make an effort to reestablish herself in the world, in *her* world. Beneath the table, her knees were shaking.

"What would you like to talk about?" he asked. His face was tired and still grimy from his shift last night and his hands were folded tightly in front of him, like a worried schoolboy facing the principal. How strange that the tables could be reversed like this, that her kidnapper might fear, even a little, something she would say.

"I . . ." Nola swallowed. Jesus, she hadn't rehearsed anything, had been so totally focused on making herself say something at all that she hadn't planned *what* to say. "I have to let my husband know I'm okay," she blurted. "He doesn't—"

"*I'm* your husband," Jesse said loudly. Now his hands were so tightly clasped that the skin of his fingers had turned white.

"You can't keep on pretending like this, Jesse. It's not going to work." The fear inside Nola was starting to build and she tried desperately to keep it at bay. If it took hold, she was doomed—she'd cower like a beaten puppy.

For a moment he only stared at her. "Three months," he said suddenly. "That's what we agreed to. If you aren't well by then, we'll go to a doc—"

"*We* didn't agree to anything," she interrupted. "*You* were the one who decided that—you never even asked me what I thought about it!"

"It doesn't matter." The look on her face must have gotten through because he quickly backtracked. "I mean, of course *that* matters, but I can't do anything about it. There's no insurance until then, don't you understand?"

"And in the meantime what is my husband supposed to do?"

"I *told* you," Jesse said hotly. "*I'm* your husband." He looked down at the tabletop, as if amazed to discover that his hands had balled into fists. "I don't think I want to talk about this anymore."

"Well, *I* do." Her purse was on the counter across the kitchen and Nola stood and strode over to it. She brought it back to the table and set it down, hard, in front of Jesse. "Look in here, Jesse. *Look.* And you'll find a whole bunch of things that will tell you who I am and what my name is—a credit card, a social security card, even a library card. A checkbook with my name—and my husband's—and our address—"

"Maybe I'll pay him a visit," Jesse said darkly.

Nola froze. "W-what?"

"Go over there and talk to him." His eyes had narrowed and there was a grim set to his jaw that Nola didn't like at all. "See what's what."

She swallowed and drew the purse away from Jesse, then felt for the chair and sank onto it. God, could she have gotten a worse idea than to bring this up? "Jesse," she said. Her voice was slow and soothing—at least she hoped it was. She was having a hard time hearing herself around the blood pounding fearfully in her eardrums. "Hurting Alec won't do any good—"

"Who said I was going to hurt him?" Jesse asked blandly. "I just said I might talk to him." He inhaled. "Maybe it could clear things up between you and me if I could get him out of the picture."

Get him out of the picture? What did that mean?

"I don't think that's necessary," Nola heard herself say. "I think you and I can work this out on our own."

"Do you, now."

She nodded, the movement jerky and graceless, as though someone was again yanking those strings from above. After all, wasn't that exactly what was happening?

Before she could stop him—not that she could have anyway—Jesse leaned across the table and pulled her purse out of her hands. "Then maybe," he said, "it would be better if we just got rid of this." When she didn't say anything, he unzipped it and took out her wallet, then extracted the little bit of cash that was left inside and tossed it in front of her. "The person this stuff belongs to isn't you," he told her. "It's someone you made up when you were sick. Having this around . . . it's just reinforcing something that's not true."

He waited, but Nola couldn't bring herself to say anything. Did he think she would agree with him? She felt exactly the opposite—that purse and what was in it were the last fragments that bound her to herself, to a personality and an existence on which she was, day by day, losing her grip. If it was gone . . .

Jesse's next words were a brutal reminder that she had to decide. "Or maybe you'd rather I did go talk to . . . what was his name? Alec."

"Go ahead and throw it out," Nola said. "I don't need it anymore." She was screaming inside, amazed that Jesse couldn't hear the anguish leaking out of her like some sort of celestial shriek.

But he only gave her a relieved smile. "All right. It's garbage day—I'll put it out with the rest of the trash."

Out with the rest of the trash, Nola thought numbly. *The last of myself.*

She watched Jesse stand and put the purse next to the kitchen garbage can, and it felt like something inside her head tore itself free and finally let go.

FEBRUARY 7--FRIDAY

Three weeks yesterday, Alec thought. Where is my wife? Is she even alive?

He immediately hated himself for thinking that, for letting a single moment of weakness and doubt taint what he had come to see as his pure and unwavering belief that he would someday see Nola again. For all these days and weeks and the mini-eternity that his existence had become, he had been able to hold his head up and stare Conroy straight in the eye, knowing that he had never, *ever* believed anything but that he and Nola would eventually walk hand in hand once more.

It was all ruined now.

Nothing could take away this blemish on his faith, no amount of self-denial would erase it. He could not hide from himself. Even if he never allowed himself to wonder about it again, Detective Conroy would see the doubt in his face, and Officer Curtis would hear it in his voice.

"Damn it," Alec hissed between his teeth, but there was no one else in the apartment to hear.

He wished, suddenly, that he were a drinker. To lose himself and his troubles in booze each day, to slip into drunken oblivion each night—how inviting it sounded, how much more comforting than the hours spent pacing the apartment and trying to read, the nights spent tossing and turning in a suddenly too-big bed. But he couldn't—damn his genetic makeup, experience had taught him that more than two glasses of wine would make him violently ill within an hour or so.

Sleeping pills then—it would be easy to convince his regular doctor that he needed something to help get him through the weeks of broken sleep and nightmares. But of these, Alec was afraid; the loneliness was too big, the despair too easily overwhelming. He'd never imagined himself in a situation where suicide would even be an option—faced with the real deal, he felt he would too easily succumb if equipped with the right tools.

He wandered from one small room to another. The

apartment wasn't big, a simple layout of a rectangle neatly divided into segments. If he stood in the dining room, he could see most of his living space—living and dining room, small, galley-style kitchen to his left, a double-door coat closet and the entrance to the bathroom on his right. There were no secrets here, no place for a missing wife to hide, no clues to be discovered as to her whereabouts.

The bedroom was the only place of real privacy, its door down the hall by the bathroom and angled away from everything else. Alec wandered in there and stood at the end of the bed, staring stupidly at the militaristic way he'd made it up—sheets cornered and tucked in tightly, bedspread pulled smooth and firm as a tabletop. Nola, neat but not so obsessive, would have had a gentler hand at it, fluffed up the pillows where he flattened them—hadn't she always done something to the top of the spread to make it look prettier? Some turn or fold of the fabric, but he couldn't remember what, and that . . . *wanting*, coupled with his traitorous earlier thought, suddenly made him absolutely enraged.

Before he could stop himself, Alec ripped the bedspread from the bed.

He didn't just pull it off and toss it aside. He really *ripped* it, felt the firsts of the inexpensive fabric tear in his hands as an unseen edge caught on something, the corner of the metal frame perhaps. The sound, the shredding of material, was like a trigger inside him, the top of a bottle unscrewed without knowing the carbonated contents had been shaken to dangerous levels.

"Damn it," he said. Then the bedspread was wadded in both hands and he was pulling and twisting and rending, *battering* it as his fury rolled out of him like explosive poison, pushed to the edge and beyond by the sight of his own too-lonely bed. "Damn it, damn it, damn it! Where *are* you?" He spun and flung the spread, now torn in a dozen places, across the room, then he went to work on the sheets and the pillows and the cases, howling—

"Where ARE you?"

—as his fingers curled into claws and found more places

in the seams where he could pull and pull and pull, until the room was a mass of ripped material and clots of soft stuffing from dead pillows. He sank to his knees in the midst of it all, tears streaking his face and his fingertips red and sore, feeling no better for the energy he'd just expended.

"Where are you?" he whispered.

*

Alec cleaned up the mess.

What else could he do but that—try to undo the damage he'd done. What would Nola say if she'd seen his display? He wanted to believe that she'd understand, but how did he know? He didn't really know her, nor she him. More than likely she would have been horrified, as shocked as he'd been drained when, at the end of the whole thing, he'd stood and gathered up what was left, bundling it into a garbage bag for later disposal. The bed seemed to stare at him—no spread or pillows or sheets, even the mattress cover had fallen under his attack. Now it was just stark blue ticking, with not even a brocade pattern, the mattress of a man alone. He felt like a prisoner, staring down at what was to be his solitary bed for the remainder of his days. Bathed in the winter sunlight streaming through the window and the curtains that no longer matched anything, it was an absurd contradiction.

"Enough," he said, and his voice came out hoarse. He pulled open the closet door and flicked on the light, found himself staring at a modest array of his and her clothes. There were, he knew, more sheets in the linen closet, but somewhere in here was where Nola had stored his old bedspread, zippered into a plastic storage bag, on one of the shelves. He found it quickly and pulled it down, then stopped and frowned at the small box revealed beneath it. Not his—he'd never seen it before. Nola's then, some personal effects she'd chosen to pack away.

Alec set the bedspread aside and lifted the box from the shelf, touching it with reverence. In here were surely secrets and details that his quiet wife had never shared with him, perhaps not with anyone. Maybe even a clue to her whereabouts, though in the face of her obvious abduction he knew distantly that he was reaching beyond what was reasonable. He set it on the bare bed and opened it, his hands trembling.

It wasn't full. Odds and ends of memorabilia and a couple of old photographs—a balding man who looked uncomfortably like an older version of himself, Nola as a child of about seven or eight, standing stiffly in front of a heavily made-up woman with deep auburn hair, a print of the same high school shot of Nola that Conroy had used in his age progression. There was a poorly mimeographed copy of Nola's birth certificate with the word "Reissued" barely legible in one corner, the result, no doubt, of her adoption and listing her mother and father as Marlo and Charles Frayne. On top of it all was an old and frayed rag doll, no recognizable child's character but well-used nonetheless, with a jaggedly repaired tear along its back and a strange rattle inside it that might have once been a primitive voice box. Alec picked it up and held it, tried to imagine his wife as a child, small and vulnerable, seeking a child's comfort in this small toy. It wasn't really that hard.

Beneath it all, at the very bottom, two newspaper clippings.

Both were dateless and yellowed obituaries, clipped away from any identifying newspaper logo and with only the opening location to reveal that they'd come from the local suburbs. Alec laid them out on the bed and read them, finally seeing a little piece of the childhood that Nola had never told him about. By its fragile and brittle texture, it was easy to pick the oldest:

> ***Bartlett***—Resident Stowe Gardell was found dead of heart failure this morning in his home by his wife, Marlo Gardell. Said his wife, "His family has a history of heart problems. He knew it was only a matter of time but no one expected it to be so soon." Doctors have ruled Mr. Gardell's death to be by natural causes. He is survived by his wife

Marlo and his daughter Nola, and will be buried in Spring Lake Cemetery in Aurora. There will be no memorial service.

And the second, an eerie echo of the first, as if somewhere in the basement of this unidentified newspaper the same ancient person had penned the notices, changing only the names and pertinent information.

Glendale Heights—Resident Charles Frayne was found dead this morning in his home by his wife, Marlo Frayne, the apparent victim of an allergic reaction to medication. Mr. Frayne had experienced a previous reaction to sulfa drugs which had hospitalized him, and been instructed by his doctor to dispose of the prescription. Said his wife, "He knew he couldn't take that sulfa drug stuff, but he had a sinus infection. I don't know why he didn't throw the old pills away. He must've gotten them mixed up in the middle of the night." Mr. Frayne's death was ruled accidental. He is survived by his wife Marlo and his daughter Nola, and will be buried in Spring Lake Cemetery in Aurora. There will be no memorial service.

Stowe Gardell—Nola's real father. One of the things that Conroy had said was that Marlo Frayne had admitted his wife's real father was a man named Stowe Gardell. Maybe what he needed to do was turn this stuff over to Detective Conroy. Alec didn't know what, if anything, it would do to help matters, but then he wasn't trained in that direction. Conroy was.

Happy to have a goal, even if only for the day, Alec went to wash the tear tracks from his face and get dressed.

Conroy studied the contents of the box that Alec had brought in, feeling the man's gaze on him from across the desk. Alec Elidad didn't look particularly hopeful, and

Conroy didn't know if that was good or bad—while it was true the man shouldn't have any false hopes, it saddened the detective to think that Nola's husband might have given up entirely. Had he and Dustine contributed to that?

The newspaper articles were interesting but didn't tell him anything he didn't already know. There was that odd bit about Nola Gardell, and Conroy had tried again on the computer only to get that same frustrating "NO INFORMATION" message. There was still nothing from the records and research clerk. The doll was nostalgic but useless; still, Conroy picked it up and looked at it, lifting an eyebrow at the odd rattle that came from its back. His curiosity heightened when he turned it over and saw the awkward stitching along the fabric. The flimsy thread gave easily when he prodded at it with a fingernail, exposing a gaping, unnaturally straight cut. Something deep inside it caught a gleam from the overhead lights and he dug into the hole with two fingers, felt something smooth and rounded, and pulled it free.

An old prescription bottle.

Conroy peered at the faded label, saw that it was from some mom-and-pop drugstore that doubtlessly no longer existed.

Bactrim—100 mg., one tablet twice a day

Bactrim . . . this was the sulfa drug that had killed Charles Frayne. What on earth was it doing sewn inside the back of young Nola Frayne's rag doll—the only toy she'd saved from her childhood?

"What is it?" Alec asked.

Conroy raised his gaze to Alec Elidad's. "Evidence."

"What am I doing here again?" Conroy had dispatched two uniformed officers to pick up Marlo Frayne, and now her voice was shrill enough to cut steel as they led her to an interrogation room. "I have rights, you know—you can't waste my time like this!" Wisely, neither of the two men responded as they showed her inside, then closed the door. Conroy caught the eye of the senior officer, whose relieved expression said it all—no doubt, Marlo hadn't been silent for more than ten seconds at a time during the entire twenty-minute ride.

There was no sense letting her stew in there—she'd only get more difficult—so Conroy grabbed his notepad and opened the door. As expected, Marlo Frayne was seated, unhappily rummaging in her purse for a cigarette. Before she could lift it to her lips, Conroy spoke.

"Sorry, Mrs. Frayne. There's no smoking in here."

She looked almost comically surprised, then her expression darkened and she shoved the cigarette back into the pack. "Fine," she snapped. "You want to tell me what the hell I'm doing here? If you wanted to know something, why couldn't you just use the telephone like everyone else?"

"I'd like to talk with you about your husband, Mrs. Frayne."

"*Ms.*, not Mrs.," the woman practically snarled. "My husband is dead and has been for a long time."

"Exactly."

Marlo stared at him suspiciously. "What's that supposed to mean?"

Conroy pulled out a chair across from her and sat. "Your husband, Charles Frayne, died . . . what did you tell me? Sixteen years ago."

"Yeah, that's right."

"And how did he die?"

"I thought I told you that already."

"You told me he died, but not what caused his death."

Beneath her makeup, Marlo's face seemed just a bit paler than it had a moment ago. "He was allergic to some medicine, an antibiotic. He keeled over in the middle of the night and I didn't find him until the next morning. They said it was heart failure or some such."

"I see." Conroy was silent for a moment. "I've done a little bit of research into this," he said. She didn't need to know just how little that was. "From what I found out, Charles Frayne knew he was allergic to sulfa drugs. How can it be that he ended up ingesting the very thing that he knew would kill him?"

"How would I know that?" Marlo Frayne demanded. "I told you, I found him dead in the morning. He was in the bathroom, all scrunched up—he must've gotten up in the middle of the night and gone in there, then collapsed."

"And what happened to the prescription for sulfa drugs?"

Her gaze shifted slightly, then came back to him. "What do you mean?"

"The bottle of pills—I believe it was Bactrim, wasn't it? Where did that go?"

"I guess I threw it out with the rest of his stuff when I cleaned out the medicine cabinet after the funeral. I didn't really pay it any mind."

"Really." Conroy dipped into his jacket pocket and brought out a plastic bag, set it on the table in front of her. Beneath the clear film was the bottle he'd found sewn into the back of the rag doll. "Could this be it?"

Marlo Frayne was a lousy actress and she couldn't hide her scowl. "I don't see how it could. I told you, I threw all that stuff out."

"Nola's husband found this in a box with a few other things from her childhood," Conroy said. "Why, I wonder, would a child save something like this?"

Marlo's expression went ugly. "Maybe because she switched the pills."

Conroy's eyebrows lifted. "You're saying that your adopted daughter killed your husband, Ms. Frayne?"

"I'm saying no such thing. I'm just speculating."

"I see. So you're *speculating* that a five-year-old child not only somehow knew the difference between two prescriptions, but intentionally substituted one for the other?"

"Could be."

"Why would she?"

"Who knows what goes on in a kid's mind?" Marlo retorted. "Some of 'em are just born bad."

"And you're saying that Nola was . . . 'born bad.' "

"Maybe."

"Well," Conroy lifted the bag and tucked it back into his pocket. "We'll soon find out. We have very sophisticated tests now, methods that can lift fingerprints and genetic material off objects decades after the crime."

A nice ploy, but it hadn't worked. Marlo shrugged. "It don't matter. You're gonna find a lot of fingerprints or whatnot on that bottle. Even mine—I'm the one who picked up the prescription for Charlie in the first place. I don't recall right off, but you got the pharmacist, and maybe a cashier. And of course, Charlie himself."

Conroy nodded. The truth was he'd already had the plastic bottle checked, but nothing had come of it—as Marlo had claimed, there were a multitude of prints on it, every one of them smeared beyond any usefulness. He stood. "All right, Ms. Frayne. You can go now—"

"And just how am I supposed to get home?" she demanded, heaving herself to her feet. "I pretty well remember my car being in my own driveway."

"I'll have a squad car drive you," he said as he opened the door for her. She pushed past him, muttering something unintelligible under her breath, then stopped short. Conroy nearly ran into her broad back.

"I know you," a familiar voice said. "You're Nola's mother—I saw you in a photograph in her things."

"Who the hell are you?" Marlo demanded.

Conroy stepped around her. "This is your daughter's husband," he said. "Alec Elidad."

Marlo's face twisted. "Well, ain't you something. An old guy like you taking up with someone as young as Nola—you ought to be arrested for that."

Conroy winced and Alec looked a little stunned, but he tried valiantly to recover. "I assure you, Mrs. Frayne, that I loved Nola very much—"

"Sure you did." Marlo's voice rose alarmingly and people around the room glanced up. "Hell, you probably *killed* her! What'd you do, get some kind of insurance—"

"That's enough," Conroy said and yanked Marlo to the side, hard enough to cut off her words. "You seem to be full of speculation, Ms. Frayne, and none of it has any basis."

"Dirty old man," Marlo spat at Alec around Conroy's shoulder. "You—"

But Alec had drawn himself up. "You're a horrid woman, aren't you. No wonder Nola didn't want to talk about her past."

"You *son of a*—"

"Alec," Conroy interrupted before this could escalate into a full screaming match, "I'd appreciate it if you'd give me a call. *Later.*"

Nola's husband shot Marlo another withering glance, then he nodded. Without another word, he turned on his heel and stalked out.

Marlo started to stomp after him, but Conroy's hand on her arm was unrelenting. "I don't think so," he said, his voice deceptively pleasant. "As I told you, someone will take you home."

Marlo yanked free of him and folded her arms, her eyes narrowed as she watched Alec leave through the door across the room. Conroy almost smiled, mentally applauding Alec Elidad for taking the woman down with one, extremely clean comment. Horrid woman? Definitely.

He thought again about the odds of Charles Frayne mixing up his medications and accidentally killing himself. Conroy thought it was much more likely that Marlo Frayne was a murderess, but only one person might be able to shed any light on that: Nola Elidad.

And God only knew if she was even alive.

FEBRUARY 11--TUESDAY

She wasn't bored.

In a way, Nola wished she could have claimed she was. While it was true that her days here had melted into one another, there was plenty—too much, perhaps—to keep her mind occupied. No longer afraid of Jesse or of the life she had here, she felt calm and better-rested than she had ever been in her life. Everything had evolved into something utterly simple, a day-to-day existence that was completely free of worries or troubles; Jesse took care of everything for her and her sole responsibility was to keep herself entertained while he was at work or when he was sleeping.

Her mind took charge of that.

Jesse had come up with more books from a small box in the basement, but Nola wasn't interested. A cursory examination had revealed that while she didn't know when or where, she'd read most of them—romances all, stories of finding true love in the face of constant adversity. While those fantasies might have once kept her occupied, the stories they told now seemed so far beyond what she could reach that she couldn't bear to so much as scan the back covers. Nola still suspected Jesse had intentionally disabled the television, and that was the way it remained while he was at work. Without what it provided—the sights and sounds of other human voices—Nola found herself returning, over and over, to the increasingly muddled landscape of her own memory.

She could no longer ignore the huge gaps, growing every day, nor the fact that each day she became more accepting of what Jesse told her. Was he wearing her down? Or was she simply running out of resistance to the truth? Surely no normal woman would lose the ability to remember the face of a man she'd claimed to be her husband, yet that was exactly what had happened. Alec Elidad? God help her, she couldn't remember a thing about him, if he was tall or short or fat or thin—she wasn't even sure how to spell or pronounce the name. It was like looking at a commonplace word for so long that suddenly the letters made no sense at all and you'd swear the word was spelled completely wrong.

Memories, Nola thought, should be crystal clear. The mind was the filing cabinet, stuffed with chronologically ordered dates, places, people, and information. Somehow her filing system had gotten upended and emptied; what she had remembered so briefly—Alec and the scrap of a life she'd had with him—was surely nothing but her own desperate attempt to replace what trauma had made her lose. A deathly illness, the loss of a child—just thinking about facing such things threatened to overwhelm her. It was not so hard to imagine that she had buckled under real-world experiences, and who was she to say they'd never happened when she couldn't even spell the name of a man to whom she had supposedly pledged herself for the rest of her life? She would have *wanted* to block out the pain, would have embraced the oblivion of forgetfulness to the point of losing her life, her husband, her *self.*

But through it all, Jesse had hung in there for her. Waiting when he had no news, taking her back when he did find her, loving her enough to forgive her the monumental failing of infidelity, something Nola could not honestly say she could have done in return. It was hard to argue a devotion that strong, a love so unflinching. He would have never gone to talk to Alec—she knew that now. It would have hurt him far too much to see the man who had been her husband and lover (something else she found she couldn't recall anything about) for a quarter of a year. A boastful threat, the human equivalent of a male bird puffing up its plumage to impress the female of its kind.

More and more, as she waited out the hours while Jesse worked, then slept fearlessly beside him each night, Nola couldn't help but begin to give credence to the idea that she might, indeed, be suffering from amnesia. Any question she asked about her missing past, Jesse could answer in detail—more than what could reasonably be explained in a make-it-up-as-you-go imagining. All the facts, the myriad things that made up a real life as opposed to a fantasy, were there, and always consistent. There seemed to be nothing that could trip him up, nothing that contradicted something he'd said the day before or last week or whenever. Obviously there was nothing wrong with *his* memory, while hers grew as indistinct as a faraway mountain on a fog-laden night. Maybe her long-ago question about what had really happened to Jesse's wife could be answered by simply looking in a mirror.

The women in the photographs . . . Nola spent a lot of time contemplating them. Oddly enough, it wasn't the idea that she couldn't remember her mother that troubled her—she had, as with so much else, accepted that and moved on. It was the other woman who disturbed her, the one Jesse had identified as Nola's aunt. "Aunt Chris," he'd said, "your mother's sister." Nola had seen her recently, she was sure of it, but the where and when of it had, like so much else in her mind, fled.

She'd had a job while she was gone, something to do with books, and she thought that might have had something to do with it. She couldn't ask Jesse, because obviously he wanted her to do nothing but forget those three months and everything that had happened during them. The woman in the photo was younger than the tall, thin stranger she barely recollected, with darker hair cut in a different hairstyle. Perhaps it was nothing more than a similarity, and even this Nola felt she could explain to herself. If the woman about whom she held such fragmented memories did, indeed, resemble her Aunt Chris, she'd probably felt drawn to her, maybe even felt the presence of the older woman, whether or not they'd been close, as vaguely comforting, like a timorous student in class who feels reassured by the presence of a teacher.

The more Nola thought about it, the more Jesse's way seemed the only explanation. Jesse felt so firmly ingrained in her memory, and as for pre-Alec memory . . . well, that just didn't exist at all anymore. And when it came right down to it, was her existence with Jesse Waite, a man who seemed only to worship everything about her, really so bad?

Once the idea that she might accept the way things were entered her head, Nola couldn't push it away. How long had this been going on, her struggle to cling to a life as someone else? She was so . . . *tired* of fighting. Even though she couldn't remember it, she *felt* like she'd been clashing with something her whole life, as though there were some great, inner war taking place and she was the battleground, the hill over which the unseen armies fought. How enticing was the thought of surrender, of just relaxing and letting happen whatever would. Her strength was not infinite, her resistance not impenetrable. Let someone else, some other woman or man, sustain themselves with willpower. She no longer could.

An hour until Jesse got home, and with hands that were reassuringly steady, she pulled open the nightstand drawer. Nothing wrong with her memory there—she recalled finding the same pad of paper and pen and writing down a telephone number on it, the one that Jesse had caught her calling using the hall phone. She'd lost that paper somewhere, hadn't thought about it in God knew how long; now it didn't matter.

Carefully she placed the pad of paper on her knee and stared at it, then picked up the ink pen. First things first, and she would at least give a token try to what she'd claimed:

Nola ~~Elle~~

Nola Ellided

She frowned, knowing that wasn't right but not knowing why. Fine, then she'd try something else.

Stacey

Strangely, once she actually wrote it out, it really wasn't so bad after all. Plus, the name seemed so . . . familiar, beyond what she felt the times Jesse stubbornly called her that. Maybe she only needed to try it on for a time, just to see how it fit.

She drew the pen across the paper again, faster this time.

Stacey Loren Newman

Not bad. One more try.

Stacey Waite

Much better.

FEBRUARY 12--WEDNESDAY

"How long has it been since you spoke with Alec Elidad?"

Lucas sat back on his chair and looked at her, then thought about it for a moment. "Friday," he said. "I had his mother-in-law brought in for questioning."

Dustine picked up on the way his lips pressed together. "Questioning?"

He nodded. "Mr. Elidad found a box of things that belonged to his wife, stuff she'd apparently kept from her childhood. There were a couple of things in there that were really unusual."

Dustine listened as he told her about the newspaper articles and the prescription bottle he'd found sewn into the back of the rag doll. "So you think the mother-in-law did this? But why would she keep the pills?"

"I don't think she did," Lucas replied. "I think Nola kept them . . . *after* she saw her adopted mother do some kind of switch with the medicine. The lab says it's been too long and the bottle's too smeared to pick up any fingerprints, but my guess is she dug it out of the garbage after Marlo tossed the bottle." Lucas's eyes were hooded. "Nola's real father was Stowe Gardell, and from what I've found so far, he seems to have died of natural causes. For the second time around, Marlo tried to pin Charles Frayne's death on Nola."

Dustine leaned against the edge of Lucas's desk. "It's not unheard of, especially in situations where the child is abused by foster or adopted parents. Is there any indication of that?"

"Oh, I'd say it's very likely that Nola went through hell as a child. Still, I don't believe she would have had the opportunity to do something like murder." Conroy pulled open a desk drawer and drew out a zippered evidence bag. Inside was a prescription bottle bearing a yellowed label and a white plastic top; he lifted it out and offered it to her. "I don't have the other bottle, the one for the antibiotics Frayne was supposed to take, but I think it's reasonable to assume it came from the same drugstore. Nola would have been five at the time. What do you think?"

Dustine took the bottle from him and examined it, noting the childproof cap. She twisted it experimentally and found it turned but wouldn't open; earlier in their use, the childproof caps had been difficult even for adults, and this one took a full, hard push against the cap to finally get it off. "I don't think she could've opened this," Dustine decided.

"Exactly." Lucas took it back. "And having an allergic reaction as severe as the one Charles Frayne supposedly endured isn't something a person forgets. What do you want to bet Charles Frayne believed he'd thrown these pills away?"

"The man might still be alive today if he'd just dumped them down the toilet."

Lucas's expression was frighteningly matter-of-fact. "If Marlo Frayne had her say in the matter, I doubt it."

What could she say to that? Instead, she pulled a business card out of her pocket and handed it to Lucas. "Anyway, the reason I asked about Alec Elidad is that the day after tomorrow is Valentine's Day. Lucas, he *needs* to talk to someone, whether he knows it or not. He will never feel so abandoned or alone as he will this coming Friday night."

Lucas nodded and fingered the card with the counseling service's number on it, the same one she'd given Elidad before. "I'll call him," he promised, "and see if I can convince him. He and Marlo Frayne ran into each other the day she was questioned—the first time they'd met—and it was downright ugly. He handled it well, but he's got to be feeling pretty battered by now." He stared at his desktop. "I know he doesn't think I'm very sympathetic."

"Don't be unfair to yourself," Dustine said, and touched him lightly on the arm. "What he's enduring is heartbreaking, but what he doesn't understand is that while he's falling apart, you *have* to keep a certain objectivity or you can't do your job properly. You know this, Lucas. People in pain are a lot like injured animals—fearful and angry, they strike at the hand that tries to help."

He nodded and slipped the business card between the handset and body of the phone, a reminder that this was to be his next call. "Back to the subject of Valentine's Day," he said.

Dustine frowned a little. "Yeah, it'll be hard—"

"Would you like to go out with me that evening?"

Caught off guard, Dustine opened her mouth to say something, then just sort of stayed that way. "For Valentine's Day," she finally managed.

"I know we haven't gone out much," he said hurriedly, "but it seems like a kind of traditional night for a date, don't you think?" He hesitated, as if something had just occurred to him. "Unless you have other plans or something."

"Well, I . . ." Valentine's Day? The whole notion of it, of the unspoken romantic element it implied, threatened to snowball her. If they did go out, would he expect—

"Well," he said, unwittingly derailing her thoughts, "you don't have to decide right now. Just let me know if you're interested."

Move it or lose it, girl. Are you going to get on with your future or let an old, despicable act overshadow everything important in your life?

"I'd like to go out," she made herself say. She found herself with her arms crossed, her fingers digging hard into her flesh, but she couldn't do much about that. "Friday. Very much."

Lucas smiled, but as always, his eyes didn't lie. He knew, he *knew*, what it had taken for her to say that. "Say seven o'clock? We'll go somewhere nice for dinner."

"Great," Dustine said, then stood. "Time to get back to my case files."

Lucas nodded, his expression grave. "Dustine, if you change your mind—for whatever reason—it's okay. Just say so."

"Of course," she said and turned to go, as if this were the most normal conversation in the world. But she would not let the rest of her days, her *future*, be ruled by old fear. She would *not*.

Dustine glanced back over her shoulder and found a small but sincere smile to give Lucas as he watched her walk away. "But I won't," she said with finality.

"Mr. Elidad—Alec—this is Detective Conroy. How are you?" The receiver felt warm in his grip and he hoped his voice wasn't too casual. Yes, he wanted to sound convincing, but he knew he couldn't go too far over the edge of friendliness or he would make the man suspicious.

"I, uh, I'm all right, I suppose." A little surprise in Elidad's voice and, as always, that sad note of hope. "Do you . . . have news?"

"I'm afraid not." Conroy tapped his pen on the desk, then dropped it and fingered the card Dustine had left. "But Officer Curtis dropped by my desk a little while ago—you remember her? The victims' counselor?"

"Yes." Elidad sounded suddenly tired, as if he knew what was coming but no longer had the strength to resist. "I remember her."

"She's very concerned about you," Conroy said. "About how you're feeling right now—"

"Because of Valentine's Day," the man interrupted. "Right?"

Conroy hesitated, but there wasn't really any way around the truth. "Yes, Alec. Because of that. She wanted to know if you'd called the group she recommended." There was a long beat of silence on the other end, and Conroy knew that there was his answer. "Right," he said. "Listen, we can't force you to call them, or anyone else. All we can do is make a suggestion because we're concerned about you and about what you're going through. I won't nag you and make you listen to the same stuff over again. Just do me a favor and give it some consideration. I know you feel that I don't understand what you're going through, and you're right—I don't. I've worked on a thousand cases but I've never had to deal with this personally. These people have, though, and they can relate to you on a level that I can't. So at least think about it, okay?"

Another beat of nothingness, but shorter this time. "All right," Elidad finally said. "I will. I still have the number."

As he hung up the telephone, Conroy felt that at least this time there had been a sliver of possibility in Alec Elidad's promise.

FEBRUARY 14--FRIDAY

She smelled the flowers before she saw them.

The townhouse had a certain scent, and Stacey—as she was making an effort to think of herself—had grown accustomed to it in the same way that she imagined a smoker got used to the smell of cigarettes in the air. The townhouse was, thankfully, free of anything like that, but it still had a scent to it, a nostalgic mixture of old country—forgotten potpourri and dried herbs—and mustiness from being shut down tightly for the winter. She found the smell both comforting and a little frustrating because she desperately wanted to air it out, roll up her sleeves and dig into a good cleaning. Jesse, unfortunately, really wasn't high on the idea of breaking his back in housework after he'd worked all night; he'd help a little but he lost patience quickly. He wanted to watch television—and thank God he'd finally broken down and repaired the bedroom connection so she could watch it while he was at work—or read bits of the newspaper to her, or just sit and talk about how things used to be and would someday be again. He didn't care if things were a bit dusty around the edges as long as the dishes were done and the garbage was taken out.

Roses—fresh ones. There was no mistaking the smell.

Sweet and powerful, a scent that could bring up memories of weddings or funerals, depending on a person's mental association. Right now all Stacey felt was surprise and a flash of dismay. Was this another way that Jesse had come up with to show her how much he cared? Maybe . . . probably. But they didn't have the money to spend on such things—Jesse had made that abundantly clear. If she was getting well enough to try wearing the name Stacey, perhaps it was time to try on the responsibility of reminding him to keep his head about things like that, as well.

The flowers were in a glass vase on the coffee table when she came down the stairs. The expected dozen, blossoms splayed like scarlet, multiwinged butterflies balanced on the tips of long, green reeds. And in the midst of the bouquet, a card, something oversized and sealed in heavy, cream-colored vellum. *For Stacey* was written across the front in a masculine scrawl that she assumed was Jesse's handwriting, although as with so many other things, she couldn't have sworn it was so.

She glanced around the room, but Jesse was nowhere to be seen. Still, Stacey could feel him—he was hiding somewhere out of sight, maybe just around the doorway to the kitchen where he could peek through a corner of the pass-through and see her reaction. They really were beautiful . . . never mind the money. These flowers seemed as much for Jesse as they were for her—how could she spoil that for him by harping on how much they'd cost?

The envelope was heavy but the flap, lined with gold and classically frayed at the edge, turned up easily when she prodded at it with her thumb. The card inside was made of the same parchment-stiff material, decorated with embossed crimson roses and writing.

Without you, I am nothing,
A blade of grass without water,
A rose untouched by sunlight.
Your smile makes the sun rise,
Your eyes furnish the glow of the moon,
The sweet sound of your voice
Sweeps the clouds from the sky.
Like the rose, and the grass,

The moon, and the sky,
Without you,
All these things are missing, and
I am nothing.
Happy Valentine's Day

It was signed *Love forever, Jesse.*

There was a noise behind her and she turned, saw Jesse standing just where she'd guessed he would be. Instead of meeting her gaze he was staring at the floor, afraid of what he might find in her eyes.

But finally he looked up, and Stacey smiled.

It was enough to make him walk hesitantly toward her, his steps slow and careful as though he were balancing on a tightrope. In a way, she thought he probably was; on one side was everything the way he wanted it to be, on the other, everything the way it was. On the painful middle line was Jesse, drawn one way but pulled back by the other, the center of a tug-of-war that he desperately wanted one side to win. She had once been that center object, but somehow the game had shifted and she had taken Jesse's place as one of the controlling players. This moment, whether she pushed or pulled right now, could determine a big part of the outcome.

Jesse stopped in front of her and waited, hands folded in front of him like a prisoner before a judge. Stacey looked at the words on the card again, knowing that he'd chosen them carefully—he was like that. How could she not be touched by his devotion and sincerity? Of all the things that had gone foggy in her mind, time, the *present,* wasn't one of them. Valentine's Day—of course. So she'd been here for just over four weeks. Twenty-nine days, yet the past about which she had been so convinced—a husband whose face she couldn't recall, a job that had surely been so monotonous and uninspiring that it, too, had fled; all the other minute parts of her so-called life—had all the strength of the last, dust-laden strands of an abandoned spiderweb. If she had ever been with anyone but Jesse, had ever truly *loved* someone, then why had that memory slipped away? What right did she have to continue to claim another existence when the undeniable truth was that she simply couldn't recollect it?

Jesse kept a respectable distance, making sure to stay out of that personal-space area of which Stacey'd been too aware in the not-so-recent past. She opened the card again and reread it, then set it on the table next to the bouquet and inhaled the heavy fragrance of the flowers. One more deep inhalation, as much for courage as to enjoy the flowers, and Stacey closed the small distance between them and put her arms around Jesse.

His expression was almost comical, a cross between disbelief and profound happiness. Before she could change her mind, Stacey lifted her face and kissed him, very softly. Jesse responded, but when his arms came up his touch was light, the hold of a man terrified of breaking the thing within his grasp. Beneath her fingers, she felt the muscles of Jesse's back tremble and wondered if it was self-control or terror that caused it, and he didn't try to stop her when she pulled away.

But Stacey had never seen him look so happy.

"Would you like to see her, Mr. Waite?"

"No," Jesse said. His voice came out hoarse and suddenly his mouth and lungs were filled with the taste of medicine, carried on the air of the hospital and somehow saturating everything inside him. "No, I wouldn't."

The look the nurse gave him was more surprised than sympathetic. For a long moment she just stood there and waited while he stared off into space, not seeing her or the faint chiffon paint of the ICU's walls. He felt like a drowning man—weren't they supposed to see their lives flash in front of them?—being suffocated by pain rather than water, watching not his own life but Stacey's streak across the forefront of his mind as though it were the world's longest and most cherished video set on fast-forward without his permission. The nurse said something else and touched his shoulder, but Jesse didn't hear her; it wasn't until she took him by the elbow and started to lead him toward Stacey's room that Jesse blinked and pulled away from her.

"I—I'm sorry," he said, frowning. For no particular reason, Jesse's eyes fixed momentarily on her name tag—Blommer. Like the chocolate company downtown. "What was that?"

"I said I know it's unpleasant," she repeated. "But you really should, you know, even if it's only for a minute. For clo—"

Something bright and hot flared in Jesse's stomach but he kept his face carefully bland. "You don't know what you're talking about, Ms. Blommer." His voice was as rigid and controlled as his expression, and its coldness was enough to make her step back. "Being with my wife has never been unpleasant."

"I—I just thought—"

Jesse held up a hand, cutting off her words. They both stared at it and for the quickest of moments Jesse had the oddest sensation that it belonged to someone else, another man who was enduring this unspeakable event. "Please," he finally said. He turned to walk away. "Don't think. Just . . . don't."

"Oh my God!"

His mother-in-law's voice was a shriek, razoring through the quiet corridor leading to the Intensive Care Unit at Alexian Brothers Hospital. He'd known she was coming, of course—how could she not?—but somehow, sitting here by himself in the meantime, he'd let himself drop into a cocoon of pain, letting it coil around him like a thousand-tentacled beast and drown out everything else in the world. How long had he been sitting here, waiting for the next chapter of pain to start in this sudden, horrible story?

Waiting for Trista?

He winced as her shriek came again—

"I am Trista Newman and she's my daughter! Where is she—where's my baby?"

—then was lost in the garble of a half dozen other voices as nurses and, Jesse hoped, doctors hurried over to quiet her down. Maybe they'd give her a sedative and make her lie on a cot somewhere until the worst of the shock wore off. This was so hard, he'd never imagined anything like it in his life, but as much as he disliked Trista his mind was still functioning enough to remember that she'd gone through this once before.

There was a lull in the noise level, then Jesse winced as the volume swelled again. When he looked up, Trista, leading a small knot of medical personnel, was coming toward him. In someone else's life, they would have comforted each other until the worst of it was past—if it ever was. Right now all he could do was stare at her twisted expression and know that things were only going to get worse.

Much, much worse.

Now his mother-in-law stood in front of him, her mouth working in an effort to make something intelligible come out. Her hair was neat, her clothes were pressed, her face was washed and lightly made up—if it'd been under any other circumstances, Jesse would have felt like a street beggar sitting in front of her. But with the situation being what it was, he could've been wearing nothing but his filthiest work clothes and he just wouldn't have cared.

When Trista finally found her voice, it was surprisingly quieter and even. "The doctors tell me that you've already had my daughter moved." She choked momentarily, then continued, instinctively detouring around the part she couldn't face. "You told them to take her away already, and so they won't let me see her." She took a deep, visibly painful breath, but this time she managed to get it all the way out. "I want to see my daughter, Jesse."

"That's not going to happen." He paused, then added, "I'm sorry, Trista."

"But . . . why not?"

Jesse's fingers twisted together, the knuckles turning more than enough to send pain spiking through both hands. Good—he needed that sensation. It would keep him grounded, at least for a little bit, while he worked through the agony of the next few hours. It would also, he hoped, keep away the memories of his parents' long-ago pseudo-serene faces. "Because I want to remember Stacey the way she was," he said evenly. "And I want everyone else to do the same. You, too. I think that would be best."

For a minute, Trista looked too stunned to say anything, then her words tumbled out, sharp and hard, almost too much to bear. "Don't you dare think you can stop me, Jesse Waite. You took her from me to begin with—this whole thing is your fault, her being sick is your fault. I don't know what you think you're doing now, but I have every right to see her and that's exactly what I'm going to do." She cut off her torrent and spun toward the doctor who had followed her down the corridor. "You," she barked. "Have your nurse or your assistant or your someone take me to where my daughter is, right this instant!"

While the doctor-on-call was young, he was not to be bullied. And why should he? He wasn't the family physician (Jesse didn't even know his name, for that matter) and beyond these walls and the next five minutes, he'd never have to face Trista Newman again. What happened over the days and weeks to come—the telephone calls and God knew what else that was surely just starting—simply wasn't any of his concern. Without looking around, he held out a hand and the nurse dropped a chart into it—presumably Stacey's—and he flipped through the pages without bothering to answer. When he finally raised his eyes, he gave the appearance of being sympathetic . . . but it was only on the surface. When Jesse looked closer, he saw that the man's expression was devoid of emotion. "According to this, you're the mother?"

Trista nodded, her chin going up and down in movements jerky enough to look painful. "That's right. I—"

"And this is the husband." The doctor indicated Jesse, but Jesse looked away, unwilling to meet that passionless gaze again.

"I'm her mother," Trista said shrilly. "I have the right—"

"As her husband, Mr. Waite had the right to decide the next course of action," the doctor interrupted. "And that's what he's done. If you have further disagreement over the matter, I'll have to ask that you settle it among the family. This facility can't be involved with matters beyond that." He closed the chart with a snap and even Trista, as upset as she was, knew that signaled the end of the debate. "I'm sorry—" His eyes, a cold jade green, swept toward Jesse and pinned him for a moment. "For both of you." He left Trista standing there, speechless, and walked away. The nurse, one of the ICU nurses who'd worked with Stacey a lot over the last week, paused to look at them apologetically, then she, too, hurried away.

Family? It was all Jesse could do to stifle a laugh. The three of them had never been a family. He and Stacey had, but certainly not Trista. Families had love for one another, families put old problems behind them and buried the bitterness of past disappointments and losses. Trista didn't know the meaning of moving on—if she knew anything, it was how to wage an ongoing battle for control and how to nourish a grudge like it was a plant that needed constant tending. She didn't want to love her son-in-law and she cared nothing about getting along with him or looking to the future. She'd never been able to see past her judgment that Jesse had stolen away the love and attention of her seventeen-year-old daughter.

Now Trista Newman leaned down and put her face close to his. "I'm not done," she hissed furiously. "You can't deny me this, you son of a bitch. I promise you that."

Oh, but he could.

And he damned well would.

Okay. He had the flowers, roses this time, but after spending damned near an hour in one of the card shops, Conroy had decided against a card. Mushy verse was out of the question because he and Dustine were way too early into their relationship—could it even be called that so soon?—to warrant that. The cards in the humor section were funny enough, but because they hadn't spent very much time together, he wasn't sure where funny might end and insult begin. He liked to laugh and he was fairly certain that Dustine did, too, but for now he'd stick with the person-to-person variety and leave the printed stuff for future use.

Sitting outside her townhouse, he checked his appearance a final time in the rearview mirror. To his eyes, nothing spectacular; just a guy who could blend in with an everyday crowd and not be noticed. Maybe a good thing for a detective, but he had serious doubts about his ability to catch a woman's eye. Still, he had to be doing something right or Dustine wouldn't have agreed to see him tonight. He'd seen the fear in her gaze, knew she was wondering about the wisdom of it. Men around the world could gripe all they wanted about how Valentine's Day was a greeting-card holiday—not true, when its origins dated back to the time of ancient Rome—but throw that line at a woman instead of a simple card . . . ? There were a lot more domestic call-ins on February 14th than people realized.

Okay. Beneath his overcoat he wore a black jacket and

dress shirt, but no tie, a dressier-than-normal pair of slacks. Conroy cracked his knuckles, then got out of the car with the bouquet in one hand. He was as ready as he was going to get, and for crying out loud, he was a grown man. How difficult could it be to take a woman out on a date for Valentine's Day?

All that self-confidence, all that *brass,* went right out the window when Dustine answered the door, and all he could do was stand there and try to recall what he'd planned on saying.

She grinned at him impishly. "I believe the normal greeting is 'Hello.' "

Conroy nodded and found his manners. "Roses," he said gravely as he offered her the bundle wrapped against the winter's chill. "To match your outfit."

"Thank you." She took the flowers and motioned him inside. "I thought I'd dress for the occasion."

"You look great," Conroy said and meant it, wondering how on earth he'd managed to get this stunning woman to agree to spend the evening with him. Her dark hair was curlier than usual, almost wild, while her dress, a long-sleeved slightly off-the-shoulder velvet thing in a shadowy pattern of black and red roses, brought out her skin's dusky quality and the deep red of her lipstick. She looked exotic and classy, way out of his league. He loved it.

Dustine closed the door behind him and stood there, smiling, until he remembered he should be taking off his coat. "Happy Valentine's Day," he finally said, still rather overwhelmed by how pretty she was tonight.

"Thanks," Dustine said again. "Come on in. Would you like something to drink, or do we have to leave right away?"

He followed her up the stairs to the living room. "To be honest, we're going to be running on luck tonight. Every place I called for reservations was booked. I know of a bunch that don't take reservations, but we're likely to spend a chunk of time waiting for a table."

Dustine leaned on the counter in the kitchen. "Going to be a tough call on Valentine's night."

Conroy nodded. "I know. I should have—"

"Do you like Chinese food?"

He blinked. "Well, sure."

Dustine's smile widened. "Great. Then I know the perfect place."

Over a dinner of kwok-tay, peppercorn shrimp, and sweet plum wine, they talked about everything under the sun.

The restaurant Dustine steered them to was a small Chinese place called the Smiling Buddha off Golf Road in Schaumburg. Out of the way and family-owned, it had been there for years, long before her friend Hilary had first visited it as a child with her father. The food was incredible: fat Chinese dumplings stuffed and browned to perfection, two oversized platters of shrimp crusted with peppercorns and garlic unlike anything he'd ever tasted before—Dustine's Chinese match for his one-of-a-kind tacos of their previous date. The plum wine, he realized, was deadly; delicious and smooth, sweet as soda pop, and bound to offer a pounding hangover if you didn't limit your intake. Still, there was nothing like a glass or two of good wine to loosen up a couple of nervous people.

"Come on," Dustine said now. "You know more about me than almost anyone else. I know zip about you. Time to 'fess up." She gave him an arched look. "Handsome, eligible, good job. Tell me you don't have a girlfriend or two stashed somewhere."

"I don't have any such thing," he retorted, amused.

"A wife, then—no, wait. An *ex*-wife."

He shook his head and chuckled. "Nope, never been married." There must've been something strained about his voice, because rather than ask another question, Dustine only waited. "I came close a couple of times," he said at last. "At least *I* thought I was close. The truth is I have a bad habit of moving too fast on someone I care about. I don't trust other people very easily, and that can sometimes be a problem."

Dustine sat back and thought about this. "You get jealous," she finally said.

Conroy almost winced. How harsh it sounded, but there was no way to tiptoe around it. "Yeah."

"Why?"

"I don't know," he said honestly. "I wish I could say that something happened when I was a kid that made me this way, or that I saw some family member screw around on their spouse and hated their behavior. But I can't—I come from a solid Irish-Catholic family, and if anyone did stuff like that, it certainly wasn't family knowledge. If I knew what made me like this, maybe I could change it."

"That's not necessarily true."

He nodded. "Of course not." Conroy shrugged, feeling self-conscious. "The bottom line is that I don't have some old girlfriend who brought it out because she cheated on me. I am what I am, and no matter how hard I try to change that, it ends up showing." He looked away for a moment. "I'm not a violent man, or a mean one, so it wasn't like that. But between that green-skinned part of me and . . . caring too soon, I bombed out both times that I thought I had something worthwhile."

Dustine sipped her wine and looked at him intently. "So now do you go the other way?"

Conroy frowned. "What do you mean?"

"Are you *too* careful now? And maybe you lie to yourself about what's going on if you're dating someone and you begin to feel a bit jealous."

Conroy considered this. "Too careful? Probably—it's hard not to be. As for the rest . . ." He shrugged. "I can't say. I haven't gotten that far a third time."

Dustine took another sip of wine and gazed at him over the rim of her glass. "Do you want to?"

Conroy started to shrug off the question, the stopped himself. Maybe it was Dustine's wine pushing the question out of her, and maybe it was his that made him want to blurt out an answer—"*Yes*"—but he wasn't about to let the alcohol keep the evening from being the very best it could be. Still, his character demanded an honest answer. He took a deep breath.

"Yes," he said finally. Conroy let his hand slide forward and cover hers. He held it briefly, then made himself draw back when the last thing in the world he wanted to do was let go of her. "Yes, I do."

"Suburban Counseling."

No flash, no frills. The female voice on the other end of the receiver was calm and unrushed. For a very long moment, Alec felt dizzy, breathless, like he'd been pushed out the open door of an airplane and was plummeting toward the Earth. If this was what skydiving felt like, he never wanted to try it. To speak required air and he had none, so he couldn't say anything.

The person on the other end of the line didn't hang up. "Hello, this is Suburban Counseling. If you'd like to talk to us, we'd very much like to help."

"I . . ." It was the best he could do.

"We're having a meeting tonight, sir. Would you like to come? It's a difficult evening to spend alone, and you wouldn't have to do anything like tell your life story to a bunch of strangers. Some of the people will talk, but you're not required or expected to, and it would get you out of the house for the evening. Would you like the address?"

The faceless woman waited, patient and unrelenting. It would have been so much easier if she'd just hung up in irritation at his continued silence. "We're easy to find," she continued without being asked. "We're in Addison on Army Trail Road, east of Route 53 about a mile and a half. The meeting starts in a half hour, but you needn't be here exactly on time. We usually have some light refreshments—soda, chips, that sort of thing."

Alec swallowed and rubbed the spot between his eyebrows. The apartment seemed to spin around him with a suddenly too-big feeling, not at all the comforting cradle he wanted it to be. "W-what's the address?" His voice sounded like a frog's croak—he hadn't spoken to anyone since Wednesday. She told him, then asked him his name. "Alec," he said, unwilling to give her any more.

It was enough. "All right, Alec," she said in that same soothing tone. "We look forward to seeing you."

He hung up without saying anything else, belatedly regretting his rudeness. Had this upheaval of his life cost him the simple skills of courtesy? He thought about this as he changed into a fresh shirt, despite knowing that it mattered little in the scheme of things. But it gave him something on which to focus other than the accusing sense that he was giving up on Nola, buckling under the unwitting cruelty of the daily nonprogress in his wife's disappearance. When he looked into the bathroom mirror Alec saw a stranger, a shadow-eyed man fifteen pounds thinner than the month before and whose brown eyes were filled with a newly found and hated doubt, a weaker twin from whom he could not escape.

But tonight, for a little while, he would at least try to distract himself.

The meeting place turned out to be nothing fancier than a small room off a coffee shop, a privately owned place rather than one of the more crowded chains. The owner, a middle-aged woman with graying hair and a quiet smile, stayed out of the way but provided two restaurant-sized coffee thermoses; the plates of cookies and crackers and plastic bowls of tortilla chips had obviously been brought by attendees. Alec forced himself to ask the woman in the coffee shop where the meeting was, and when she pointed him in the right direction, he stood in the doorway indecisively. Did he really want to do this?

"You must be Alec," someone said from behind him.

Caught, he turned and faced a trim, attractive woman who might have been two or three years older than himself. Reddish blonde curly hair just brushed the tops of her shoulders and framed brown eyes set in a square-jawed face. Her smile showed just a hint of a dimple on the left side. She held out her hand. "Marietta Cale. I'm the one who picked up your call."

Reluctantly, Alec shook her hand. "I'm Alec . . . Elidad." He'd felt a great reluctance about revealing his last name, as if it were an admission of something, a way to trace an imagined infidelity. He cleared his throat. "How did you know it was me?"

Marietta touched his elbow to urge him into the room. "You're the only new face. We have a great group, but thankfully not a lot of new members. Would you like a cup of coffee?"

He nodded. "Black is fine." There was an old wooden table in the center of the room with chairs around it; most were taken but she guided him to one off to the side, an upholstered thing that seemed like it ought to have been in someone's living room rather than here. There were a couple of others like it here and there, some occupied, some not. Marietta came back in a moment and handed him a mug. He took it, then glanced worriedly at the others. A few were looking at him curiously but made a point to drop their gazes after an acknowledging nod. "What do I have to do?"

"Nothing," she said. "Just listen; speak only if you want to. In that regard, I guess we're kind of like Alcoholics Anonymous. If talking to the group makes you uncomfortable, I'll be glad to listen. I'm not in charge—we have a licensed counselor if someone really needs guidance—but I'm sort of the 'first contact' person."

Alec stared at his coffee. "I don't think I'm ready for that yet."

"Then don't say anything," Marietta said gently as she turned to join the men and women seated around the table. "Just listen to the others and spend an evening with some company other than your own. It'll take your mind out of the house."

Well, he couldn't argue with that need. But that's all it was—an urge to get away from his empty apartment, especially on Valentine's night when Nola should have been there with him, when they should have been celebrating their first February 14th. It was *not* a concession to the idea that his wife might be anything but alive, that she would not, somehow, soon be found. Because she would be. He needed her, and therefore, someday, she *had* to be.

And so while Alec didn't join in, he listened. And for a while, he almost forgot his own troubles.

It was more a discussion group than a one-at-a-time recitation. Because of this, he didn't get a whole story from anyone, just heartbreaking bits and pieces that made him remember, for the first time since his wife's disappearance, that he wasn't the only one in the world facing such a horrific situation. This group, it seemed, was about learning to cope with loss on a day-to-day basis rather than trying to change it, and in a vague way that made him angry with Detective Conroy all over again. Still, the stories touched him—he knew their pain, the shattered sense of having the nexus around which your world revolved suddenly yanked out of place and secreted away. Runaway children, missing friends and relatives, others; from what he could gather, a few of the tales, Marietta's included, were more disastrous—murdered spouses or loved ones who would never be coming back, and these were the ones that Alec feared most, although he wouldn't, *couldn't,* acknowledge that. Nola, he told himself over and over, is *not* dead. She *will* be found, and she *will* be all right when she is.

But, God help him, his sense of surety, of *righteousness* about this was no longer there. It didn't matter what the rest of the world thought or how many doubts Detective Conroy and Officer Curtis had. What did matter was himself, and sitting silent in the corner as he looked around the room at the others, Alec suddenly felt like he was lying to himself. And of all the people who could see through his thin charade, it was most certainly the man he faced in the mirror every morning.

The group broke up after a couple of hours, with some of the people detouring into the coffee shop to continue quiet conversations. Marietta joined Alec as he pulled on his coat. "How are you doing?" she asked.

He opened his mouth, fully intending to lie. What came

out—"Not good"—clearly surprised him more than her. When he stood there, appalled at his own honesty, she only nodded sympathetically.

"It's difficult to lose someone you care about," she began.

"They'll find her," Alec said automatically. But that's just what it was—*automatic,* a trained response in which he was fast losing his faith. He tried again, not very successfully. "They *will.* It hasn't been that long."

Marietta nodded again, but Alec knew she neither agreed nor disagreed. "This is your wife?"

"Nola," he told her. "We were married last October."

"So you're still newlyweds," she commented. "What a nightmare." Marietta studied him. "Do you have family, Alec? People to help you out?"

He looked at his shoes. "No. Nola . . . there isn't anyone else."

Marietta's gaze slid away from him and touched on a few people around the room before returning. "Sometimes," she said carefully, "talking to the police only makes what's inside you worse. The pain and the worry build like a poison, until people can barely function anymore." She folded her hands in front of her. "Would you like to talk to me, Alec? Tell me what happened to . . . Nola?"

Alec started to refuse—this woman was a total stranger, someone he might never see again after tonight. How could he share the agony of not knowing where Nola was, reveal the traitorous uncertainty that made him despise his own face?

"I know you heard pieces of it tonight," she said suddenly, as if she was aware of the turn his thoughts were taking, "but two years ago my husband Andy was murdered on his way home from work. The police said it was an attempted carjacking, but Andy pushed the panic button and the alarm went off so the two men didn't take the car. The best guess is that they were so angered by the alarm that they took it out on him. They stabbed him fourteen times."

Alec frowned. "Best guess?"

"They never caught the men who did it." Marietta's eyes clouded over briefly. "For a long time all I could do was wonder what went through Andy's mind while this was happening. If he thought about me, about the things we'd had planned, why he just didn't hand them the damned keys and walk away." Her voice broke for a moment and she inhaled, then blinked.

"I'm sorry," Alec said quietly.

Marietta turned her gaze, now clear, on him. "During the first year after his death, the only thing that kept me going was hatred, the belief that someday his murderers would be brought to justice." She looked down at her hands. "I still believe that, Alec, so I understand why you can't let go of your convictions about Nola. And you shouldn't—you have every right and reason to hang on to them for as long as you need to. God knows I did. The difference between the woman I was then and who I am now is that I no longer let the past rule my life." She paused, and despite the kind tone of her voice, Alec wanted to flinch away from her final words. "But the most important thing is *you*—you have to hang on to your future. Don't let go of yourself because of something that happened in the past that you'll never, ever be able to change. It just isn't a fair trade-off."

FEBRUARY 17--MONDAY

"Well, I'll be damned," Conroy said.

He lifted the clear plastic bag he'd found on his desk and peered at the contents, then snatched up the small folder of paperwork next to it and scanned through it. His initial shot of hope crashed quickly into the realization that he was going to have to pass this latest bit of bad news along to Alec Elidad. Not a chore he found particularly appealing.

A shadow momentarily blocked his light and Conroy looked up to find Frank Drosner standing next to his desk. "A uniform went over and took the report earlier this morning," the older man explained.

"It's been tagged and examined?" Conroy asked.

"Yeah. I saw the name and ran it through first thing. Forensics didn't find anything they could point at—it's a pretty big mess."

Conroy nodded. "Thanks."

As Drosner walked away, Conroy reached into his bottom drawer and found a pair of disposable latex gloves, then spread the top of the bag apart. As he pulled out Nola Elidad's purse, he wrinkled his nose at the smell and glanced at the report again. Location: found jammed in the side corner of a garbage truck, and there was no denying that was the truth. He went through it methodically, but there was nothing spectacular about the contents: a few pieces of identification and her credit card—the same unused one he'd carefully monitored since her disappearance—a few light cosmetics, her wallet, all covered with filth and smashed until they were barely recognizable. The only interesting thing was the lack of cash in the wallet, but a dozen hands could've gone through it between the time it'd been dumped and the time the uniformed cop had bagged it as evidence. Pinning her disappearance on a robbery motive would be a real stretch, and Conroy hadn't forgotten about the Pik-Kwik clerk's story.

Stripped of money, but there'd been no use of Nola Elidad's credit card, even on the day she'd been abducted. No ransom note and no body, but now they had the purse she'd been carrying. It didn't look good; even the dubious theory that she'd left on her own was further weakened by this discovery—fleeing her husband, she might've thrown out the credit card and even her identification, but it was highly doubtful she'd have tossed her entire purse. No, someone had taken it away from her and disposed of it. The odds that they would ever find this woman alive had just moved into almost nonexistent.

Conroy resealed the bag and steeled himself for the call he had to make to Alec Elidad.

FEBRUARY 20--THURSDAY

Stacey found the slip of paper with the telephone number on it.

It was under the bed, just behind the leg—easy to miss something that small and insignificant in the times that she'd searched the room. Jesse's shift was over and he was in the shower, following a routine with which they'd both become familiar. With the hum of the water in the background, Stacey sat on her side of the bed and smoothed out the rumpled piece of paper. Her writing, of course, but the woman who'd written these numbers seemed a world apart from her, a distant relative with whom she had so little contact that Stacey could do nothing but label her a stranger. She didn't even remember the name of the person, presumably a policeman, to whom this number was tied, and she certainly felt no compulsion to call him. Just as well, since Jesse had disconnected the hall telephone and she still had no idea where it was.

This phone number—it was a tie to the outside world. Yet that same world had apparently forgotten about her, or about Nola, the woman she'd thought she was. In this small Chicago suburb, more of a small town than anything else, wouldn't someone have found her by now if she truly was anyone other than Stacey Waite? Beyond that long-ago notice in the paper, no one seemed to have searched, least of all the faceless man still vaguely in her memory who, supposedly, had been her husband.

And Jesse . . . he had been so good to her, endlessly patient with her rantings and stubbornness. How much had all of this hurt him, to see her and love her but be afraid to touch her—all the while knowing in the back of his mind that another man had done just that. Surely his biggest fear of all was that she might decide she preferred the stranger she'd married by mistake. If the situation were reversed, would she not be just as afraid?

Stacey heard the water stop in the background and her fist closed around the tiny scrap of paper, crushing it. Hurriedly, knowing Jesse might open the door at any second, she yanked open one of the drawers in the dresser and shoved the wadded ball underneath a stack of slips. If she needed it, she'd remember where it was this time. It would be like a little security blanket, the key to her freedom if she felt it were really, truly necessary.

She'd closed the drawer and sat back down on the edge of the bed just before the door to the bathroom opened and Jesse stepped out. When he saw her, he smiled, slightly uncertain. He spent so much of his time around her like that—cautious about what he said and did, as if she were the eggshell upon which he had to step every day. The amount of patience and love that must take suddenly struck Stacey as enormous, yet what did she give him in return? Not much, and it would cost her so little to actually try.

"Are you tired?" she asked and stood. "I could make breakfast this morning."

Jesse shrugged and stopped next to her, then glanced at his shirtless reflection in the mirror. His hair was wet and tousled, still uncombed although he'd slipped on a clean pair of jeans. "I'm okay. And I don't mind cooking for you."

She smiled. "That wouldn't be a way of saying my cooking is lousy, would it?"

He peered at her, not sure whether or not she was kidding. "No—I wouldn't—"

"Come on," she said. "Admit it. You'd rather eat three-day-old leftovers than face what I do to eggs."

"That's not true," he said, surprised. "I like your cooking just fine." Despite his denial, Stacey caught a hint of something beneath his voice, a tinge of humor. She tried to remember the last time she'd heard Jesse laugh, but nothing came to mind.

"Yeah?" She cocked one eyebrow. "You ought to see what I can do with roadkill."

Jesse's eyes widened. "What?"

"Roadkill," she repeated. "Go scrape up a deer and I'll show you."

His mouth worked. "Scrape up a *deer*? Stacey, what—"

"You're afraid of my cooking," she said accusingly.

"I am no such thing!"

"Then let me cook for you this morning."

He folded his arms and gave her a mock scowl. "No. I refuse to eat deer and potato patties. I want sausage."

Stacey shook her head—if they were going to play, she was going to take it as far as she could. "It's Thursday. Have you forgotten? I don't do sausage on Thursdays—deer only. Maybe skunk."

"I don't like skunk," he retorted. His face remained deceptively bland but his eyes were laughing. "I could do . . . hedgehog. Yeah, hedgehog would be okay."

"But they're spiny!"

"They're crunchy."

"Pokey."

He squinted at her. "Pokey?"

She nodded gravely. "They poke you in the nose when you try to bite into them."

"Ow!"

"Exactly. Skunk would be better." He wrinkled his nose but before he could say anything, Stacey spoke again. "Smashed skunk hash. I guarantee you've never tasted anything like it."

Jesse pushed his fingers through his hair. "Can I hold out for the sausage? I think I'm allergic to skunk hash—something I just developed."

Stacey tried to look comically thoughtful. "Hmmm. Well, there's always pos—"

Jesse backed up to the edge of the bed and sat, then held up a hand to stop her. "You know what? I think I'm losing my appetite."

She grinned down at him. "I knew I'd get out of cooking if I tried hard enough."

Finally, Jesse laughed. "You're wicked—you offered in the first place!"

She shook her head. "Not so. I'm just being strategic."

"Like a fox!"

Stacey shrugged, suddenly out of clever responses, then sat next to him. She could feel him shake every now and then, still chuckling over their ridiculous exchange, and they sat there in comfortable silence. Neither said anything in this rare, remarkably-free-of-tension moment, and facing the mirror, Stacey could see both their reflections. She looked the same as always, dressed a little earthier than she might've chosen on her own in the jeans and soft, button-down shirt with the sleeves rolled up into which she'd changed while Jesse showered. Jesse looked good, a huge improvement over the wild-eyed man who'd taken her from the parking lot. His dark, damp hair was a little long and shaggy, and he'd started combing it straight back from his forehead; he'd picked up a few pounds, his work shift adding a little muscle here and there while leaning out the small roll of padding he'd begun to develop around his middle. Sitting next to him, Stacey caught the scent of his skin—slightly steamy and clean, still holding the faint residue of the all-natural soap he preferred. His arm rested casually against hers, and the contact made her skin tingle slightly.

Desire slid over her, unexpected and hot, like the sudden, shocking shift in the temperature when stepping into the blistering sun from a shadowed spot on a summer day. She jerked in surprise at the same time that Jesse did, as though something he was feeling had also changed, perhaps in response to her. The movement made her lose her balance, and when she started to slip off the edge of the bed, Jesse's hands instinctively reached to catch her.

Stacey found herself facing him with his hands around her upper arms, their noses nearly touching. Jesse froze and stared at her, as if he wasn't quite sure what was happening. "Stacey, I—"

She leaned forward and kissed him.

His lips were soft, then more insistent as his mouth opened and his tongue sought hers. She felt the overnight growth of his dark beard against her face, surprisingly soft, as his hands left her arms and slid around her back, drawing her close. This time, Stacey had no thought of resisting; her hands swept through his hair and she pulled him harder against her, feeling the muscles of his chest and arms and suddenly desperate to be with him, starving for his touch and taste, curious to find out everything she'd been terrified of only a few short weeks ago.

His mouth still on hers, Jesse pressed her down on the bed. When one hand moved hesitantly to the buttons on her shirt, Stacey pressed his palm over her breast, then was vaguely shocked as her body arched in response to the heat that swept through her.

For Jesse, the movement was like a key turning in a lock; suddenly his hands were everywhere he hadn't been able to touch, his mouth and tongue following along until Stacey was dizzy with need, barely able to breathe. When her blouse and jeans came off, she registered it only because it let her get closer to Jesse, finally gave her the sensation of her skin against his. Her pulse felt like it was skyrocketing and perspiration slicked them both, tasting salty and sweet in her mouth as her teeth trailed along his neck and shoulder, her nails unwittingly raked his back. She had no last-minute hesitation as his body covered hers, felt only the fire exploding in both of them as he filled her and they both cried out.

And afterward, their bodies still tightly entwined, Jesse cried in her arms.

Jesse could smell the formaldehyde in the air.

He shifted on his chair, trying for no good reason to recall the details. It's what they used, right? There was no mistaking the scent—he remembered it well from biology class. Unfortunately the recollection of the stinging, unpleasant aroma brought with it a number of other memories that he would have preferred to leave alone, things like stainless steel scalpels and dissection trays, the sight and feel of flesh parting beneath the blade.

"It stinks in here," he muttered to his friend John. "Can you smell it?"

John Aldwin glanced first at him, then around the room to which they'd been escorted by the receptionist. He and John had been best friends since grammar school, and now John's round face was creased with worry, his brown eyes a mirror of Jesse's misery. "No," he answered in a low voice. "What is it?"

Jesse started to respond, then shook his head as the door opened and Raymond Pitofsky walked in. The director of Pitofsky & Sons Funeral Home was a tall, blonde man, younger than Jesse had expected, dressed in a seemingly perfect dark gray suit over a smooth white shirt and plain, black silk tie. His expression was mild and somber, professional. Maybe it was Jesse's ravaged features that tipped him off, but when both Jesse and John stood, he knew exactly which man to address.

"Mr. Waite, I'm Raymond Pitofsky," he said quietly as he offered his hand. Jesse took it and shook; the man's grip was as in sync with his surroundings as the rest of him: warm with just the right amount of pressure. Nothing to remember or offend. "I'm so very sorry for your loss."

Jesse had expected these words, but the resentment he'd thought he would feel didn't surface. Yes, this man made a living from the sadness of others, but suddenly Jesse realized that someone had to do it, someone had to . . . take care of this part of it, didn't they? There was a sense of inner competence, of understanding in Pitofsky, and it didn't matter whether it was there because of his training or because it came to him instinctively. It was just there, and Jesse was very, very grateful for it.

Raymond Pitofsky turned to John and shook his hand too, his expression politely questioning. "This is John Aldwin," Jesse said. "He's an old friend."

Pitofsky nodded. "It's good to have someone with you through these difficult times." He indicated the two chairs in front of his desk as he went behind it and sat down. "Please, make yourself comfortable."

Jesse and John sat again. Comfortable? Maybe other people believed differently but Jesse thought the chair, one of those dark leather things trimmed with brass fasteners, was hard and unyielding. The rest of the office followed the style, different from what he would have expected in suburban Addison, showing lots of dark, Victorian-type furniture and deep brown leather. The walls were paneled and hung here and there were a few carefully chosen floral paintings in muted colors; the single window was covered by cream-colored sheers and flanked by heavy, deep blue velvet drapes that matched the plush carpeting. Pitofsky's desk was smaller than expected, the surface clear of all but a few essentials.

When Jesse didn't say anything, the director leaned forward and folded his hands on the desktop. "To make these arrangements," he said matter-of-factly, "I'll need to have you fill out some forms once you've let me know what your preferences are. It won't take long, but the law requires the home to have this information." He looked at Jesse, waiting for his nod of acceptance before continuing. When it came, Pitofsky lifted a plastic-sheathed piece of paper from the neat stack of items on his right and held it out. "This is our price list, Mr. Waite. If you want to look this over and think about what you want, I'll complete what I can of the paperwork for you. Then you can take it from there."

Jesse watched his hand reach out and accept the price list, but when he tried to read it, none of the words or figures wanted to sink in. Price list? Was he really here—was this really happening?

Stacey . . .

"I don't have a lot of money." He heard the words come out of his mouth and hated himself for it, despised the fact that this devastating moment in his life, the death of the one person he treasured above everything else, should be reduced to a matter of dollars and cents. What kind of a world was this?

"I understand," Pitofsky said. "And making arrangements for a loved one isn't an easy thing to begin with, and it becomes much more difficult when means are limited. But you needn't feel you have no options, Mr. Waite. We have a number of choices for you to consider, including affordable financing—"

Pitofsky droned on, his monotone voice maintaining a professionally soothing tone during his no doubt well-rehearsed speech. Jesse blinked and continued to stare at the paper in front of him, stuck now on the phrase "affordable financing." How absurd that he might have to finance the death of his wife. Yet, wasn't that exactly what the hospital had already done, with its doctors and the rounds of endless medicine and intensive care supervision—

"Jesse," John said quietly.

He forced himself to look up. "I'm sorry . . . I missed what you were saying."

"He wanted to know if there was a plan on the sheet that you thought would be okay."

Jesse nodded and ran his gaze down the column on the right side of the paper again, then cleared his throat. "This one," he answered, choosing the one that was one above the least expensive. "One up from the bottom." He thought that their savings account ought to cover it, although it wouldn't leave much behind. But it didn't matter—what did he have to spend it on now but this?

"A fine choice," Raymond Pitofsky assured him as John leaned closer to look at the sheet Jesse held. Jesse handed it to his friend and saw him scan it—a simple, blue cloth-covered casket, short ceremony, obituary, various pickups and deliveries, copies of the death certificate, interment. No doubt things like a memorial stone would be extra—everything would be extra—but he would think about that later. Pitofsky made a few more check marks on the form he was filling out, then offered the clipboard to Jesse. "If you would please complete the areas I was unable to fill in, we can finalize this matter. I know you must want to get back to your family."

There was that word again, and Jesse choked back a bitter laugh. He felt uncomfortable, slightly warm and claustrophobic despite the cold, stiff leather on which he was sitting and the fairly spacious room. Still, he just nodded and looked at the form, trying to make himself concentrate on answering the questions. He did the best he could, a passable job considering he felt like someone had taken his mind and run it through a paint-can shaker, mixed up everything bright and beautiful in his world until it was a sad and uniform gray. He made his final marks and handed it back, waiting with John at his side while the young director carefully checked his answers. At the end of the form, Pitofsky's youngish face creased.

"It says here you want a closed casket, Mr. Waite?"

"Yes."

Pitofsky sat back. "As I understand it, your wife's appearance is . . . satisfactory," he said carefully. "According to what you've filled out, there are several family members on your wife's side. I know this is a terribly painful time, but I do want to point out that this may cause some disagreements."

"It's not their decision," Jesse interrupted. His voice had an

edge to it that made John look at him nervously. "It's mine, and I want her casket closed. I want to remember her as she was alive, and that's the way I want everyone else to remember her, too."

Pitofsky nodded. "Many people think that way at first, Mr. Waite. But for some family members this leaves an area of dou—"

"This is not open to discussion and I don't want to hear any more about it." He felt like it was someone else speaking, the words being forced through his tightly clenched teeth. "I don't want to see her, and I don't want anyone else to see her either—I will not have my wife stuck in a box and stared at, and if this is a problem, then I'll take her somewhere else. I don't want—"

"Jesse."

John's hand on his arm grounded Jesse again. He took a deep breath and realized he was standing—when had he gotten up?—leaning over Pitofsky's fancy desk and nearly shouting at the funeral director, who was staring at him in dismay. "Excuse me," he said abruptly. He looked around, a little wildly. "Is there a rest room where I can, uh, rinse my face?"

"Of course." Pitofsky stood as if nothing had happened and motioned for Jesse to follow him to the door, where he indicated the subtly lit hallway. "If you'll just take this to the end and turn left, you can't miss it."

"Thank you." Jesse's voice was shaking, but he'd be damned if he was going to apologize for this. He would not be pushed into doing something he was so totally against—Stacey, who'd known his feelings about the hideous custom of viewing corpses, would never have wanted him subjected to this because of her.

It was darker and cooler in the hallway, and Jesse's mood immediately calmed. He shouldn't have flown off the handle in there, should have realized that Pitofsky was used to dealing with people who wanted what Jesse considered to be the most morbid ritual ever invented by mankind. Before making the turn at the end of the hall, he paused and glanced back. The door to Pitofsky's office was like a square of light in the gloom, and instead of returning to his seat, the director was standing next to John's chair, speaking earnestly with his hands spread, no doubt trying to persuade John to somehow change Jesse's mind. As he stared, John suddenly looked up and gave Jesse a reassuring smile at the same time that Pitofsky saw Jesse watching them. Whatever he'd been saying got cut off in mid-sentence and he, too, smiled . . . perhaps a little more nervously. It's okay, Jesse told himself, forcing his shoulder muscles to untense. John and he had been the best of friends for over a decade and he knew the other man would never fail him, and as if to confirm that, John sent him a slight nod.

In the small, tastefully decorated rest room, Jesse adjusted the water temperature then splashed his face a few times, welcoming the coolness against his hot, dry skin. Stubble grated against his fingers and it occurred to him that it'd been at least three days since he'd shaved—there just hadn't been time to worry about trivial things like appearances. The pain of losing Stacey was like a huge, glass-encrusted softball in the center of his chest, but he'd have to get past it somehow, at least pull himself together for the service. He couldn't embarrass Stacey's memory with another outburst like the one he'd just had in Pitofsky's office. The truth was, when the time came Trista would probably do enough of that for both of them.

He rinsed his face a final time, then dried it with paper towels. As an afterthought he pulled out his comb and forced it through his mop of dark, overlong curls. Even the sensation made him remember his wife and the way she used to run her fingers through his hair all the time, always teasing him and saying that if life were fair she would have his hair and he would have hers.

If life were fair, indeed.

Jesse's eyes started to burn and he squeezed them shut and gripped the edge of the sink as hard as he could, willing himself to find enough self-control to get through the rest of this appointment at the funeral home. He would not go back in there and raise his voice again. He would handle this in a reasonable manner and he would get what he wanted because there just wasn't any other way. End of problem, and as he put away his comb, Jesse nodded at his image in the mirror as if to confirm it.

When he got back to Raymond Pitofsky's office, the funeral director was seated and waiting for him. Jesse lowered himself onto his chair and opened his mouth to speak, but nothing came out. This whole viewing thing . . . was it really that important? Why?

He couldn't answer that, other than to point at the horrible mental picture he'd been carrying around for half of his life, the one of his parents in their caskets. He'd thought he'd grow out of it and leave it behind . . . but it hadn't happened. How could he face the prospect of having that same image of Stacey in his head twenty years from now, swallowing up all the good memories he should be cherishing instead?

"All right," Pitofsky said when Jesse didn't say anything. "If you'll just sign at the bottom of the form and decide what time you want the service, I think we can finish this up."

"What?" Jesse asked blankly. No more arguments?

Pitofsky slid the clipboard toward him and indicated a line at the bottom of the form. "Right here."

"But the viewing," Jesse said in confusion. Despite his intentions, he could hear his voice starting to rise. "I never agreed—"

"It will be a closed casket, of course," Pitofsky said. His voice was gentle. "In accordance with your wishes."

Jesse stared at him mutely, then glanced at John. His friend reached over and squeezed his arm reassuringly. Jesse thought, as he so often did, of Stacey, and the image that filled his mind was a random one, something from earlier in the summer when they'd gone shopping at the Pik-Kwik. She'd said something to him in the parking lot, a comment a little on the ribald side and totally unexpected that had made him laugh on and off for half an hour.

Relief spread through him, and for the first time since the charge nurse at the ICU had given him the awful news, Jesse felt the agony around his heart ease the tiniest bit. Yes, these were the kinds of things that he wanted to—and would—remember over the coming years.

He wrapped up the details while in the embrace of a pleasantly numbing fog, refusing the newspaper obituary and specifying two hours of visitation in the home's chapel tomorrow morning followed by a short memorial service. He barely looked at the form before signing it, and was proud of himself for being able to hold back the semihorrified laughter that wanted to escape when he paid for the whole thing—all thirty-five hundred dollars of it—with his Visa. Such details as how to finance Stacey's death had escaped him this morning and he hadn't remembered to bring the checkbook or given any thought to transferring money from the savings account to cover a check that large. It wasn't until John leaned forward and offered to write his own check to pay for it that

Jesse came to his senses enough to stop him, recalling the small, discreet decal he'd seen elsewhere in the funeral home. It seemed like only a few more minutes before the three men were shaking hands again and saying good-bye, and even though he knew he'd be back here in a few short hours, Jesse was never so glad to leave a building behind.

The mid-September sun was bright and painful after the comforting gloom that had permeated the interior of the funeral home, like bright wrapping paper camouflaging the aura of bleakness that had taken over everything in Jesse's life. All it did was hurt his eyes and make him long for Stacey—she'd loved the sun, had always thrown open the blinds around the townhouse and to hell with the air-conditioning bill. She should be here now, with him, maybe deciding what they were going to do this weekend—

"Why don't I stay at your place tonight?" John's voice broke into Jesse's thoughts. "I can just camp out on the couch and in the morning I'll run back to my place and pick up some clean clothes. Or you can come home with me."

For a long moment his friend's words didn't process, then Jesse finally understood. He shook his head. "No, but . . . thanks. I'll be okay. There's a lot I have to get done before tomorrow."

John frowned. "Jesse, I'm not sure you ought to be by yourself—"

"I'll be fine," Jesse interrupted. He gave John a small smile that felt more like a painful lifting of one side of his mouth, but the emotion behind it was sincere. "Thanks for the offer, though, and for coming with me today."

"You needed someone," was all John said. Jesse could hear the gruffness in his voice, though, and he knew his buddy was thinking about Trista. She had family of her own, people—not many, but a few—who would help her through this unthinkable thing that was cracking the foundation of Jesse's existence. In someone else's life, he and Trista would have been friends or had a little affection for each other—they could have drawn strength from one another and lessened the pain, if only a bit.

But not in this one.

John pulled his car over to the curb and stopped, then shifted into PARK, *and Jesse was surprised to see that they were already back at the townhouse he had shared with Stacey since their marriage four years earlier. He stared at it for a few long moments through the window, thinking that it already looked like Stacey's touch was missing. The small, two-story structure nestled between its neighbors was as tidy as always, the grass and bushes neatly trimmed, and the two pots of white petunias that Stacey had planted in the spring still thrived. The white blooms waved gaily in a breeze that was warm for the season but still carried an edge to it, a reminder that colder times were ahead. But the flowers were a lie—everything about the townhouse still looked . . . brown somehow. And sad, like one of those antique, sepia-toned photographs in which no one smiled but everyone stared at the camera as though they were frozen in time,. That's what Jesse felt like now: frozen, only instead of his prison being a hundred-year-old photograph, it was his own life.*

Cold times were coming, all right, Jesse thought morosely.

"Jesse?" John asked gently.

He took a depth breath, then found a semblance of a smile. "Okay, I'm off. I'll see you at the funeral home tomorrow."

John shook his head. "Nonsense. I'll pick you up at ten and drive you. It'll be one less thing for you to worry about."

Jesse started to protest, then shrugged. John was right, of course. Hell, he couldn't even remember if the Impala—Stacey's car, not his—had gas in it. "Thanks," he said again.

John nodded. He'd always had a boyish face, but the last few days had aged him. The world had a way of doing that. "See you tomorrow." He hesitated. "Jesse, are you sure—"

"I'm fine," Jesse cut in. "Really." He got out of the car and closed the passenger door before John could continue, afraid that the next question might be the one to push him over the edge, to make him break down and wail out loud like he really wanted to. He kept his back straight as he went up the walkway, knowing John was watching him; there was too much turnover in the rentals to forge any friendships, so thankfully the neighbors around here minded their own business. As he unlocked the door, he glanced back and gave John a dutiful nod. His friend inclined his head in return and pulled away as Jesse stepped inside.

He might as well have stepped into hell.

There were no fires of damnation or evil demons waiting to torture him, but Jesse thought that would have been preferable to the cold, dark silence crouching inside what had been his and Stacey's home. This had to be hell, a place where everything of value and color had fled and left behind only shadows sliding through rooms filled with silent emptiness.

The door swung shut behind him and Jesse stood there, frozen with the dread of all the nothing that awaited him in the days and months and years to come.

All those nights, Stacey thought, of lying quietly and feeling Jesse tremble if her arm brushed his . . . it was that, and the Valentine's Day flowers and card, his patience and control and unconditional love. These were the things that had finally made her take this irreversible step. And it was *so* much that—unchangeable, unforgettable, fueled by unacknowledged desire and curiosity, and the final realization that all she wanted in the world was to know what it would be like to be held by a man like Jesse, who wanted nothing more than to love her and please her, and would accept without question whatever crumbs of affection she could offer in return.

Now she watched Jesse sleep. Her body was sated, her mind drowsy but not quite ready to yield to sleep. His hair fell over his forehead in damp strings and his cheek was pressed into the pillow, his content expression making him look like an overgrown boy. The way he'd loved her and touched her . . . it was amazing, as though he'd been doing the same thing for years and was totally familiar with every part of her body. She felt as fulfilled as Jesse looked, complete not just physically but emotionally, as though Jesse had somehow closed the black hole that had become her memory. And while it was true that not everything had fallen into place, Stacey finally felt a serene acceptance, an *assurance*, that it all eventually would.

Maybe, Stacey thought sleepily, not remembering Jesse,

not remembering my life with him, is what created that black hole in the first place.

She smiled and snuggled closer, heard him murmur in his sleep before his arm folded warmly over hers. She'd come so far; surely she just needed to hold on and wait for the rest to come to her.

5

Dislocation

The truth that survives is simply the lie that is pleasantest to believe.

—H. L. MENCKEN

FEBRUARY 21--FRIDAY

Tonight the table was gone from the room, taken away by the coffee shop's owner, so Alec sat in on the circle with the counseling group. But he couldn't look at them; his elbows were on his knees, his head down, hands clasped. All he could do was stare at the floor and try to get the words out. It was like trying to speak around a tennis ball.

"I think my wife . . . may be dead."

There was no collective gasp or murmur of sympathy. The feelings were there—he knew that—but the others only sat quietly and waited, ready to listen if he wanted to say more. He did.

"The police found her purse on Monday," he continued, still staring downward. "Everything was still in it except the money. There's never been a ransom note or anything like that, and the day she disappeared there was a kid in the grocery store—I'd dropped her off in the parking lot—who said he saw a guy drag a woman into his car. He thought it was just a couple arguing and didn't pay any attention to it." There was a crack in the oak flooring beneath his shoe and Alec found himself focusing on it, following the split up and down. "It doesn't look good."

He lapsed into silence, and after a few moments the counselor, a pleasant-faced man named Kurt, cleared his throat. "And how does that make you feel?"

It was a standard psychology-type question. Alec had

known it would eventually come up, and he'd expected to feel the same sort of rage that he'd directed toward Detective Conroy. Not this time. Well, he did, but at least it wasn't directed toward the person who'd asked the question.

"Anger," he said. "Disbelief." He made himself look away from the crack, vaguely aware that he was giving himself a headache. "I have this question running through my head constantly—'Why me?' " He glanced around the circle, suddenly ashamed. "I guess that's selfish."

"Not at all," said someone else, a young woman Alec didn't know. "I promise you we've all felt that way. Happiness is easy to share, and everyone wants to. Misery is a solo thing. Friends, even relatives, have a marvelous way of disappearing. And then it's just you, and what happened, and no explanation."

"And there isn't anything that *can* make you feel better," added someone else. "You hear a lot about how it'll get easier as time passes, and maybe that's true. But in the meantime, you've still got to endure each hour of each day."

Alec nodded as someone else added his thoughts, and then someone else after that. Everyone had suffered here, and everyone understood. And while he really didn't feel any *better,* he felt less . . . stressed, less *guilty* about the idea that he might be taking his first tenuous steps down a path leading to a life without Nola. In some ways he still felt like a turncoat—would she have given up on him so easily?

The night wore on, but for a change it wasn't at a snail's pace. Listening to the stories of the others didn't remove his pain but it did mute it—instead of one person drowning alone, suddenly he had company in the water, a dozen or so companions all trying to keep their heads above the surface. For the first time since that terrible evening in mid-January, Alec no longer felt utterly alone.

"I think we'll wrap it up for tonight," he heard Kurt say. Alec glanced at his watch and was shocked to see it was ten o'clock, nearly two and half hours since the start of the meeting. He gathered his coat, scarf, and cap and milled about with the rest of them, watching most of them say their good nights and head into the parking lot while a few others drifted into the coffee shop section of the small building. In spite of the painful topics of conversation, for him the evening had been a blessing, something to keep him out of the empty apartment and away from his own bleak thoughts. The truth was, he was practically desperate to keep it going.

"Would you like to have a cup of coffee?"

Alec turned and saw Marietta standing a couple of feet away with her coat over one arm. Her smile was somewhere between welcoming and cautious, as if she didn't know how he would react. As far as he was concerned, she was a godsend. "That'd be great," he said.

He followed her through the door and she chose a small table by the window, halfway down the room. It struck Alec as being sort of neutral territory—not so close to the register as to be public, but not far enough back to be intimate. "Is this okay?"

"It's great," he said again, then held out the chair for her. He draped his coat over the back of the other chair, and gestured to the chalkboard menu behind the counter. "What . . . ?"

"Decaf," she said. "With cream, please. Nothing fancy."

Alec nodded and stepped into the short line, wondering briefly what he was doing here. Having coffee with an acquaintance, he told himself. Someone to talk with who knows what I'm going through. It was a comforting thought.

When he returned with their coffees—he'd decided to have the same—Marietta's small smile made him, again, glad he'd accepted her invitation. "So what did you think of the meeting tonight?" she asked as he settled across from her. Funny how everyone in the group steadfastly insisted on calling their evenings "meetings" rather than "sessions."

"It was nerve-wracking," Alec answered, surprising himself. He hadn't intended to be so blunt, but wasn't that the whole point? He couldn't lie to himself, and he shouldn't lie to Marietta. "I didn't know what to expect. I suppose I thought I'd end up being psychoanalyzed or something."

She nodded, her expression gone serious. "That's how I

felt, too. And it carried over to several meetings. But it's like anything that you participate in with the same group of strangers—classes, for instance. After three or four times you might not really know them, but they aren't quite strangers anymore either. You begin to realize they won't attack." She was silent for a moment, idly running a plastic stirrer through the liquid in her cup. "It must be hard," she said at last. "Not knowing."

Alec felt a muscle in his jaw tense and he made himself relax. This was what he'd wanted—someone to talk to, a sympathetic ear and a viewpoint that didn't try to rush him into accepting things he wasn't yet ready for. When he nodded, he felt like a robot jerking his head up and down, a piece of machinery controlled via remote by someone unseen. Not so bad, really, a way to distance himself from his own mental agony. "It is," he heard himself say. "There's no closure here—I go day by day, jumping every time the telephone rings or someone knocks on the door. Preparing for the worst but hoping for the best, then calling myself an idiot when I end up with neither."

Marietta shook her head. "You're not an idiot, Alec. And you're not alone in hanging on to hope—do it as long as you need to. No one else can tell you when it's the right time to let go, to change your outlook."

"The detective on the case—"

"—is a pessimist by nature," she interrupted. "It doesn't make him bad, it's just what he sees every day in his job. He can't help it, and he believes in preparing you for the worst."

Alec nodded. "I suppose so. He probably thinks he's helping, but from where I sit, he's just rushing. I don't know . . . sometimes I think he believes it ought to be easier for me because Nola and I didn't know each other that long."

She tilted her head. "Maybe from the outside looking in, it seems like that ought to make a difference. But when you love someone and that person is taken away, it hurts just as much."

"Yes," Alec agreed. "It does." For all the man's efforts, Detective Conroy had an unconscious way of making Alec feel embarrassed about his marriage to Nola. Maybe it was because they'd married so quickly, or maybe it was Nola's age—perhaps in his own subconscious, Alec felt uncomfortable about both those things. Not tonight, though, not here with Marietta or earlier in the group. Acceptance was much more comforting than judgmental sympathy. Marietta and the others . . . they knew how painful it could be to lose someone you loved and face the world alone, uncertain about the future—with them he could express his pain and sorrow at Nola's disappearance fully, in ways he never could with the detective.

Another refill on the coffees, a little more talk. Nothing too deep or hurtful, as though Marietta saw the first hint that there might be healing on Alec's part and had no wish to rip the wound wide again. Ten minutes, then twenty—a half hour tops, yet Alec felt better than he had in days, soothed and strengthened by the calm presence of the woman across the table.

"Here's my number," Marietta said when they stood and pulled on their coats. "You're not alone, Alec. If you need to call, if you need to talk, it doesn't matter what time it is. Lost sleep is something we can easily put behind us. Despair isn't."

Alec nodded gravely and accepted her card, tucking it into his wallet. He walked her to her car—for the rest of his life, he knew he would never again drive away without assuring himself that someone he was with was safe—then stood for several long, cold minutes under the bluish lights in the nearly empty parking lot after she'd pulled off. Snow dusted his shoulders, just enough to intensify the moisture in the frigid air and make him shiver inside his coat.

He unlocked his car and climbed inside, shivering even more as he started the engine and waited for it to warm up. What had Marietta said to him at the end of the evening last Friday? Something about hanging on to the future and not losing himself because of what had happened. He felt as if there'd been a turning point inside himself, enough so that he was even ready to end the leave of absence and go back to work on Monday. It would be the first, awkward step toward trying to acknowledge what might be a very painful truth.

Nola is probably dead.

Alec put his hands on the wheel and felt the cold seep through his gloves, forced himself to look straight ahead and put the car in gear when his shoulders would have slumped.

Going to the group's meetings was one small step; making himself go back to work was another. Two steps, and only a start.

Because he could say the words aloud all he wanted, but he still had a ways to go before he actually believed and accepted them in his heart.

MARCH 3--MONDAY

Jesse should've known it couldn't last.

"I'm okay now," Stacey told him as he got ready to leave for work that night. "Don't lock me in anymore."

Jesse looked at her mutely, wondering if the terror blasting through his heart showed in his eyes. Every instinct he had screamed at him not to listen to her, to make her go into the bedroom and padlock the outside of the door just as he had for the last six-odd weeks, keep her safely tucked away like a fragile, treasured piece of crystal is hidden from the visiting grandchildren.

And yet, how could he blame her? All week he'd been pulling longer shifts, going in early and staying late to make an eleven-hour day, being damned grateful for the overtime that was helping, week by week, to put them back on their financial feet. But Stacey . . . Jesus. Could he really expect her to just live with being alone so much, just accept the endless hours of solitude inside that single, small room?

He *had* to chance it. The thought of walking out of here with Stacey free made his heart pound wildly, but there wasn't any other choice. He couldn't lock her in forever, couldn't force her to play the part of his perpetual prisoner. Wasn't there some old, stupid saying about letting something go and if it loved you, it would come back? But what if he did just that, and she went . . . and just kept on going?

The past twelve days—he'd counted each and every one of them—had been paradise for him. His wife was back, in his heart and mind and arms, and if there was any shadow in his life at all, it was that small part of him that worried over Stacey's frame of mind. With this—

"I'm okay now. Don't lock me in anymore."

—it had all come to a head. Whether the end was good or bad remained to be seen.

What if, asked a dark voice in his brain, all the progress you've made up to now is nothing but a ruse on Stacey's part so she can escape? Staring at her now, knowing she was waiting for his answer, Jesse felt like he was on the parachute drop ride at Great America in Gurnee, the one where your seat was lifted two hundred feet in the air and then simply let go, leaving you and your co-riders to hurtle toward the ground at some ungodly speed until the brakes kicked in and stopped you from certain death. To escape . . . dear God, would she actually make love with him, so many times since the week before last, to accomplish this? Jesse couldn't—*wouldn't*—let himself believe that.

He looked at her, and then at the padlock in his hand, the one he always snapped into the hasp on the outside of the master bedroom door after she went inside. He saw himself lower his hand to the coffee table and open his fingers, watched but really couldn't feel it as the padlock rolled out of his palm.

Either Stacey wanted to stay, or she didn't.

The smile Stacey gave him was half normal, half relief. The only thing she could think as she warmly kissed him good-bye was that thank God she wouldn't be stuck in the bedroom again tonight. Something inside her had reached a tolerance limit in the wee hours of the last morning, the one too many in a long series of sanity-stretching nights;

Stacey wasn't sure what she would've said had Jesse refused her request, but she was convinced it wouldn't have been pretty.

And then, almost in the blink of an eye, Jesse was gone.

The door closed and Stacey locked it behind him automatically with the key he'd left, as if she'd been doing just that for half a decade. Then, startled at the sudden, stark silence, she simply stood there and stared at the foyer around her.

It seemed . . . *different* somehow, bigger without Jesse's strong presence to fill it. For a moment her vision did something weird and the room elongated in front of her, leading away to impossible shadows in its farthest corners. She squeezed her eyes shut and opened them again and it was back to normal. Just an entry foyer leading to a living room, and not a particularly large one at that. The tiny, unused dining area and pass-through off to the right, and beyond that the kitchen, compact and barely big enough for the table that she and Jesse ate breakfast at each morning.

Stacey stepped forward and the whisper of her tennis shoes on the carpet sounded as loud as bricks being dragged across a concrete sidewalk. The air in the room pressed against her, uncomfortably heavy, and for a moment she had the urge to run to the bedroom and lock *herself* in, anything to get away from this overwhelming feeling of fear. It was completely irrational, nearly suffocating—enough so that the only way Stacey could stop herself from doing just that was to drop to her knees on the carpet and fold herself over, as though she were praying for unseen salvation.

The minutes ticked by, and gradually she could breathe again.

She pulled herself slowly to her feet and leaned against the hallway wall. Her future was, finally, hers again: The front door was a few feet away, there was a telephone on the kitchen wall, and Jesse had probably stored the other phone in one of the closets. She could put on her coat and walk out of here, or simply pick up the phone and wait for deliverance.

But . . .

Well, for one thing, she didn't know where to go, couldn't think of any address in the world other than this one, which Jesse had told her repeatedly. It was cold outside, freezing, and even if she'd had another destination in mind—which she didn't—she had no transportation since Jesse took the car to work every night. Sure, she could go in the bedroom and retrieve that piece of paper with the police number on it, but try as she might, Stacey still couldn't remember the name of the detective that went with the number. Wouldn't she have to ask for someone in particular? And how would it sound when she couldn't say who? They'd think she was crazy, a woman calling in to report a situation that she couldn't possibly find a way to explain.

911—she could dial that, the saving grace of all urban emergencies. But that would hurt Jesse so badly, and things between them had gotten . . . well, they were *good,* damn it, better than any other time in her life that she could remember. And there was still his original promise—she knew he'd stick by it, the one where he'd agreed to take her to a psychiatrist when the insurance kicked in if she still had problems about the way things were going in her life. If she just rode with it awhile, Stacey had this feeling that things could end up really . . . special. Look how much time had already passed—there was probably less than six more weeks to go. She could hang in there for that short a time, couldn't she? Especially now that she'd regained a semblance of normal freedom?

Stacey glanced around the room again, absorbing the silence. Did she still have doubts about who she was or once had been, or about who Jesse believed she would be? Yes—there was no denying it. But what small doubts lingered didn't really have anything to do with identity—that would work itself out in time. Instead, they were more a sort of rebellion at the way Jesse had made her stay here for so long, for keeping her in detention like a naughty student. She felt like a child taken into a foster home who'd discovered that it wasn't so bad after all, and who finally had to admit that the world she came from wasn't the paradise she'd wanted to believe.

No, she thought, it wouldn't hurt to just . . . go with the flow for a while longer, the other half of the promise Jesse had given her. Whether she waited it out or left tonight, the truth wasn't going anywhere; eventually she'd find it. That other personality, Nola—what if that was nothing more than something her fevered brain had cooked up? If she left tonight only to discover that was so tomorrow, she would have hurt Jesse for nothing. For his sake, to return some of the caring this man had given to her, was it really the end of the world to completely be the woman he wanted her to be—Stacey Waite—for a little while longer?

There were only a handful of people in attendance.

Jesse had specifically told John not to tell anyone else, for the same reason he'd instructed Pitofsky not to run a newspaper obituary—he didn't want flowers and cards and a whole bunch of empty, insincere wishes. He couldn't bear the thought of trying to deal with that. Better this private and sparsely attended service where he didn't have to listen to the hypocrites who would have come out of the woodwork like cockroaches to feast on his grief, the same so-called, platitude-filled friends who hadn't been in touch for literally years but who would now show up

I'm so sorry to hear about this.

with offers of help they didn't really mean.

Let me know if I can do anything, anything at all.

He'd been through all that when his mom and dad had been killed, and Stacey's death had made the memory fresh. Jesse didn't think he could take it again, didn't think he was strong enough to simply forget the promises that would never be kept and the upcoming, crushing loneliness that would increase by a hundred every time he thought of the people who never picked up the telephone.

Things were bad enough in the here and now, with Trista and her small family—he could never think of her as Stacey's family—and the constant, darker undertone that permeated the service at every turn because of her.

"Jesse," she said now. "Please. Mr. Pitofsky won't listen to me—he says that as Stacey's husband, you have the final say in the matter. So I'm asking you this as Stacey's mother, Jesse. Let me see my daughter. *Don't you understand—how can I believe she's really gone unless I actually see her?"*

He shook his head, wishing he could make her believe that he wasn't doing this just to be difficult, or to torment her. He knew, he knew, *from firsthand experience how much damage a memory like that could do. Why couldn't she understand that he'd ordered the casket closed and sealed for her own good, for the good of everyone who'd known and loved Stacey? He understood her pain—God knows he did—and despite all the years of bad blood between them, he even felt sorry for her. Someday she'd thank him, even if right now she just . . . hated him. "I'm sorry," was all he said, and he meant it.*

He knew it wasn't going to be enough.

Trista was a small woman like Stacey had been, although her features were fairer than his wife's and her hair several shades lighter. There was a strong enough family resemblance—nearly identical blue eyes, a gently squared jawline, finely shaped lips—that it hurt Jesse to see Trista's expression twist into one of fury.

"Damn you, Jesse Waite," she said under her breath. Her hands opened and closely uselessly at her side. "I don't know what my daughter ever saw in you, and now you do her the final disrespect by packing her up and shoving her in a cold grave like she's something nasty you need to get rid of."

"Trista, that's not how it is at all. If you'll just listen—"

"I've heard everything I'm going to from you," she said icily. "If you can't say the right words—the ones that'll get that casket opened—then don't you ever talk to me again."

The last part of her sentence had been loud enough to make the few others in the oversized room look toward them as she turned and stalked away. Jesse stared after her, but the sadness he'd felt for her was gone. Even now, in this darkest of hours, she was still trying to control Stacey, albeit through him. Stacey had grown up under Trista's iron will and unrelenting eye; if she knew anything about what he was going through now from wherever she was, he hoped she knew not only how much he still loved her but how difficult it was to continue to protect her. That was the ultimate proof of his devotion, because it would have been so much easier to give in . . . but Stacey hadn't wanted to lie in a box and be stared at—by anybody—any more than he'd wanted to put her in one.

Jesse took a deep breath, then looked at the casket again. He and Stacey had had so many plans—love, a family, a future—and in another hour and a half even the pretty, satin-covered coffin, his wife's final bed, would be gone. Something inside him hurt so bad that he was vaguely surprised that he could still breathe. He wanted to crawl in a hole somewhere and die himself, find out once and for all if there really was an afterlife, if Stacey was waiting for him somewhere else. Closing his eyes to blackness had to be better than enduring what was going on here, in this awful funeral home.

*Jesse squeezed his eyes shut, then opened them again, waiting quietly for the service to start and looking dully at the blanket of red roses—*From Your Loving Husband*—lying across the top of Stacey's coffin. From where he sat across the room, he could clearly hear Trista's angry, grief-crazed voice as she talked to her husband, sister and brother-in-law, and anyone else within earshot—*

"Why is that son of a bitch keeping the casket closed? My girl was beautiful, even at the end—there's nothing to hide. How can I believe she's really gone unless I actually see her?"

And the worst suggestion—

"How can my baby be in that awful box—what if she's not really in there?"

—the one that wormed its way into the bruised recesses of his mind and heart and kept repeating over and over, despite his own common sense—

"What if she's not really in there?"

—where it nestled deep and festered like an unclean wound, and nearly paralyzed him with guilt and fear.

"What if she's not really in there?"

MARCH 4--TUESDAY

Late night at the shop really wasn't that bad—a little noisy but not the thunderous racket that Jesse knew could exist during the day, at the height of the first shift working a full crew. MC Tooling was a smallish outfit like the one he'd apprenticed at years earlier, and the graveyard shift was empty but for a few guys like himself, desperate to work and willing to take any hours to get that bonus on their paycheck. Tonight's hot job was machining a cast housing for an experimental aircraft engine, a small but essential piece of the whole and something that had to be completed in time for the day shift to move on with the next step and ship the parts out by the end of Wednesday.

Christ, Jesse thought. What's Stacey doing right now?

Standing at the Bridgeport milling machine, he clamped a ten-inch magnesium casting into place and hit the power switch, cursing at himself under his breath for letting his attention wander. He needed to focus, damn it, or he'd screw this up and delay the entire schedule.

But what if she really did leave—what would he do then? Was she really that sure of herself? He was having a hard time believing it. No, it was a lot more likely that the police would be waiting when he got home. The thought made Jesse cringe—Stacey would be hysterical or worse . . . cold and vengeful, a stranger like the woman he'd found in the parking lot that day. Everything he'd worked so hard on since then, all the progress that he'd imagined he and Stacey had made, it'd be gone. In its place would be a huge mess—the shambles of his life, a mental disaster for Stacey, and when all he'd tried to do was protect her, *save* her, and help her find herself again. And what about the police? Could they arrest him for reclaiming his own wife? He didn't think so, but that brought him no comfort.

The whine of the cutter momentarily filled his ears as he finished milling a slot inside the casting, then the noise jumped to a sudden scream as the cutting edge hit an inclusion. Sparks scattered from the casting and over the worktable, and an instant later the small pile of magnesium chips left from his previous cut went up in white-hot flames.

Jesse's response was automatic, too rapid to even bother including a curse. An arm's reach away was a chemical fire extinguisher and he had it poised and spraying within two seconds; in its wake it left minimal smoke and a casting that was probably ruined from whatever the cutter had run into, not to mention the end cutter itself. A pain-in-the-neck loss, but nothing he could have avoided, and the other three guys barely noticed the incident.

Jesse cleaned up the worktable and changed the cutter, then clamped another casting in place. This fire . . . so small. What if there was a fire at the townhouse while Stacey was sleeping? They had two smoke detectors, of course, but were there even fresh batteries in them? God, what an idiot he'd been—all those weeks of leaving her not just locked in the townhouse but *trapped* in the bedroom. He could have unwittingly been the cause of a tragedy far worse than anything they'd been through so far.

For a moment, a very long one, it was all Jesse could do not to panic and walk out. But life, the reality of it, interfered. Not only did they need his paycheck, but he *had* to be able to work and leave Stacey at home as though the two of them had a perfectly normal marriage.

Whether he was ready for it or not, their time as captor and captive was over.

Weekends were the worst.

Jesse walked out of the machine shop where he worked in Elk Grove Village at three-thirty every Friday afternoon, and he couldn't come back until six-thirty on Monday. People always thought of a weekend as being a couple of days off and too short, but in reality it was sixty-three hours of agony from the time he left work until the time he could go back. Sixty-three hours of a house filled with echoes and memories and loneliness, of empty moments strung together like a noose that just kept getting tighter and more painful as each week passed.

He'd done the overtime bit at first, and it had been a blessing, just the thing to keep him occupied and burn away the hours, help soften the blow of the bills that came in—the Visa charge and leftover medical bills that the insurance wouldn't cover, co-pays and everything under the sun that had been disallowed—without totally destroying the savings account. Jesse was too shattered to fight, and there were just too many bills—he put the notices and statements in a pile on the kitchen table, and every Friday, after he deposited his paycheck and set aside money for rent, utilities, and food, he went through the stack and paid the oldest ones. It was a routine, but he didn't look forward to it. He dealt with this stuff because it was there, not because he cared.

Then business went sour at the shop and the overtime dried up—bad management and worse decisions—and now the owner was talking about selling the business and the shop supervisor didn't even have work for Jesse to do when he didn't want any money for it. His friend John had a wife and a family and he'd already moved on, found himself a position at another shop two suburbs over before the hammer hit. Jesse didn't have the strength to do anything but stay; John still called Jesse when he could, but business at the new place was hopping and his own life was taking priority. That was as it should be and Jesse didn't want anyone to be his perpetual baby-sitter anyway—he could do just fine at this shop, minding his business and doing his job amid the other guys and the roar of the machinery. The sound was like white noise in his head, an up-close-and-personal version of the snow on the TV screen when you flipped to a dead channel. Yeah, from Monday to Friday he could handle it just fine.

But the weekends . . . God.

Not this time, Jesse told himself. He had passed the carnival when he drove west on Irving Park Friday afternoon and barely registered its presence. The blinking lights and the noise—people screaming with glee on the rides, the laughter of the crowd and the canned music—it all slipped into his head as an afterthought when he caught the light at that weird little intersection where Maple met Irving Park at an angle to the train station's main entrance. He didn't realize that the memory of the carnival had stuck until the next afternoon, when he was sitting in the living room of the townhouse and staring at the television, already thinking about popping open a can of beer.

The thought both appealed to him and horrified him. For Christ's sake, it was barely past one o'clock—if he started drinking now, he'd be tanked by six, probably sooner. That was ridiculous, unthinkable. Didn't they say drinking alone and early in the day was a sign of alcoholism? He didn't hide bottles or anything—he never had liked the hard stuff—but to start this early in the day . . . Jesus, he'd end up passed out by eight or nine o'clock.

Some little part of his mind that he hadn't known existed whispered to him suddenly, suggesting that this was a good thing because then he could sleep, on and on for as long as he could stretch it . . .

. . . then start all over tomorrow.

Jesse got off the couch so quickly that his foot caught the leg of the coffee table and almost overturned it. The remote slid to the carpet along with the TV Guide, *and when Jesse picked up the small magazine he saw the issue was two weeks old—he hadn't even noticed. The drapes were closed—he hadn't opened them since the day he'd taken Stacey to the hospital for the last time—and the living room was dark and stale, a little too warm because he'd left the thermostat set too high. He thought again about having a cold beer, then grabbed his wallet and got the hell out of there.*

It was odd the way a man could be lonely while in the company of several thousand people.

Jesse felt like he was walking down the midway and surrounded by something he couldn't see, an . . . aura, maybe. Whatever it was, it was surely black, and deadly, and made everyone else in the world want to be talking to anyone but him—he couldn't even get anyone to make eye contact with him. Not that he really wanted to, of course, and he didn't particularly want to strike up a conversation. But it would have been nice to lose the feeling that he didn't exist in the world anymore, that he might even be just a bit invisible to the people milling around him. They all had someone to talk to and laugh with, someone to hold hands with, someone to be *with.*

He tried to find some joy in the beautiful fall day, in the sights and smell of carnival food and the giddiness of the kids running madly in all directions, but he couldn't. Instead, it was those same children—chasing each other while their parents chased them—that made it suddenly sink in what a monumental mistake it'd been to come here. For God's sake, it was practically all couples and families and groups of friends—even the gothic teenagers who wore black lipstick plastered across their mouths and glared at everyone seemed to have some form of a significant other. Retired moms and pops trailed after grandkids while men and women of all ages explored the game booths and the tents selling greasy fast food. But the hardest for Jesse to bear were the hundreds of Mr. and Mrs. Joe Averages, those couples close to his own age and who sometimes carted the toddlers, the tiny sons or daughters who made them into the complete family that he and Stacey would now never be. The whole carnival, despite the gaily blinking lights and the noise and the cheap food and the hawkers braying at passersby, was nothing but a nonstop reminder of everything Jesse had lost. Compared with this, with the companionship so apparent in everyone around him, his life was a bleak hole where Stacey had once been, a constant state of painful disbelief because of what had happened last month.

But if he didn't stay here, what else would he do? Why, go back to the townhouse, pop open that can of beer, move on to the next, and the next, and pretty soon he'd be working on a double six-pack. He'd been doing so much of that lately, and he wasn't so far gone that he couldn't see it, and even hate himself a little for it. His old man used to drink like that, knocking back a case per weekend, half on Saturday and half on Sunday. There, Jesse believed, was no doubt the reason his mom had insisted they go out every Friday evening; if not, it would surely have been a night where the old man poured down another twelve cans. She knew that while they were out, away from the television and Garvey's favorite chair, his father was less likely to knock 'em back, much like Jesse right now. Oh, he'd drink, all right . . . but not at the usual feel-sorry-for-himself pace. And let's face it: If he did end up getting tanked, the Metra parking lot where the carnival was being held just couldn't be any more convenient. He'd have to be pretty soused not to be able to handle the fifteen-minute stagger that would get him home.

Jesse wandered around for a while, knowing he ought to eat something to soak up the alcohol—a hot dog, at least—but nursing a plastic cup of bottom-line beer instead as he tried not to look miserable. It was so hard, though, to see all these happy people when he couldn't seem to find the turning point to get on with his life, the switch inside his head that would make him accept the devastation and move into repair mode. Maybe Trista and that funeral home director had been right—maybe he should have let there be a viewing. Maybe he'd needed to see an open casket where a last, horrid image of Stacey would have pushed him into action simply out of a desire to be rid of it. Maybe—

He saw her standing in line for one of the rides.

Later, Jesse wouldn't be able to remember which of the rides she'd been waiting for, if she'd already been there with the man she spent the day with, or had met the guy somewhere at the carnival. Right now, all he could do was stand and stare across the width of a double sidewalk.

Jesse's hand tightened around the thin plastic and he looked down stupidly as beer exploded from between his fingers. He dropped the crumpled cup and wiped his fingers on his jeans without knowing it, oblivious to the foamy stain spreading down the front of his shirt. He was already moving, headed right for her across the packed midway, when he realized what he was doing and yanked himself to a stop, visibly jerking as if some unseen cable had pulled tight. Knock it off, he told himself. Get a grip on reality—

That's not Stacey, you idiot. She's dead.

Thank God for the hundreds of people streaming between them. The crowd afforded Jesse some bit of insulation from the shock, the smallest moment of hesitation as his brain tried to make sense of the information his eyes were feeding it.

She's dead.

But . . . damn. The resemblance was right, so eerie. Only the hair was different, shorter and slightly darker, with none of the sun's highlights in it that Stacey's had had—

As though she's been hiding somewhere for a month.

Her style of dress was completely changed, too, with the tan slacks and white shirt she wore so bland they bordered on dowdy. Stacey would never wear something that dull; she liked patterns and color, preferably the pastels that were so prominent around Easter. But everything else, the face, build, the eyes—

Oh, God. The eyes.

And suddenly it wasn't Stacey that Jesse thought of at all, but her mother. He hadn't really talked to her since the service at the funeral home—he'd tried, but she certainly wasn't interested in talking to him. Now her voice rang in his head as though she had a fiber-optic line straight to everything inside him that mattered:

"What if she's not really in there?"

....

He almost couldn't go inside his own home.

By the time his shift was over it was light outside, but the townhouse looked unaccountably dark, the curtained windows like cold, vacant eyes, the front door like a mouth shut tight against him. Dirty patches of snow dotted the still, winter-brown landscape and a heavy March cloud cover blocked any inkling of sun—it could have been eight in the morning or four in the afternoon. Standing with his key in the lock, Jesse could find nothing welcoming about the place he'd called home for the past four years.

Every nerve in his body was screaming as he twisted the knob and walked into the cool darkness of the entry foyer. Jesse couldn't take it, couldn't stand facing whatever awaited without at least the small benefit of light. A flick of his wrist gave him that, but little else—

—except the sight of the telephone on the hall table.

The last time he'd seen this, he'd hidden it in the coat closet after Stacey had thrown it at him. The evidence of her anger was still there in the form of a thin crack that ran diagonally across the plastic receiver, unsightly but not enough to destroy the telephone. She must have been going through the closets and found it.

Jesse's legs felt suddenly weak and he leaned against the wall, feeling the silence surround him like a suffocating pillow. It wasn't the sight of this phone that crashed it all home—there was another in the kitchen, the wall phone he'd never taken down and had just been careful to monitor. Instead, it was everything, the realization that whatever he found in the next ten seconds would unequivocally determine the course of the rest of his life.

A lump of loss was already forming in his throat as he climbed the steps soundlessly toward the master bedroom, preparing for the misery that was surely to come. That doorway, set at the end of the upstairs hall, was darker than anywhere else, the entrance to a terrifying cave. Jesse paused for a moment and rubbed his face, felt anxiety sweep over him and fill him with vertigo. But there would be no more waiting—he would know, once and for all, just where they were, or weren't, going.

He slapped at the switch on the wall and light cut through the room, enough to make him squint. On the bed, rolled into the comforter like a cocoon, Stacey blinked sleepily up at him, then smiled. "Cleaned up a little around here," she mumbled. "Found the phone and it still worked, so I plugged it in. How was work?"

Nearly paralyzed with relief, Jesse could only stand there for a long moment. *Cleaned the house, how was work?* Jesus, could there be a more normal Hi-honey-I'm-home conversation? Was he really standing here seeing everything he wanted in the world coming *true*?

Stacey mumbled something else that might have been a question and he leaned over and stroked her hair. "No—sleep late today," he whispered. "I'll come to bed in a few minutes."

" 'Kay," she said drowsily and snuggled deeper into her pillow. He stood there and watched her for awhile, loving the pillow creases along one cheek and her sleep-scrunched hair. Finally, numb with gratitude, Jesse stripped off his dirty work clothes and climbed into the shower, barely feeling the water wash away the evening's grime. It'd been a hard method—the way he'd grabbed her back, then kept her shut away—and maybe his technique wouldn't be considered orthodox by most people. But the end result had worked as well as any psychiatrist's treatment, and it hadn't put them in the poorhouse, either.

Showered and dry, Jesse crawled into bed and curled up behind the warm body of his wife. When it came right down to it, he'd only done what was right for both of them.

MARCH 7--FRIDAY

Around her, the world felt huge.

For late winter, it was a beautiful day. The air was clear

and crisp but not too cold, the sun almost blindingly bright after nearly a week of oppressive cloud cover. There was scattered birdsong in the air and a few people going here and there, filling her ears with the sound of car engines and occasional conversation.

It was also Stacey's first step outside the door of the townhouse since January.

She breathed deeply, enjoying the chilly air and the slightly tipsy sensation of being out in the open. Cabin fever—she'd had it and not even known, had been concentrating so hard on the mental part of herself that she'd suppressed the physical need to move beyond the confines of her environment. Now every noise seemed overly loud, the sunshine warmer than the month of March would ever allow it to be, and she couldn't help grinning as she followed Jesse to the Impala and stopped with him by the driver's door.

He unlocked it, then said "Here," and pressed the keys into her hand. "You drive."

Stacey's smile faded and she looked at him, confused. "I don't drive," she said reproachfully.

Instead of taking back the keys, Jesse only stared at her. His face lost a little of its high color and his happy expression was replaced by worry. "Well, sure you do," he said carefully. "Honey . . . this is your car, not mine."

Stacey shook her head and thrust the keys at him. "No." Without waiting for a response, she pulled open the door and climbed into the cold car, sliding across the front seat to the passenger side. "I don't even have a driver's license," she muttered to herself. Darn him for bringing it up—he'd ruined the feeling of contentment she'd had, the anticipation of going outside for the first time in practically forever.

But Jesse heard her. "Of course you do. Look." He pulled out his wallet and flipped it open, dug through it until he came up with a small laminated card to hand her. "I kept it in my wallet so I'd know where it was when you needed it. Go ahead—take it."

Stacey took it wordlessly and studied it. The standard Illinois driver's license with the requisite info—name, address, description. It all matched, as did the picture of her own, impishly smiling face. It wasn't even going to expire for another six months.

"Are you sure you don't want to dri—"

"I can't remember how!" Her voice was louder than she'd intended, edged with panic.

"It's no big deal," Jesse said quickly. He shoved the key into the ignition and cranked the engine, and Stacey listened to the car start up. They sat there in uncomfortable silence while the engine warmed, then Jesse smiled over at her as he buckled his seat belt and motioned at hers. "Guess we'll have to re-teach you. Think of it as an opportunity to spread chaos and destruction on the streets of Roselle."

Stacey couldn't help but laugh. "Could be fun."

"And we're off." Their moment of awkwardness forgotten, Stacey watched with interest as he wound his way out of the townhouse development. She tried to bring up a memory of the route, but there was nothing—apparently it'd gone the way of her driving skills, into that nasty black abyss that she didn't want to think too much about. When Jesse's turns brought him to Plum Grove Road and he headed north, then turned west and went over to Roselle Road, the mental map she'd been so desperate to find sunk into place at last. The Jewel Food Store lot that he pulled into was as familiar as the sight of her own face in the mirror each morning.

Thank God, Stacey thought. For a while I thought I was losing myself all over again.

Jesse wasn't sure how it happened, but Stacey sort of . . . took over in the store, snagging a grocery cart and charging off toward the fresh vegetable aisle as though she'd been shopping with him last Thursday instead of eight months ago. He followed behind her, half breathless and half worried as he watched her pick and choose a few apples, a couple of oranges, a bag of pre-chopped salad lettuce and three plum tomatoes, before moving deeper into the store.

It was a fascinating thing, this grocery trip with his wife, a relearning experience about the woman who'd dropped out of his life for nearly a third of a year. Half of him wanted to watch everyone around them, terrified that someone from her *other* existence might think they recognized her; the other half wanted only to tag along on this strange variation of a joyride through the supermarket. Until now Jesse had been doing all of the shopping and errand running, and it was marvelous to see her picking up the more mundane pieces of the puzzle as if nothing in the world had ever been wrong. His only fear remained recognition and with that, an almost paranoiac fear that she might relapse in the face of it. Feeding that had been the sight of one of the damned posters, still tied around a light pole at the front of the parking lot. But that was okay—the wet winter had taken its toll and the paper had disintegrated into little more than shreds.

The thought that she might slip *back*, however, nagged at him. Until now, in the midst of this grocery superstore, he hadn't even considered it, had taken the fact that she'd stayed of her own free will and reinitiated their man-and-wife relationship as the gospel truth that an overnight miracle had occurred. Clearly that wasn't so, and the bad time earlier about her being able to drive had been like a smack to the side of his head. He was, unfortunately, still going to have to be careful about when and where he took her out.

But it won't be like that forever, Jesse told himself. And we're okay here so far—we don't have any choice but to be so. Tension made sweat trickle down his back beneath the too-many layers of his shirt, sweater, and jacket. What he and Stacey were enduring . . . well, it was a nearly unimaginable situation between a husband and a wife. If they were to survive it and move on, Stacey needed to be able to heal without his criticisms or comments, and he *had* to be flexible with the mannerisms and preferences she'd learned—even if they never went away. She'd been gone only a few months, but he would, Jesse knew, be attributing things to that time period for the rest of their lives. Those things would be the scars, visible and ugly, but eventually fading to only a pale shadow of what they had once been.

MARCH 20--THURSDAY

Stacey had stopped being surprised by all the things she couldn't remember—driving, for instance, or incidents that had happened between her and Jesse that he talked about. Jesse himself had become a fixture in her life, and while she couldn't necessarily remember things from their past, in some ways she couldn't think anything but that he'd always been there, supporting her, accompanying her, loving her. Their wedding had become as alive in her mind as if she could remember it, the photographs—which she'd taken back down and now studied religiously—making the entire event unfold in her head to the point where she imagined she could hear the music, taste the champagne and wedding cake, and feel herself dancing in Jesse's arms. But still . . .

Damn it, she ought to remember her mother.

She'd thought she could accept that shortfall, but she couldn't—day by day, it bothered her more. Of course it would—it was the other half of the two main things in her life. She'd recovered herself with Jesse, her husband; now it was time to do the same with her family.

Easter. It was ten days away, and Jesse had mentioned it was for this one holiday that she had, as a matter of tradition, always invited her small family over for dinner. It was obvious right from the start that Jesse was sorry he'd brought it up, but once the words were out there, they couldn't be taken back. They preyed on Stacey's mind, frustrating her with the insinuation that here wasn't just one more thing she couldn't remember, but a *major* piece of her life, something tied up with family and childhood, a chunk around which all those missing parts should coalesce.

"Tell me about them," she said over dinner. She almost regretted asking when Jesse lowered his fork and she saw the distressed expression on his face. But damn it, she needed to know these things if she was ever to get the fragments to come together properly. She couldn't sidestep the chasms forever.

When he finally spoke, he sounded almost petulant, like a child forced to do something he wanted to avoid. "I don't know why it's so important," he said. "You've been ill—you should skip it this year, or at least postpone it. It wouldn't hurt to have them over for, say, Thanksgiving."

Stacey sat back and considered this, but the answer was the same. "No," she said. "That's eight months away. I want to get things back on track now."

Jesse's eyes went dark. "They haven't been very good to you, Stace."

She frowned. "Are you saying I don't like my mother? Or that *you* don't."

"Both."

"Ah." She looked at him steadily. "But I still need to know, Jesse. I know you remember things I don't, but that doesn't mean you can live for me. I need to make my own decisions."

He stared at her and she had to grit her teeth against the guilt she felt—she was desperate to learn about herself, but she hadn't seen him look this miserable in a long time. Finally, though, he nodded. "You're right, of course. I guess I just thought we could postpone it—"

"I don't think so," she cut in. "It's best to get things back to the way they were as quickly as possible."

"Maybe," he said, staring at the uneaten food on his plate.

"If we always had Easter dinner," Stacey continued, "then this seems like the perfect time, don't you think?" She waited, but he just sat there stubbornly. All right, so maybe he wouldn't agree; he didn't have to. "So tell me what I don't remember."

Jesse drew a deep breath. "It's a . . . difficult thing," he said carefully. "You and Trista—your mom—it's been years since you got along well. I told you she never liked me and, well, I always thought it was like you had this yearly dinner thing just to aggravate her."

Stacey shrugged. "Maybe I did. I can't say." Trista—the name, as always, sounded familiar but not familiar, like something she'd known a long time ago. She licked her lips and asked her next question. "What about my father?"

"Tadd Newman. Your stepfather, but he seems like an okay guy. You never complained about him. I don't know anything about your real father."

Tadd Newman? The name brought nothing—no spark, not even a hint of curiosity. "Who else?"

"You've got an aunt and an uncle, Krystin and Ken." For a second he grinned. "Sounds like a couple of Barbie dolls, doesn't it? Anyway, they don't have any kids. You always seemed to get along with her—do you recall her at all?"

Stacey thought carefully. Krystin, the woman in the photographs who looked so familiar. She did remember her . . . but at the same time, she didn't. "I—I'm not sure," she answered. "What else can you tell me about her?"

Jesse looked blank. "Not much. Let's face it, your mother practically hates me. The rest of the family might be okay, but they kind of stay away because of that." He brightened a little. "I do know she's a librarian. Does that help?"

Stacey blinked. Maybe there was something to that—maybe she'd somehow worked with the woman, gotten a job that would let her be close to her? No, that didn't make any sense. Stacey had been missing—if she'd shown up, Krystin Parker would have recognized her and done something about it, called Jesse, her sister, the police. Called *some*one. "Not really," she said at last. "Is there anyone else—brothers or sisters?"

The hesitation on Jesse's face was impossible for him to hide. Stacey didn't say anything, just waited. He had to know by now that she wasn't going to let this go. "A sister," he finally admitted. "A twin. But you never knew her."

She sat forward and stared at him in amazement. "I had

a *twin*? For God's sake, Jesse—why didn't you tell me? What's her name?"

Jesse lifted his chin, trying not to look defensive. "I didn't mention it because it doesn't affect anything—she died as a result of heart problems as a toddler. Her name was Tammy, but you've been through so much—losing our baby, being sick and what all—I just didn't want to throw even more at you."

Stacey was silent for a moment, then she said softly, "That heart thing again."

"It's not the same as what happened to you," Jesse said sharply. "I don't know the details since your mother never much talked about it, but your problem came more because of the fever than anything hereditary. You're not going to kick over and die tomorrow."

A corner of Stacey's mouth turned up. "I hope not." Then her face grew serious again. "I just wish I could remember, Jesse. It seems like it must've happened to someone else, like I've been in a bubble for the last twenty years."

"You don't remember anything from school, or from when you were younger?"

She hesitated. "Flashes now and then. From a *long* time ago. It's like I know the people in the memories are my mother and father, but I can't really see them." She stopped before she could tell him about some of the other stuff she remembered, feeling slightly ashamed for holding back. But he didn't need to know the details—hadn't he already said she and her mother didn't get along? The flashbacks she sometimes had were dark, filled with fear and the overwhelming presence of a woman that everything in her fought to *not* recall. If these were associated with Trista, telling him about them would only give him more reason to despise her mother.

Jesse nodded, rubbing his hands nervously. "From what you told me, your mother kind of wigged out over your sister's death. It's sad, when you think about the reason—twenty years ago the doctors and treatment available to everyday people without much money wasn't that great. Trista was so afraid that what happened to Tammy would happen to you that she became smothering and super-possessive. For a little girl that was probably okay, but when you started getting interested in boys, she knew that meant she'd eventually lose you to someone." He smiled and leaned over to stroke her cheek. "You were as pretty then as you are now—I wasn't the only guy who tripped over my feet when I first saw you. But I *was* the lucky one." He sat back again. "Or, if you ask your mother, the devil who took you away from her."

"Maybe," she said. One of these days, she would work up the courage to call her mother. Who she'd find on the other end of the telephone remained to be seen, but there was nothing like the loss of everything to make a person want to stitch up a few wounds. After all that had happened, she couldn't help but think that, and she said as much. "But maybe it'll be different this time."

"I don't know," Jesse began skeptically.

Stacey reached over and squeezed his hand. "Because you're also the devil who brought me back."

It wasn't Stacey, of course. The idea was preposterous, a painful and short-lived fantasy cooked up by his heart, one that flickered into existence only because he was still so shattered by Stacey's death.

It wasn't her, of course.

Of course.

Jesse knew this even as he ambled after her, drawn by the remarkable resemblance of this young woman and hungry for the nearness of this stranger who looked so much like his lost wife. He kept a dozen or more people between himself and her and stayed far enough behind so that she never noticed him, and somewhere along the line he became aware of the man she was with, an okay-looking guy with brownish hair receding at the forehead who was at least ten years older than she was. The sight of her companion fueled rather than broke Jesse's impulse to follow her; he felt a combination of longing, sadness, and envy of the guy that damned near took his breath away and only made him that much more determined not to let her out of his sight.

The Ferris wheel, the Tilt-A-Whirl, a dozen or more of the small and, with the exception of the carnival's mini-version of a roller coaster, not very exciting rides. The noise and smells of the crowd faded in Jesse's mind; nothing mattered but the couple he was carefully shadowing—what they did, where they went, even what they ate. He forgot about beer and food for himself as he mingled with the carnival-goers and kept the couple in sight, and when the two left the festivities behind and crossed Irving Park to duck into Piper's Restaurant, his own hunger pangs went unnoticed. Piper's was a small place that had been in the same location for as long as Jesse could remember, and as he walked casually past the window Jesse saw a waitress pour coffee for the quiet-looking man and the woman who looked like his wife. Their faces were flushed from the crisp air and the hours in the sun, and Jesse felt a stab of jealousy—again—at how easily it could have been Stacey sitting in that booth.

Stop it, he told himself suddenly. Go home—you're acting like a fool, or a stalker, or both. What the hell's wrong with you?

Without letting himself think about it, Jesse turned and headed back home—

—where he picked up the car and came back to sit and wait in the parking lot outside the restaurant.

They stayed in Piper's for a long time, nursing cups of coffee and talking about God knew what. Jesse didn't mind the wait, and the truth was, he wasn't sure what he was waiting for. Maybe it was just something to do that would keep him out of the townhouse for a change, something on which he could focus while he sat in his car in the sun, happy to turn his thoughts away from the haunting image of that powder blue casket. The memory always came complete with the cloying smell of funeral roses, a recollection that his brain translated into a far too realistic scent he found increasingly suffocating. He'd never been a particularly patient man, but he found patience now, or maybe it was simply his own version of limbo. He didn't know why he was here or what he thought he was going to accomplish; he simply was. For now, that was enough.

The couple never ordered dinner, but they stayed in Piper's until nearly six o'clock. Jesse, lulled by the afternoon's passing and the long time in the car's warm, sunny interior, was so startled when he saw them stand that he nearly hit the horn with his elbow. Nerves jangling, he had the Impala running before they came outside, not wanting to draw their attention while he waited for their next move. They strolled east on Irving Park and Jesse timed the traffic so that he could limp along behind them without too much trouble, looking like nothing more than someone in a too-old beater with engine problems. When they turned into the Springhill Apartments a few blocks up and the man ushered her into a fancy car that was a couple of years old, a light blue Lexus, it became a game of follow the leader as he paced them, making sure he stayed far enough back so that he wouldn't be noticed.

He wasn't sure how many times he asked himself what he was doing, but it was a useless question that got him nothing but nonsensical, bullshit answers—he was killing time, it was a free country and he was just driving around, he was making sure this woman was going to be okay. That last one was so far from reality he even laughed out loud when the thought flitted across the front of his brain. For a moment, he almost hit the brakes and pulled over, then he reminded himself that what he was doing was harmless, a little something to do on a Saturday to occupy his grief-frozen brain. Hell, kids did it all the time when they first started driving, picked a car at random and followed it to wherever it ended up with no thought but to drive and be amused. It was nothing more than that.

The drive wasn't long, maybe twenty minutes down familiar roads clogged with early evening traffic. Jesse committed the route to memory without consciously realizing it—Irving Park west to Roselle Road, then down to Lake Street where they headed west yet again. They turned south on Gary Avenue and Jesse thought they were headed into the affluent suburb of Bloomingdale; then the Lexus turned again, this time into the smaller, sometimes unlabeled streets of Keeneyville. Although he'd lived in this area all his life, Jesse'd never been to either side of Gary Avenue, and the area was a surprise. Most of it was shadowed and shabby, a neighborhood he would have expected to find in the more tired parts of Chicago to the east. Here and there he saw newer houses, but they all stood out like new clothes on a child whose face and hands were still dirty. When the Lexus finally slowed and stopped, the dingy and ill-kept house beyond the curb matched the others around it, although Jesse barely noticed. His eyes were fixed on the couple in the front seat, and he watched with undisguised relief as the young woman climbed out of the passenger side without kissing her companion good-bye. A quick, last wave toward the driver of the Lexus idling on the street, then she disappeared into the house.

Jesse sat in the car and watched the dim, silent house until it was too dark to see anymore.

He called his boss at home on Sunday and said he needed some time off from the machine shop, and the guy was completely understanding.

"Take all the time you need, Jesse. We all thought you should have done that when . . . well, you know." He broke off, and Jesse heard him awkwardly clear his throat. "Take all the time you need," he repeated. "Your job will be waiting for you when you get back."

Jesse wouldn't know until it was too late that his boss was lying, and by then it wouldn't have mattered anyway.

He'd burned the woman's address into his memory, again not as an outright decision but as something that happened all by itself, a subconscious sort of flash that left it etched indelibly in his mind, glowing softly below the surface all the time. Jesse spent most of Sunday doing a whole lot of nothing, wandering around the townhouse and turning the television off and on every twenty minutes or so just to see if anything interesting was on, even though he wouldn't have wanted to watch it. Late in the afternoon he drove over to the supermarket and bought some stuff to make sandwiches and a thermos to keep his coffee hot, and the whole time he was shopping he kept up a running mental dialogue of denial about what he was doing. He wasn't loading up on supplies to keep himself comfortable in his car, no sir—he was just replacing a thermos he'd cracked at the shop over a year ago and forgotten about, and what did buying supplies for lunch have to do with anything, for God's sake? He hadn't stepped out on his job because he was going to stalk her, for crying out loud; he just needed, as his boss had pointed out, the time off that he should've taken back when Stacey had died. A little rearranging in his life, a little time out, that was all. There was nothing sinister or evil going on, and everything was as it should be.

On Monday morning the alarm went off at the same time it always did when he got up for his seven-to-three shift at the machine shop. By six-thirty a.m., the Impala was parked in the darkness of a mid-October morning across the street from the woman's house and Jesse was pouring himself a cup of still-scalding coffee from his new thermos.

He spent the next week and a half finding out everything he could about her. The learning curve for a do-it-yourself detective didn't seem to be too tough; after all, she had no reason to hide and no clue that she was being followed, and by the end of that first day Jesse already knew that she worked for the Roselle Library and what her hours were and how they ran with the Pace bus schedules. He even knew when she took her lunch break because although she brown-bagged it, as long as the weather was passable she'd carry her food outside and sit on a bench in the small, ornately bricked courtyard that ran the length of the side entrance to the library building. He wanted to go inside and find out more, see if she was a clerk or held some other position he didn't know existed, but he didn't dare. Roselle might be a suburb on the outskirts of a city of twelve million, but it was still like living in a small town where you ran into someone you knew at every turn. If he didn't have his wires crossed, Trista's sister worked in the library, and outside of Trista herself, she was the last person Jesse wanted to run into. It nagged at him that this Stacey look-alike had actual ties to his dead wife's family, but surely it was nothing more than a bizarre coincidence.

Surely.

That problem aside, there were other things to worry about, like the fact that she had dinner every night with the man Jesse had seen her with at the carnival. That haunted him, then he found something new to fret over when she climbed in a cab one day on her lunch hour and went over to a medical building in Bloomingdale. She was in there for only a half hour, but it was enough for Jesse to imagine all sorts of dire things, a hundred horrible scenarios. Uppermost in his mind was the way the last month or so of Stacey's life had rippled out of control, like dropping something that looked smooth and delicate into a pond of calm, clean water and finding out that the object was really something nasty and soft and polluting. He couldn't very well march into the unknown doctor's office and demand an explanation, so there wasn't anything to be done about it but wait and see what happened—was she going to get sick? Or was she sick now?

Jesse already felt oddly disconnected from his life and his job and everyone he knew, as though he were invisible and standing in a world where everyone else—Trista and the rest of Stacey's family, his boss, John and the handful of other friends he had—all flowed ignorantly past, never noticing or knowing how much he suffered. In some ways, this young woman who looked so much like Stacey was his only tie to everything, the rope that kept him grounded in the world and prevented him from fading entirely into a sort of wide-awake hell.

But even that, Jesse found, was short-lived and fragile.

A day shy of two weeks since he'd first set eyes on her, thirteen short days, and he saw her routine break as her boyfriend picked her up at work in the middle of a Friday afternoon. The Lexus was freshly washed and shining, the guy wore a tailored suit over a sharply pressed white shirt and a tasteful tie; when the woman who looked like Stacey came out to meet him, Jesse remembered the plastic dress bag she'd carried into the library with her that morning and he saw she had changed into a plain but lovely pink dress. The man opened the passenger side door for her and presented her with a small bouquet of flowers, but Jesse couldn't, wouldn't, allow himself to think of what that meant. To do so would be a silly jump to conclusions on his part; the guy had to be nearly forty years old, a white-collar business type, for God's sake, and they just didn't move that quickly—

Numb, Jesse followed the driver of the Lexus and sat staring as he pulled into a parking slot in front of the Roselle Village Courthouse, literally unable to process what he was seeing although he knew in his gut exactly what it meant. But his soothing cocoon of unreality let go when the couple emerged, this time holding hands and smiling. The woman was blushing and laughing prettily each time she glanced at her companion, glowing with a happiness that Jesse, frozen behind the wheel of the Impala, envied so much it was beyond his ability to put a name to it.

And as Jesse trailed them to the fancy Wyndham Hotel in nearby Itasca where they settled in for the rest of the weekend, he still couldn't let himself admit the truth of what had taken place practically in front of his own tear-filled eyes . . .

Just before midnight, Stacey lay in bed next to Jesse, content in body if not in soul. No overtime for him tonight, and for a change he'd been home before eleven-thirty; a quick shower and he'd joined her in bed. Their love-making was sweet and sure, as it always was, and now she balanced on the edge of that relaxed state just before full sleep, swinging half in and half out of wakefulness with her eyes closed.

Children's laughter, her own and someone else's, the high-pitched tones of little girls. There was sunshine and the sense of happiness, the spin of a merry-go-round in the park. She fell off and landed on her back in the sand, opened her mouth to laugh—

—and a hand covered it and swung her through a sudden, startling darkness filled with a woman's panicked scream. Jesse lifted her and ran, his fingers bruising her face as he carried her through woods lit by a huge, white moon—

—then it was just her, and she was a child, and she was hiding out of sight around the corner of the hallway, where she could see—only just—into the tiny bathroom. There a faceless woman quickly pulled a single pill from a prescription bottle in the pocket of her apron and dropped it on top of the medicine in another bottle in the cabinet. She knew the feel of this woman's hand, the way the edges of her fingernails cut into the tender skin of her scalp, and she started to back away. But a noise from the bedroom drew the attention of the woman, who hastily tossed the first bottle in the waste-basket and left. A moment later she crept into the bathroom and took the bottle from the garbage. But the top was funny and she couldn't get it open, so she carried it back to her room and hid it, thinking that someday, it might be important . . .

Stacey woke in a cold sweat, the images still whirling behind her eyes. She could feel Jesse's presence next to her, like an anchor in her sea of bad dreams. So many images and hardly any of them good—underlying all of it had been something akin to constant fighting, the unpleasant and constant bickering of people who were never meant to try and coexist.

Be that as it may, there was that one sweet recollection, fading far too fast, of another child. Had this been a sliver of memory about her twin sister, some small event that had taken place in their lives before the girl had passed away? It seemed right, although nothing in the rest of what had passed through her mind supported the idea that her sister had died. Rather, she was just . . . *gone,* a child's game of a now-you-see-it, now-you-don't that gave her no answers in the present.

Sighing, Stacey moved closer to Jesse and closed her eyes, determined to sleep. Dreams, that's all, with no ties to the here and now. And she certainly couldn't base what would happen in her future on something that had likely never taken place in her past.

MARCH 21--FRIDAY

"I thought it was a good meeting tonight," Marietta said. "How about you?"

Alec thought about it for a moment, then nodded. "Yes," he said. "I thought so, too." He held the door open for her and she stepped into the main coffee shop, then paused and looked at him questioningly. He nodded slightly before following her across the room to what had, Alec supposed, become their "usual" table, that same spot in the middle where they'd talked after that first Valentine's night meeting. Tonight had been the sixth time he'd attended—wasn't there something significant about that number? He'd read somewhere that it took three weeks to instill a new routine or make a new habit, but all he could equate with "six" was that a lot of self-education classes ran for six weeks. Perhaps the counseling sessions—meetings—were just that: self-education in the craft of continuing your life.

There had been no more progress on the case. It'd been over a month since Nola's purse had been found, and the truth was that there hadn't been any significant breaks in the lack of information before that. Nola had been gone for nine weeks and one day, and while Conroy didn't say it outright, the detective might as well have had *Your Wife Is Presumed Dead* tattooed across his forehead the last time Alec had seen him. Marietta and the people at these meetings—they were his life preserver; their support and fellowship were the only things that had pulled him back from the edge of unthinkable hopelessness. He had, without words, asked them to break the loneliness of his solitary life; they had complied, and he had begun to depend on them.

"So," Marietta said when he'd returned with their cups of decaf, "what are you doing for Easter? Do you have family to visit?"

No games or stalling—it was an important question and Marietta wasn't going to tiptoe around it. It was the same way with his answer. "I don't have any plans," he said. "I was the stereotypical surprise late-life baby and my parents passed away some time ago. There's a very elderly aunt who lives out of state, but she's in a nursing home and we're not close." He gave her a rueful smile. "I guess the lineage ends with me."

Marietta leaned her elbows on the table. "I hope this doesn't sound pushy, but why don't you have Easter dinner with me and my family? There are so many of us and people are always bringing friends—it wouldn't be like you were the only new face staring down the table."

Easter with Marietta and her family? Alec didn't know what to say. "It might be overwhelming," she continued, unknowingly voicing his thoughts, "for someone not used to the chaos of a houseful of people—and I do mean house *full*—but it might be good for you, a distraction." Her gaze flicked away from him momentarily, a move that made her seem oddly nervous. "And Brian would love to meet you. He's always asking about the man he talks to on the telephone."

Brian . . . Marietta's seven-year-old son. Alec had, in his darkest of emotional times, taken advantage of her offer to lend an ear. At Brian's age, the boy was prone to running for the telephone every time he heard it ring, then doing his best to carry on a conversation with the caller. No stranger to children, it had been easy for Alec to draw the boy out, no matter how badly he'd felt himself. In fact, Alec had begun to look forward to talking with Brian.

Just as he had with Marietta.

He cleared his throat. "I appreciate the invitation, but I don't really think I'm up for that just yet."

"I understand," she said, although he caught a flash of the disappointment that shadowed her face before she covered it. Marietta changed the subject then, deftly moving away from what suddenly seemed uncomfortably close to a personal invitation. It hadn't been, of course—she'd only been trying to occupy him, keep him from sitting at home alone and thinking about his missing wife on a holiday. Another half hour and they parted, sharing a chaste hug as they always did before driving in opposite directions.

When Alec got home, he opened the door of the apartment and stood there for a few moments, listening. And as it had been since that bleak evening in January, he heard not a sound.

He'd left two lights on, one in the living room and the other over the stove. He shut off the one in the kitchen, thinking about this habit he'd started about a week after Nola's disappearance, his mouth twisting in reluctant bitterness when he realized there must be dozens, maybe hundreds, of songs that had been written about people leaving lights on for lost lovers. One in particular crossed his mind, a country tune called "Years" by Barbara Mandrell that his mother had listened to when he was a teenager. According to the song, the woman had turned on the hall light every night; now, a sliver of the words—*"In case you come back home . . .*"—ran annoyingly through his mind. Was that what he was going to do—spend years waiting for a woman who in all probability he would never see again?

Discouraged, Alec went into the living room and sat on the couch. The room was so empty, so *quiet.* God, how he would have liked to accept Marietta's Easter invitation, let himself be "overwhelmed" by something other than Nola's disappearance. But if he did, it would be a sort of . . . surrender, a veiled acknowledgment that yes, the worst has happened. Right now, he thought he could—barely—still claim that he believed otherwise.

But . . . then there was Marietta.

There was no denying she was an attractive woman, but that realization had come after the fact, a sort of bonus to a growing awareness of how much he enjoyed her company, how close he felt to her. They shared a bond that few others did, the strength, born of necessity, to survive some of the worst circumstances that fate could toss at them. It had made them friends beyond that which he had ever known with anyone else, male or female, co-survivors of an unnatural life disaster that few ever endured.

And that was where the fear came in.

Irrational, maybe, but Alec couldn't help wonder if he saw Marietta not only as a comrade but a substitute for Nola. Was what he felt, the part of him that wanted to undeniably, *unwillingly,* go beyond companionship, really genuine? Or, as he dreaded most, if he were someone else looking at himself, would he see nothing but a desperate man clinging to the extended helpful hand for all the wrong reasons?

Dear God, he hoped he was clearheaded enough not to do that, not to make a fool of himself and so shamefully abuse Marietta's support. He thought that given enough time, and should his circumstances remain the same—should his wife not be found—he and Marietta could ultimately find something more than friendship.

It was an idea that Alec found both appealing and hideous, because above all, this filled him with a deplorable sense of disloyalty to Nola.

MARCH 24--MONDAY

The trail was dead cold.

But Conroy just wasn't ready to put the Elidad file in the unsolved drawer yet. He knew Alec Elidad thought the police had given up. Privately he didn't believe for a second that the man's wife was still alive. Everything was against that, from the blood in the shoe to the purse with the credit card still in it. His contact in the records department still hadn't come through, and while she seemed as mystified about the misplaced records as he was, Conroy had to admit that finding them probably wouldn't contribute much to Nola Elidad's current whereabouts.

Sitting in his car, the detective stubbornly spread the contents of the Elidad file on the seat. Was there something he'd missed, some thread on which he hadn't followed up?

The first suspect, of course, was Alec. No matter what the law said, spouses always fell conveniently into the guilty until proven innocent purview. Conroy had been keeping track of him, and Dustine's contacts reported that he'd started going to counseling in February, then kept attending. He was back at work—he'd called Conroy to make sure the detective had the number there in case something came up—and was presumably trying to get on with his life.

Marlo Frayne was probably a murderess and a social security scammer. Conroy wasn't through with her yet, but he didn't believe she had anything to do with her adopted daughter's disappearance.

Nola's supervisor at the library, Krystin Parker—he could think of nothing there to pick up on, despite that hunch that she was holding something back on him. Whatever her secret was, Conroy still had his suspicions that it somehow tied to Trista Newman, and through her, to Jesse and Stacey Waite. Flipping through the pages of the notes he'd made—not much there, either—Conroy came across one of his scribbles, then stopped. *MC Tooling, Bensenville*—what was that? He scanned down a few lines and remembered that this was where Jesse Waite worked—had he followed up on that? No, because when he'd talked to Waite the man had mentioned it was a new job and he hadn't wanted to make waves. But that had been back in January and now it was March; he'd have to think up a reason to ask about Waite, but the man ought to have been on the job long enough by now so his poking around a little wouldn't endanger anything.

MC Tooling was a smallish machine shop, one of a line of concrete block buildings just a little past Foster and Thomas, where the noise of the planes arriving and departing from O'Hare Airport directly to the east split the air every few minutes. Nothing fancy about the place, and when Conroy walked into the office, he could see through the room's windows that the day shift was in full swing. The machines thrummed and the men looked busy, something any small-business owner would be gratified to cope with, and the guy who glanced up from a pile of paperwork in the office looked pleasant enough. "Help you?"

Conroy nodded and offered his hand, noting the name *Fred* embroidered on the man's shirt. "My name's Conroy. I'm from the Roselle Police Department. Are you the boss?"

Fred stood and accepted Conroy's hand and shook it briefly. "That's me, Fred Schultz. What can I do for you?"

"I have a couple of questions about one of your men, if you don't mind, a guy named Jesse Waite." Conroy glanced at one of the chairs in front of the cluttered desk. "May I?"

"Be my guest," Fred Schultz said as he settled back on his own chair. Fred was a round-faced man in his upper fifties, still pretty fit. His eyes were blue and sharp. "So, Jesse Waite. I don't know what I can tell you about him except that he's a good worker and he hasn't missed a day's work since I hired him. The truth is I don't have to deal with him much because he works the night shift. What do you want to know?"

Conroy nodded and cracked his knuckles. Careful here—he didn't want to screw things up for Waite. "Well, to be honest, I'm just looking for a general rundown on him, what he's like. It's too complicated to explain, but his name's come up in a case we're working on." Conroy made a pretense of hesitating. "I'm not really at liberty to say more than that, other than to say that Waite's not in any trouble or anything. I'm just trying to cover all the loose ends."

Fred nodded, accepting his explanation, but Conroy could see the curiosity in his eyes. He unsnapped a ring of keys from his belt and swiveled in his chair, then unlocked a drawer in one of the file cabinets behind him. He thumbed through the folders inside and lifted one out. "Well, let's see. Personally I can tell you he seems like a stand-up guy. Skilled help, wants to work and does a good job of it, keeps his work area clean. He's never had any problems with anyone else. His start date was January twentieth, emergency contact is his wife, Stacey. That's about it."

Conroy nodded. "How about his previous employer? Maybe I could talk to someone there."

Fred flipped through the papers. "Well, here's his job application. He used to work at a place called C&H Machinery in Itasca—that's where we would've gone for references. I don't recall anything special, but they must've checked out or I wouldn't have hired him."

Conroy pulled out his notebook and wrote down the name. "You have a number for this outfit?"

Fred read him what was on the application. "You're sure Jesse's not in any trouble?"

Conroy put his notebook away. "No, he's fine. Like I said, this is all just background stuff on this other file, cleaning up loose ends. But I'd appreciate it if you didn't tell him I was asking about him—I wouldn't want him to get the wrong impression." And what, he wondered, was that, really? Nothing more than a strange feeling in his gut that although there wasn't anything truly *wrong* about Jesse Waite, there was also something not quite *right*.

While he'd kept his face impassive, Conroy didn't think the man was fooled. Fred nodded anyway. "Sure thing. If you have any more questions, feel free to give me a call. Here's the shop's card."

"Thanks," Conroy said. He took the business card, then

offered one of his own. "And the same here—if you think of anything we didn't talk about today, this is where I can be reached."

Fred nodded and the two men shook hands again before Conroy left. Outside, Conroy tapped *C&H Machinery* into the police car's computer and it gave him an address, but when he pulled up in front of the Itasca building twenty minutes later, he found an empty structure, smaller than MC Tooling, with a FOR SALE sign out front that looked like it'd been there at least a month. He drove around back but there was nothing to point anyone toward a new address; more than likely, C&H had sold out—maybe the owner had retired—and the crew had moved on.

Another damned dead end.

"Mr. Schultz, this is Detective Conroy. I came by your office this morning?" Conroy leaned back on his chair, trying to keep the frustration out of his voice. He'd done his best to track down anyone from C&H. No luck. "Listen, I went by that C&H Machinery where you told me Jesse Waite used to work and it's closed down. You wouldn't have any idea where they might've gone, would you?"

There was a pause while Schultz thought about it. Then, *"No, I sure don't, and come to think of it, I should've remembered about C&H—I think they closed before I even hired Jesse Waite. But there's a guy who works the second shift here name of John Aldwin. He was also one of Jesse's references, used to work with him at that C&H place a long time ago—yeah, that's where I got the reference for Jesse. He's on some kind of long weekend thing with his family so he won't be around until later this week, but I'll have him give you a call as soon as he comes in. How's that?"*

"I'd appreciate it," Conroy said sincerely. "That would be very helpful."

"One thing, though—Aldwin is a good friend of Jesse's, so you might want to be careful what you say to him. Just in case Jesse's in any trouble. And I'm sorry for the mix-up about C&H. Like I said, I should've remembered."

"No problem. And thanks again." Conroy hung up and wrote this new name on a fresh sheet of paper. It wasn't exactly a clue, but at least it wasn't a blank page anymore.

No matter what Jesse had said, Stacey still felt strange driving a car.

He'd sworn to her that it was like that old cliché about riding a bicycle—once you learned, you never forgot—but try as she might, Stacey couldn't come up with a single recollection or reach any real level of comfort while sitting in the driver's seat. She was okay now only because Jesse had driven her to the oversized commuter train parking lot for several nights and taken her through his version of driver's ed. She still wasn't up to any major trips and traffic made her nervous, but she felt she could handle taking the Impala out on her own today. She couldn't expect Jesse to ferry her everywhere, all the time.

Her sleep schedule had finally completely shifted to match his—Stacey slept when he did, spent time with him when he was home, and usually stayed up all night while he was at work, doing household stuff, reading, or watching late-night cable. Today, however, she'd made a special effort to get up "early" and go to the store; she wanted to pick up a few things and make a special dinner—steak, maybe—a sort of secret celebration even if she wasn't ready to share her news.

Stacey was convinced she was pregnant.

She was only a week late but she was certain her body had been regular as clockwork before now. Still, she would wait until she was absolutely positive before telling Jesse. She wasn't sure how he would react, but she had an idea that the biggest response was going to be fear. In a way she couldn't blame him, but look at her now—physically she couldn't have been any healthier, her attitude was good, her outlook positive. There were lessons to be learned from what had happened last year—the strep throat, the fever, and finally the miscarriage. There wasn't going to be a repeat of that—the first time she so much as skinned her knee, she'd run for the doctor so fast there'd be a stream of smoke behind her.

Excitement filled her, going beyond the zing of tension driving alone put into her muscles. She knew what she wanted from the store and it wasn't complicated—no need to travel any farther than the Pik-Kwik on Irving Park. She turned into the lot and parked, then hurried into the store and away from the damp, March wind. If they were lucky they'd get through the rest of the month and into April without any more snow and finally see an end to the gray winter clouds. She couldn't wait for spring and the sunshine it would bring, the blue skies—could anyone be happier than she was now? She had a husband who adored her and she him, and now, at last, they would take that love to the next level and become a real family.

Being inside the store made Stacey smile even wider as she grabbed a cart and headed down the aisles. It felt . . . *right* in here, as though she'd stopped here dozens of times. One more thing to add to the sense of well-being that was increasing every day. She only needed a few things—egg noodles, a bottle of Lawry's Seasoned Salt, then a couple of good-looking if slightly overpriced strip steaks. She finished up with the makings of a salad and added a few fancy touches—a decadently expensive gold bell pepper and jicama—then found a bottle of tangy raspberry vinaigrette. That she knew where everything was just made it all the more perfect.

Stacey zipped through the checkout line and paid with a check, offering her driver's license as identification. The clerk was a teenager who, strangely enough, kept staring at her and peered at the picture on her driver's license with a bit more intensity than seemed reasonable. Finally, though, he gave it back and ran her check through.

Weird, she thought as she hurried back to the Impala. But forgettable—she had much more wonderful things to worry about in her life than some overly intense teenager who probably thought she resembled his mother or something.

Things like how on earth she was going to manage to keep her secret from her husband.

He had to wait until his next break to look for it, but Brent finally scrounged around in all the baskets beneath the registers until he came up with that cop's card—Detective Conroy, that was the guy's name. Yeah, he might be nuts and maybe it was only a weird karma thing, but he remembered that woman's face from the poster somebody had tacked up on the outside bulletin board back in January. They were saying she'd been abducted right out there in the parking lot, and that he'd seen it and not paid any attention. Well, maybe he'd fucked up back then by not getting a license number or something, but he sure wasn't going to run a repeat this time.

"This is Detective Lucas Conroy. I'm not available right now, but please leave me a detailed message. If this is an emergency—"

Shit, he'd gotten the man's voice mail. Whatever.

"Yeah, uh, hi. My name is Brent and I talked to you a couple of months ago, when you were asking about that woman who's missing? And I couldn't tell you anything because I didn't see it? Anyways, this lady just came into the store, right, and like I don't know for sure if the name is the same or anything, but I could swear it's the same woman on the poster that was hanging up here awhile back." He paused, not really knowing what else to say to the machine. "So, like, if you want it, she wrote a check for her stuff and so I've got her name and where she lives. The store closes at ten, but I'm here until eleven stocking shelves."

Brent hung up and stood there indecisively. Then, just in case the cop didn't pick up the message until tomorrow, he went to the register and copied down the woman's name, address, and driver's license number.

Conroy almost fell off his chair.

". . . but I could swear it's the same woman on the poster that was hanging up here awhile back."

Had he heard that correctly? He replayed it, just to be sure, then ran it a third time. Then he grabbed his coat and ran to his car.

"And you got this information from where?"

The teenaged Brent was looking at him like Conroy had two heads, but that was okay. Someday the kid would learn patience. "I told you—I copied it off her check." He pointed at the slip of paper, already crumpled and smudged. "And that's her driver's license number."

"And you think it's the same woman on the posters we hung around Roselle a couple of months ago."

"Yeah." Brent's chin lifted stubbornly. "Yeah, I do. Look, I know you think I'm a dumb-ass for not paying attention when that woman got snatched in the parking lot, so I'm not going to do anything to make you think that again. Until it got all wet and fell apart, I had to look at that poster every day when I came in, and I always felt like maybe it was kinda my fault." He shuffled his feet. "Or that at least she would've been found if I'd have gotten the plate number or something. I'm telling you, this woman"—he poked at the piece of paper in Conroy's hand again—"looks exactly like her. Go see for yourself."

Conroy folded the piece of paper and tucked it into his pocket. "Thanks," he said after a moment. He looked at his watch—seven o'clock. His timing had never been better. "I think I'll do just that."

Conroy rang the bell and Nola Elidad answered the door.

"May I help you?"

Small and fragile-looking; dark, shoulder-length wavy hair. Her eyebrows were more straight than arched, and from this close, Conroy could see the gray and green flecks in her blue eyes, the exact color Alec Elidad had described.

For a long second, Conroy didn't know what to say—a

first in his career as a cop. Then, just to throw everything into place right now, he asked exactly what he wanted to know.

"Nola Elidad?"

But her expression in response to his question was nothing more than quizzical. "I'm sorry—who? I think you have the wrong house."

She started to back up and close the door, then stopped when Conroy pulled out his badge and held it up. "My mistake. Could I ask you a few questions, Mrs . . . ?"

"Waite," she said. "My name is Stacey Waite." She peered at his badge intently, then shrugged. "I guess you can come in. My husband and I were just sitting down to dinner, so I hope this won't take long."

"It won't," Conroy promised.

She motioned him inside and closed the door behind him. Conroy could see the living room, well-cleaned and tidy, and a small dining room. The table was set—plates, silver, even candles—and the smell of broiling steak was quite appetizing. "Jesse," she called. "We have company."

"Celebrating something?" Conroy asked mildly as he waited for Jesse Waite to make his appearance.

Stacey Waite shrugged delicately. Her smile was soft and, to Conroy's practiced eye, not quite truthful. "Not . . . really. It's just kind of a splurge."

He heard footsteps from down a hallway he couldn't see, and Jesse Waite hurried into the room. "Who—" He froze when he saw Conroy, then did his best to smile. "Detective," he said. "What brings you here again?"

Conroy glanced at Stacey. "I don't know if you recall, Mr. Waite, but the last time I stopped by I asked you if you knew a woman named Nola Elidad."

Jesse nodded. "I remember. And I'm pretty sure I told you I didn't."

"Right." Conroy folded his arms. Was that a tremor he'd heard in Jesse Waite's voice? "Today I got a message from one of the cashiers at the Pik-Kwik grocery store saying that he thought Nola Elidad, who's been missing since

January, came in and bought some groceries." He turned toward Stacey. "The name and address he gave me was yours, Mrs. Waite."

Stacey tilted her head. "Well, I can't imagine why he would do that."

"To hear him tell it, you and Nola Elidad bear more than a passing resemblance." He didn't know what kind of a response he'd expected, but Stacey only stood there, looking blank. "Could I see your driver's license, ma'am?"

"I'll get it," she said, and headed out of the living room.

Turning to Jesse, Conroy pulled out his notebook and opened it. "So how long have you and . . . Stacey been married?"

"Uh, four years," he said. "Almost four and a half."

"Really." Conroy's pen was poised over the paper. "And the date of your marriage was what?"

"July—"

"—twenty-seventh," Stacey finished for him as she came back and handed her driver's license to Conroy. "At St. Walter's. You know where that is?"

Conroy nodded and examined the license. It was all right there, name, address, physical description. He couldn't decide which was more freaky—the fact that this woman might have been a perfect double for Nola Elidad or that they shared the same birthday. The picture, which showed a Stacey Waite with waist-length hair, was yet more proof that the license was over three years old, issued long before Alec Elidad met his wife. Another six months and it would expire. He handed it back. "Thank you."

Stacey looked at him expectantly. "Is there anything else, Detective? I don't mean to be rude, but our dinner's getting cold."

Conroy studied her. "Mrs. Waite, would it be possible for you to talk to Alec Elidad, the husband of the missing woman?"

Out of the corner of his eye Conroy saw Jesse's face drain of color, but Stacey only frowned. "Why in heaven's name would I do that? I know the police sometimes have unorthodox methods, Detective, but if I really do look as much like his wife as you claim, I can't imagine anything more cruel to do to the man. Absolutely not."

He hadn't expected her to consent, but he had to admire the way she'd thoroughly chastised him. Jesse tried to hide it, but it was obvious he was relieved. "You're right, of course," Conroy said. "It's probably not a good idea."

Stacey Waite stepped past him and put her hand on the front doorknob. "Unless there's something else?"

"Thanks for your help," Conroy said, nodding to her and her husband. He started to say "Call me if you think of anything," but he had an idea it would be a useless gesture. "Have a good evening."

"Thank you."

And, with the door now closed solidly behind him, Conroy stood in the cold March darkness and wondered what the hell was going on.

6

DISINTEGRATION

I can tell you the past is
a bucket of ashes.

—CARL SANDBURG

MARCH 27--THURSDAY

It was a good life.

Except, still, for the part about her mother.

She had so many questions—the main one being why hadn't her mother called her in all this time—but she was afraid of the answers. Jesse had been clear about the fact that she and Trista just didn't get along, and he'd also told her that Easter, which was now only three days away, was their traditional time for getting together. Whether the outcome was good or bad, he'd told her, through the years the routine had been maintained.

Well, today was Thursday and all the grocery sales for the upcoming holiday had started. There couldn't be any more screwing around; she had to decide what to fix for Easter dinner and make a shopping list around the menu. It was time to finalize.

But . . . would her mother prefer ham? Or a roast? Stacey had no idea—for all she knew her mother could be one of these people who had an unshakable aversion to pork and she would be committing the biggest faux pas of their relationship by gracing the table with a clove-studded hunk of the stuff. And what about her stepfather—did he love or hate green vegetables? And her Aunt Chris: If Stacey fixed a chocolate cake for dessert, would the woman have to remind her that chocolate gave her migraines? She felt overwhelmed, her plans for Easter dinner shaky at best, the whole idea utterly terrifying.

For God's sake, Stacey thought as she paced in front of the telephone in the hall, she still couldn't *remember* the woman, or her stepfather, or anyone else in the family. Memory gaps—they worried at her on a level that she wouldn't admit, always there but most times unacknowledged because she simply had no way to explain them. They were like a splinter in a finger—you always knew it was there, but it only stabbed you when you touched it the right way.

Like now.

She stopped her pacing and glanced worriedly at the bedroom door. Jesse was still sleeping, but he might get up at any moment. She should make the call to Trista now, before he woke—he'd be so against it that she didn't think she could do it with him hanging over her, yet without his presence in the house, even sleeping, she lost all courage. It was like the other day, when that detective had shown up—she was quite proud of herself and the smooth, unconcerned answers she'd given him. Inside, however, her pulse had been jackhammering inexplicably and thank God he hadn't tried to shake her hand—her palm had been wet with hot perspiration. She didn't know why she'd suddenly been so frightened. And the way he'd asked her to talk to that man whose wife was missing—was he crazy?

But somehow, and she didn't dare tell Jesse this, she had the feeling she *should* have. Ridiculous, of course—her comment to Detective Conroy about the cruelty of a move like that had been heartfelt, her horror at the suggestion sincere. Stacey knew she'd sounded sure of herself when she'd refused, and yet she couldn't help wonder if in some strange way she'd turned her back on someone who'd needed help. Another absurd notion—what help could she have possibly given a stranger?

Enough thinking about that, darn it. There were things she needed to do, and issues she needed to resolve—worrying about someone she didn't know and glaring at the telephone wouldn't accomplish anything. It was time to call her mother and get reacquainted. Jaw set with determination, Stacey pulled open the drawer of the hall table and took out the old telephone directory that Jesse kept there. It embarrassed her to have to look up her own mother's telephone number, but there was nothing to be done about it.

There were two numbers for her mother, one for home and one for work, and Stacey's hands were shaking as she dialed the work number. When it started ringing, she actually lost her breath for a moment, nearly panicked because she thought that when the time came, she wouldn't be able to speak.

"Trista Newman speaking."

That voice—did she remember it? She thought she might, but it seemed like it was from another lifetime. Pushing her words out felt like the hardest thing she'd ever had to do, but Stacey made herself talk. "H-hi, Mom." She cleared her throat, trying to get around the lump that had sudden clogged it up. "It's S-stacey."

There was silence on the other end. Then, finally, a faint "What?"

Had it been that long since they'd talked? Well . . . yes. Stacey tried to imagine how her mother looked right now—shocked? Annoyed? She had no idea. But whatever their last conversation, surely it hadn't been intended as a permanent good-bye.

Stacey took a deep breath. "I was c-calling about Easter, to f-find out if you were coming over." Darn it, she wished she could stop stuttering. "And what you'd like me to fix." There, that was better. The menu was neutral ground—no matter what their differences, they had to be able to discuss food.

Still, there was no reply. Stacey frowned and pressed the receiver of the telephone harder against her ear. Had they been disconnected? No—she thought she could hear breathing on the other end. "Mom?"

"*Who is this?*" her mother whispered.

Stacey blinked, caught off guard. "It's me, Mom. Stacey. I know we haven't talked in a while but—"

"Is this some kind of *joke?*" Trista's words tumbled over the line, momentarily silencing Stacey. "You think this is *funny?*"

"No, I—"

"How *dare* you call me like this!" Her mother's voice grew stronger, rising nearly to a shriek. "What gives you the *right?*"

Suddenly Stacey was aware that Jesse was there—he must've heard her talking on the phone, maybe her voice had risen to match Trista's, maybe she was shouting right back. She didn't know. "M-mom, wait—"

"Don't call me that!" Trista screamed. *"I don't know who you are and don't you ever call me that AGAIN! You—"*

Stacey slammed the phone down.

Then collapsed into Jesse's arms.

Jesse managed to hold his temper until he got Stacey calmed down and in bed, wrapped in the quilt and with a hot cup of tea on the nightstand. But his anger was like a beast pounding dully against the inside of his skull, and he knew he'd have his say with Trista Newman. And it would be tonight, damn it, not tomorrow or the next day, or sometime next week. Since his last conversation with her, he'd convinced himself that it was more sad than anything that she had refused to listen to him the night he'd tried to tell her he'd found Stacey; now he was convinced she *had* believed him, but through some twisted sense of viciousness she was acting like this to punish her daughter.

"Take a nap, honey," Jesse said quietly. He smoothed the hair back from her face, pulling tear-dampened strands off her cheeks. "You'll feel better when you wake up." He was proud of the way he kept his voice level, the perfect actor. Exhausted from crying, his wife nodded and mumbled something into the covers that he didn't catch, then her eyes flickered and closed. He sat there with her, willing his hands not to tremble and his breathing to stay regular; both were telltale signs that Stacey would catch in an instant. When he was sure she was asleep, he stood and took a deep, slow breath, keeping it as quiet as he could. The fury he felt at his mother-in-law was nearly overpowering, the stress gifting him with an immense headache, enough so that he took a couple of aspirins before walking calmly to the kitchen phone and dialing the number.

"Trista Newman speaking."

His mother-in-law's voice sounded strained and for a second Jesse simply stood there, relishing the idea that for whatever reason, something in this hateful woman's life was difficult. She deserved it.

"Hello, Trista." The greeting came out through his teeth, with his jaw so tightly clenched that the muscles ached all the way down his neck.

It must have been the fury she heard in his voice, but Trista didn't say anything for several seconds. Then, however, she started with the same venomous tone she must've used on Stacey. "Jesse, just what the hell do you think you're—"

"I have something to say to you, Trista, so you just shut the fuck up until I'm through." There was a shocked silence, then an indrawn breath. Before she could spew again, Jesse continued, unconsciously leaning into the phone and putting every ounce he had into making her know how much he despised her. "I called you in January and tried to tell you that I'd found Stacey and brought her home, but you wouldn't listen. After all these years, you're still so full of hate that no one's voice counts but yours, no matter *what's* going on. I don't know if you didn't believe me or if there was something else going on in your head, and frankly, I don't give a shit. Now you've gone and hurt Stacey with your nasty mouth and your evil games. No one hurts my wife, damn it, not even you. It wasn't enough that your paranoia smothered her when she was a kid and you couldn't let her have a life of her own. You had to have your fingers into every part of it, didn't you?" Dimly, Jesse realized his voice was rising dangerously toward a shout, and he tried to bring it back down.

"She's been *so* sick all these months, and where the hell were you? Nowhere, when she could've used you in her life. Now that she's recovered on her own, she comes to you and what do you do? You push her away, that's what. For Christ's sake, can't you just make up your mind?"

"Jesse," Trista stammered. "I don't know what you're ta—"

She sounded near hysteria. Good. "You are never, *ever* welcome in this house again," Jesse cut in brutally. "If you come near here, or near Stacey, I'll strangle you with my own two hands."

He was yelling at the end. He couldn't help it—hell, maybe he'd been yelling the entire time. But even so, he hung up the receiver very, very gently.

"I heard you on the phone," Stacey said.

Jesse turned, but the expression on his face wasn't guilty. Defiant, perhaps triumphant, but she saw no regrets or shame.

"I'm sorry you had to hear that," he said, "but I needed to tell her what I thought. She deserved it."

She'd dragged the quilt off the bed with her and now she stood there uncertainly, feeling like a child clutching her security blanket. "What did you mean when you were talking about her paranoia smothering me and she wouldn't let me have a life of my own?"

Jesse's face hardened. "Maybe it's just as well you don't remember, Stace. She was like a vulture, always hovering over you after Tammy died, like she thought you were going to vanish into thin air or something. She watched you constantly, always demanding to know where you were going and who you'd be with every minute of every day. It got to be a real problem once you hit high school and started wanting to date, and then when you met me . . ." He shrugged and she got the message.

"So it was a battle for independence," Stacey said softly.

"For years, then the fight went into astronomical proportions when we decided to get married. I wasn't kidding when I said your mom thought I was the devil," Jesse said quietly. "I never meant to be, but I suppose I was the catalyst that really sent her out of control. It was always obvious that she loathed me for taking you away from her.

"And because of the way she felt about me, you told me you hated her."

"Excuse me, are you Detective Conroy?"

Conroy looked up to see a youngish looking guy with a round face and kindly brown eyes standing next to his desk. "That's me. What can I do for you?"

The other man offered his hand. "My name's John Aldwin. My boss is Fred Schultz at MC Tooling? He said you might want to talk to me—something about my friend Jesse."

Conroy stood and shook Aldwin's hand, then gestured at him to sit. He checked out Aldwin as he retrieved the Elidad file—late twenties, medium height with close-cropped hair, a husky build that said he might be involved in a weekend sport like football or soccer, little bit of a beer belly. He was in an MC Tooling uniform and wore a wedding ring on his left hand; there was a sort of general-nice-guy aura about him that put Conroy at ease. Aldwin waited patiently while Conroy flipped a few pages back and forth.

"I just have a few questions about Jesse," Conroy finally said. "I understand you knew him from working with him before, at C&H Machining?"

" 'Machinery,' " Aldwin corrected automatically. "Actually, I've known Jesse a lot longer than that. We went to high school together." Concern flickered across the younger man's features. "Jesse didn't do anything wrong, did he? I have to tell you, it's pretty unnerving to have the cops asking about him . . . no offense."

Conroy smiled slightly, liking the guy's honesty. "None taken. And no, I don't believe he's in trouble."

"Then . . . ?"

Conroy hesitated. "To be honest with you, Mr. Aldwin—"

"John."

"John, then. I can't tell you *what* it is about Jesse that's striking me funny. What I'm trying to track here is nothing but a really screwed-up paper trail that starts with another case. As far as I can tell, Jesse doesn't even know these people, yet the name 'Waite' keeps popping up in their files."

Aldwin looked both relieved and puzzled. "That's weird. Who are these people—that is, if you can tell me, of course."

"The Elidads," Conroy answered. "Nola and Alec Elidad. Like I said, it's just a twisted string of names that keeps coming back to Jesse." He folded his hands on the desk, deciding to keep the details to himself. "I've talked to Jesse but I can't find anything there. So I thought I'd try to dig a little deeper."

Aldwin nodded. "That's good. Jesse . . . well, he's got a temper and he can get pretty loud if you tick him off, but he's not a physical guy—he'd never hurt anyone. Like I said—we went to high school together. We were best friends for years and I helped get him the job at MC after he left C&H Machinery. I was best man at his wedding, the whole schmeel." He looked like he didn't know where else to go with the conversation. "All in all, it's a pretty normal past."

"You said you 'were' best friends," Conroy said. "Has that changed?"

Aldwin momentarily looked at a loss for words. "It's . . . kind of hard to explain, Detective Conroy. Jesse is a good man, but he's had more than his fair share of misery this last year or so. I tried to be there for him, but now . . ." Aldwin bit his lip, obviously reluctant to say the words, almost as if he were embarrassed on behalf of his friend. "Well, I don't want to give you the wrong impression, but the truth is that Jesse's one seriously messed-up guy. It seems like we've been friends forever, but jeez, I just don't know what to say to him anymore."

Conroy frowned. "I'm not sure I follow. Messed up—what do you mean by that? I've talked to him a couple of times and he seems okay."

Aldwin looked away, his expression pained. "He . . . keeps talking about the things he and Stacey—that's his wife—are doing, what they're planning . . . all the things you'd expect from a guy seriously in love." Now Aldwin scrubbed at his face with his hands before raising his troubled gaze to Conroy's.

"But Detective Conroy, Jesse's wife is *dead.* She died last fall—I went to her funeral."

Conroy's mouth dropped open in shock. "She's *dead*?"

Aldwin nodded, his shoulders slumping. "It was an awful thing—I can't even describe what Jesse went through. He—"

"I'd like to show you a picture of someone," Conroy interrupted. He turned his chair toward the computer and banged out a driver's license information request on Stacey Waite; it was only a matter of seconds before the photo from her license came up on the screen, along with the usual statistics. "Is this Jesse's wife?"

Aldwin stepped around to where he could see the screen. "Sure, that's Stacey."

"And what about this?" Conroy pulled out a small mock-up of one of the *Missing/Abducted* posters the department had made up in January.

Aldwin's eyes widened. "Damn!" He peered at the piece of paper. "Nola Elidad? This is the woman you mentioned before—she's *missing*?"

Conroy nodded and Aldwin went back and sat heavily on the chair. "Oh, this sure doesn't look good. Him talking about his wife and what have you, and then this . . . Christ."

"The thing is," Conroy said, leaning forward, "I've talked to a woman at Jesse's house who claims she's Stacey Waite. She looks just like her"—he pointed to the computer screen—"and her." Aldwin looked completely flabbergasted, and Conroy cracked his knuckles thoughtfully, trying to work through this. Maybe this was why he hadn't been able to come up with any information on Stacey Waite—some kind of hang-up in the death records. Or maybe the woman wasn't dead at all. But then, where did that leave Nola Elidad? Could he be dealing with some kind of multiple personality thing here?

"That's why I was so surprised when you said she was dead," Conroy finally continued. "I wonder if something happened—maybe Stacey didn't die after all. If she and Jesse were having marital problems that no one else knew about, maybe she ran, tried to start a new life for herself with someone else. And maybe Jesse tried to cover it up, and now they've worked it out."

"No," Aldwin cut in. "That's not possible." At Conroy's questioning look, he continued. "It was an awful thing, Detective. Jesse could barely handle it, and he and his mother-in-law—"

"Trista Newman."

"Right. They were fighting all the time—she blamed him for Stacey being sick, he blamed her for not being there for Stacey. They'd hated each other for years anyway. When the doctor told him she'd passed away, Jesse refused to let Trista or anyone else see Stacey's body, and he wouldn't go see it himself, not even at the funeral home."

Conroy's eyebrows raised. "Then how do you know she really died—how does *anyone* know?"

"Because *I* saw the body, Detective. Jesse was so adamant about everyone remembering Stacey the way she was, so determined that no one could see her dead, that the funeral director pulled me aside while Jesse was in the men's room. He hustled me into the back and asked me to view the body, said that according to state law someone *had* to, just to make sure that the hospital had transported the right body to the home. Jesse never knew I did it." Aldwin looked completely miserable at the memory. "I'd known Stacey almost as long as Jesse had, and there was *no* mistaking that it was her in that coffin."

When Krystin answered the phone, her sister was crying on the other end.

She sat up straight. "Trista, what's the matter—are you all right? Did something happen—"

"It's Jesse," Trista sobbed. "He c-called me and—oh, God, Krys, you wouldn't believe the things he said!"

Jesse? Krystin held the phone to her ear and fought with the cord as she scooted around her desk and toed her office door closed. She'd always liked Jesse, had thought he worshiped Stacey in every way. Privately, she'd also always thought her sister acted like an idiot about him and should've been happy that Stacey'd found someone who so obviously adored her. "What?" she asked. "What did he say?"

"It started with a telephone call from this woman. She sounded so *much* like Stacey, and she was acting like she was." Trista was obviously on the edge of hysteria. "Krys, she claimed she was my daughter! I lost it and accused her of being a crank caller. She hung up on me."

When Krystin sat there, speechless, Trista continued. "About a half hour later, Jesse called me and started screaming at me over the phone. He was furious, said all kinds of crazy things about Stacey being home and how he tried to tell me in January—"

"January?" Krystin asked. "What's this about January?"

Trista sniffed. "I didn't tell you—I didn't tell *any*one. I know you and Ken, even Tadd, think I've been too hard on Jesse all these years, and I thought you'd just think I was being the same way as always. But last January, Jesse called me practically in the middle of the night—well, really early in the morning."

"What did he say?"

"I . . . well, I hung up on him," her sister admitted. "I just didn't want to deal with him, and he woke me up, and . . ." Her voice faded out.

Krystin swallowed. "What did he say in January?"

There was a pause on the other end, and Krystin could hear the line humming emptily. It sounded like she and her sister were separated by an unseen abyss. "He tried to tell me that he'd found Stacey, but I wouldn't listen," Trista said softly. "And he said that now if I ever came near her again, he'd kill me."

"There are a couple of things I need to tell you."

Krystin sat across the table from Trista, but she couldn't meet her sister's eyes. Even in Trista's own home, the one place where she'd said she had always felt safe, Trista now looked haggard and frightened, like someone who'd unexpectedly realized she was walking on a thin crust of cooled lava over an active volcano.

Trista's mouth trembled. "Oh, God, Krys—I don't know if I can take any more stress today."

Krystin reached across the table and took her sister's hand, held it tight. "I'm sorry, but you're going to have to."

Trista pulled out of her grasp and hugged herself protectively. Still, she couldn't do any more than nod.

Now that she had to, Krystin didn't know where to start. "There was a young woman who applied for a job at the library last fall," she finally said. "Her name was Nola Elidad."

Trista frowned at her. "Wait—I've heard that name before, haven't I?"

"If you have, it wasn't from me." Krystin stared at the table, again unwilling to meet her sister's gaze. "I—"

"I think I remember," Trista said suddenly. "It was in a phone message from a police officer, asking if I knew anything about her. I called him back but he wasn't there, and of course, I didn't know what he was talking about." She peered at Krystin from below lids swollen from crying. "What does this have to do with Jesse—why did you drive all the way out here to tell me this?"

Krystin took a deep breath, trying to calm her singing nerves. "I hired her because she looked exactly like Stacey."

"What!"

"Don't jump to crazy conclusions," Krystin rushed on. "She *wasn't* Stacey. She was just a young girl who looked like her, quiet and conservative, and who wanted the library clerk position. She said she'd studied library science in high school but didn't have any experience. It didn't pay much so I offered it to her and she took it."

Trista stared at her, trying to understand. "But . . . I still don't understand what this has to do with Jesse."

Krystin drew her hands down over her mouth, hardly believing herself what she was about to say. "The young woman I hired disappeared in January, Trista. She's never been found."

Trista looked at her blankly for a moment, then her eyes widened in understanding. "Oh my *God,* Krys—you don't think Jesse had something to do with that!"

She leaned toward Trista. "I don't know, but . . . listen to what you're telling me. He calls you and says he 'found' Stacey? I had no idea—if I'd have known about this in January, I'd have told the detective about it. As it was, I couldn't tell him anything—I never even checked references on the girl, and I certainly never thought about Jesse." She shuddered slightly. "Krys, we have to call that Detective Conroy—I wrote his name on my calendar—and tell him about this. This could be the thing they need to find Nola Elidad."

"But what if it's not her?"

Krystin stared at her sister. "I'm sorry—what? Who else could it be?" When Trista answered, Krystin had to strain to hear the words.

"It could be Stacey."

Conroy had been on his way out the door to pay the Waite household another visit when he'd gotten the call from Krystin Parker. Now he sat across from her and her sister Trista and tried to pull enough pieces out of the story so that it all made sense.

Trista Newman was a neatly kept middle-aged woman with gray-touched brown hair and blue eyes. She was a little soft around the middle, but her age showed most of all in the worry lines across her forehead and the tense wrinkles around her mouth, indentations that seemed to deepen every time she crossed her arms and hugged herself, which was frequently. "I really don't think we need to be here, Detective Conroy," she said now. "This is a family matter." She shot Krystin a severe look. "It should be handled by us."

Conroy said nothing, content for now to sit and listen to the discourse between the two sisters. He could see Trista's strong resemblance to the woman who claimed to be Stacey Waite . . . whoever she was.

Krystin Parker shook her head vehemently and pushed

a stray lock of hair back from her forehead. "Trista, I'm telling you. I worked with Nola Elidad five days a week. If it'd been Stacey, I would have known it."

"No," Trista said stubbornly. She turned her nearly exuberant gaze on Krystin. "Stacey was ill, don't you remember? She had a dangerously high fever—the doctors warned us about brain damage. I should have listened to Jesse when he called that morning in January. He probably wouldn't let me see her at the hospital because he knew something we didn't. Maybe she ran away—that's what it sounded like he was saying today on the phone."

Conroy frowned. "Ran away? Mrs. Newman, I'm sorry to sound harsh, but it was my understanding that your daughter died last year."

"But no one ever saw the body," Trista said. Her finger stabbed at the desktop for emphasis. "Jesse wouldn't allow it, not even at the funeral! Plus, he wouldn't let a death notice be published—almost no one knew about it."

"John Aldwin saw her." Trista's face went white and Conroy immediately regretted being so blunt. Belatedly he realized the woman had probably been holding on to this far-fetched hope since last September, nearly half a year. "I'm sorry," he added.

"He . . . saw my daughter?" Trista asked faintly. "At the hospital?"

"At the funeral home," Conroy told her gently. "The home required a positive identification from someone, and when Jesse refused to cooperate, the director went to John without Jesse's knowledge."

"Oh." Trista didn't say anything else, just sat there staring at her hands.

Krystin Parker rubbed at her mouth. Her eyes were wide and enigmatic as she looked first at Conroy, then at her sister. "Trista," she said in a voice that was almost a whisper, "do you think that Nola Elidad could be . . . Tammy?"

Trista's head whipped toward Krystin at the same time as Conroy sat forward. Tammy Gardell, he thought. *No information.*

"Is this your idea of a joke?" Trista snapped at her sister.

Krystin looked as though she'd been slapped. "No, of course not."

"Who's Tammy?" Conroy cut in. His tone of voice made it clear he wasn't fooling around anymore.

When Trista just sat there looking furious, Krystin offered him the information. "Tammy was Stacey's twin sister, the younger of the two."

He looked at the women, surprised. "Stacey has a twin?"

"Had," Trista said sharply. "Tammy's dead. She died when she was a toddler."

"How do you know?" Now Krystin looked as stubborn as her sister.

"Because I was *told* by that man Stowe worked with on the construction site!" Trista cried. "And we saw it in the papers! Damn it, Krys—"

"Stop," Conroy interrupted. He slapped a fresh notebook on the desktop. "No more arguing. Just tell *me* what's going on. What I'm getting here is that you had another daughter but someone else told you she died, and that just doesn't make sense."

The women looked at each other, but Krystin only raised her chin and stayed silent. Finally Trista sighed and, hugging herself again, filled him in. "Stacey and Tammy were twins," she said. There was a great reluctance in her voice, as if just saying the names of her children filled her with too much pain to bear. "Their father—"

"Stowe Gardell?" Conroy guessed. Nola Gardell, he thought. *No information.*

"Right. We were young and we just couldn't get along. We fought all the time and finally had enough sense to get a divorce. The judge gave us joint custody but said the girls should live with me." She rocked a little on her chair. "Stowe was enraged. He wanted both his children, and he wanted them all the time. The divorce had hardly been final, only a couple of weeks, when he broke into the house in the middle of the night and tried to take them." A single tear slid down her cheek but she didn't seem to notice.

"The girls had separate rooms and he only got Tammy—he knocked something off a table and I heard him. But by the time I got there, he was gone. I called the police, but this was almost twenty years ago. Back then, they weren't interested in parental abductions, and besides, it was right there in the divorce papers that he had joint custody. They felt that he had a right to take her, and that he'd probably come back in a week or two, after he found out how hard it was to care for a toddler." She gave a short, caustic laugh. "I remember the cop that night telling me I ought to be grateful because I still had the other one."

Conroy scowled but made himself concentrate on finding out what happened next. "And?"

"Well, I got word in a week or two, all right." She glared at Krystin, who stared back unflinchingly. "Stowe was a construction worker, a laborer who just went from site to site. A guy who'd worked with Stowe off and on knocked on the door one morning and told me they were both dead, said Stowe'd taken Tammy and headed out west, but their plane had gone down."

Conroy cracked his knuckles. "And you verified this?"

"That son of a bitch was the consummate con artist," Krystin threw in before Trista could reply. "Yeah, there had been a plane crash out of O'Hare going to Texas the day before, but it was in all the papers and there was no proof that Stowe was on it. His 'friend' told her that Stowe had bought the airline ticket under a fake name, and he didn't need a ticket for Tammy if he held her on his lap, said he didn't know what name Stowe had used. So she couldn't verify anything. *Ever.*"

Conroy looked at Trista. "Is that true?"

"I did the best I could," Trista said defensively. "I called the airline but they couldn't tell me anything other than there was no one by that name on the list. I checked the passenger list when they made it public but that didn't help either. It was a terrible crash, over a hundred and fifty people, and there were three men on the list who had no next of kin to contact. I went to the site where Stowe was working but they said he picked up his check one day, went home, and never came back. The police wouldn't help and I was young and broke, so I couldn't afford a private detective." She was crying unabashedly now.

"I had no choice but to accept it and move on. I told Stacey that her sister had gone away to God, and when she got older I just kept up the lie and said it was related to her heart. It was easier than admitting her own father had kidnapped her, and Stacey had always had a heart murmur—it ran in the Gardell family. I thought it would make her be a little quieter, not be so prone to over-exerting herself. I was terrified something would happen to her, too."

Next to her, Krystin's face softened and she touched Trista's shoulder. "I'm sorry—I didn't mean to be so hard on you." She looked to Conroy. "I just . . . I never trusted Stowe. I know she loved him when they were together, but I always felt every word that came out of the man's mouth was a lie. I guess I couldn't believe that this wasn't either."

Conroy pulled a box of tissues out of his desk and passed it to Trista, who swiped roughly at her eyes. "So," he said to Trista, "essentially your daughter Tammy just disappeared with your ex-husband."

She nodded. "I never saw either one of them again. What was always strange was that Stacey used to wake up crying in the middle of night, telling me she had bad dreams about her twin. They faded—finally—when she got to be about . . . I don't know, maybe ten years old. But I always thought that if my daughter really were alive, I'd have felt it."

So much for maternal instinct, Conroy thought grimly. He pictured a terrified toddler, kidnapped in the middle of the night and renamed by a father who died only a few months later, then renamed again and raised—only a few miles away—by a despicable and murderous stepmother. When history repeated itself almost two decades later, it was no wonder the young woman had no clue who she was anymore.

It was time to tell the truth. He leaned forward. "Mrs.

Newman—Trista—from what you're telling me, and from the information I've gathered, I have a reasonable suspicion that the young woman living with Jesse Waite is your missing daughter Tammy."

"What we want you to do," he told Trista Newman, "is go in there and talk to them. In spite of how angry he is, Jesse doesn't fit the profile of someone prone to violence. I think if you apologize and appeal to his wife's forgiveness, for her sake he'll accept you again."

On the other side of his desk, Trista sat hunched on her chair, looking miserable. "But what will I say?" she asked in a small voice. "God, I don't even *know* her."

"Exactly," Conroy pointed out. "And she doesn't know you—so she won't be able to point a finger at any mistakes you make. What I'm looking for here is an idea of her state of mind. We already know what Jesse's is, but how fragile is Stacey's—or Tammy's? Whether you know her or not, you'll be able to talk with them on a level that I can't."

Krystin looked from her sister to Conroy, her eyes shadowed with anxiety. "And then what does she do?"

"Then she comes back out to us and tells us what she found," he said with total calm. "And then we go in."

It was cold and dark outside, the wind edged with a nasty bit of last-effort winter for this late-March night. Silence surrounded Trista as she stood before the door to the townhouse, and the knowledge that Conroy and her sister, as well as a number of other police officers, were parked in the shadows behind her brought no comfort. There had been a time not so long ago that Trista had thought she would never knock on this door again, much less ask to come inside; that she was doing so now was nearly unthinkable, a testament to the fact that destiny can sometimes laugh in the face of the most determined plans.

She'd been standing here, unmoving, for almost five

minutes. The cold was seeping past the fingers of her gloves and becoming painful, and she could think of no more reason to stall, so she set her jaw, raised her hand, and knocked hard on the door.

While the last few years of her life hadn't been difficult, except for Stacey's death, things in general hadn't been easy. The divorce from Stowe, the disappearance of one of her daughters, and raising a child alone until her remarriage had forced her to be strong. But nothing she'd endured so far had prepared her to meet the young woman who answered the door.

It was Stacey . . . or was it?

No, not quite, and for a long second all Trista could do was stand there, paralyzed, and return the woman's quizzical stare.

"Hi, what . . . can I do for you?"

Not Stacey, of course—she would have recognized her own mother, no matter how sick she'd been. Trista opened her mouth to say something, anything, but her chance was lost when Jesse stepped into the light behind the woman who was calling herself his wife. "What are you doing here?" he demanded harshly. "I told you that you weren't welcome here anymore."

Trista was not as strong as she thought.

She tried, again, to speak, but the sound was lost in a sob. Jesse started to step forward and shut the door in her face, but Stacey—or whoever she was—blocked his path. "Mom?" She looked back at Jesse. "Jesse, is this my mother?"

Jesse's face was thunderous. "Yeah. But look how much she's hurt you—tell her to go away."

"No." The young woman reached out and took Trista's arm, then pulled her into the townhouse. "Come in," she said. "Here, let me take your coat."

Still unable to speak, Trista slipped off her coat and held it out. She couldn't take her eyes off the Stacey look-alike—Tammy? Because she hadn't been around her while she was growing up, it was strangely like seeing a clone of her daughter rather than a twin. But . . . not quite: The hair was different, shorter, and she had fewer lines around her eyes and mouth, as if whcrever she'd been all these years, there had been very little laughter. "H-hello," Trista finally managed. She shivered, the cold air outside still skittering along the inside of her clothes. "I . . . I came over b-because I'm so s-s-sorry about earlier." She fought against the sudden urge to just drop to her knees and bawl. "I—I—"

"That was an awful thing you did," Jesse said coldly.

"Crank calls," Trista blurted, snatching at the first idea that came to mind. "I've been getting them over the last couple of weeks, but you didn't know that, how could you? I thought this was another one, and it wasn't until you called back that I realized how wrong I was." She looked at them both pleadingly. "I didn't call back because I thought you'd just hang up on me. Which you would have had every right to do," she added hastily.

Jesse was silent and she could see the indecision in his face. Stacey—Trista tried to force herself to think of her like that—looked from him to her, then back; it was heartbreakingly clear that she desperately wanted Jesse's support in this.

Finally, he shrugged. "Whatever," he said. He sounded like a sullen little boy. "I just want Stacey to be happy, so it's up to her. If she's okay with it, with you being here, then I can live with it."

Stacey's smile was radiant. "I *knew* we'd be okay. Come on—let me make you some tea." She hesitated. "Or . . . coffee? Would you rather have that?"

"Tea is fine," Trista said, following her hesitantly toward the kitchen. Jesse trailed behind with his hands shoved in his pockets, as if he didn't know where to go or what to do with himself, but he was damned sure going to be around to protect Stacey. Trista hadn't been in the townhouse since the end of last summer, back when her daughter had told her she was pregnant. That had actually been a happy time, one of the few for Trista since Jesse and Stacey had gotten married; Stacey had been glowing with delight over the coming baby. Not much had changed about the place since then, except winter had made it a bit darker and drearier; the furniture and floor were as spotless as her daughter had always maintained them.

Her daughter . . . were Krystin and Detective Conroy right? Could it really be true that the woman living with Jesse now was Tammy, still alive after all these years? What other explanation could there be?

If only it were that simple, Trista thought as she watched 'Stacey' go through the motions of making tea, feeling the presence of her son-in-law the entire time. What had happened to him—what twists and turns had gone on in his mind—to make him believe that this really was Stacey? He'd said something about finding her after she'd been sick; did he really believe she'd somehow walked out of the hospital with nothing more devious than amnesia? It was as if he had brainwashed himself into believing the thing he wanted most in the world to be true. Which brought up the other, just as ominous question:

What on earth had he done to this young woman to convince her that she was someone she wasn't?

And yet . . . she seemed okay. Healthy, happy—happier this evening than when she'd called her on the phone earlier today. It was so *hard* to see Tammy—if that's who she was—wearing Stacey's clothes, acting like Stacey, being affectionate toward Jesse as though they really had been married for years. On the surface, there were only tiny differences, nothing that someone other than, say, her mother would notice. Could there be any more evidence than what was in front of her that Jesse was treating her well, that he wasn't dangerous?

"Here you go." Trista, lost in her thoughts, blinked as Stacey set a mug in front of her, then carefully lowered a tea bag into it. "Would you like sugar?"

"N-no," Trista said. "Thanks." She watched as Stacey put her own mug down, then sat across from her. She seemed completely at ease here, as though she'd been the one to rent and furnish this townhouse with Jesse four years ago, as if she were the woman whose hands had crocheted the afghan thrown over the couch in the living room. If it hadn't been for Detective Conroy telling her that John

Aldwin had actually seen her daughter in her coffin, Trista thought she might have easily believed this young woman was Stacey.

The two of them stared at each other awkwardly, with Jesse looming in the background like some kind of dark guardian. Finally Trista coughed into her hand, then tried to start a conversation. "How . . . how are you feeling?" It seemed as good a place as any.

"Fine," Stacey said brightly. "Never better." She glanced at Jesse but her smile didn't hold; when she looked back at Trista, she actually seemed ashamed. "I don't remember you," she admitted in a low voice. "I've been sick. I'm—I'm sorry."

Trista's eyes filled with tears and she squeezed them shut, knowing Stacey couldn't have known the impact of those words, how they would tear at her mother's heart, or for what reason. Stacey was gone, but Tammy sat only a few feet away and was completely turned around in the world, far beyond Trista's ability to fix things for her. And wasn't that what every mother wanted for her beloved children? To fix what was wrong, to heal what was hurt. How could Trista repair the damage done here?

She felt something warm on her hands and opened them to see Stacey's—or Tammy's—fingers covering her own. God help them all. Before this night was over, all three of them would find out if they could do just that, whether they wanted to or not.

"Here she comes," said a voice over the radio.

From his parking spot at the curb at the end of the driveway, Conroy looked up and saw that the door to the townhouse had opened and he heard Krystin, sitting on the passenger side, inhale sharply. For a few moments, three people were caught in the light from inside, their silhouettes meshing into a single, multilimbed form. Then they broke apart and one stepped away—Trista—and began walking rapidly toward the line of parking spaces.

For a moment the door stayed open as Jesse and the woman he was calling his wife watched her leave.

He couldn't say for sure until he talked to Trista, but Conroy was guessing that things had gone well. From Trista's description of her conversation with Jesse earlier, Conroy figured it was a good bet that Jesse would've thrown her out of the house had she and Stacey ended up arguing, or had Stacey become upset in any way. He had told Trista to take her time and do whatever was necessary to make the visit seem normal, and he'd been prepared, absent any reason to do otherwise, to wait for several hours—after all, this was a woman ostensibly catching up with a daughter whom she not only hadn't seen in six-plus months, but whom she had believed was dead. Reunions like this didn't happen in fifteen minutes, and it hadn't unsettled him that Trista had been in there for over an hour; in fact, he was surprised to see her so soon.

As he'd instructed her, she got in her car and started it up. He monitored the townhouse carefully, but there was no sign that Stacey or Jesse was watching through the window, and after a moment Trista backed out of the parking space. Instead of turning to go out of the complex, she drove in the opposite direction until she stopped a quarter of a block down, across the street from where Conroy was parked but, because of the angle, out of view of the front of the townhouse. Conroy got out of his car and slipped across the street, and when he stepped up to the window, he saw she was crying.

"Are you all right?" he asked softly.

Trista nodded, but the glow of the streetlight five yards away illuminated the moisture smeared across her cheeks. He couldn't imagine what this woman was going through right now, and that went a long way toward explaining why he'd elected *not* to get in touch with Alec Elidad until he actually had his wife in custody. He knew Alec had finally returned to work, and Dustine had told him that Suburban Counseling reported he was attending meetings every week, finally finding the strength to pull himself through this. Whatever progress he'd made—whether he'd accepted the idea that his wife was dead or just learned to wait and not think about it as much—tonight's situation was going to force him to do a complete about-face. Worse yet, he'd have to be told that his wife not only didn't remember him, but had now taken on another's woman's identity and was living with her kidnapper. He had to be told all this, and Nola had to be told who she really was—both now and in her past. And what would Alec do if Nola didn't react immediately, if she didn't somehow figure out who she really was?

Trista finally nodded when Krystin reached around Conroy and squeezed her shoulder. "I'm okay," she said shakily. She leaned her head on the steering wheel for a moment, then sat back up. "Believe it or not, they seem like they always were. A couple of married kids, in love, in an everyday townhouse." She gave a strained little laugh. "Except it's not Stacey. I don't know who it is—if it's Tammy, or Nola, or someone else. It's just . . . not Stacey."

Conroy nodded, then glanced at Trista. "You want to stay with Krystin? I think it's time to wrap this up once and for all."

Trista exhaled, her breath a stream of white mist in the cold night air. "Yes, of course."

He left the two women and went back to his car, then leaned in the door and thumbed on the radio transmitter. The channel was already set. "Let's go," he said simply. He heard two engines start farther down the street, knew that one would be here within seconds to back him up while the other would drive around to the end of the row of townhouses; from there the two officers would make their way along the deserted backyards until they got to the Waite residence, where they would stay to make sure no one tried to escape out the back.

When the uniformed car rolled up to the curb and its occupants got out, Conroy nodded and motioned at them to follow him up to the door. Standing there, ready to knock, he considered carefully whether he needed to bring out his weapon, then decided against it. He hoped it wouldn't come to that, but if it did, he'd just try to get to Nola Elidad and count on the two officers behind him for firepower.

Conroy raised his hand and knocked, hard, on the front door.

This time it was Jesse who answered it, looking as though he expected to find Trista returning for some last-minute comment. He started when he saw Conroy, then his gaze flicked to the two serious-faced police officers flanking him.

"Jesse Waite," Conroy said steadily. "I'm going to have to ask that you and . . ." He faltered for just an instant, not wanting to make things as bad as they could get right away. "Your wife," he finally said, "come with me to the Roselle Police Station."

Jesse's chin lifted, but he made no move to let them inside. "What's this all about?" he asked instead.

"We'd like to talk to you, that's all. Clear up a few things—"

The voice of the woman Conroy had talked to earlier in the week cut him off as she hurried into the foyer. "Jesse, who is it—oh!" She stopped when she saw Conroy. "What's going on here?"

Jesse had turned toward Stacey's voice, and now Conroy used the opening in the doorway to step inside. "I have to ask that the two of you come with me to the police station," he repeated.

Jesse scowled, but didn't try to bolt. "And if we don't care to?"

"I'm afraid I'll have to insist."

Jesse started to say something, but it was lost in Stacey's sharp words. "I don't think so, Detective. I believe you have to have a reason for *insisting,* as you put it. And I don't think we're going anywhere until we hear it." She crossed her arms and looked at him defiantly. "And I *don't* recall inviting you into my house!"

Christ, Conroy thought. Isn't this fun? He stepped forward even more, crowding Jesse; when the other man automatically backed up, a single gesture made the two uniformed officers hustle into the foyer. With five people clustered into it, the place suddenly seemed the size of a small bathroom, and it didn't help things when the two officers decided on their own to grab Jesse.

"Hey!" he protested. He pulled against them, but it wasn't really a fight, just surprise. "Let go!"

"Is there a charge, Detective Conroy?" Stacey demanded. She came forward until she was right in front of him, and for a second Conroy thought she was going to poke him in the chest with her finger. "If not, you let my husband go and get out right now."

"Ma'am," Conroy said as gently as he could, "this man is not your husband."

"What!"

"And you are *not* who he's led you to believe you are. If we can just all go down to the station, we can start getting this straightened out."

"We're not going anywhere!" Her voice was rising uncomfortably toward a shriek. "You can't just march into someone's house and pull them out for no reason, damn it!"

"All right." Conroy looked over to one of the officers, both of whom still had a firm grip on Jesse's arms. "Handcuff him. The charge is suspicion of kidnapping."

Jesse, who'd been standing calmly as though he'd expected his wife to explain everything, finally tried to shake out of the hold. He was too late and overpowered anyway—they had him locked down long before he could accomplish anything. "No, that's not right, I didn't—"

"Kidnapping *who*?" Stacey demanded. "What the hell are you talking about?"

She reached for Jesse, but Conroy stepped in between them and faced her. "For kidnapping you," he said, intentionally blunt. "Nola Elidad."

She gaped at him, then began to shake her head and back away. "No," she told him. "No, no—that's not my name. You're wrong."

"Stacey—" Jesse began.

"Get him out of here now," Conroy said without turning around. Jesse protested louder as they hauled him out the door, but Stacey seemed to have forgotten Jesse even existed. Her eyes were wide and round, filled with terror.

"Don't do this," Stacey said in a low, desperate voice. She backtracked until the couch stopped her and she dropped onto it. "You don't know what you're doing. We're fine—we don't need your help."

"I'm sorry," Conroy said, and he really meant it. He reached for her, hoping to God that she wouldn't fight and make it all that much worse. His fingers closed around her arm and she tensed. "But right or wrong, tonight's the night we set it all straight."

After a long moment, her gaze dropped from his and she nodded. As unjust and cruel as it might seem to her, Conroy supposed she knew there was nothing to do but surrender to these sudden strangers in her life, and see what the world would do to her.

Black holes, Nola thought as she sat at an institutional-type table and drank bitter, black coffee from an institutional-type cup, are supposed to exist in space. She remembered this from science classes, basic astronomy: a star collapses and everything around it is sucked into it—nothing escapes. There was also a lot of speculation about worm holes and whether, if such things existed, you might enter on one side and come out on the other in another part of the universe. But what would happen to the traveler in the meantime?

These things—black holes and worm holes—were not supposed to exist in her mind.

For many months, she had likened the increasing gaps in her memory to bits and pieces of herself disappearing into one of those spatial black holes, as unseen in her head as a real one was in space to an astronomer. Now, however, it seemed much more probable that the universe inside her brain was divided into two sections, one attached to the other by that terrifying, speculative worm hole. Were she to believe what she was being told, she had been pushed back and forth through this fantastic mental passageway for years, each time landing somewhere different, each time changing herself in response to her surroundings. When the traveling was done this time, what would she be like?

The two men sitting before her—Detective Conroy and the police psychologist—regarded her patiently. They seemed to be waiting for her to say something. "I'm sorry—what was the question?"

The psychologist, Dr. Jason Shea, regarded her gravely. "I asked if you know who you are."

She blinked. "I . . . guess I'm Nola Elidad."

"You guess?"

She folded her hands tightly, then relaxed them, afraid it would look too much like she was praying. She didn't think she believed in God anymore. She might have once, but what kind of a god would put her through this? A cruel one, indeed—it was safer, saner, to believe things happened just because they did, not because some supreme being pulled strings somewhere for no reason other than heartless amusement. "This is what you've told me, and you've laid out all the facts," she said carefully. "I've always been a logical person. It all . . . makes sense."

Dr. Shea leaned forward. "You believe this makes sense?"

She stared at the table and thought about her answer, afraid they were trying to trap her. "Not that it happened," she finally said. "But *how* it happened."

Conroy looked at the doctor and the doctor nodded his okay. "Nola, do you remember your husband Alec at all?"

She frowned. "After everything you've told me, I know that he exists. But I can't remember what he looks like. I—I'm sorry." She was silent for a moment. "I guess you've called him by now."

Dr. Shea nodded. "He's on his way here."

Nola tried to digest that. Alec Elidad, her husband. She hadn't been lying about knowing him—now that they'd spread out all the facts for her, her mind was trying to pick up the pieces, tuck-pointing the cracks in her past one level at a time. But the gaps that still remained were huge and frightening: This man coming to take her home—a place that, like him, she knew existed but couldn't recall—what would he expect of her? He would expect her to be the same as he had known her, of course, make an instantaneous return to the woman he'd married in a civil ceremony that to her was only a faraway tickle of remembrance. And when they went back to their home—what then? Would he want to hold her, kiss her, make love? She shuddered.

The movement wasn't lost on Dr. Shea. "What are you feeling now, Nola?"

"Fear," she said without hesitating. "I don't know him."

"That's understandable," Dr. Shea said calmly. "From what we've talked about and what Detective Conroy has unearthed, you were subjected to some very extreme conditions as a child, and now again as a young woman. Many would say that you've been brainwashed. How do you feel about that?"

Nola lifted her gaze to his with difficulty. "I'm *tired.* It just seems like it never ends."

Dr. Shea nodded in understanding. "You don't feel that being reunited with Alec Elidad is going to end it?"

She tried to look him in the eye but couldn't hold it. He didn't know about the baby, of course—no one did, not even Jesse. "No," she said softly. "I don't think it's going to end it at all."

Detective Conroy's face darkened with concern. "Can I ask why? Do you think Jesse will try something else?"

Nola tried to think of an answer that he'd find acceptable, but nothing came to mind. "No, of course not. I just meant that it kind of seems to be my lot in life, don't you think? To be handed from one person to another and told who I'm supposed to be."

A lie, but in retrospect maybe there was more truth to it than she'd realized. How bizarre that she'd ended up thinking she was her own twin sister—that she even *had* a twin sister to begin with. Dr. Shea had pointed out that it was a verifiable fact that twins separated at birth or as young children often led lives that were uncannily similar in every respect—mates, careers, preferences, sometimes personalities. Yet of her twin, she had no memory at all; whatever methods her adopted mother had used to wipe her mind after her father had kidnapped her, they must've been much more effective than Jesse's gentle persuasion. "My mother," she said suddenly. "I mean, Marlo. Is she coming in, too?"

"Actually, she's outside," Dr. Shea told her. "Detective Conroy had her brought in about an hour ago." He studied her. "Do you remember her at all?"

"Bits and pieces," Nola said automatically, but that wasn't quite truthful either. They were more like large, jagged chunks, figurative asteroids hammering through that worm hole in her mind. The knowledge that the woman was outside didn't lift her spirits at all. "Do I have to see her?"

"Not if you don't want to," Dr. Shea said, although Conroy looked less than pleased. "How do you feel about it?"

"Not good." She glanced at Conroy, wondering what was going on in *his* head. She didn't know why he seemed to want her to go face-to-face with Marlo Frayne, but sooner or later she was sure to find out. In the meantime, she couldn't hide from the rest of the real world forever, but she could drag it on. And on. Did she really want to do that? "But I will. In fact, let's get it over with now."

Both men looked surprised. "Nola, are you sure?" Dr. Shea asked. "This is a lot for you to absorb in one evening—"

"Yes," she interrupted. "I'm sure." She looked at Conroy. "Why don't you bring her in?"

Conroy glanced from her to the psychologist. "If you think it's okay," he finally said. The doctor didn't look thrilled but he nodded, so Conroy got up and went to the door. He stepped outside and left it cracked open; almost immediately Nola could hear a woman's piercing, scolding voice. Far too quickly, the voice was in the room with her.

"Well, look at who's finally decided to come back among the living!"

Nola looked up from her seat at the table and felt her jaw clench as countless unwanted memories swarmed over her, all about as welcome as biting mosquitoes. The formidable woman looming in front of her fit neatly into a huge percentage of those blank slots in her mind, and damned near every one of them made Nola want to sit there and tremble.

"Well," Marlo Frayne demanded, "don't you have anything to say for yourself? Where've you been, anyway?"

"It doesn't matter," Nola said.

Marlo snorted and sent both Conroy and the doctor a triumphant look. "Doesn't that just beat all—*it doesn't matter.* The girl causes everybody in the world a whole barrel of trouble, and she thinks it doesn't matter."

A strange sense of calm slid over Nola, quieting her nerves and giving her strength. "It doesn't," she repeated, "because it's over now. I'll get everything straightened out and move on."

"You think so, do you?" Her adopted mother jabbed at the tabletop with a fingernail long enough to be a knife and Nola flinched. "You just up and walk out on me, then you up and walk out on that old guy you married, and you think it's all right to cause me all this trouble, get me dragged down here—*twice*—"

"Ms. Frayne," the doctor interrupted. "I hardly think Nola needs to be put under any more stress—"

Marlo spun toward him. "I don't think I was talking to you," she snapped. She seemed determined to vent her aggravation on anyone within reach—how well Nola remembered that now. "I don't mind saying that you don't know shit about my daughter—"

"I'm not your daughter," Nola cut in. Her voice was cold and firm, and she couldn't ever remember talking to someone in that tone before. "And you can leave now."

Marlo's face went slack with shock, and out of the corner of her eye Nola thought she saw Conroy hide a smirk behind his hand. "*What!*"

"I think I put up with enough of you while I was growing up," Nola said. She enunciated her next words very clearly, relishing them. "I don't have to do that anymore."

"You ungrateful little *brat,*" Marlo snarled. She reached out a thick hand, tipped with all those sharp fingernails, toward Nola. A dozen more memories—a hundred—suddenly exploded through Nola's mind, all of them associated with pain and Marlo's unique methods of discipline. "I'll teach you to—"

Dr. Shea gasped and Nola threw herself backward at the same time as Detective Conroy's strong fist locked around Marlo's wrist. "I don't believe you'll be teaching Nola anything," he said grimly. He spun her roughly and propelled her toward the door. "I'll have a squad car drive you home." Marlo's face twisted into an ugly scowl and she opened her mouth to speak, but Conroy held up a finger to stop her. "Shut up, Ms. Frayne," he said bluntly. "No one wants to hear it."

As Conroy hauled Marlo out of the room, Nola swallowed and pulled her chair back up to the table—she hadn't realized it at the time, but she'd scooted a good four feet away in her effort to stay out of Marlo's range. When she rubbed at her mouth, she found a line of perspiration across her upper lip—how often had she experienced that in her life with Marlo? But no more.

A minute or so later, Conroy was back. "Your husband is outside," he told her. "Are you ready for this?"

"As ready as I'll ever be," she said, sounding a lot more flippant than she felt.

Conroy nodded and cracked his knuckles absently. "Before I bring Alec in," he said, "I'd like to ask you about something that happened when you were a child and living with Marlo. I realize you might or might not remember the incident."

It was all Nola could do to agree—God, how she wanted to leave that segment of her life behind, even if it meant charging into the frightening, unknown part that was next. "All right."

Conroy pulled out his chair and sat, watching her carefully. "From the records, I think you would have been about five years old at the time I'm talking about." When Nola nodded, he continued. "I have some . . . questions about what happened to your stepfather—your *adopted* stepfather, Charles Frayne. I've researched his death and found out that he died of an allergic reaction to medicine that he'd been warned not to take. To be honest, I'm wondering just how he could have—"

"She killed him," Nola said flatly.

Dr. Shea had been quiet for some time, but now he sat forward. "You believe your adopted mother killed her husband?"

"I *know* she did," Nola corrected. "I saw her."

"What exactly did you see?" Conroy asked. His expression had gone narrow and intense.

Nola rubbed her eyes. "It was in the middle of the night," she told them. "I never slept well as a child—I was always afraid of the dark but I couldn't go to Marlo or Charles for comfort. I would hear noises and make myself get up and see what they were on my own, because if I didn't, I wouldn't be able to fall asleep at all. Anyway, I heard a noise one night and I snuck out of bed to see what it was. Marlo was in the bathroom, and I saw her open a bottle, take out a pill, then put it into a different bottle. She put that one back in the medicine cabinet, and then *she* heard something—Charles, maybe getting out of bed. So she dropped the first bottle in the garbage and went back to her bedroom." Nola hugged herself. "I took it out of the wastebasket and saved it."

Conroy nodded. "We found it with your things."

"I thought so," Nola said. She looked off into space, reluctantly remembering. "It was years later that I found the newspaper with his obituary in it, thrown on the shelf in the hall closet with some other old stuff, including one for Stowe Gardell. I took it and saved it. Charles was a quiet little man, kind of sickly. He was no match for Marlo, but he was always nice to me."

No one said anything for a moment, but Nola knew what was on Conroy's mind. Before he could say anything, Dr. Shea spoke again. "What are your feelings about this, Nola? About being a witness to what your adopted mother did?"

She shrugged. "It's a tragic thing," she said, then looked at Conroy. "But I'm not going to testify against her."

"Nola—" Conroy began.

"No," she said firmly. "I'm *done* with her, Detective. Done with that part of my past, and I'm done being manipulated by other people to get what *they* want. I was a child then, and face it—who's going to believe me now, after what I've been through? I can't remember who I really am most of the time, and I just spent three months thinking I was my dead sister. Do you really think a judge or a jury would convict her based on that?"

Conroy scowled but said nothing—it was obvious she was right. Nola took a deep breath. "May I see my husband now?"

Alec felt dizzy, high, and nauseous all at once. His head was pounding and his blood pressure was probably high enough to cause a coronary, but none of that mattered—

Nola had been found!

The door to the interrogation room behind him opened and Alec spun, catching a glimpse of his reflection in the window on his left as he turned. He was a frightening spectacle—wild-eyed and nearly crazed, unable to stop his jerky pacing in the small waiting area. He should have combed his hair, rinsed his face—done something so his wife wouldn't be reunited with a man who looked like a maniac. Conroy stepped out, but closed the door before Alec could rush through.

"Alec," he said. "There are a few things you need to know before you see your wife."

"What?" Alec demanded. "Is she all right—was she hurt? Was she raped? What happened to her? What—?"

He started toward the door he'd seen Conroy close, but the detective stopped him with a firm hand on his arm. "Let's go in here and talk for a minute," he said and pulled Alec, hard, toward a different door to the left of the interrogation room. Confused and impatient, Alec had no choice but to comply. The instant the door closed behind them, he turned to tell the policeman just what he thought of this, and then—

—he saw Nola.

She was sitting at a table with another man, on the other side of a window that Alec belatedly realized must be a two-way mirror. The man was older and slender, in his late fifties, with sparse, close-cropped gray hair and a darker beard. Scholarly-looking glasses, bifocals perhaps, were balanced on the end of his nose, and he was talking earnestly to Alec's wife. Nola looked about the same as she always had—better, maybe. Her hair was longer and more relaxed, and there was a sort of fresh, nearly makeup-free glow to her skin that Alec had never seen before.

"Who's he?" Alec rasped. It was the first question that crossed his mind.

"His name is Dr. Jason Shea," Conroy replied. "He's the Roselle P.D.'s staff psychologist."

"Psychologist," Alec repeated. Okay, he should have expected that—Nola had been abducted, had gone through God knows what in the time since he'd last seen her. But why did he have a feeling that there was something wrong here, something a whole lot bigger than what appearances would have him believe, and much worse than the worst that he had expected? "You want to fill me in, Detective Conroy?"

"Why don't you have a seat—"

"I'll stand, thank you," Alec said. His hands were gripping the ledge below the window as he watched his wife talk to . . . what was his name? Dr. Shea. He couldn't hear what they were saying, but even through the window he could tell that she seemed different, more outgoing and self-assured.

Instead of arguing, Conroy joined him at the window and watched with him for a few moments, not saying anything. Finally he cleared his throat. "This is a very unique situation, Alec, and it's going to take a lot of understanding on your part. What happened here isn't something that's going to be resolved overnight."

"I didn't think it would be."

Conroy pressed his lips together. "Your wife was abducted by a man because he thought she was his wife," he said with brutal simplicity.

When Conroy waited to see what his reaction would be, Alec only nodded. "Go on."

Conroy cracked his knuckles, making Alec start. "You told me quite emphatically that you knew very little about Nola's past. You'll find out all the details soon enough, but Nola was also abducted as a child."

Alec's eyes widened and for the first time he turned his gaze away from the window and faced Conroy. "Really? That's incredible!"

Conroy nodded. "This is . . . complicated, Alec. More than you ever imagined. Nola's real name was Tammy, and she had a twin sister who was left behind. That twin sister died last fall. Her name was Stacey, and she was . . . married to the man who kidnapped Nola."

"My God," Alec whispered, staring first at Conroy, then at Nola. "A twin? I had no idea."

"Neither did she," Conroy told him. "She doesn't remember anything about her."

"So this man who took her, he was just nuts because his wife died," Alec said. He was trying desperately to find some sympathy for this faceless stranger, but it was so *hard.* "So he didn't mean to hurt her or . . ." His voice trailed off momentarily. "He didn't, did he? Hurt her?"

Conroy inhaled. "Alec, Nola went through some situations as a child, things that the woman who raised her did to her, that made it . . . very easy for her abductor to convince Nola of certain things."

A pulse began to throb in Alec's temple. "What *things*?"

Another horrifying pause. "When we found her," Conroy said softly, "your wife truly believed she was her sister Stacey."

Nola instantly recognized the man who walked in the room. She felt like some kind of child's interconnected puzzle, where she'd been given a good shake and now all the pieces were suddenly starting to fall into the right slots. This was Alec, of course—she'd lived with him at the Springhill Apartments since their marriage last October, and he was the one who had let her out in the Pik-Kwik parking lot the night Jesse had found her. How they'd met, alas, was a little fuzzy, as if the farther back she went, the more frayed the memories became. Perhaps she'd been ready to let go of them altogether when the police had found her.

Alec stared longingly at her, then looked back to Detective Conroy, who nodded and motioned for him to go over to the table. When he pulled out the chair and sat on it, his movements were jerky, as though he were exercising great restraint. Thank God for that—she'd been afraid he would rush to her and smother her in an unwanted embrace. "Nola," he said awkwardly. "How—how are you? Are you, uh, okay?" His brown eyes were dark pools of concern.

"I'm okay," she said and nodded, although she wasn't sure if it was true or not. "I—I'm sorry you had to go through this," she added.

"Oh, no!" he exclaimed. Without warning, he reached out and grasped her hands, held on tight; she forced herself not to yank away from his warm, dry touch. "I just—I was so crazy with worry over you, not knowing if you were all right." He inclined his head toward Conroy. "And what he's told me, the awful things you've been through—" His grip tightened; now her fingers were grinding painfully together. "We can get a handle on this, Nola. I know we can, if you just—"

"You're hurting me, Alec."

He let go of her as if he'd been shot. "Oh, God—I'm *sorry*—"

"Why don't we slow down a little," suggested the psychologist. He held out his hand to Alec. "I'm Dr. Shea. I gather Detective Conroy has explained?"

Alec nodded, his gaze cutting back to Nola. "Yes."

"Then I'm sure you understand why we need to take matters one step at a time," Dr. Shea said. "Your wife—"

"I'd just like to go home now," Nola said.

Alec and the other two men stared at her, startled. "Nola," said Dr. Shea, "don't you think that might be a bit hasty?"

"I just want to put what happened behind me and get on with my life," she said firmly. Hadn't she said that earlier?

"Well," Alec said. He sounded absurdly cheerful, considering the circumstances. "That settles it, then. If someone will just get my wife's coat, we'll be off." He stood, then paused. "I assume that her abductor will be charged with whatever's appropriate?"

Conroy's eyebrows raised. "We haven't actually determined that yet."

"Mr. Waite is a very troubled individual and he's already being detained in a Streamwood psychiatric facility," the doctor added. "While a prison term might satisfy your anger over what happened to your wife, it certainly won't help him."

"That's not our problem," Alec snapped. "He's dangerous and he needs to be locked up."

"Stop it!" Nola barked. She stood and Alec turned, his expression going from anger to surprise. "No one's going to lock Jesse up. Like Dr. Shea said, he has mental problems. He needs help." Her husband's eyes went bright with anger, in a way she'd never seen before. *Keep going,* she thought. *And you'll find out a few things about me you never knew before either. None of us did.*

Alec exhaled sharply. "Nola, I'm sorry for the difficulties this man went through in his own life," he said stiffly, addressing both her and Detective Conroy, "but he had a terrible impact on ours and I think he's dangerous. I'm afraid I'm going to demand that—what's his name? Jesse Waite, right—that Jesse Waite be charged. We can start with kidnapping and move on from there, and this will at least keep him off the streets."

Nola reached back and found the chair that had pushed out when she stood, pulled it forward, and sat down again carefully. That same sensation of composure that she'd felt with Marlo earlier returned now, steadying her thoughts and giving everything around her a clear, sharp edge. It was all nicely defined—where she was, the roles that Detective Conroy and Dr. Shea played in her life, the position Alec now held.

"You don't have the right to demand anything, Alec," she said. Her voice was deceptively placid. "This didn't happen to you, it happened to me. And I will not press charges."

"Well, *I* will!" he cried, his cheeks filling with color. "As your husband, I will!"

"If you try, I'll tell the prosecutor that I went with Jesse Waite willingly," she said flatly. "And that I knew who I was the entire time and only acted like Stacey Waite to get away from you."

For a long moment, no one in the room moved. Then they all started talking at once.

"Stacey," Dr. Shea began. "You—"

"My name is Nola," she snapped immediately. "Stop trying to trick me."

"Nola, what are you saying?" Alec demanded loudly. "I can't believe what I just heard!"

"Perhaps it would be better if we all just calmed down and thought about this overnight." Conroy's voice overrode all of theirs. "You're both upset, and you've both gone through your own form of hell. Jesse isn't going anywhere, Alec—he's under psychiatric care, and he doesn't need to be formally charged with anything for that to continue."

"But he *kidnapped* her!"

"He's also my brother-in-law," Nola reminded him sharply. "My dead sister's husband. It's not the black-and-white television cop story you seem to think!"

"That's the most ridiculous thing I've ever heard!"

"That's enough, Alec," Conroy said. "In this instance I'm going to agree with the doctor and take a 'wait and see' position. Frankly, I don't believe Jesse is dangerous, and so far the doctors who've examined him agree. The fact is, Nola would be the key witness in any felony kidnapping charge; without her testimony"—he glanced at her and she lifted her chin defiantly—"there really is no case."

"And I would add that such charges and a trial would significantly prolong the ordeal for your wife," Dr. Shea reminded Alec. "I'm sure you don't want her to endure any more distress than she has already."

That seemed to take a little of the air out of Alec's argument and his shoulders slumped. When he looked at Nola, there was a different, more cautious light in his eyes and his expression was pleading. "Nola, I . . ." He coughed into his fist, and she knew it was a ploy to give him time to search for the right words. "I'm sorry I blew up like that. I just . . . didn't think it through, I suppose."

"Never mind," she said lightly. She rose and carefully pushed the chair under the table. "It's all behind us now."

Dr. Shea looked at her, his expression the most suspicious of them all. "I would strongly suggest that we talk further," he said, and pulled a card out of his shirt pocket. "Please, call my office to schedule an appointment? You should also have a more thorough physical examination."

"Certainly," Nola said and took the card, knowing full well that she'd neither call him nor submit to a detailed physical exam. She walked around the table and stood next to Alec, then forced herself to tuck her hand into the bend of his elbow. "As soon as Detective Conroy brings me my coat, we'll go home."

MARCH 28--FRIDAY

God help me, Alec thought.

I don't know this woman anymore.

But if the truth were told . . . had he ever?

He and Nola sat at the dining room table, but they didn't look at each other. Instead, they studied the walls, their coffee cups, the carpet, the furniture—anything else. The comfortable morning routine that had existed before that disastrous day in January was gone, perhaps forever. They'd gotten home—scratch that, it didn't feel like home anymore. They'd gotten back to the *apartment* last night, but they hadn't talked then, either. It'd been nearly midnight and so they went to bed; Nola had changed into pajamas behind a closed and presumably locked bathroom door, then climbed into bed and rolled over to face away from him. He'd had the distinct impression she was as far away as she could get without actually falling out of their bed.

And now . . . well, here they were.

He'd called in at school, of course, and now he wished he hadn't. Doing otherwise had been unthinkable—he was full of the unreasonable fear that if he went to work, she would be gone again when he came home, a horrible, fast-motion repeat of last January 16th. He'd thought that having her back would fix everything, but this was somehow worse; the one time he'd tried to take her in his arms, when they'd come inside the apartment last night, she'd backed away from him and said, "Please, Alec—I'm not ready for that yet. We have to get to know each other again."

And there it was, the truth that underscored what was wrong between them right now. She'd been gone for as long as they'd been married—longer, actually. Could people forget what they knew about each other under circumstances like those? It certainly seemed so. For all his longing to see her again, to know she was all right and have her back, the long weekend that now stretched before him seemed like an eternity.

"The paper's probably here," he said, standing. When Nola jumped, Alec realized how loud his voice sounded, even though he'd thought he was speaking normally. "I'll go down and get it." She nodded but didn't say anything, then looked back toward the double glass doors in the living room, as though she were a caged animal that knew freedom was out there somewhere. He thought she was making a concentrated effort to look pleasant, to keep her features arranged in neutrality.

The hallway outside was chilly and too dark, the result of a burned-out bulb in one of the light fixtures. Even so, Alec stood there for a long while after he'd gone down to the front foyer and picked up his newspaper. There was so much to think about, so much to reconcile. He couldn't do it while he was around her, sitting next to her. Part of him wanted so much to reach out, to pull her into his arms and kiss her; the other froze up at that thought, was paralyzed with jealousy and revulsion when he realized she'd been living as the wife of—*sleeping* with the man who'd kidnapped her. The reasons for doing so—psychosis, confusion, brainwashing, whatever—might excuse it, but they couldn't make it go away. When they finally made love, would he be able to tell, to see or feel the influence of Jesse Waite? And what about how she touched him, her rightful husband—had she somehow been *changed* by her time away?

Maddening questions, and all of them enough to make him want to do anything but go back inside the apartment and be with his wife.

I should at least *try*, Nola thought as the door closed behind Alec. After all, I'm Alec's wife and this is where I started out. It's his right to—

To *what*?

Own her? Lay claim to the rest of her life? For God's sake, everything was different now—more than Conroy or Alec or even Jesse knew. The proof of that was nestled secretly within her body, and wasn't *that* going make for a congenial scene between her and Alec when he found out? She was sure that somewhere within his brittle outer shell was a compassionate man, but no one could blame him if he couldn't find it within himself to extend that benevolence toward Jesse. The man had damned near stolen his wife, his *life*.

She sighed and wandered around the apartment, knowing that Alec was probably standing out in the cold hallway, trying to come up with a topic of conversation. They ought to be talking about the two of them, their marriage, their future. Did they have one anymore? It was hard to say, and for this Nola's heart went out to Alec. He'd thought her dead—she'd seen that in his eyes when he'd first greeted her—and had given up on their future; now it had been, he thought, handed back to him. Could she so cruelly take it away again?

She didn't want to be here, but she had to try. Alec deserved at least that for the pain he had gone through.

But . . . the trying part, even that bothered her. Wasn't it just one more incidence in her life where she was to be molded to someone else's whims? First as a child, then by Jesse—yes, even him—and now here she was again, trying to forcefully reshape herself back into the Nola Elidad/ Alec's Wife pattern. She was a puppet over which someone else, it seemed, always controlled the strings.

Nola heard the door to the apartment open behind her and passed a hand over her stomach before turning around. This time, she thought, if and when the time comes, I'm going to wield the scissors that will cut those strings once and for all.

7

REALIZATION

A pleasant illusion is better than a harsh reality.

—CHRISTIAN NESTELL BOVEE

APRIL 1--TUESDAY

Jesse could, once he'd thought about it, pinpoint the time he'd gone over the edge.

That one, he thought. She looks just like Stacey.

Three tables over, a man and a woman talked animatedly while they ate, with both of them shooting glances at the basketball game on the overhead tube every now and then. Jesse watched her while he drank a little more of his beer and waited for his burger to arrive, envious of the ease with which they touched and laughed, little moves that advertised to the world how long they'd been together. Jesse peered at them, trying to see clearly through his building alcohol level and the lights from the Christmas decorations still blinking erratically around the bar. Did she really look that much like his dead wife? Or—

"Here you go, pal."

Jesse jerked and almost upended the bottle of Amstel as the bartender slid a plate of hot food in front of him, one of the oversized cheeseburgers that Bud's Eatery was known for, fries done well the way he'd asked, some kind of coleslaw cup on the side.

"How's your Amstel holding up?"

"Bring me another one."

The bartender nodded and moved away, leaving Jesse to look at his food and wonder why he'd ordered it in the first place. He could smell it—hot, fresh, probably cooked just right—but it did nothing for him. Instead, he took a pull from the bottle and turned back to stare again at the couple at the table. How many beers had he had now? Three, that was it—and the bartender was bringing him a fourth. That wasn't so bad, was it? Or maybe it was five that he'd had, and his sixth was on its way? Whatever.

Jesse turned back to his food and picked up the burger without much enthusiasm, took a bite and chewed. If he didn't get something in his belly, he'd end up ten sheets to the wind and barely able to find his car, much less drive the few blocks home. Roselle wasn't the kind of 'burb where the residents or cops took kindly to folks staggering down the sidewalk in the middle of the night. A cab, maybe that was the ticket. But . . . no, he really couldn't afford it, shouldn't even be in here drinking and ordering a meal. Hell, he hadn't worked for months, and his savings were down to almost nothing. He just hadn't felt like cooking, hadn't felt like another late evening of sitting by himself at home or in the car while the rest of the world went on with its life.

This place, though—it was more of a pub than a bar. Crowded for after-Christmas, and the food took longer than expected, and he'd knocked back more beer than he'd realized. And suddenly he started noticing all the Christmas decorations, the twinkling lights, and especially, especially, *all the couples, at least a dozen paired off at the tables around the room. That had made him start thinking about Stacey—didn't everything?—and it hadn't taken long to make him bleed inside. Now the food had finally arrived, and he really ought to eat it and just go home before he got any drunker.*

Jesse picked up the burger, then set it down again. Sometime during the last few minutes, the bartender had popped open another bottle for him and removed his latest empty, so Jesse went for that instead. When he checked, the couple he'd been watching was gone, with nothing left to mark their place beyond dirty dishes and a few bucks left as a tip. It didn't matter, Jesse thought blearily. His gaze skipped over the room and found someone else, a woman sitting at the table closest to the door. She was another one who looked a little like Stacey, although her hair color was wrong—

"Get you another one, pal?"

Jesse looked up and found the bartender, a young guy with reddish curls above a heavily boned face, studying him. He looked like an athlete, clean-cut but strong, the sort of man's man Jesse expected to find doling out beers and burgers in a place like this. He glanced at his beer—almost gone. He really shouldn't. "Yeah."

"So what's the deal?" the bartender asked curiously. "You look like a man with woman problems."

Jesse shrugged. He'd cut himself off from everyone early on because he couldn't bear to talk about Stacey, but now part of him desperately needed to talk to someone. Maybe this guy was just the ticket, a man who knew nothing of Stacey or her family, or the way he'd quit his job to follow someone around just because she looked like the woman he'd loved more than anything.

But that was the very same thing that stopped Jesse. This man was a total stranger. How could he share this oh-so-personal pain with this trim twenty-something-year-old who was building up a degree in barroom psychology? Jesse looked back at the woman across the room, but drunk as he was—no sense in denying it—this time she didn't look a bit like Stacey. What the hell had he been thinking? No, the woman who looked like Stacey, who could be Stacey, wasn't even in Bud's. Now she lived with someone over in the Springhill Apartments.

"My wife's gone," Jesse said suddenly. His voice was hoarse.

"Ah." The man's tone was knowing. "Dumped you, huh? That sucks."

Jesse shook his head. "No, nothing like that." He started to keep going, then changed his mind and stared at the scarred top of the bar instead. The whole thing was too complicated and personal to explain to a stranger, and this guy, no matter how warm he tried to seem, was too callous. Too cold. How would he ever be able to understand just how deeply Jesse hurt? He couldn't even say the real words. "She just . . . left."

Instead of responding, the bartender swung a bottle around and uncapped it with professional smoothness, then slid it to a stop in front of Jesse. "Same thing, pal," he said after a moment. He leaned on the bar and looked at Jesse intently. "I see way too many guys come in here drinking themselves stupid when what they oughta do is get out there, find their woman, and straighten things out." Without warning, the guy laughed, and the sharp sound hurt Jesse's ears. "Telling customers to leave—guess I'm not real good for business, huh?"

Jesse stared at him without answering, then his gaze flicked back to the last table he'd been staring at, the one by the far wall. The woman who'd been sitting there was gone, but the wheels were rolling now, weren't they just—grinding away in Jesse's head like he'd fired up a rusty machine at the shop that hadn't been started in way too many months. And all thanks to this bartender who he'd thought at first was a jerk—maybe the guy was onto something. After all, this entire thing with Stacey in the hospital, it had happened so *quickly—almost too fast to believe. And then there was that other thing, the Stacey look-alike who had wormed her way inside his head and his heart, and about whom he thought nearly every time he took a breath—*

"What if she's not really in there?"

Jesse couldn't believe Trista's voice was still in his head after all this time.

Without warning his eyes began to burn, and Jesse struggled against the urge to put his face in his hands and bawl like a baby. For God's sake, he thought a little desperately. I'm a grown man in a public bar. Get a grip on it, fool.

The bartender leaned close enough so that Jesse could smell wintergreen and cigarette smoke on his breath, the sweetness of one not quite enough to overcome the other. "Hey man, you gonna sit here and cry in your beer, or you gonna go out there and fix things up with her?"

Fix it? The urge to cry disappeared abruptly, strangled by a bray of laughter that Jesse somehow managed to lock inside his throat. When he had it under control, he opened his mouth to tell the guy that no, what happened couldn't be fixed, not now, not ever . . .

But he wanted exactly that, didn't he?

In his mind, Jesse could still see Stacey, could still remember the sweet desert scent of her skin and recall the warm taste of her mouth. He remembered the straight shape of her eyebrows, the lighter shade of blue that surrounded the irises of her eyes, the way her dark hair always wanted to part just slightly to the right, the indentation in the center of her full bottom lip. The way she had a tendency to tilt her head to the right when she smiled. All the things that most men took for granted about the woman they loved were burned into his brain as though God had reached down and applied the universe's biggest, most painful branding iron.

The bartender started to say something else, then someone down the counter called out and he shrugged and moved away instead, leaving Jesse to his thoughts. Jesse ground his teeth and watched him go, then felt his grip tighten around the bottle of beer. He felt . . . weird—half numb, half enraged, like something had been opened up inside him, or maybe born. His fingers spasmed and he realized that his hold on the bottle was so tight that his hand was shaking. He released his fingers one by one—if he didn't the bottle was going to break, and there was no sense in making a spectacle of himself.

People shouldn't just go away overnight, he thought with careful deliberation. Without consciously deciding to do it, Jesse brought out his wallet and counted out the cash to pay for his barely tasted food and the lineup of alcohol. A man's life was his own and it was precious, something you put together like a meticulously constructed model. It shouldn't be ripped apart and left in pieces like his had been, no matter what the reasoning—the second person in a pair didn't have the right to just step outside of everything and to hell with the consequences. A married man and woman had responsibilities and if one of them tried to walk away from them . . . well, it wasn't proper, and sometimes a person had to stand up and do something about it. Still, fixing things, the way it had gone . . . wrong with Stacey, it just wasn't that simple.

Was it?

Jesse stood and felt the room tilt a little, slipped his hand casually against the edge of the bar to steady himself. He'd gotten really good at maintaining appearances over the last few months, and a six-pack of beer, give or take a bottle, wasn't enough to break the habit. He got his jacket on without a problem, even zipped it all the way up like he really cared if it was cold outside.

Being careful not to sway, Jesse carefully made his way out of Bud's Eatery.

This isn't happening, Jesse thought now. Please God, tell me I didn't really do this. It had to be some kind of tangible form of hell—he'd been through a psychiatric exam, endless police questioning, and God knew what was going to happen to his job.

But the worst of it was the truth he was hearing now,

coming to him live—breathing and speaking and telling him a whole lot of what he'd never wanted to hear.

"It's not Stacey," he said, echoing Detective Conroy's words. "But—"

"Jesse," John Aldwin interrupted. "Stacey *did* die last year. I saw her, in her casket at the funeral home. You wouldn't do it, so I had to identify her remains for the funeral director."

John had seen Stacey's corpse? Her *remains*? Jesse shook his head. "No, this can't be right. I—I couldn't make a mistake this *big*, it's too . . ." He broke off, his mind spinning uselessly. If it wasn't Stacey he'd been living with for the last three months, then *who was it*?

The psychologist they'd brought in to talk to him last night, Dr. Shea, had returned this morning with Conroy and his friend John. Now he leaned forward. "Jesse," he said gently, "don't be too hard on yourself. Considering the amount of strain you were under and the circumstances, it's not difficult to understand how this happened."

Jesse looked at him and the other two men in astonishment. "Understand? Well, that's *great*. I wish someone would fill me in so I could understand it, too! For God's sake, first you tell me the woman I brought home with me last January *isn't* my wife—which makes me a kidnapper—then you say you understand why I did it." He sat back on the chair, fighting the urge to slam his fists on the table. God, this was so *frustrating*.

John looked at the doctor, who nodded. "Jesse," his friend said carefully, "the woman you thought was Stacey was her sister."

"What!"

Conroy leaned forward. "This is something your mother-in-law lied to Stacey about all her life, for a number of reasons. The truth is that Stacey's twin sister, Tammy, didn't die as a child. She was kidnapped by her father and Trista never saw her again—in fact, she did believe Tammy was dead, but not from any heart condition. Apparently the girls' father was a con artist, and he concocted a pretty elaborate scheme, tied in with an airline crash, to cover his trail and make her think that both he and Tammy had been killed. He knew that back then Trista didn't have the money to hire anyone to dig deeply enough to see if it was true. To make a long story short, Tammy was adopted and her name was changed to Nola—the young woman you saw in the Pik-Kwik parking lot and mistook for your wife."

"Nola," Jesse repeated. God help him, but he could still hear the words she'd tried to tell him, over and over—

"That's not my name!"

—until, out of sheer persistence and blundering fate, he'd actually managed to convince her she was wrong. "My God," he said hoarsely. "What did I do to that poor woman?"

"She's going to be fine," Dr. Shea put in, and when Jesse glanced at him, he found the sincerity in the doctor's face comforting. The man was a professional—surely he knew what he was talking about, could tell if Jesse had done something really terrible to Stacey—no, *Nola.* "Also, you can't blame this entire situation on yourself. Nola went through some things as a child that made her particularly responsive to your belief that she was your wife."

"Easy to victimize, you mean." Jesse was surprised at the anger in his voice. How could he have been so blind, so *stupid*? That double question kept running through his mind, stuck on some internal infinity track.

"I think that's far too strong a term," Dr. Shea said. "There's a difference between being victimized and being influenced. Nola Elidad has a history of identity trauma. This made her prone to believing things that someone else in the same situation would have never accepted."

Jesse was silent. How could he argue when he didn't know all the facts, and why bother anyway? It wasn't going to change what had happened, what he'd done. "So what now?" he asked resolutely. "I go to jail, right? For how long?" Not that it mattered much, anyway. Stacey was dead, *really* dead, and now that he'd found out the truth, Jesse thought he could look Nola Elidad in the face and know she wasn't Stacey. In fact, reality had settled in at an alarming pace—all those days and weeks and months, there'd been a thousand tiny things about 'Stacey's' behavior that had been off, or just downright wrong. He'd ignored every one, found a thousand ways to rationalize behavior and aspects of her personality that his real wife had never possessed. What a fool.

"You aren't going to jail, Jesse."

He blinked and looked at the psychologist, then at Detective Conroy. "I'm not?" He tried to digest this and when the explanation came to him, it was almost as bad. "Some kind of mental care facility, then."

"No," said Conroy. "Dr. Shea believes—and I agree—that you aren't a threat to Nola Elidad anymore. She doesn't want to bring charges and since Nola wasn't harmed, the district attorney doesn't see the point in pursuing this any further. So even though you'll have to undergo court-ordered psychiatric treatment, you may be able to put this behind you and get on with your life."

John leaned forward, his eyes bright. "You can make a fresh start, Jesse. I talked to Schultz and told him what happened and why you didn't show for work but I left out the details. He's willing to cut you some slack. Your job's still there."

Jesse nodded but stayed silent. He wanted to say make a *sane* start, but it was probably best if he just kept quiet. A fresh start—with what? With pretty much the same as last year after Stacey died, before his hold on reality had cracked: nothing.

They were looking at him expectantly. "That's great," Jesse said.

"Jesse," said Dr. Shea, "I know it must seem very dismal now. You probably feel like you lost your wife not once, but twice. This is where I can help you, so don't give up too soon. All right?" Jesse swallowed, slightly unnerved at the ease with which the psychologist had pinpointed his emotions.

Across the table, Conroy rose. "Your mother-in-law is here to see you," he told Jesse. "She's waiting outside."

"Trista? But . . . why?"

John and Dr. Shea stood and went to the door with Conroy. "Why don't you just talk to her," suggested the doctor. "You've both been through a lot." He smiled slightly. "And keep something in mind, Jesse. Despite your rather unique way of doing things, you've actually *helped* this woman by reuniting her with the daughter she thought was dead. It's hard to be the bad guy when the results come out like this."

Jesse stared at him. Trista . . . and Nola. God, he hadn't even thought about that. So maybe Trista wouldn't hate him as much for putting her through this mini-hell. "Okay," he said.

John paused, then came back and clapped Jesse on the shoulder. "You're gonna be all right, man. You'll see. And you call me if you need anything—don't sit around and sink by yourself this time."

"Okay," Jesse said again, and this time he managed a ghost of a smile. Conroy and Dr. Shea nodded at him—no doubt he'd be seeing them both again, probably many times—then stepped outside. For a long moment he was alone in the room, and he thought with sudden clarity that this was how it had all started, with him alone in a room at home, no one to talk to and help keep him grounded. I'll be okay, he decided solemnly, if I just don't let that happen again.

"Jesse?"

Trista was standing uncertainly in the doorway, but she wasn't the same woman he'd seen Thursday night; this morning her face was makeup-free, her eyes red and swollen. He wanted to get up and go to her, hug her, but he was . . . well, he was too damned scared. "Hi." It came out sounding like a croak, but instead of trying again he motioned for her to come in.

She crossed the room and pulled out a chair, then sat and folded her hands like a teacher getting ready to talk to a wayward student. "How . . . how are you doing?" she finally asked.

"I'm getting a few things straightened out," he said honestly. They sat for a few seconds without saying anything.

"Trista, I'm so *sorry,*" he finally blurted. "Boy, you always thought I was a screw-up, and I guess I really did it this time."

Trista lowered her face to her hands, but when she looked up again, her eyes were dry. "Don't be sorry, Jesse. You've . . ." She gave a short, amazed laugh. "You found Tammy—Nola—when I'd given her up for dead almost twenty years ago. Don't you realize what a gift that is?"

"But I—" He shook his head abruptly. "Jesus, I can't even *say* it!"

She leaned forward, her face earnest. "But it's all *okay* now, or it will be, after everyone has a little time to heal. Even you'll be okay." Now it was his turn to be astonished as she reached across the table and clasped his hand. "Jesse, I can't even tell you how wrong I was all these years. I was so . . . paranoid after Tammy was kidnapped that I carried that fear over to every aspect of Stacey's life. When the two of you got married, I was insanely jealous, because as far as I could see it you'd taken away my little girl just the same as Tammy's father had taken her away from me. I'm the one who's *sorry,* Jesse. For all the grief I gave you both."

She squeezed his fingers. "What happened here with you and Nola was my fault, too—I had no right to blame you for Stacey's death, and I should have never, ever left you alone afterward. I had people to help me through it—my husband and Krystin. You had no one." She hesitated, but didn't let go. "Jesse, if you can stand to be around me, I'll make it up to you. This time I won't leave you to deal with Stacey's death by yourself."

He stared at her, not knowing what to say. Even putting aside what he'd done—and that wouldn't be easy—could he forget the years of arguments and bitterness? He didn't know . . . but he damned sure wanted to try. A month or a year ago, he would've never imagined this woman offering to help him with anything, nor would he have dreamed he'd be grateful for it. He finally found enough air to speak. "That'd be wonderful."

Trista stood. "They've told me you can go home tonight—"

His eyes widened. "Tonight? Already?"

"I think it's too soon for you to go back home by yourself," she said, startling him even more. "If you'd consider it, I'd like you to stay with Tadd and me for a few days, or however long you want. I can drive you home and you can pick up a few things and get your car—I know you'll need it to get to work on Monday."

Stay with Trista and her husband? It wasn't something he'd ever considered, but . . . well, it was so much preferable to the once-again too-big, too-empty townhouse. If she came through on even half of what she was promising—to help him and be there for him if this double loss of Stacey became too much—why, he might come out of this with that fresh start that John had so emphatically promised a little while ago. Because according to Conroy and Dr. Shea, no matter what he'd done, he had never truly hurt Nola Elidad.

Jesse met Trista's eyes and wouldn't let himself look away from the pain and regret he saw there. "I'd like to stay with you for a while," he said. He stood and carefully pushed the chair under the table. "Yes . . . I'd like that very much."

"So that's how it ended," Conroy finished. He and Dustine were back at the Smiling Buddha—Dustine's request—and winding down a slow, easy dinner during which he'd filled her in on the last of what was going on with the now-closed Nola Elidad case. "Trista Newman picked up her son-in-law and is now trying to undo way too many years of damage." He pushed his well-cleaned plate away and picked up his glass of plum wine, then raised it in a small salute. "I hope she succeeds."

"Me too," said Dustine. "For her sake as well as Jesse's. He sounds like he could use a hand." She sipped her wine thoughtfully. "What about Alec and Nola—how are they doing?"

Conroy spread his hands. "I haven't a clue. Asking questions like that—way out of my realm."

"Well, hopefully they'll pick up some kind of couples' counseling. I've got a feeling he and Nola are going to need it."

"Yes," Conroy agreed. He drained the last of his wine, then put the glass aside and leaned toward her. "But enough work talk. Have I told you how pretty you look tonight?"

She grinned. "Yes. But you can tell me again if you like."

"You're beautiful."

"Feeling brave, are we?"

"Completely enamored."

Dustine had to laugh. "Just how—"

"Can I clear these for you?"

They looked up as one of the waitresses—who was probably also one of the owners—stepped up to the table.

"Sure," Conroy said, then inclined his head toward Dustine. "Look—isn't she beautiful? She doesn't believe me."

"Lucas!"

"Oh, yes," the waitress said agreeably, her words carrying a heavy Asian accent. "Very beautiful." To Dustine she said, "He is good, yes?"

Dustine smiled wryly. "He's good, all right."

"I was just telling her the obvious," Conroy said as the woman disappeared with their dinner plates.

"What's obvious is that you've had too much wine," she said, smiling.

"No more than you," he pointed out. "Two glasses. Just enough to make me feel a little warm."

"Over-heated," she said beneath her breath. But my, wasn't she—

"Excuse me?"

"I said you were over-relaxed."

He snickered. "I don't think so."

She frowned at him. "You're not relaxed?"

"Don't I look relaxed?"

"You just said you weren't."

"Actually, I said 'I don't think so,' and I wasn't referring to that."

"I'm confused."

"I know."

"Lucas!" She stared at him, half laughing, half exasperated. "What the heck are you doing?"

"Messing with your mind," he said comfortably. "Just to see if I can get you off balance."

"Why?" she demanded.

"Why not?" he shot back.

"I am not here for you to play with," she said archly.

"Darn," he said, his voice mild. "And I thought we could play together."

Now Dustine knew it had to be the wine talking. He'd never said anything like that before—in fact, she'd been starting to wonder if she'd been relegated to the dreaded best bud category.

Or maybe she was just misinterpreting his words.

Coward, she thought. That's what I am—what I've been all along in this relationship.

"How're you doing?" Conroy asked. He peered at her, puzzled, perhaps, by her silence. "Do you want dessert? Or another glass of wine?"

Dessert, she thought with a sudden flash of hidden wickedness. Yeah, that's what I want. Aloud she said, "Actually, I think I'm ready to head home."

Cold and dark, with no hint of a break in what still felt like winter weather. Perfect.

"It's pretty chilly outside," she said at the door to her place. "Why don't you come in."

Conroy looked at her hesitantly, then glanced back at his car. There was a tenseness between them, an undercurrent that Dustine had felt begin to build back at the restaurant. "I don't know," he said. "It's late, and I can really feel those two glasses of wine."

Now who was nervous? "What is it you always say to people who aren't cooperating with you?" she asked with a gentle smile. She turned the key in the lock, then pushed open the door. Welcome, warm air spilled over them. She wrapped a hand around one of his wrists and gave him a good, hard tug. "I *insist.*"

"Whoa!" he said as he stumbled inside. Still holding his wrist, Dustine slipped around him and quickly twisted the dead bolt, then turned back and pulled his coat down to his elbows, giving him no choice but to straighten his arms so she could tug it off. "Well," he said, recovering and gallantly reaching for her coat in return. "Then let's have a cup of coffee."

Dustine shrugged out of her coat and let both hers and his drop to the floor before Conroy could catch them. "Let's not," she said, and stepped into his arms.

They had kissed before, a number of times. The feeling, the *chemistry* had always been there, but Dustine had always held it in check and had relied on Conroy to do the same. What he did or didn't do tonight, however, was entirely up to him. She was through holding back, tired of being afraid of her own desires and of the needs of someone else. She wanted to give for a change, and to get something in return from someone she cared about. And she definitely cared about Lucas Conroy.

She felt how startled he was from the way he tensed, but instead of drawing away, Dustine slid her arms around his back and pressed herself more firmly against his chest. A second passed, feeling like an eternity—would he pull away? She'd always thought of herself as being the one with the hang-up, but what if Lucas wasn't ready for her?

Then his arms encircled her and what she'd offered him in her kiss was returned, and more. That unseen element that had been building between them for the last two-plus months rose to the surface like liquid just starting to boil. Her hands slid in between his sweater and shirt and she felt lean muscle through the fabric. At the same time, the scent of him settled all around her—clean and masculine, cologne-free, unlike anything else she could recall. All it did was make her want to get closer to him.

"Dustine—wait," Conroy said against her mouth. His hands slid to her arms and he held her slightly away while he looked intently into her eyes. Desire was etched in every line of his face, but there was that control—sometimes damnable—of his. "This is . . . I don't want to push you too soon. It's up to—"

"Me," she said, and smiled at him. She left their coats on the floor, took his hand, and led him into the darkened townhouse.

"I know, Lucas. I know."

APRIL 2--WEDNESDAY

Despite the incredible evening the night before, or maybe because of it, Conroy's mind was sharp and clear.

The Elidad file was spread across his desk again, because he wasn't quite through with it—not yet. There was that one last thing that he needed, somehow, to tie up, and the answer, that final deadly stab, had come to him on the drive into work from Dustine's townhouse this morning.

Dustine . . . now there was something he'd never thought he'd see in his life. A woman he cared about and who seemed capable, perhaps due to her background in dealing with problematic people, of withstanding his intensity. Everyone else he'd gone out with had been literally overwhelmed by him, by his strength and his simple presence, a brutal degree of honesty in both giving and taking that most women couldn't handle. Dustine could do both, and wasn't that an amazing thing considering the trauma and disappointment she'd been subjected to as a young woman?

And that thought brought him back to contemplating the problem of Marlo Frayne.

The first thing he'd done this morning was make a phone call to Mrs. Peterson to tell her that Stacey Waite had died in September, probably about a week before that placeholder had been put in the slot where her records ought to be. Armed with that information, it had taken the elderly woman only an hour to call him back with the news that she'd located the records, which had been pulled for updating by one of the junior clerks. He had held the physical file and put a block on the computer file because the one thing he needed to close Stacey Waite's record was the date and location of her published obituary. When he couldn't find it, he'd simply kept pushing the task of locating it to the bottom of his priority pile to avoid the bother of calling around to the local newspapers. With a married young woman like Stacey Waite, it had never occurred to the young man that the family wouldn't have had one published.

With that out of the way, and with closure—bizarre or otherwise—for the "no information" tag on Tammy Gardell, Conroy pulled out a telephone book and flipped it open. His finger ran down the government listings until he found what he was looking for, then he made sure he had all four of the social security numbers he needed—Marlo Frayne's, Charles Frayne's, Stowe Gardell's, and the young Nola Frayne's—before he dialed the number. Calls like this always meant you got transferred three or four times, and as he worked his way through the ranks at the Social Security Administration, he thought about what Nola had told him about the things Marlo had done and Nola's own questionable memory. She was right, of course; there would be no justice for the murdered Charles Frayne. Marlo Frayne might remain a free woman, but Conroy planned on making the next few years for her miserable indeed.

"Fraudulent Claims Investigation Division."

There, finally, was exactly what he wanted to hear.

"Hello," he said pleasantly. "This is Detective Lucas Conroy of the Roselle Police Department. I'd like to talk to someone involving a probable case of social security theft. The woman involved is Marlo Frayne, and I believe she may have illegally collected social security from two, possibly three sources at once.

"Yes." Conroy smiled to himself, then leaned back in his chair until he was comfortable. "Of course I'll hold."

APRIL 3--THURSDAY

Boy, wouldn't this would make Alec go nuts if he found out?

For someone else, *any*one else, it might have been a perfectly normal Thursday morning. For Nola, however, sitting at a table with her real mother, and with her dead sister's husband and her own former kidnapper, it was the strangest experience of her life.

Nola hadn't told Alec, but Trista had taken a week's vacation and she'd been calling her mother at home every other day or so—how could she not? She wanted to get to know this woman, her good points, her faults—learn all the things she'd been denied while she was growing up. Trista had told her that Jesse was staying there and that she was trying to help him work things out; Nola thought that said a lot about the effort the woman was making to fix the wrongs of the past.

And yesterday, when Trista had hesitantly asked her if she wanted to come to the house in Streamwood and have lunch with them, Nola had jumped at the chance. Since she knew how to drive, she'd made Alec take her to get her driver's license last Saturday, and now she drove him to work and kept the car; she wasn't yet ready to go back to the library even though Aunt Krys—how odd to call her that and realize how wrong she'd been to assume the woman's name was 'Aunt *Chris*'—had said her job was waiting.

When she pulled into the driveway at Trista's house, logic told her that this place hadn't been the paradise it appeared to be. A tidily kept white split-level, its windows shone with cleanliness and the bushes and dormant lawn were still neatly trimmed—no peeling paint marred the eaves or metal railing along the small riser of steps. But no matter what her head told her, it was hard to reconcile the difference between this and the tiny, dingy houses that Marlo had always favored, with their tobacco-stained rooms and drawn curtains.

Inside it was bright and clean, a pleasing mix of lace curtains and not-too-stiff Early American furnishings, with lots of yellow and white in the kitchen. While both Trista and

Jesse had testified that life here had held its share of pain, the place still seemed bright and hopeful. Someday, Nola thought, I would like to live in a house like this.

Lunch—a homey combination of tomato soup served with turkey sandwiches and slices of apple—was over and the dishes were cleared; now the three of them sat at the kitchen table and tried to get to know one another.

"There isn't much to know," Nola said. Hers was the last of the tales each had told. "I spent a lot of time alone while I was growing up, and I wasn't allowed to bring friends home. I got the name 'Frayne' from the man Marlo married after my father died—she went through formal adoption proceedings and had it changed. God knows what she did on paper to get it to go through. Not too long after that, he died too." She didn't bother to elaborate. What was the point?

"And I thought I was bad," muttered Trista. "At least I didn't keep Stacey jailed up like an inmate." She shot a glance at Jesse. "Although it probably felt that way to her."

Jesse looked at Nola thoughtfully. "Yeah, it did. But I guess we realize now that Stacey had no idea how much worse it could have been. Nola, that must have been a terrible way to live."

She shrugged. "It was what it was—I didn't know anything different. The day I met Alec, it was a total deviation from my routine. I never planned on going to the carnival, but I'd overheard a couple of kids talking about it at the library and I knew it was within walking distance. So I decided to go."

"And that's when everything changed," Trista said.

Nola nodded. "Alec and I were paired on the Ferris wheel because neither of us had partners, and we just kind of stayed together so we could go on the rides. I didn't mean to, but subconsciously I probably saw Alec as a way out of the awful prison I was in with Marlo. And he was good to me—kind and considerate. No one had ever . . . cared about me before. It wasn't very long before he asked me to marry him, and I said yes. I thought I loved him."

"And now?" Trista looked at her carefully.

"Now we've got some issues to work out," Nola finally answered. "I've learned things about myself and my family"—she raised her eyes to them—"that affect how I feel. I've even learned things about Alec."

Jesse stared at the tabletop. "We've all made some discoveries."

Trista nodded and they sat there in companionable silence for a little while. Nola felt nervous and comfortable at the same time—Trista was the mother she'd never had, and she needed to get to know her from the ground up. How different things might have been for all of them had her father not abducted her—Trista wouldn't have been nearly as protective; Stacey, and later Jesse, would've been happier; she herself would have been entirely different.

And Jesse . . . Nola saw him now in an entirely different light. She'd known him as so many things: first as her kidnapper, then her pseudo-husband and lover, and now finally as the husband of the dead twin sister she didn't remember. When she considered it, everything he'd ever told her had been, in a fashion, true: his love for her when he believed she was his wife, his need for her, his desire for nothing more than the continuation of a normal and secure life with the person he treasured. How could she blame him when these were the very things that she had always wanted, too? It was tragic to see Jesse now, trying to put the pieces back together because the biggest loss of his life had overwhelmed his ability to think clearly.

Without meaning to her gaze met his and locked. Something in Jesse's eyes made her suddenly blush—perhaps the unspoken memory of all those nights they had lived and loved as man and wife. Apologetic and embarrassed he might be, but there was no denying the sense of longing and more that she saw there, the unspoken message that although he knew she wasn't Stacey, he could, and would if she would allow him, cherish her just for who she really was.

Seeing this, and feeling it, it wasn't so difficult for Nola to understand what the dead Stacey Waite had found so wonderful in the man she loved and ultimately married.

APRIL 5--SATURDAY

This was the most animated she'd seen Alec in the entire time she'd been back home.

Nola wasn't that great of a cook, but she'd actually learned a thing or two while living with Jesse, and it had been her idea for Alec to invite Marietta Cale over for dinner. She'd also thought it was a good thing when Alec told her he was going to go to a few more of the Friday evening counseling sessions, plus she wanted to meet this woman about whom Alec talked constantly, whether he realized it or not. Nola wanted to learn more about the counseling and, frankly, about Marietta.

So now she chopped vegetables for a salad and puttered around the kitchen, having no idea what Alec was up to in the other room beyond moving his computer off the table. She had no desire to ask. How sad that there had been no miracle recovery and return to normalcy for her and Alec—surely he had expected no less. But her ordeal had changed them both, and while Alec seemed like a pleasant enough man, Nola was seeing him from a completely new perspective—much the same way she'd come to alter her view of Jesse. Now Alec was like a stranger to her. Had he changed that much in the time she'd been gone? Or had she?

And more important, could she salvage her feelings for him, find the love she'd thought only three short months ago would last forever?

It was hard to believe that could happen. She and Alec argued—a lot. He seemed reluctant to make the first move toward her, and she simply couldn't find it in herself to offer her body. It seemed false somehow, a bribe that would ultimately accomplish nothing. In the meantime, her husband talked constantly of his support group and its members, particularly Marietta. Every other sentence seemed to be some quote of their advice or some recollection of the sympathy and strength they'd given him. Yes, it had been a painful time, but now she was back—was it cold of her to feel only impatience and irritation about the support group, and want only to move on?

Whatever her feelings, it was clear that the support group had taught Alec to be more open with his feelings, if not understanding about what she had gone through. Their arguments were frequent and heated, and the topics left Nola feeling drained and defensive. She didn't know how to answer his veiled accusations about unfaithfulness, and she flatly disagreed with his claim that had she shared her past with him, she would have been stronger and able to "keep herself" in the face of what she'd gone through. And while she knew he would never admit it, it was clear to her that before she'd been found, Alec had finally accepted that she was gone forever—he'd believed she was dead and he'd been ready to move on with his life. Now there was no doubt that he felt much closer to the people from the support group—and to Marietta—than to her; they, he told her, were always totally up front about everything, with no secrets, good or bad. He hadn't realized it when the words came out of his mouth, but the most damaging thing Alec had said was that she should be more like the people in his group.

Nola didn't want to be *like* anyone else. Not anymore. Not *ever.*

What had happened to her was exactly because of that—someone else, *again,* had tried to make her into someone *they* wanted her to be. She had survived it, and now she was ready to go on. This time, however, moving on was *not* going to mean molding herself into an ideal for someone else.

"Marietta will be here any minute," Alec said, breaking into her train of thought. He stood in the doorway to the kitchen, freshly shaved and wearing a navy and light blue striped shirt that was quite becoming. She didn't recall seeing it before. "Can I help with anything?"

"I don't think so," Nola said. "Everything's ready." It would be a simple meal of crock-pot beef stew and a fresh salad, served with crusty Italian bread. For dessert she'd picked up an apple pie, which was warming slowly in the oven. She glanced up when Alec didn't say anything; he was looking off toward the rest of the apartment, staring into space with a vaguely sad expression. Maybe, she thought, he was remembering a time when dinner for the two of them had been as natural as the sun setting each evening. Not anymore.

The doorbell rang and Alec started and pulled his gaze away from the softly lit living room. "I'll go down and get her," he said. "She won't know which way to turn in the hallway."

Nola nodded and watched him go, then dried her hands and nervously smoothed the front of her slacks. Did she look okay? Above cream-colored slacks she wore a sweater with a cornflower-blue paisley pattern on it—perhaps she should have worn something else. Just how, she wondered with sudden black humor, was a rescued kidnap victim expected to dress?

Waiting in the dining room, Nola heard voices in the hall, a smattering of light laughter, then the door to the apartment opened and Alec ushered in Marietta.

"Nola, this is Marietta Cale," Alec said. "Marietta, this is my wife."

"Hi," Marietta said with a smile and extended her hand.

Nola shook it and smiled. "It's nice to meet you. Alec has said some wonderful things about you and the group."

Marietta's smile got a little bigger and Nola thought she saw the woman actually blush. "Alec, why don't you put away her coat and I'll get us something to drink."

Small talk then, an evening of decent food and weak drinks while they discussed the weather, the news, a hundred other completely nonsensical and safe topics, not a single one of which Nola could later remember. She felt a twinge of jealousy that had nothing to do with her husband almost every time she looked at this slim, attractive woman. Alec and Marietta somehow interacted with each other, and while Marietta wasn't everything Nola wanted to be, she damned sure had a lot of it down. Without being overbearing, she was poised and self-confident—

there didn't seem to be a shy bone in her body. Was it the group that had done this? Or—Alec had told her about Marietta's husband—the tragedy that each had endured? Marietta knew Alec and he knew her, not physically but *mentally;* theirs was a connection on a level that Nola and Alec had never achieved. Whether it had never had a chance in the first place or had died because of their unexpected separation was immaterial.

They said their good nights and Alec walked Marietta down to her car while Nola cleaned up the dinner dishes. He was gone a good fifteen minutes, but Nola didn't mind; no doubt there were things he'd wanted to talk over with Marietta—things about Nola and things about his life in general—that he hadn't been able to discuss at the dinner table. These things, Nola felt certain, were forever out of her reach because it was so very obvious that Alec would be much happier with Marietta. The sad truth, the thing that Alec would never admit, was that he didn't want Nola because he loved her. He wanted her because he thought he *should.*

When he finally came back inside there was a mix of emotions playing across his face, and she, who'd felt so few of them before this simple man had come into her life, could read every one: giddiness from a good conversation with Marietta, happiness that the evening had gone smoothly, pain because he couldn't fix what was wrong with his wife and his life, guilt because the bald truth was that he'd rather be with the woman who'd just left than with the woman wearing his wedding ring. The two of them, Nola knew with sudden sorrow, were completely doomed.

But outwardly she did her best to smile. "That went well, don't you think? She seemed to enjoy herself."

"Yeah," Alec said. "She did." He stood there for a moment, as if he didn't know what to do with himself.

"Why don't you go watch some television or something," she said. "I'm going to finish up in here, then take a shower." Had she really just suggested that to her husband, a man who'd turned the television on perhaps six times that she could recall? Still, he nodded, clearly relieved, and practically rushed into the living room.

A shower, dragged out for as long as possible—there could be no more perfect example of two people suddenly imprisoned in a too-small box masquerading as an apartment. And then bed, finally, another night where she lay on her side of the mattress and Alec on his, neither daring—or wanting—to touch the other. There was no denying it ate at Alec that she had slept with another man, no matter what the reason, and perhaps that destroyed his desire.

On her part, Nola felt a great longing for Jesse, for the warmth and love that had somehow leaked away from her and Alec during her absence, or had been destroyed by the blatant facts of her rediscovery. Lying awake and staring into the darkness, watching the LED display of the clock as it ticked away another quarter hour, she knew it was up to her to take the next step, to somehow make right what her return had forced off track. God help them both, but Alec would stubbornly stay with her until the day he died, stonewalling his own heart's knowledge that she was no longer the woman he'd once loved. She couldn't let him do this, couldn't allow him to be trapped with her the same way she had, in one way or another, been trapped by other people all her life.

And all during that same life, Nola had let others decide what and who she should be.

Enough.

Sometime during the last half hour, Alec had fallen asleep. She could hear him breathing, deeply and evenly, and she hoped he was dreaming good things. She got out of bed and dressed without waking him, then quietly packed a small bag; what little remained, she could come back for some other time.

In the bathroom, Nola looked at herself in the mirror and saw a woman changed because of what had happened. But it wasn't only her—Alec had changed because of it, Jesse had changed, even Trista had changed. Among them, only Alec seemed determined to hang on to something that no longer existed, even though it was time to let go and grow. No matter what his intentions, she knew Alec had fallen in love with Marietta Cale, and she with him; he *needed* Marietta in a way that he had never needed Nola.

And yet Nola, above all else, needed to *be* needed. As she had admitted to her mother and Jesse, she'd seen Alec as a rescuer, someone to get her away from Marlo, and she would always love him a little and be grateful to him for being just that. Had it not been for the circumstances which followed, had they been left to be only with each other, that might have been enough. Now, however, she still cared for Alec, but she had to admit that she no longer loved him.

And as for Jesse . . .

Jesse was alone now. It seemed so unfair that he'd lost Stacey, and then lost Nola, too. She knew how he was in day-to-day life—good-natured and full of humor, life, and love—and it wasn't hard to believe that, given the support of Trista and the rest of Stacey's small family, he would soon be able to get his life back on an even track.

And when he did, well, he would make a fine and wonderful father for the child Nola carried in her womb.

It wasn't an easy or a frivolous decision, and Nola fully expected a range of responses—hurt, anger, shock. But she'd thought long and hard about it and she knew, she *knew,* that ultimately this was right, that buried far below the surface a lot of people would eventually find, because of her and what she did tonight, happiness. For her, there was no other right choice—the baby she would bear was not Alec's. She could not have it raised by a man who was not its father—she would *not* start this helpless, unborn child along essentially the same path on which she'd been placed when her own parents divorced so long ago. Already her husband couldn't deal with her intimacy with Jesse—how would he face the fact that she was pregnant with Jesse's child? And even if he could accept that, where was it written that he would be able to love the child of what he considered to be her infidelity?

It was unthinkable. Nola wanted this baby to be raised where it would be most wanted, most *loved.* And she knew exactly where that would be.

In the bedroom Nola heard Alec mumble something in his sleep, then he quieted. She closed the bedroom door and went to sit in the living room with a pen and a sheet of paper. When she finished her good-bye letter to Alec, she thought she would carry her suitcase up to the phone booth by the Pik-Kwik and call Jesse to come and get her.

REPRISAL

Better by far you should forget and smile
Than that you should remember and be sad.

—CHRISTINA ROSSETTI, "REMEMBER"

SEPTEMBER 1--MONDAY, LABOR DAY

Nola had never dreamed she could be this happy.

At seven and a half months pregnant, she felt like she took up the space of two people, and the backyard of the townhouse was small anyway, barely big enough for them and their company. Today was hotter than normal for September, but despite her mother and Jesse fluttering around her like bumblebees guarding a prize flower, she wasn't uncomfortable. In fact, she was having the time of her life, sitting on a lawn chair and watching Jesse diligently tend the barbecue. For such a capable man, it was damned comical to see him try so hard *not* to burn the chicken . . . which everyone knew he was going to burn anyway, because he *always* did.

Also crammed into the tiny yard, mindful of the flowers Nola had planted along the fence line, were Trista and Tadd, Aunt Krys and her husband Ken, plus John Aldwin and his wife Melissa, who had accepted her without reservation despite the strange circumstances of her and Jesse's marriage last month. Melissa kept a close eye on her two small girls, and Nola was glad to pitch in and help provide damage control.

Every now and then, as she looked around at the small group of people who had become her family and friends, Nola still felt a small shiver of disbelief. Somehow, without regrets or guilt, she had left behind a past filled with pain and bleakness. The divorce between her and Alec had been swift and unremarkable, and she'd even talked to him now and then before they'd finally drifted apart for good.

Alec was a good man, and wherever he was now, Nola hoped he'd finally found happiness.

My God, Alec thought, I've never seen so many kids outside of one of my classes!

One of them barreled up to him now, nothing at all shy about her. "Uncle Alec! Uncle Alec!" she screamed as loud as her three-year-old lungs would allow. Alec swung her up and into his arms and couldn't help the grin that spread across his face as he turned and saw Marietta arguing with one of her cousins about the potato salad, or maybe it was the ham salad—some salad, anyway. There were probably another half a dozen good-natured disagreements going around the clearing that Marietta's family had reserved in the forest preserves outside of northwest Chicago for their annual Labor Day shindig. There had to be a hundred people here—family, friends, far-family, and friends of friends. Some of the kids had brought along two or three more of their own buddies, there were boom boxes going in two corners and Frisbees were cutting through the air like brightly colored flying saucers. And the food—they could have fed a small army!

My God, Alec thought again. What the heck would it be like to deal with a family like this for the rest of his life?

Marietta looked up and caught his eye, then laughed at him when her little niece—there were simply too many for him to remember their names this soon—twisted in his arms and yanked on his ear.

The rest of his life?

Alec was smiling so wide that his face hurt.

"How did this happen?" Conroy complained. "How come I get the holiday off and you end up having to work an evening shift?"

"Luck of the draw, I guess," Dustine said cheerfully. "Now what's this secret 'fun' you've been teasing me about all week?"

With Dustine slated to work second shift, later they would go out to lunch. Right now Conroy gave her a goofy grin and handed her a book of matches. "Look what I've got!" he crowed. He waved his surprise—an oversized firecracker left over from last summer's Fourth of July celebration—past her nose, intentionally too fast for her to get a good look at it. "It's called a Patriotic Crackling Floral," he said proudly. "It has really cool red, white and blue sparkles that we probably won't see very well in the sunlight, because *someone* has to go to work today and we can't set it off tonight."

Dustine laughed and folded her arms, trying to look stern. "Detective Lucas Conroy, you know perfectly well that fireworks are illegal. I may have to place you under arrest and confiscate the evidence."

Conroy gave her a look of exaggerated shock. "Illegal? Oh my *God*! Don't arrest me! Here—" He tossed the molded ball to her. "You'll have to take it off my hands, then."

Dustine laughed again and snatched it out of the air, then stopped short and peered at what was in her hand. When she held it up to the sunlight, the object tied to the firework's overly long fuse sent out its own shower of fiery sparks:

An engagement ring.

Conroy smiled. "Dusty . . . do I have to ask?"

Yvonne Navarro is a Chicago area novelist who has been writing for longer than she'll admit. This is her tenth published novel, and she's also had over fifty short story pieces published. Her first and second novels, *AfterAge* and *deadrush,* were both finalists for the Bram Stoker Award.

Yvonne has written the novelizations of *Species* (for which actor Alfred Molina picked up the 1996 Audie Award for Best Solo Performance in an audiobook reading), *Species II, Aliens: Music of the Spears,* and *Buffy the Vampire Slayer: The Willow Files, Vol. I.* She also authored *The First Name Reverse Dictionary,* a reference book for writers.

Readers are still requesting a sequel to *AfterAge,* as well as a third book to continue the unintentional mini-series of the award-winning *Final Impact* and its follow-up, *Red Shadows.* In early 2000, DarkTales Publications published her novel, *DeadTimes.* In her goal to please everyone, she's planning to write a sequel to almost every solo novel she's ever written. Right now she's completing an original Buffy the Vampire Slayer novel and trying to decide what's next.

Someday Yvonne plans to move out of the Chicago area and get a big dog. In the meantime she writes, studies martial arts, and shivers a lot. Yvonne also maintains an extensive website at *http://www.para-net.com/~ynavarro* which includes announcements, message boards, excerpts, and fun photos. Please visit!